HILARY MANTEL wa ... ed at a convent and l ... oad in Africa and the ... in 1985 to make a career as a writer.

From the reviews of *Beyond Black*:

'Magnificent . . . one of the greatest ghost stories in the language. A novel of desperate truthfulness – a majestic work' PHILIP PULLMAN

'Laceratingly observant, a masterpiece of wit . . . It is also glorious, insolent and slyly funny: full of robust, uncluttered prose and searing moments' *Independent*

'A deep, disturbing, violently amusing and subversive work, testimony to the formidable strength of Mantel's imagination' *Daily Telegraph*

'Hilary Mantel has done something extraordinary. She has taken the ethereal halfway house between heaven and hell, between the living and the dead and nailed it on the page . . . She persuades, she convinces, she offers an alternative universe, she uses the extraordinary descriptive skills that are her trademark – Mantel does "seedy" as no one else' FAY WELDON, *Guardian*

'Mantel always writes with scalpel-sharp observations and a prodigal gift for imagery' MAGGIE GEE, *Sunday Times*

'Pins elusive Middle England to the page in all its creepiness: a place bland and disconnected, yet fatally self-absorbed' RACHEL COOKE, *Observer*

'An elegant, atmospheric tale and a nuanced portrait, full of sly ironies' *Tatler*

'Wickedly funny and often unsettling . . . Strikingly intelligent and original . . . The comedy is very black, but Hilary Mantel writes so beautifully, and with such penetrating psychological insight, that in her hands the obese medium becomes a genuinely tragic figure. That she has written a gripping contemporary ghost story, which is also a searing comment on a complacent nation that has ceased to believe in anything, demonstrates her versatility and range as a novelist' *Literary Review*

'Has the kind of gallows humour that makes you laugh out loud . . . A real page-turner, a darkly humorous take on the enduring effects of childhood trauma' *Mslexia*

'A very clever novel, full of vitality. It fizzes with energy [and] is written with bravura and conviction . . . The everyday life of prosperous, seedy, post-industrialist England is acutely and wickedly observed'

ALLAN MASSIE, *Scotsman*

'Darkly comic . . . a powerful meditation on death, grief, power and charisma . . . This reader can't help but be drawn in – and feel a little terrified' *Red*

'A remarkable novel: an intricately structured portrait of the secret dreads and desires of Middle England, written with a kind of comic fury whose energetic grotesquerie trembles in a fine balance with Mantel's fierce powers of observation and her mimic's ear for dialogue . . . A fiction of ominously memorable elegance'

JANE SHILLING, *Sunday Telegraph*

'Wonderfully funny' D.J. TAYLOR, *Spectator*

'An illuminating study of what can happen when you try to confront the past with honest choices made in the present. Told with much verve and originality' *Time Out*

'Savage, startlingly subversive and raucously funny'
M. JOHN HARRISON, *TLS*

By the same author

Every Day is Mother's Day
Vacant Possession
Eight Months on Ghazzah Street
Fludd
A Place of Greater Safety
A Change of Climate
An Experiment in Love
The Giant, O'Brien
Learning to Talk

NON-FICTION
Giving Up the Ghost

HILARY MANTEL

Beyond Black

HARPER PERENNIAL
London, New York, Toronto and Sydney

This edition produced for The Book People Ltd,
Hall Wood Avenue, Haydock, St Helens, WA11 9UL

Harper Perennial
An imprint of HarperCollins*Publishers*
77–85 Fulham Palace Road, Hammersmith, London W6 8JB

www.harperperennial.co.uk

This edition published by Harper Perennial 2008
1

First published in Great Britain by Fourth Estate 2005
First published in paperback by Harper Perennial 2005

A catalogue record for this book is available from the British Library

ISBN 978-0-00-781540-1

Set in Meridien with DeVinne BT display by
Palimpsest Book Production Limited, Grangemouth, Stirlingshire

Printed and bound in Great Britain by Clays Ltd, St Ives plc

FSC
Mixed Sources
Product group from well-managed forests and other controlled sources
www.fsc.org Cert no. SW-COC-1806
© 1996 Forest Stewardship Council

FSC is a non-profit international organisation established to promote the responsible management of the world's forests. Products carrying the FSC label are independently certified to assure consumers that they come from forests that are managed to meet the social, economic and ecological needs of present and future generations.

Find out more about HarperCollins and the environment at
www.harpercollins.co.uk/green

To Jane Haynes

'There are powers at work in this country about which we have no knowledge.'

H.M. the Queen (attributed)

ONE

Travelling: the dank oily days after Christmas. The motorway, its wastes looping London: the margin's scrub-grass flaring orange in the lights, and the leaves of the poisoned shrubs striped yellow-green like a cantaloupe melon. Four o'clock: light sinking over the orbital road. Teatime in Enfield, night falling on Potters Bar.

There are nights when you don't want to do it, but you have to do it anyway. Nights when you look down from the stage and see closed stupid faces. Messages from the dead arrive at random. You don't want them and you can't send them back. The dead won't be coaxed and they won't be coerced. But the public has paid its money and it wants results.

A sea-green sky: lamps blossoming white. This is marginal land: fields of strung wire, of treadless tyres in ditches, fridges dead on their backs, and starving ponies cropping the mud. It is a landscape running with outcasts and escapees, with Afghans, Turks and Kurds: with scapegoats, scarred with bottle and burn marks, limping from the cities with broken ribs. The life forms here are rejects, or anomalies: the cats tipped from speeding cars, and the Heathrow sheep, their fleece clotted with the stench of aviation fuel.

Beside her, in profile against the fogged window, the driver's face is set. In the back seat, something dead stirs, and begins to grunt and breathe. The car flees across the junctions, and the space the road encloses is the space inside her: the arena of combat, the wasteland, the placc of civil strife behind her ribs. Heart beats, the tail lights wink. Dim lights shine from tower blocks, from passing helicopters, from fixed stars. Night closes in on the perjured ministers and burnt-out paedophiles, on the unloved viaducts and graffitied bridges, on ditches beneath mouldering hedgerows and railings never warmed by human touch.

Night and winter: but in the rotten nests and empty setts, she can feel the signs of growth, intimations of spring. This is the time of Le Pendu, the Hanged Man, swinging by his foot from the living tree. It is a time of suspension, of hesitation, of the indrawn breath. It is a time to let go of expectation, yet not abandon hope; to anticipate the turn of the Wheel of Fortune. This is our life and we have to lead it. Think of the alternative.

A static cloud bank, like an ink smudge. Darkening air.

It's no good asking me whether I'd choose to be like this, because I've never had a choice. I don't know about anything else, I've never been any other way.

And darker still. Colour has run out from the land. Only form is left: the clumped treetops like a dragon's back. The sky deepens to midnight blue. The orange of the street lights is blotted to a fondant cerise; in pastureland, the pylons lift their skirts in a ferrous gavotte.

TWO

Colette put her head round the dressing-room door. 'All right?' she said. 'It's a full house.'

Alison was leaning into the mirror, about to paint her mouth on. 'Could you find me a coffee?'

'Or a gin and tonic?'

'Yes, go on then.'

She was in her psychic kit now; she had flung her day clothes over the back of a chair. Colette swooped on them; lady's maid was part of her job. She slid her forearm inside Al's black crêpe skirt. It was as large as a funerary banner, a pall. As she turned it the right way out, she felt a tiny stir of disgust, as if flesh might be clinging to the seams.

Alison was a woman who seemed to fill a room, even when she wasn't in it. She was of an unfeasible size, with plump creamy shoulders, rounded calves, thighs and hips that overflowed her chair; she was soft as an Edwardian, opulent as a showgirl, and when she moved you could hear (though she did not wear them) the rustle of plumes and silks. In a small space, she seemed to use up more than her share of the oxygen; in return her skin breathed out moist perfumes, like a giant tropical flower. When you came into a room she'd left – her bedroom, her hotel room, her dressing room backstage – you felt her as a presence, a trail. Alison had gone, but you would see a chemical mist of hairspray falling through the bright air. On the floor would be a line of talcum powder, and her scent – Je Reviens – would linger in curtain fabric, in cushions and in the weave of towels. When she headed for a spirit encounter, her path was charged, electric; and when her body was out on stage, her face – cheeks glowing, eyes alight – seemed to float still in the dressing-room mirror.

In the centre of the room Colette stooped, picked up Al's shoes. For a moment she disappeared from her own view. When her face bobbed back into sight in the mirror, she was almost relieved. What's wrong with me? she thought. When I'm gone I leave no trace. Perfume doesn't last on my skin. I barely sweat. My feet don't indent the carpet.

'It's true,' Alison said. 'It's as if you wipe out the signs of yourself as you go. Like a robot housekeeper. You polish your own fingerprints away.'

'Don't be silly,' Colette said. 'And don't read my private thoughts.' She shook the black skirt, as if shaking Alison.

'I often ask myself, let's see now, is Colette in the room or not? When you've been gone for an hour or two, I wonder if I've imagined you.'

Colette looped the black skirt on to a hanger, and hung it on the back of the long mirror. Soon Al's big black overshirt joined it. It was Colette who had persuaded her into black. Black, she had said, black *and perfectly plain.* But Alison abhorred plainness. There must be something to capture the gaze, something to shiver, something to shine. At first glance the shirt seemed devoid of ornament: but a thin line of sequins ran down the sleeve, like the eyes of sly aliens, reflecting black within black. For her work on stage, she insisted on colour: emerald, burnt orange, scarlet. 'The last thing you want, when you go out there,' she explained, 'is to make them think of funerals.'

Now she pouted at herself in the glass. 'I think that's quite nice, don't you?'

Colette glanced at her. 'Yes, it suits you.'

Alison was a genius with make-up. She had boxfuls and she used it all, carrying it in colour-coded washbags and cases fitted with loops for brushes and small-size bottles. If the spirit moved her to want some apricot eyeshadow, she knew just which bag to dip into. To Colette, it was a mystery. When she went out to get herself a new lipstick, she came back with one which, when applied, turned out to be the same colour as all the others she had; which was always, give or take, the colour of her lips. 'So what's that shade called?' she asked. Alison observed herself, a cotton bud poised, and effected an invisible improvement to her underlip. 'Dunno. Why don't you try it? But get me that drink first.' Her hand moved for her lipstick sealant. She almost said, look out, Colette, don't tread on Morris.

He was on the floor, half sitting and half lying, slumped against the wall: his stumpy legs were spread out, and his fingers playing with his fly buttons. When Colette stepped back she trampled straight over him.

As usual she didn't notice. But Morris did. 'Fucking stuck-up cow,' he said, as Colette went out. 'White-faced fucking freak. She's like a bloody ghoul. Where did you get her, gel, a churchyard?'

Under her breath Alison swore back at him. In their five years as partners, he'd never accepted Colette; time meant little to Morris. 'What would you know about churchyards?' she asked him. 'I bet you never had a Christian burial. Concrete boots and a dip in the river, considering the people you mixed with. Or maybe you were sawn up with your own saw?'

Alison leaned forward again into the mirror, and slicked her mouth with the tiny brush from the glass tube. It tickled and stung. Her lips flinched from it. She made a face at herself. Morris chuckled.

It was almost the worst thing, having him around at times like these, in your dressing room, before the show, when you were trying to calm yourself down and have your intimate moments. He would follow you to the lavatory if he was in that sort of mood. A colleague had once said to her, 'It seems to me that your guide is on a very low vibratory plane, very low indeed. Had you been drinking when he first made contact?

'No,' Al had told her. 'I was only thirteen.'

'Oh, that's a terrible age,' the woman said. She looked Alison up and down. 'Junk food, I expect. Empty calories. Stuffing yourself.'

She'd denied it, of course. In point of fact she never had any money after school for burgers or chocolate, her mum keeping her short in case she used the money to get on a bus and run away. But she couldn't put any force into her denial. Her colleague was right, Morris was a low person. How did she get him? She probably deserved him, that was all there was to it. Sometimes she would say to him, Morris, what did I do to deserve you? He would rub his hands and chortle. When she had provoked him and he was in a temper with her, he would say, count your blessings, girl, you fink I'm bad but you could of had MacArthur. You could have had Bob Fox, or Aitkenside, or Pikey Pete. You could have had my mate Keef Capstick. You could of had Nick, and then where'd you be?

Mrs Etchells (who taught her the psychic trade) had always told her, there are some spirits, Alison, who you already know from way back, and you just have to put names to the faces. There are some spirits that are spiteful and will do you a bad turn. There are others that are bloody buggering bastards, excuse my French, who will suck the marrow out your bones. Yes, Mrs E, she'd said, but how will I know which are which? And Mrs Etchells had said, God help you, girl. But God having business elsewhere, I don't expect he will.

Colette crossed the foyer, heading for the bar. Her eyes swept over the paying public, flocking in from the dappled street; ten women to every man. Each evening she liked to get a fix on them, so she could tell Alison what to expect. Had they pre-booked, or were they queuing at the box office? Were they swarming in groups, laughing and chatting, or edging through the foyer in singles and pairs, furtive and speechless? You could probably plot it on a graph, she thought, or have some kind of computer program: the demographics of each town, its typical punters and their networks, the location of the venue relative to car parks, pizza parlour, the nearest bar where young girls could go in a crowd.

The venue manager nodded to her. He was a worn little bloke coming up to retirement; his dinner jacket had a whitish bloom on it and was tight under the arms. 'All right?' he said. Colette nodded, unsmiling; he swayed back on his heels, and as if he had never seen them before he surveyed the bags of sweets hanging on their metal pegs, and the ranks of chocolate bars. Why can't men just *stand*? Colette wondered. Why do they have to sway on the spot and feel in their pockets and pat themselves up and down and suck their teeth? Alison's poster was displayed six times, at various spots through the foyer. The flyers around advertised forthcoming events: 'Fauré's *Requiem*', giving way in early December to '*Jack and the Beanstalk*'.

Alison was a sensitive: which is to say, her senses were arranged in a different way from the senses of most people.

She was a medium: dead people talked to her, and she talked back. She was a clairvoyant; she could see straight through the living, to their ambitions and secret sorrows, and tell you what they kept in their bedside drawers, and how they had travelled to the venue. She wasn't (by nature) a fortune teller, but it was hard to make people understand that. Prediction, though she protested against it, had become a lucrative part of her business. At the end of the day, she believed, you have to suit the public and give them what they think they want. For fortunes, the biggest part of the trade was young girls. They always thought there might be a stranger on the horizon, love around the corner. They hoped for a better boyfriend than the one they'd got – more socialised, less spotty: or at least, one who wasn't on remand. Men, on their own behalf, were not interested in fortune or fate. They believed they made their own, thanks very much. As for the dead, why should they worry about them? If they need to talk to their relatives, they have women to do that for them.

'G & T,' Colette said to the girl behind the bar. 'Large.'

The girl reached for a glass and shovelled in a single ice cube.

'You can do better than that,' Colette said. 'And lemon.'

She looked around. The bar was empty. The walls were padded to hip height with turquoise plastic leather, deep-buttoned. They'd been needing a damp cloth over them since about 1975. The fake wood tables looked sticky: the same applied. The girl's scoop probed the ice bucket. Another cube slinked down the side of the glass, to join its predecessor with a dull tap. The girl's face showed nothing. Her full, lead-coloured eyes slid away from Colette's face. She mouthed the price. 'For tonight's artiste,' Colette said. 'On the house, I'd have thought!'

The girl did not understand the expression. She had never

heard 'on the house'. She closed her eyes briefly: blue-veined lids.

Back through the foyer. It was filling up nicely. On their way to their seats the audience had to pass the easel she had set up, with Al's super-enlarged picture swathed in a length of apricot polyester that Al called 'my silk'. At first she'd had trouble draping it, getting the loops just right, but now she'd got it off pat – a twist of her wrist made a loop over the top of the portrait, another turn made a drift down one side, and the remainder spilled in graceful folds to whatever gritty carpet or bare boards they were performing on that night. She was working hard to break Al's addiction to this particular bit of kitsch. Unbelievably tacky, she'd said, when she first joined her. She thought instead of a screen on to which Al's image was projected. But Al had said, you don't want to find yourself overshadowed by the special effects. Look, Col, I've been told this, and it's one bit of advice I'll never forget; remember your roots. Remember where you started. In my case, that's the village hall at Brookwood. So when you're thinking of special effects, ask yourself, can you reproduce it in the village hall? If you can't, forget it. It's me they've come to see, after all. I'm a professional psychic, not some sort of magic act.

The truth was, Al adored the photo. It was seven years old now. The studio had mysteriously disappeared two of her chins; and caught those big starry eyes, her smile, and something of her sheen, that inward luminescence that Colette envied.

'All right?' said the manager. 'All humming along, backstage?' He had slid back the lid of the ice-cream chest, and was peering within.

'Trouble in there?' Colette asked. He closed the lid hastily and looked shifty, as if he had been stealing. 'See you've got the scaffolding up again.'

'C'est la vie,' sighed the manager, and Colette said, 'Yes, I dare say.'

Alison kept out of London when she could. She would fight her way in as far as Hammersmith, or work the further reaches of the North Circular. Ewell and Uxbridge were on her patch, and Bromley and Harrow and Kingston upon Thames. But the hubs of their business were the conurbations that clustered around the junctions of the M25, and the corridors of the M3 and M4. It was their fate to pass their evenings in crumbling civic buildings from the sixties and seventies, their exoskeletons in constant need of patching: tiles raining from their roofs, murals stickily ungluing from their walls. The carpets felt tacky and the walls exhaled an acrid vapour. Thirty years of freeze-dried damp had crystallised in the concrete, like the tiny pellets from which you boil up packet soup. The village hall was worse of course, and they still played some of those. She had to liaise with village-idiot caretakers, and bark her shins and ankles hauling chairs into the semicircle Al favoured. She had to take the money on the door, and tread the stage beforehand to detect comic squeaks, and to pull out splinters; it was not unknown for Al to kick off her shoes partway through the first half, and commune barefoot with spirit world.

'Is she all OK back there on her own?' asked the manager. 'A large gin, that's the ticket. Anything else she needs? We could fill the place twice over, you know. I call her the consummate professional.'

Backstage, Al was sucking an extra-strong mint. She could never eat before a show, and afterwards she was too hot, too strung-up, and what she needed to do was talk, talk it all out of her system. But sometimes, hours after she had put out the light, she would wake up and find herself famished and nauseous. She needed cake and chocolate bars then, to pad her flesh and keep her from the pinching of the dead, their peevish nipping and needle teeth. God knows, Colette said, what this eating pattern does to your insulin levels.

I'd really like my gin, she thought. She imagined Colette out there, doing battle for it.

Colette was sharp, rude and effective. Before they joined up, Al was thrust into all sorts of arrangements that she didn't want, and was too shy to speak out if things didn't suit her. She never did soundchecks unless the management told her to, and that was a mistake; you needed to insist on them. Before Colette, nobody had tested out the lighting, or walked out on stage as her surrogate self, to judge the acoustics and the sight lines from the performer's point of view. Nobody had even checked underfoot, for nails or broken glass. Nobody made them take the high stool away – because they were always putting out a high stool for her to perch on, not having realised she was a big girl. She hated having to hoist herself up, and teeter like an angel on a pinhead: getting her skirt trapped, and trying to drag it from under her bottom while keeping her balance: feeling the stool buck under her, threatening to pitch her off. Before Colette, she'd done whole shows standing, just leaning against the high stool, sometimes draping one arm over it, as if that were the reason why it was put there. But Colette just minced the management when she spotted a stool on stage. 'Take it away, she doesn't work under those conditions.'

Instead, Colette asked for an armchair, wide, capacious. Here, ideally, Alison would begin the evening, relaxed, ankles crossed, steadying her breathing before her opening remarks. At the first hint of a contact, she would lean forward; then she would jump up and advance to the front of the stage. She would hang over the audience, almost floating above their heads, her lucky opals flashing fire as she reached out, fingers spread. She'd got the lucky opals mail order but, if asked, she pretended they'd been left to her family by a Russian princess.

She had explained it all, when Colette first joined her. Russia was favourite for ancestors, even better than Romany, nowadays; you didn't want to put anxiety in the clients' minds, about fly-tipping, head lice, illegal tarmac gangs, or motorhomes invading the green belt. Italian descent was good, Irish was excellent – though you must be selective. In the Six Counties hardly anywhere would do – too likely to crop up on the news. For the rest, Cork and Tipperary sounded too comic, Wicklow and Wexford like minor ailments, and Waterford was too dull – 'Al,' Colette had said, 'from where do you derive your amazing psychic gifts tonight?' Al had said at once, in her platform voice, 'From my old great-grandmother, in County Clare. Bless her.'

Bless her and bless her, she said, under her breath. She looked away from the mirror so Colette wouldn't see her lips moving. Bless all my great-grandmothers, whoever and wherever they may be. May my dad rot in hell, whoever he may be; whatever hell is and wherever, let him rot in it; and let them please lock the doors of hell at night, so he can't be out and about, harassing me. Bless my mum, who is still earthside of course, but bless her anyway; wouldn't she be proud of me if she saw me in chiffon, each inch of my flesh powdered and perfumed? In chiffon, my nails lacquered, with my lucky opals glittering – would she be pleased? Instead of being dismembered in a dish, which I know was her first ambition for me: swimming in jelly and blood. Wouldn't she like to see me now, my head on my shoulders and my feet in my high-heeled shoes?

No, she thought, be realistic: she wouldn't give a toss.

* * *

Ten minutes to go. Abba on the sound system, 'Dancing Queen'. Glass of gin held in one hand, the bottle of tonic looped by her little finger, Colette peeped through a swing door at the back of the hall. Every seat was full and space was tight. They were turning people away, which the manager hated to do but it was fire regulations. How does it feel tonight? It feels all right. There'd been nights when she'd had to sit in the audience, so Alison could pick her out first and get the show going, but they didn't like doing that and they didn't need to do it often. Tonight she would be flitting around the hall with a microphone, identifying the people Al picked out and passing the mike along the rows so she could get clear answers out of them. We'll need three minimum to cover the space, she'd told the manager, and no comedians who trip over their own feet, please. She herself, fast and thin and practised, would do the work of two.

Colette thought, I can't stand them now: the clients, the punters, the trade. She didn't like to be among them, for any purpose. She couldn't believe that she was ever one of them: lining up to listen to Al, or somebody like her. Booking ahead (all major cards accepted) or jostling in a queue by the box office: a tenner in her fist, and her heart in her mouth.

Alison twisted her rings on her fingers: the lucky opals. It wasn't nerves exactly, more a strange feeling in her diaphragm, as if her gut were yawning: as if she were making space for what might occur. She heard Colette's footsteps: my gin, she thought. Good-good. Carefully, she took the mint out of her mouth. The action left her lips sulky; in the mirror, she edged them back into a smile, using the nail of her third finger, careful not to smudge. The face does disarrange itself; it has to be watched. She wrapped the mint in a tissue, looked around, and looped it hesitantly towards a metal bin a few feet away. It fell on the vinyl. Morris grunted with laughter. 'You're bloody hopeless, gel.'

This time, as Colette came in, she managed to step over Morris's legs. Morris squawked out, 'Tread on me, I love it.'

'Don't you start!' Al said. 'Not you. Morris. Sorry.'

Colette's face was thin and white. Her eyes had gone narrow, like arrow slits. 'I'm used to it.' She put the glass down by Alison's eyelash curlers, with the bottle of tonic water beside it.

'A splash,' Al directed. She picked up her glass and peered into the fizzing liquid. She held it up to the light.

'I'm afraid your ice has melted.'

'Never mind.' She frowned. 'I think there's someone coming through.'

'In your G & T?'

'I think I caught just a glimpse. An elderly person. Ah well. There'll be no lolling in the old armchair tonight. Straight on with the show.' She downed the drink, put the empty glass on the countertop with her strewn boxes of powder and eyeshadow. Morris would lick her glass while she was out, running his yellow fissured tongue around the rim. Over the public address system, the call came to switch off mobile phones. Al stared at herself in the mirror. 'No more to be done,' she said. She inched to the edge of her chair, wobbling a little at the hips. The manager put his face in at the door. 'All right?' Abba was fading down: 'Take a Chance on Me'. Al took a breath. She pushed her chair back; she rose, and began to shine.

She walked out into the light. The light, she would say, is where we come from, and it's to the light we return. Through the hall ran small detonations of applause, which she acknowledged only with a sweep of her thick lashes. She walked, slowly, right to the front of the stage, to the taped line. Her head turned. Her eyes searched, against the dazzle. Then she spoke, in her special platform voice. 'This young lady.' She was looking three rows back. 'This lady here. Your name is – ? Well, Leanne, I think I have a message for you.'

Colette released her breath from the tight space where she held it.

Alone, spotlit, perspiring slightly, Alison looked down at her audience. Her voice was low, sweet and confident, and her aura was a perfectly adjusted aquamarine, flowing like a silk shawl about her shoulders and upper arms. 'Now, Lee, I want you to sit back in your seat, take a deep breath, and relax. And that goes for all of you. Put on your happy faces – you're not going to see anything that will frighten you. I won't be going into a trance, and you won't be seeing spooks, or hearing spirit music.' She looked around, smiling, taking in the rows. 'So why don't you all sit back and enjoy the evening? All I do is, I just tune in, I just have to listen hard and decide who's out there. Now if I get a message for you, please raise your hand, shout up – because if you don't it's very frustrating for the spirits trying to come through. Don't be shy, you just shout up or give me a wave. Then my helpers will rush over to you with the microphone – don't be afraid of it when it comes to you, just hold it steady and speak up.'

They were all ages. The old had brought cushions for their bad backs, the young had bare midriffs and piercings. The young had stuffed their coats under their chairs, but their elders had rolled theirs and held them on their knees, like swaddled babies. 'Smile,' Al told them. 'You're here to enjoy yourselves, and so am I. Now, Lee my love, let me get back to you – where were we? There's a lady here called Kathleen, who's sending lots of love in your direction. Who would that be, Leanne?'

Leanne was a dud. She was a young lass of seventeen or so, hung about with unnecessary buttons and bows, her hair in twee little bunches, her face peaky. Kathleen, Al suggested, was her granny: but Leanne wouldn't own it because she didn't know her granny's name.

'Think hard, darling,' Al coaxed. 'She's desperate for a word with you.'

But Lee shook her bunches. She said that she didn't think she had a granny; which made some of the audience snigger. 'Kathleen says she lives in a field, at a certain amount of money. Bear with me. Penny. Penny Meadow, do you know that address? Up the hill from the market – such a pull, she says, when you've got a bagful of potatoes.' She smiled at the audience. 'This seems to be before you could order your groceries online,' she said. 'Honestly, when you think how they lived in those days – we forget to count our blessings, don't we? Now, Lee, what about Penny Meadow? What about Granny Kathleen walking uphill?'

Leanne indicated incredulity. *She* lived on Sandringham Court, she said.

'Yes, I know,' Al said. 'I know where you live, sweetheart, but this isn't anywhere around here, it's a filthy old place, Lancashire, Yorkshire, I'm getting a smudge on my fingers, it's grey, it's ash, it's something below the place you hang the washing – could it be Ashton-under-Lyne? Never mind,' Alison said. 'Go home, Leanne, and ask your mum what Granny was called. Ask her where she lived. Then you'll know, won't you, that she was here for you tonight?'

There was a patter of applause. Strictly speaking, she hadn't earned it. But they acknowledged that she'd tried; and Leanne's silliness, deeper than average, had brought the audience over to her side. It was not uncommon to find family memory so short, in these towns where nobody comes from, these south-eastern towns with their floating populations and their car parks where the centre should be. Nobody has roots here; and maybe they don't want to acknowledge roots, or recall their grimy places of origin and their illiterate fore-mothers up north. These days, besides, the kids don't remember back more than eighteen months – the drugs, she supposed. She was sorry for Kathleen, panting and striving, her wheezy goodwill evaporating, unacknowledged; Penny Meadow and all the terraced rows about seemed shrouded in a northern smog. Something about a cardigan, she was saying. A certain class of dead people was always talking about cardigans. The button off it, the pearl button, see if it's dropped behind the dresser drawer, that little drawer, that top drawer, I found a threepenny bit there once, back of the drawer, it gets down between the you-know, slips down the whatsit, it's wedged, like – and so I took it, this threepence, and I bought me friend a cake with a walnut on top. Yes, yes, Al said, they're lovely, those kind of cakes: but it's time to go, pet. Lie down, Kathleen. You go and have a nice lie-down. I will, Kathleen said, but tell her I want her mum to look for that button. And by the way, if you ever see my friend Maureen Harrison, tell her I've been looking for her this thirty year.

Colette's eyes darted around, looking for the next pickup. Her helpers were a boy of seventeen, in a sort of snooker player's outfit, a shiny waistcoat and a skewed bow tie; and, would you believe it, the dozy little slapper from the bar. Colette thought, I'll need to be everywhere. The first five minutes, thank God, are no guide to the evening to come.

Look, this is how you do it. Suppose it's a slow night, no one in particular pushing your buttons; only the confused distant chit-chat that comes from the world of the dead. So you're looking around the hall and smiling, saying, 'Look, I want to show you how I do what I do. I want to show you it's nothing scary, it's just, basically, abilities that we all have. Now can I ask, how many of you,' she pauses, looks around, 'how many of you have sometimes felt you're psychic?'

After that it's according to, as Colette would say, the demographics. There are shy towns and towns where the hands shoot up, and of course as soon as you're on stage you can sense the mood, even if you weren't tipped off about it, even if you've never been in that particular place before. But a little word, a word of encouragement, a 'don't hold back on me'; sooner or later the hands go up. You look around – there's always that compromise, between flattering stage lighting, and the need to see their faces. Then you choose a woman near the front, not so young as Leanne but not so old she's completely buggered up: and you get her to tell you her name.

'Gillian.'

Gillian. Right. Here goes.

'Gill, you're the sort of woman – well,' she gives a little laugh and a shake of her head, 'well, you're a bit of a human dynamo, I mean, that's how your friends describe you, isn't it? Always on the go, morning, noon and night, you're the sort of person, am I right, who can keep all the plates spinning? But if there's one thing, if there's one thing, you know, all your friends say, it's that you don't give enough time to yourself. I mean, you're the one everybody depends on, you're the one everybody comes to for advice, you're the Rock of Gibraltar, aren't you, but then you have to say to yourself, hang on, hang on a minute, who do *I* go to when *I* want advice? Who's there for Gilly, when it comes to the crunch? The thing is, you're very supportive, of your friends, your family, it's just give give give, and you do find yourself, just now and then, catching yourself up and saying, hang on now, who's giving back to me? And the thing about you, Gillian – now stop me if you think I'm wrong – is that you've got so much *to* give, but the problem is you're so busy running round picking up after other people and putting their lives to rights, that you haven't hardly got any opportunity to develop your own, I mean your own talents, your own interests. When you think back, when you think back to what made you happy as a young girl, and all the things you wanted out of life – you see, you've been on what I call a Cycle of Caring, and it's not given you, Gill, it's not given you the opportunity to look within, to look beyond – you really are capable, now I'm not telling you this to flatter you, but you really are capable of the most extraordinary things if you put your mind to it, if you just give all those talents of yours a chance to breathe. Now am I right? Say if I'm not right. Yes, you're nodding. Do you recognise yourself?'

Gillian has of course been nodding since the first time Al paused for breath. In Alison's experience there's not a woman alive who, once past her youth, doesn't recognise this as a true and fair assessment of her character and potential. Or there may be such a woman, out in some jungle or desert: but these blighted exceptions are not likely to be visiting Alison's Evening of Psychic Arts.

She is now established as a mind-reader; and if she can tell Gillian something about herself, her family, so much the better. But she's really done enough – Gillian's brimming with gratification – so even if nobody comes through from spirit, she can just move right on to whoever is her next target. But long before this point Alison has become conscious of a background mutter (at times rising to a roar) situated not there in the hall but towards the back of her skull, behind her ears, resonating privately in the bone. And on this evening, like every other, she fights down the panic we would all feel, trapped with a crowd of dead strangers whose intentions towards us we can't know. She takes a breath, she smiles, and she starts her peculiar form of listening. It is a silent sensory ascent; it is like listening from a stepladder, poised on the top rung; she listens at the ends of her nerves, at the limit of her capacities. When you're doing platform work, it's rare that the dead need coaxing. The skill is in isolating the voices, picking out one and letting the others recede – making them recede, forcing them back if need be, because there are some big egos in the next world. Then taking that voice, the dead voice you've chosen, and fitting it to the living body, to the ears that are ready to hear.

So: time to work the room. Colette tensed, forward on her toes, ready to sprint with the mike. 'This lady. I feel some connection with the law here. Do you have to see a solicitor?'

'Constantly,' the woman said. 'I'm married to one.'

There was a yell of laughter. Al joined it. Colette smirked. She won't lose them now, she thought. Of course she wanted Al to succeed; of course I do, she told herself. They had a joint mortgage, after all, financially they were tied together. And if I quit working for her, she thought, how would I get another job? When it comes to 'your last position', what would I put on my CV?

'Who's got indigestion at the back?' Al's forehead was damp, the skin at the nape of her neck was clammy. She liked to have clothes with pockets so she could carry a folded cologne tissue, ready for a surreptitious dab, but you don't usually get pockets in women's clothes, and it looks stupid taking a handbag out there on stage. 'This lady,' she said. She pointed; the lucky opals winked. 'This is the one I'm speaking to. You're the one with the heartburn, I can feel it. I have someone here for you who's very happy in spirit world, a Margo, Marje, can you accept that? A petite woman wearing a turquoise blouse, she was very fond of it, wasn't she? She says you'll remember.'

'I do remember, I do,' the woman said. She took the mike

gingerly, and held it as if it might detonate. 'Marje was my aunt. She was fond of turquoise and also lilac.'

'Yes,' and now Al softened her voice, 'and she was like a mother to you, wasn't she? She's still looking out for you, in spirit world. Now tell me, have you seen your GP about that indigestion?'

'No,' the woman said. 'Well, they're so busy.'

'They're well paid to look after you, my love.'

'Coughs and colds all around you,' the woman said. 'You come out worse than you went in – *and* you never see the same doctor twice.'

There was an audible smirk from the audience, a wash of fellow feeling. But the woman herself looked fretful. She wanted to hear from Marje; the dyspepsia she lived with every day.

'Stop making excuses.' Al almost stamped her foot. 'Marje says, why are you putting it off? Call the surgery tomorrow morning and book yourself in. There's nothing to be frightened of.'

Isn't there? Relief dawned on the woman's face; or an emotion that would be relief, when it clarified; for the moment she was tremulous, a hand on her ribs, folded in on herself as if to protect the space of the pain. It would take her a while to give up thinking it was cancer.

Now it's the glasses ploy. Look for a woman in middle age who isn't wearing glasses and say: have you had your eyes tested recently? Then the whole world of optometry is at your command. If she had an eye test last week, she'll say, yes, as a matter of fact I have. They'll applaud. If she says no, not recently, she'll be thinking, but I know I ought to . . . As for the woman who says she wears no glasses ever: oh, my love, those headaches of yours! Why don't you just pop along to Boots? I can see you, a month from now, in some really pretty squarish frames.

You could ask them if they need to see the dentist, since everybody does, all the time; but you don't want to see them flinch. You're giving them a gentle nudge, not a pinch. It's about impressing them without scaring them; softening the edges of their fright and disbelief.

'This lady – I see a broken wedding ring – did you lose your husband? He passed quite recently? And very recently you planted a rose bush in his memory.'

'Not exactly,' the woman said, 'I placed some – in fact it was carnations—'

'—carnations in his memory,' said Al, 'because they were his favourite, weren't they?'

'Oh, I don't know,' said the woman. Her voice slid off the mike; she was too worried to keep her head still.

'You know, aren't men funny?' Al threw it out to the audience. 'They just don't like talking about these things, they think it means they're oversensitive or something – as if we'd mind. But I can assure you, he's telling me now, carnations were his favourite.'

'But where *is* he?' the woman said: still off the mike. She wasn't going to quarrel about the flowers; she was pressed against the back of her seat, almost hostile, on the verge of tears.

Sometimes they waited for you afterwards, the punters, at the back exit, when you were running head down for the car park. In the ghastly lights behind the venue, in the drizzle and the rain, they'd say, when you gave me the message I didn't know, I didn't understand, I couldn't take it in. 'I know it's difficult,' Al would say, trying to soothe them, trying to help them, but trying, for God's sake, to get them off her back; she would be sweating, shaking, desperate to get into the car and off. But now, thank God, she had Colette, to manage the situation; Colette would smoothly pass over their business card, and say, 'When you feel ready, you might like to come for a private reading.'

Now Alison fished around in the front rows for somebody who'd lost a pet and found a woman whose terrier, on an impulse three weeks ago, had dashed out of the front door into the traffic. 'Don't you listen,' she told the woman, 'to people who tell you animals have no souls. They go on in spirit, same as we do.'

Animals distressed her, not cats, just dogs: their ownerless whimper as they padded through the afterlife on the trail of their masters. 'And has your husband gone over too?' she asked, and when the woman said yes, she nodded sympathetically but pulled her attention away, throwing out a new question, changing the topic: 'Anybody over here got blood pressure?'

Let her think it, that dog and master are together now; let her take comfort, since comfort's what she's paid for. Let her assume that Tiddles and his boss are together in the Beyond. Reunion is seldom so simple; and really it's better for dogs – if people could just grasp it – not to have an owner waiting for them, spiritside. Without a person to search for, they join up in happy packs, and within a year or two you never hear from them individually: there's just a joyful, corporate barking, instead of that lost whine, the sore pads, the disconsolate drooping head of the dog following a fading scent. Dogs had figured in her early life – men, and dogs – and much of that life was unclear to her. If you knew what the dogs were up to, she reasoned, if you knew what they were up to in spirit world, it might help you work out where their owners were now. They must be gone over, she thought, most of those men I knew when I was a child; the dogs, for sure, are in spirit, for years have passed and those kind of dogs don't make old bones. Sometimes in the supermarket she would find herself standing in Pets, eyeing up the squeaky toys, the big tough chews made for big friendly jaws; then she would shake herself, and move slowly back towards organic vegetables, where Colette would be waiting with the trolley, cross with her for vanishing.

She will be cross tonight, Al thought, smiling to herself: I've slipped up again about the blood pressure. Colette has nagged her, don't talk about blood pressure, talk about hypertension. When she'd argued back – 'they might not understand me' – Colette lost her temper and said, 'Alison, without blood pressure we'd all be dead, but if you want to sound like something from the remedial stream, don't let me get in your way.'

Now a woman put her hand up, admitted to the blood pressure.

'Carrying a bit of weight, aren't we, darling?' Al asked her. 'I've got your mum here. She's a bit annoyed with you – well, no, I'm pitching it a bit high – concerned, would be more like it. You need to drop a stone, she's saying. Can you accept that?' The woman nodded: humiliated. 'Oh, don't mind what *they* think.' Al swept her hand over the audience; she gave her special throaty chuckle, her woman-to-woman laugh. 'You've no need to worry about what anybody here's thinking, we could most of us stand to lose a few pounds. I mean, look at me, I'm a size twenty and not ashamed of it. But your mum now, your mum, she says you're letting yourself go, and that's a shame, because you know you're really, look at you, you've got such a lot going for you, lovely hair, lovely skin – well, excuse me, but it seems to me your mum's a plain-spoken lady, so excuse me if I offend anybody, she's saying, get up off your bum and go to the gym.'

This is Al's public self: a little bit jaunty and a little bit crude, a bit of a schoolmistress and a bit of a flirt. She often speaks to the public about 'my wicked sense of humour', warning them not to take offence; but what happens to her sense of humour in the depth of the night, when she wakes up trembling and crying, with Morris crowing at her in the corner of the room?

Colette thought, you are a size twenty-six. And you *are* ashamed of it. The thought was so loud, inside her own head, that she was amazed it didn't jump out into the hall. 'No,' Al was saying, 'please give the mike back to this lady, I'm afraid I've embarrassed her and I want to put it right.' The woman was reluctant, and Al said to her neighbour, 'Just hold that mike steady under her chin.' Then Alison told the fat woman several things about her mother, which she'd often thought but not liked to admit to. 'Oh, and I have your granny. Your granny's coming through. Sarah-Anne? Now she's an old soul,' Al said. 'You were five when she passed, am I right?'

'I'm not sure.'

'Speak up, my love.'

'Small. I was small.'

'Yes, you don't remember much about her, but the point is she's never left you, she's still around, looking after the family. And she likes those cabinets you've got – I can't quite make this out – a new kitchen, is it?'

'Oh my God. Yes,' the woman said. 'Yes.' She shifted in her seat and turned bright red.

Al chuckled, indulging her surprise. 'She's often with you in that kitchen. And by the way, you were right not to go for the brushed steel, I know they tried to talk you into it, but it's so over and done with, there's nothing worse than a dated kitchen when you come to sell, and besides it's such a harsh look at the heart of the home. Sarah-Anne says, you won't go wrong with light oak.'

They burst into applause: the punters, the trade. They are deeply appreciative over information about their kitchen fittings: they marvel at your uncanny knowledge of where they position their bread bin. This is how you handle them;

you tell them the small things, the personal things, the things no one else could really know. By this means you make them drop their guard: only then will the dead begin to speak. On a good night, you can hear the scepticism leaking from their minds, with a low hiss like a tyre deflating.

Someone in uniform was trying to get through. It was a policeman, young and keen, with a flushed face; he was eager for promotion. She worked the rows, but no one would own him. Perhaps he was still earthside, employed at the local station: you did get these crossed wires, from time to time. Something to do with radio frequencies, perhaps?

'This lady, have you got ear trouble? Or ear trouble somewhere in the family? Slowly, the barmaid lurched across the hall in her platform shoes, the mike held out at arm's length.

'What?' the woman said.

'Ear trouble.'

'The boy next door to me plays football,' the woman said, 'he's done his knee up. He was getting in trim for the World Cup. Not that he's playing in it. Only in the park. Their dog died last year, but I don't think it had ear trouble.'

'No, not your neighbour,' Al insisted. 'You, someone close to you.'

'I haven't got anyone close to me.'

'What about throat trouble? Nose trouble? Anything in the ENT line at all? You have to understand this,' Al said, 'when I get a message from spirit world, I can't give it back. I can't pick and choose. Think of me as your answering machine. Imagine if people from spirit world had phones. Now your answering machine, you press the button and it plays your messages back. It doesn't wipe some out, on the grounds that you don't need to know them.'

'And it records the wrong numbers, too,' said a pert girl near the front. She had her friends with her; their sniggers ruffled adjacent rows.

Alison smiled. It was for her to make the jokes; she wouldn't be upstaged. 'Yes, I admit we record the wrong numbers. And we record the nuisance calls, if you like to put it that way. I sometimes think they have telesales in the next world, because I never sit down with a nice cup of coffee without some stranger trying to get through. Just imagine – double-glazing salesmen . . . debt collectors . . .'

The girl's smile faded. She tensed. Al said, 'Look, darling. Let me give you a word of advice. Cut up that credit card. Throw away those catalogues. You can break these spending habits – well, you must, really. You have to grow up and exercise some self-control. Or I can see the bailiffs in, before Christmas.'

Al's gaze rested, one by one, on those who had dared to snigger; then she dropped her voice, whipped her attention away from the troublemaker and became confidential with her audience. 'The point is this. If I get a message I don't censor it. I don't ask, do you need it? I don't ask, does it make sense? I do my duty, I do what I'm here for. I put it out there, so the person it applies to can pick it up. Now people in spirit world can make mistakes. They can be wrong, just like the living. But what I hear, I pass on. And it may happen, you know, what I tell you may mean nothing to you at the time. That's why I sometimes have to say to you, stay with that: go home: live with it. This week or next week, you'll go, oh I get it now! Then you'll have a little smile, and think, she wasn't such a fool, was she?' She crossed the stage; the opals blazed. 'And then again, there are some messages from spirit world that aren't as simple as they seem. This lady, for example, when I speak about ear trouble, what I may be picking up is not so much a physical problem – I might be talking about a breakdown in communication.'

The woman stared up at her glassily. Al passed on. 'Jenny's here. She went suddenly. She didn't feel the impact, it was instantaneous. She wants you to know.'

'Yes.'

'And she sends her love to Peg. Who's Peg?'

'Her aunt.'

'And to Sally, and Mrs Moss. And Liam. And Topsy.'

Jenny lay down. She'd had enough. Her little light was fading. But wait, here's another – tonight she picked them up as if she were vacuuming the carpet. But it was almost nine o'clock, and it was quite usual to get on to something serious and painful before the interval. 'Your little girl, was she very poorly before she passed? I'm getting – this is not recent, we're going back now, but I have a very clear – I have a picture of a poor little mite who's really very sick, bless her.'

'It was leukaemia,' her mother said.

'Yes, yes, yes,' Al said, swiftly agreeing, as if she had thought of it first: so that the woman would go home and say, she told me Lisa had leukaemia, she knew. All she could feel was the weakness and the heat, the energy of the last battle draining away: the flickering pulse at the hairless temple, and the blue eyes, like marbles under translucent lids, rolling into stillness. Dry your tears, Alison said. All the tears of agony you've shed, the world doesn't know, the world can't count them; and soberly, the woman agreed: nobody knows, she said, and nobody can count. Al, her own voice trembling, assured her, Lisa's doing fine airside, the next world's treated her well. A beautiful young woman stood before her – twenty-two, twenty-three – wearing her grandmother's bridal veil. But whether it was Lisa or not, Al could not say.

Eight fifty, by Colette's watch. It was time for Al to lighten up. You have to start this process no less than eight minutes before the end of the first half. If the interval catches you in the middle of something thrilling and risky, they simply don't want to break; but she, Al, she needed the break, to get back there, touch base with Colette, gulp a cold drink and redo her face. So she would begin another ward round now, picking up a few aches and pains. Already she was homing in on a woman who suffered from headaches. Don't we all? Colette thought. It was one of the nets Al could safely cast. God knows, her own head ached. There was something about these summer nights, summer nights in small towns, that made you feel that you were seventeen again, and had chances in life. The throat ached and clogged then; there was tightness behind her eyes, as if unshed tears had banked up. Her nose was running, and she hadn't got a tissue.

Al had found a woman with a stiff left knee, and was advising her on traditional Chinese medicine; it was a diversion, but they'd go away disappointed if she didn't throw in some jargon about meridians and ley lines and chakras and feng shui. Gently, soothingly, she was bringing the first part of the evening to a close; and she was having her little joke now, asking about the lady standing at the back, leaning against the wall there, the lady in beige with a bit of a sniffle. It's ridiculous, Colette thought, she can't possibly see me, from where she's standing. She just, somehow, she must just simply know that at some point in the evening I cry. 'Never mind, my dear,' Al said. 'A runny nose is nothing to be ashamed of. Wipe it on your sleeve. We're not looking, are we?'

You'll pay for it later, Colette thought, and so she will; she'll have to regurgitate or else digest all the distress that she's sucked in from the carpet and the walls. By the end of the evening she'll be sick to her stomach from other people's chemotherapy, feverish and short of breath; or twitching and cold, full of their torsions and strains. She'll have a neck spasm, or a twisted knee, or a foot she can hardly put on the floor. She'll need to climb into the bath, moaning, amid the rising steam of aromatherapy oils from her special travel pack; and knock back a handful of painkillers, which, she always says, she should be allowed to set against her income tax.

Almost nine o'clock. Alison looked up, to the big double doors marked EXIT. There was a little green man above the door, running on the spot. She felt like that little green man. 'Time to break,' she said. 'You've been lovely.' She waved to them. 'Stretch your legs and I'll see you in fifteen.'

Morris was sprawled in Al's chair when she came into her dressing room. He had his dick out and his foreskin pushed back, and he'd been playing with her lipstick, winding it up to the top of the tube. She evicted him with a dig to his shin from her pointed toe; dropped herself into the vacated chair – she shuddered at the heat of it – and kicked off her shoes.

'Do yourself up,' she told him. 'Button your trousers, Morris.' She spoke to him as if he were a two-year-old who hadn't learned the common decencies.

She eased off the opals. 'My hands have swelled up.' Colette watched her through the mirror. Al's skin was bland and creamy, flesh and fluid plumping it out from beneath. 'Is the air conditioning working?' She pulled at bits of her clothing, detaching them from the sticky bits of herself.

'As if carnations were anybody's favourite!' Colette said.

'What?' Al was shaking her hands in the air, as if they were damp washing.

'That poor woman who was just widowed. You said roses, but she said carnations, so then you said carnations.'

'Colette, could you try to bear in mind, I've talked to about thirty people since then?'

Alison held her arms in a 'U' above her head, her naked fingers spread. 'Let the fluid drain,' she said. 'Anything else, Colette? Let's have it.'

'You always say, oh, keep a note, Colette, keep your eyes

open, listen out and tell me what goes right and what goes wrong. But you're not willing to listen, are you? Perhaps it's you who's got the hearing problem.'

'At least I haven't got a sniffle problem.'

'I can never understand why you take your shoes off, and your rings off, when you've got to force them back on again.'

'Can't you?' Al sipped her blackcurrant juice, which she brought with her in her own carton. 'What can you understand?' Though Al's voice was lazy, this was turning into a nasty little scrap. Morris had lain down across the doorway, ready to trip up anyone who came in.

'Try thinking yourself into my body,' Al suggested. Colette turned away and mouthed, *no thank you.* 'It's hot under the lights. Half an hour and I'm fit to drop. I know you've been running around with the mike, but it's easier on the feet to be moving than standing still.'

'Is it really? How would you know that?'

'It's easy, when you're thin. Everything's easier. Moving. Thinking. Deciding what you'll do and what you won't. You have choices. You can choose your clothes. Choose your company. I can't.' Al drank the end of her carton, with a little sound of sucking and bubbling. She put it down, and squashed the tip of the straw, judiciously, with her forefinger.

'Oh, and the kitchen units,' Colette said.

'What's your problem? I was right.'

'It's just telepathy,' Colette said.

'*Just*?'

'Her granny didn't tell you.'

'How can you be sure?'

She couldn't, of course. Like the punters out there, she could entertain simultaneously any number of conflicting opinions. They could believe in Al, and not believe in her, both at once. Faced with the impossible, their minds, like Colette's, simply scuttled off in another direction.

'Look,' Alison said, 'do we have to go through this every time? I would have thought we'd been on the road together for long enough now. And we've been making the tapes, haven't we? Writing this book you say we're writing? I'd have thought I'd answered most of your questions by now.'

'All except the ones that matter.'

Al shrugged. A quick dab of Rescue Remedy under the tongue, and then she began to repaint her lips. Colette could see the effort of concentration needed; the spirits were nagging in her ear, wanting to stake out their places for the second half.

'You see, I'd have imagined,' she said, 'that sometimes, once in a while, you'd feel the urge to be honest.'

Alison gave a little comic shiver, like a character in a pantomime. 'What, with the punters? They'd run a mile,' she said. 'Even the ones with the blood pressure would be up and charging out the door. It'd kill them.' She stood up and pulled down her clothes, smoothing the creases over her hips. 'And what would that do but make more work for me?'

'Your hem's up at the back,' Colette said. Sighing, she sank to her knees and gave the satin a tug.

'I'm afraid it's my bottom that does it,' Al said. 'Oh dear.' She turned sideways to the mirror, resettled the skirt at what passed for her waistline. 'Am I OK now?' She held up her arms, stamped her feet in her high heels. 'I could have been a flamenco dancer,' she said. 'That would have been more fun.'

'Oh, surely not,' Colette said. 'Not more fun than this?' She nudged her own head at the mirror, and smoothed down her hair; damp, it lay on her head like strings of white licqorice.

The manager put his head around the door. 'All right?' he said.

'Will you stop saying that?' Colette turned on him. 'No, not all right. I want you out there for the second half, that girl from the bar is useless. And turn the bloody air conditioning up, we're all melting.' She indicated Alison. 'Especially her.'

Morris rolled lazily on to his back in the doorway and made faces at the manager. 'Bossy cow, ain't she?'

'So sorry to disturb your toilette,' the manager said, bowing to Alison.

'OK, OK, time to move.' Colette clapped her hands. 'They're out there waiting.'

Morris grabbed Al's ankle as she stepped over him. She checked her stride, took a half-pace backwards, and ground her heel into his face.

The second half usually began with a question-and-answer session. When Colette first joined Al she had worried about this part of the evening. She waited for some sceptic to jump up and challenge Al about her mistakes and evasions. But Al laughed. She said, those sort of people don't come out at night, they stay at home watching *Question Time* and shouting at the TV.

Tonight they were quick off the mark. A woman stood up, wreathed in smiles. She accepted the microphone easily, like a professional. 'Well, you can guess what we all want to know.'

Al simpered back at her. 'The royal passing.'

The woman all but curtsied. 'Have you had any communication from Her Majesty the Queen Mother? How is she faring in the other world? Has she been reunited with King George?'

'Oh yes,' Alison said, 'she'll be reunited.'

In fact, the chances are about the same as meeting somebody you know at a main-line station at rush hour. It's not 14 million to one, like the National Lottery, but you have to take into account that the dead, like the living, sometimes like to dodge and weave.

'And Princess Margaret? Has she seen HRH her daughter?'

Princess Margaret came through. Al couldn't stop her. She seemed to be singing a comic song. Nothing derails an evening so fast as royalty. They expect to make the running, they choose the topic, they talk and you're supposed to listen. Somebody, perhaps the princess herself, was pounding a piano, and other voices were beginning to chime in. But Alison was in a hurry; she wanted to get to a man, the evening's first man, who'd got his hand up with a question. Ruthless, she gave the whole tribe the brush-off: Margaret Rose, Princess Di, Prince Albert, and a faint old cove who might be some sort of Plantagenet. It was interesting for Al that you got so many history programmes on TV these days. Many a night she'd sat on the sofa, hugging her plump calves, pointing out people she knew. 'Is that really Mrs Pankhurst?' she'd say. 'I've never seen her in that hat.'

The man had risen to his feet. The manager – pretty quick round the room now Colette had given him a rocket – had got the mike across the hall. Poor old bloke, he looked shaky. 'I've never done this before,' he said.

'Take it steady,' Al advised. 'No need to rush, sir.'

'Never been to one of these,' he said. 'But I'm getting on a bit myself, now, so . . .' He wanted to know about his dad, who'd had an amputation before he died. Would he be reunited with his leg, in spirit world?

Al could reassure him on the point. In spirit world, she said, people are healthy and in their prime. 'They've got all their bits and whatsits. Whenever they were at their happiest, whenever they were at their healthiest, that's how you'll find them in spirit world.'

The logic of this, as Colette had often pointed out, was that a wife could find herself paired with a pre-adolescent for a husband. Or your son could, in spirit world, be older than you. 'You're quite right, of course,' Al would say blithely.

Her view was, believe what you want, Colette: I'm not here to justify myself to you.

The old man didn't sit down; he clung, as if he were at sea, to the back of the chair in the row ahead. He was hoping his dad would come through, he said, with a message. Al smiled. 'I wish I could get him for you, sir. But again it's like the telephone, isn't it? I can't call them, they have to call me. They have to want to come through. And then again, I need a bit of help from my spirit guide.'

It was at this stage in the evening that it usually came out about the spirit guide. 'He's a little circus clown,' Al would say. 'Morris is the name. Been with me since I was a child. I used to see him everywhere. He's a darling little bloke, always laughing, tumbling, doing his tricks. It's from Morris that I get my wicked sense of humour.'

Colette could only admire the radiant sincerity with which Al said this: year after year, night after bloody night. She blazed like a planet, the lucky opals her distant moons. For Morris insisted, he insisted that she give him a good character, and if he wasn't flattered and talked up, he'd get his revenge. 'But then,' Al said to the audience, 'he's got his serious side too. He certainly has. You've heard, haven't you, of the tears of a clown?'

This led on to the next, the obvious question: how old was she when she first knew about her extraordinary psychic gifts?

'Very small, very small indeed. In fact, I remember being aware of presences before I could walk or talk. But of course it was the usual story with a sensitive child – sensitive is what we call it, when a person's attuned to spirit – you tell the grown-ups what you see, what you hear, but they don't want to know, you're just a kiddie, they think you're fantasising. I mean, I was often accused of being naughty when I was only passing on some comment that had come to me through Spirit. Not that I hold it against my mum, God bless her, I mean, she's had a lot of trouble in her life – and then along came me!' The trade chuckled, en masse, indulgent.

Time to draw questions to a close, Alison said; because now I'm going to try to make some more contacts for you. There was applause. 'Oh you're so lovely,' she said. 'Such a lovely, warm and understanding audience, I can always count on a good time whenever I come in your direction. Now I want you to sit back, I want you to relax, I want you to smile, and I want you to send some lovely positive thoughts up here to me . . . and let's see what we can get.'

Colette glanced down the hall. The manager seemed to have his eye on the ball, and the vague boy, after shambling about aimlessly for the first half, was now at least looking at the trade instead of up at the ceiling or down at his own feet. Time to slip backstage for a cigarette? It was smoking that kept her thin: smoking and running and worrying. Her heels clicked in the dim narrow passage, on the composition floor.

The dressing-room door was closed. She hesitated in front of it. Afraid, always, that she'd see Morris. Al said there was a knack to seeing spirit. It was to do with glancing sideways, not turning your head: extending, Al said, your field of peripheral vision.

Colette kept her eyes fixed in front of her; sometimes, the rigidity she imposed seemed to make them ache in their sockets. She pushed the door open with her foot, and stood back. Nothing rushed out. On the threshold she took a breath. Sometimes she thought she could smell him; Al said he'd always smelled. Deliberately, she turned her head from side to side, checking the corners. Al's scent lay sweetly on the air: there was an undernote of corrosion, damp and drains. Nothing was visible. She glanced into the mirror, and her hand went up automatically to pat her hair.

She enjoyed her cigarette in the corridor, wafting the smoke away from her with a rigid palm, careful not to set off the fire alarm. She was back in the hall in time to witness the dramatic highlight; which was always, for her, some punter turning stroppy.

Al had found a woman's father, in spirit world. 'Your daddy's still keeping an eye on you,' she cooed.

The woman jumped to her feet. She was a small aggressive blonde in a khaki vest, her cold bluish biceps pumped up at the gym. 'Tell the old sod to bugger off,' she said. 'Tell the old sod to stuff himself. Happiest day of my life when that fucker popped his clogs.' She knocked the mike aside. 'I'm here for my boyfriend that was killed in a pile-up on the sodding M25.'

Al said, 'There's often a lot of anger when someone passes. It's natural.'

'Natural?' the girl said. 'There was nothing natural about that fucker. If I hear any more about my bastard dad I'll see you outside and sort you out.'

The trade gasped, right across the hall. The manager was moving in, but anyone could see he didn't fancy his chances. Al seemed quite cool. She started chatting, saying anything and nothing – now, after all, would have been a good time for a breakthrough ditty from Margaret Rose. It was the woman's two friends who calmed her; they waved away the vague boy with the mike, dabbed at her cheeks with a screwed-up tissue, and persuaded her back into her seat, where she muttered and fumed.

Now Alison's attention crossed the hall, rested on another woman, not young, who had a husband with her: a heavy man, ill at ease. 'Yes, this lady. You have a child in spirit world.'

The woman said politely, no, no children. She said it as if she had said it many times before; as if she were standing at a turnstile, buying admission tickets and refusing the half-price.

'I can see there are none earthside, but I'm talking about the little boy you lost. Well, I say little boy. Of course, he's a man now. He's telling me we have to go back to, back a good few years, we're talking here thirty years and more. And it was hard for you, I know, because you were very young, darling, and you cried and cried, didn't you? Yes, of course you did.'

In these situations, Al kept her nerve; she'd had practice. Even the people at the other side of the hall, craning for a view, knew something was up and fell quiet. The seconds stretched out. In time, the woman's mouth moved.

'On the mike, darling. Talk to the mike. Speak up, speak out, don't be afraid. There isn't anybody here who isn't sharing your pain.'

Am I? Colette asked herself. I'm not sure I am.

'It was a miscarriage,' the woman said. 'I never, I never saw. It wasn't, they didn't, and so I didn't—'

'Didn't know it was a little boy. But,' Al said softly, 'you know now.' She turned her head to encompass the hall: 'You see, we have to recognise that it wasn't a very compassionate world back then. Times have changed, and for that we can all be thankful. I'm sure those nurses and doctors were doing their best, and they didn't mean to hurt you, but the fact is, you weren't given a chance to grieve.'

The woman hunched forward. Tears sprang out of her eyes. The heavy husband moved forward, as if to catch them. The hall was rapt.

'What I want you to know is this.' Al's voice was calm, unhurried, without the touch of tenderness that would overwhelm the woman entirely; dignified and precise, she might have been querying a grocery bill. 'That little boy of yours is a fine young man now. He knows you never held him.

He knows that's not your fault. He knows how your heart aches. He knows how you've thought of him,' Al dropped her voice, 'always, always, without missing a day. He's telling me this, from spirit. He understands what happened. He's opening his arms to you, and he's holding you now.'

Another woman, in the row behind, began to sob. Al had to be careful, at this point, to minimise the risk of mass hysteria. *Women,* Colette thought: as if she weren't one. But Alison knew just how far she could take it. She was on form tonight; experience tells. 'And he doesn't forget your husband,' she told the woman. 'He says hello to his dad.' It's the right note, braced, unsentimental: 'Hello, Dad.' The trade sighed, a low mass sigh. 'And the point is, and he wants you to know this, that though you've never been there to look after him, and though of course there's no substitute for a mother's love, your little boy has been cared for and cherished, because you've got people in spirit who've always been there for him – your own grandma? And there's another lady, very dear to your family, who passed the year you were married.' She hesitated. 'Bear with me, I'm trying for her name. I get the colour of a jewel. I get a taste of sherry. Sherry, that's not a jewel, is it? Oh, I know, it's a glass of port. Ruby. Does that name mean anything to you?'

The woman nodded, again and again and again: as if she could never nod enough. Her husband whispered to her, 'Ruby, you know – Eddie's first wife?' The mike picked it up. 'I know, I know,' she muttered. She gripped his hand. Her fluttering breath registered. You could almost hear her heart.

'She's got a parcel for you,' Al said. 'No, wait, she's got two.'

'She gave us two wedding presents. An electric blanket *and* some sheets.'

'Well,' Al said, 'if Ruby kept you so warm and cosy, I think you could trust her with your baby.' She threw it out to the audience. 'What do you say?'

They began to clap: sporadically, then with gathering force. Weeping broke out again. Al lifted her arm. Obedient to a strange gravity, the lucky opals rose and fell. She'd saved her best effect till last. 'And he wants you to know, this little boy of yours who's a fine young man now, that in spirit he goes by the name you chose for him, the name you had planned to give him . . . if it, if he, if he was a boy. Which was,' she pauses, 'correct me if I'm wrong, which was Alistair.'

'Was it?' said the heavy husband: he was still on the mike, though he didn't know it. The woman nodded. 'Would you like to answer me?' Al asked pleasantly.

The man cleared his throat, then spoke straight into the mike. 'Alistair. She says that's right. That was her choice. Yes.'

Unseeing, he handed the mike to his neighbour. The woman got to her feet, and the heavy man led her away, as if she were an invalid, her handkerchief held over her mouth. They exited, to a fresh storm of applause.

'Steroid rage, I expect,' Al said. 'Did you see those muscles of hers?' She was sitting up in her hotel bed, dabbing cream on her face. 'Look, Col, as you quite well know, everything that can go wrong for me out there, has gone wrong at some-time. I can cope. I can weather it. I don't want you getting stressed.'

'I'm not stressed. I just think it's a landmark. The first time anybody's threatened to beat you up.'

'The first time while you've been with me, maybe. That's why I gave up working in London.' Al sat back against the pillows, her eyes closed; she pushed the hair back from her forehead, and Colette saw the jagged scar at her hairline, dead white against ivory. 'Who needs it? A fight every night. And the trade pawing you when you try to leave, so you miss the last train home. I like to get home. But you know that, Col.'

She doesn't like night driving, either; so when they're outside the ring of the M25, there's nothing for it except to put up somewhere, the two of them in a twin room. A bed and breakfast is no good because Al can't last through till breakfast, so for preference they need a hotel that will do food through the night. Sometimes they take pre-packed sandwiches, but it's joyless for Al, sitting up in bed at 4 a.m., sliding a finger into the plastic triangle to fish out the damp bread. There's a lot of sadness in hotel rooms, soaked up by the soft furnishings: a lot of loneliness and guilt and regret. A lot of ghosts too: whiskery chambermaids stumping down the corridors on their bad legs, tippling night porters who've collapsed on the job, guests who've drowned in the bath or suffered a stroke in their beds. When they check into a room Alison stands on the threshold and sniffs the atmosphere, inhales it: and her eyes travel dubiously around. More than once, Colette has shot down to reception to ask for a different room. 'What's the problem?' the receptionists will say (sometimes adding 'madam') and Colette, stiff with hostility and fright, will say, 'Why do you need to know?' She never fails in her mission: challenged, she can pump out as much aggression as the girl in the khaki vest.

What Alison prefers is somewhere new-built and anonymous, part of some reliable chain. She hates history: unless it's on the television, safe behind glass. She won't thank you for a night in a place with beams. 'Sod the inglenooks,' she once said, after an exhausting hour tussling with an old corpse in a sheet. The dead are like that; give them a cliché, and they'll run to it. They enjoy frustrating the living, spoiling their beauty sleep. They enjoyed pummelling Al's flesh, and nagging at her till she got earache; they rattled around in her head until some nights, like tonight, it seemed to quiver on the soft stem of her neck. 'Col,' she groaned, 'be a good girl, rummage around in the bags and see if you can find my lavender spray. My head's throbbing.'

Colette knelt on the floor and rummaged as directed. 'That woman at the end, the couple, the miscarriage – you could have heard a pin drop.'

Al said, '"See a pin and pick it up and all the day you'll have good luck." My mum told me that. I never do, though. See a pin. Or find money in the street.'

That's because you're too fat to see your feet, Colette thought. She said, 'How did you do that thing with the name? When you were going on about mother love I nearly puked, but I have to hand it to you, you got there in the end.'

'Alistair? Well, of course, if he'd been called John, you wouldn't be giving me any credit. You'd have said it was one of my lucky guesses.' She sighed. 'Look, Colette, what can I tell you? The boy was standing there. He knew his own name. People do.'

'The mother, she must have been thinking his name.'

'Oh yes, I could have picked it out of her head. I know that's your theory. Mind-reading. Oh God, Colette.' Al slid down inside the covers. She closed her eyes. Her head dropped back against the pillows. 'Think that, if you find it easier. But you will admit I sometimes tell people things they've yet to find out.'

She hated that phrase of Al's: 'Think that, if you find it easier.' As if she were a child and couldn't be told the truth. Al only seemed dense – it was part of her act. The truth was, she listened to Radio 4 when they were on the road. She'd got a vocabulary, though she didn't use it on the trade. She was quite a serious and complicated person, and deep, deep and sly: that was what Colette thought.

Al seldom talked about death. At first when they started

working together, Colette had thought the word would slip out, if only through the pressure of trying to avoid it. And sometimes it did; but mostly Al talked about passing, she talked about spirit, she talked about passing into spirit world; to that eventless realm, neither cold nor hot, neither hilly nor flat, where the dead, each at their own best age and marooned in an eternal afternoon, pass the ages with sod all going on. Spirit world, as Al describes it to the trade, is a garden, or to be more accurate a public place in the open air: litter-free like an old-fashioned park, with a bandstand in a heat haze in the distance. Here the dead sit in rows on benches, families together, on gravelled paths between weedless beds, where heat-sozzled flowers bob their heads, heavy with the scent of eau de Cologne: their petals crawling with furry, intelligent, stingless bees. There's a certain 1950s air about the dead, or early sixties perhaps, because they're clean and respectable and they don't stink of factories: as if they came after white nylon shirts and indoor sanitation, but before satire, certainly before sexual intercourse. Unmelting ice cubes (in novelty shapes) chink in their glasses, for the age of refrigeration has come. They eat picnics with silver forks; purely for pleasure, because they never feel hunger, nor gain weight. No wind blows there, only a gentle breeze, the temperature being controlled at a moderate 71° F; these are the English dead, and they don't have centigrade yet. All picnics are share and share alike. The children never squabble or cut their knees, for whatever happened to them earthside, they are beyond physical damage now. The sun shall not strike them by day nor the moon by night; they have no red skin or freckles, none of the flaws that make the English so uncouth in summer. It's Sunday, yet the shops are open, though no one needs anything. A mild air plays in the background, not quite Bach, possibly Vaughan Williams, quite like the early Beatles too; the birds sing along, in the green branches of the seasonless trees. The dead have no sense of time, no clear sense of place; they are beyond geography and history, she tells her clients, till someone like herself tunes in. Not one of them is old or decrepit or uselessly young. They all have their own teeth: or an expensive set of implants, if their own were unsightly. Their damaged chromosomes are counted and shuffled into good order; even the early miscarriages have functioning lungs and a proper head of hair. Damaged livers have been replaced, so their owners live to drink another day. Blighted lungs now suck at God's own low-tar blend. Cancerous breasts have been rescued from the surgeons' bin, and blossom like roses on spirit chests.

Al opened her eyes. 'Col, are you there? I was dreaming that I was hungry.'

'I'll ring down for a sandwich, shall I?'

She considered. 'Get me ham on brown. Wholemeal. Dab of mustard – French, not English. Dijon – tell them cupboard on the left, third shelf. Ask them for – do they do a cheese plate? I'd like a slice of Brie and some grapes. And some cake. Not chocolate. Coffee maybe. Walnuts. It has walnuts on top. Two at the rim and one in the centre.'

In the night Al would be out of bed, her large outline blocking the light that leaked in from the hotel forecourt; it was the sudden darkness that woke Colette, and she would stir and see Al outlined, in her chiffon and lace, against the glow from the bedside lamp. 'What's the matter, what do you need?' Colette would murmur: because you didn't know what was happening, it could be trivial, but then again . . . Sometimes Al wanted chocolate out of her bag, sometimes she was facing the pangs of birth or the shock of a car crash. They might be awake for minutes or hours. Colette would slide out of bed and fill the plastic kettle, jerking its cord into its socket. Sometimes the water remained unboiled and Al would break off from her travail and say, 'Plug switched on at the socket, Col?' and she would hiss, yes, yes, and shake the bloody thing so that water slopped out of the spout; and quite often, that would make it go: so temper, Al said, was just as good as electricity. Then while Al rolled towards the bathroom to retch over the bowl, she would forage for dusty tea bags and tubs of UHT; and eventually they would sit side by side, their hands wrapped around the hotel cups, and Al would mutter, 'Colette, I don't know how you do it. All your patience. These broken nights.'

'Oh, you know,' she'd joke. 'If I'd had kids . . .'

'I'm grateful. I might not show it. But I am, sweetheart. I don't know where I'd be now, if we'd never met.'

At these times, Colette felt for her; she was not without feeling, though life had pushed her pretty far in that direction. Al's features would be softened and blurred, her voice would be the same. She would have panda eyes from the night's make-up, however diligent she'd been with the cotton-wool pads; and there was something childlike about her, as she made her apologies for the way she made her living. For the bad nights Colette carried brandy, to ward off fresh nausea and bouts of pain. Crouching to slide a hand into her overnight bag, she'd think, Al, don't leave me, don't die and leave me without a house and a job. You're a silly cow, but I don't want to do this world on my own.

So, after a night more or less broken, they would fight back to wakefulness, somewhere around seven thirty, side by side in their twin beds. Whatever had happened during the night, however many times she had been up and down, Colette's sheets were still tucked in tight, as if her body were completely flat. Al's bed looked, more often than not, as if there had been an earthquake in it. On the floor by their slippers they would find last night's room-service plates, with a pallid half-tomato and some crumbled potato crisps; cold sodden tea bags in a saucer, and strange grey-white fragments, like the ghosts of boiled water, floating in the bottom of the kettle. Colette would put on breakfast TV to swamp the traffic noise beyond the window, the sigh of tyres, the rumble of distant aircraft approaching Luton: or Stansted, if they had headed east. Al would lever herself, groaning, from the wreck of her bed, and begin the complex business of putting her persona in place; then she would go down for her breakfast. Colette would kick the remnants of room service out into the corridor, begin picking up after them and packing their bags. Al brought her own towelling robe, and now it was damp and perfumed after her bath, and bulked out the case; hotel robes didn't fit her, she would have needed to tie two together in some sort of Siamese twin arrangement. She always travelled with two or three pairs of scissors, and her own sewing kit; as if she were afraid that she might begin to unravel. Colette would pack these items away; then she would put the lucky opals in the case, count the bracelets, fit the make-up brushes snugly into their tabs and crevices, retrieve the hairpiece from where it was lying; pull from the closet her own insignificant crease-free outfits, flop them over her arm and drop them into her bag. She could not eat breakfast; it was because, when she had been with her husband Gavin, breakfast had been prime time for rows. She would forage for more tea, though often the allocation of room supplies was so mean that she'd be left with the Earl Grey. Sipping it, she would raise the window blind, on Home Counties rain or vapid sunshine. Al would tap on the door to be let in – there was only ever the one key in these places – and come in looking fat, full of poached eggs. She would cast a critical eye over the packing, and begin, because she was ashamed of it, to haul her bed into some sort of shape, dragging up the blankets from the floor and sneezing gently as she did so. Colette would reach into her bag and flip over the antihistamines. 'Water,' Al would say, sitting down, as if exhausted, among the poor results of her labour. Then, 'Steal the shower caps,' because, she would say, 'you can't get them these days, you know, and they're only good for twice.' So Colette would go back into the bathroom to pocket the shower-cap supplies; they left the shampoos and the slivers of soap, they weren't cheap or petty in that way at all. And her mind would be running, it's 8.30 and Morris not here, steal all shower caps, check behind bathroom door, 8.31 and he's not here, out of bathroom looking cheerful, throw stolen shower caps into bag, switch off TV, say are we right then, 8.32 and Al stands up, 8.32 she wanders to the mirror, 8.33 she is dropping the sodden tea bags from the saucer into the used cups, Al, she says, what are you doing, can we not get on the road please . . . and then she will see Al's shoulders tense. It's nothing she's done, nothing she's said: it's the banging and cursing, audible only to Al, that tells her they have been rejoined by Morris.

It was one of the few blessings Colette could count, that he didn't always stay the night when they were away. The lure of strange towns was too much for him, and it was her job to provide him with a strange town. To stray up to a five-mile range from their lodging didn't seem to bother him. On his bent, tough little legs, he was a good walker. But reservations at room-only motor lodges were not his favourite. He grumbled that there was nothing to do, stranded somewhere along the motorway, and he would sit in the corner of their room being disgusting. Al would shout at him for picking his feet; after that, she would go quiet and look furious, so Colette could only guess what he might be doing. He grumbled also if to get to his evening out he had to take a bus ride or find himself a lift. He liked to be sure, he said, that if need be he could get back to her within twenty minutes of the pubs closing. 'What does he mean, if need be?' she'd asked. 'What would happen if you were separated from Morris? Would you die?' Oh no, Al had said; he's just a control freak. I wouldn't die, neither would he. Though he has already, of course. And it seemed that no harm came to him on the nights when he would fall in with some other lowlifes and drift off with them, and forget to come home. All next day they'd have to put up with him repeating the beery jokes and catchphrases he had picked up.

When she'd first joined Al, she'd not understood about Morris. How could she? It wasn't within the usual range of experience. She had hoped that he'd just lurch off one night and not come back; that he'd have an accident, get a blow on the head that would affect his memory, so he'd not be able to find his way back to them. Even now, she often thought that if she could get Al out of a place on the dot of eight thirty, they'd outsmart him; hurtle back on to the motorway and leave him behind, cursing and swearing and walking around all the cars in the car parks, bending down and peering at the number plates. But somehow, try as she might, they could never get ahead of him. At the last moment, Al would pause, as she was hauling her seat belt over her bulk. 'Morris,' she would say, and click the belt's head into its housing.

If Morris were earthside, she had once said to Al, and you and he were married, you could get rid of him easily enough; you could divorce him. Then if he pestered you, you could see a solicitor, take out an injunction. You could stipulate that he doesn't come within a five-mile radius, for example. Al sighed and said, in spirit world it's not that simple. You can't just kick out your guide. You can try and persuade him to move on. You can hope he gets called away, or that he forgets to come home. But you can't leave him, he has to leave you. You can try and kick him out. You might succeed, for a while. But he gets back at you. Years may go by. He gets back at you when you're least expecting it.

So, Colette had said, you're worse off than if you were married. She had been able to get rid of Gavin for the modest price of a DIY divorce; it had hardly cost more than it would to put an animal down. 'But he would never have left,' she said. 'Oh no, he was too cosy. I had to do the leaving.'

The summer they had first got together, Colette had said, maybe we could write a book. I could make notes on our conversations, she said. 'You could explain your psychic view of the world to me, and I could jot it down. Or I could interview you, and tape it.'

'Wouldn't that be a bit of a strain?'

'Why should it be? You're used to a tape recorder. You use one every day. You give tapes of readings to clients, so what's the problem?'

'They complain, that's the problem. There's so much crap on them.'

'Not your predictions?' Colette said, shocked. 'They don't complain about those, surely?'

'No, it's the rest of the stuff – all the interference. People from spirit, chipping in. And all the whizzes and bangs from airside. The clients think we've had a nice cosy chat, one to one, but when they listen back, there are all these blokes on the tape farting and spitting, and sometimes there's music, or a woman screaming, or something noisy going on in the background.'

'Like what?'

'Fairgrounds. Parade grounds. Firing squads. Cannon.'

'I've never come across this,' Colette said. She was aggrieved, feeling that her good idea was being quashed. 'I've listened to lots of tapes of psychic consultations, and there were never more than two voices on there.'

'That doesn't surprise me,' Al had sighed. 'My friends don't seem to have this problem. Not Cara, or Gemma, or any of the girls. I suppose I've just got more active entities than other people. So the problem would be, with the tapes, could you make the words out?'

'I bet I could. If I stuck at it.' Colete thrust her jaw out. 'Your pal Mandy's done a book. She was flogging it when I went down to see her in Hove. Before I met you.'

'Did you buy one?'

'She wrote in it for me. Natasha, she put. "Natasha, Psychic to the Stars."' Colette snorted. 'If she did it, we can.'

Al said nothing; Colette had made it clear she had no time for Mandy, and yet Mandy – Natasha to the trade – was one of her closest psychic sisters. She's always so smart, she thought, and she's got the gift of the gab; and she knows what I go through, with spirit. But already Colette was tending to push other friendships out of her life.

'So how about it?' Colette said. 'We could self-publish. Sell it at the psychic fayres. What do you think? Seriously, we should give it a go. Anybody can write a book these days.'

THREE

Colette joined Alison in those days when the comet Hale–Bopp, like God's shuttlecock, blazed over the market towns and dormitory suburbs, over the playing fields of Eton, over the shopping malls of Oxford, over the traffic-crazed towns of Woking and Maidenhead: over the choked slip roads and the junctions of the M4, over the superstores and out-of-town carpet warehouses, the nurseries and prisons, the gravel pits and sewage works, and the green fields of the Home Counties shredded by JCBs. Native to Uxbridge, Colette had grown up in a family whose inner workings she didn't understand, and attended a comprehensive school where she was known as Monster. It seemed, in retrospect, a satire on her lack of monster qualities; she had in fact no looks at all, good or bad, yes or no, pro or con. In her school photographs, her indefinite features seemed neither male not female, and her pale bobbed hair resembled a cowl.

Her shape was flat and neutral; fourteen passed, and nothing was done in the breast department. About the age of sixteen, she began to signal with her pale eyes and say, I'm a natural blonde, you know. In her English classes she was praised for her neat handwriting, and in maths she made, they told her, consistent progress. In religious studies she stared out of the window, as if she might see some Hindu deities squatting on the green mesh of the boundary fence. In history, she was asked to empathise with the sufferings of cotton mill operatives, plantation slaves and the Scots foot soldiers at Flodden; it left her cold. Of geography, she had simply no idea at all; but she learned French quickly, and spoke it without fear and with the accent native to Uxbridge.

She stayed on after sixteen, because she didn't know what she would do or where she would go once she left the classroom; but once her virginity was lost, and her elder sister moved out, leaving her with a room and a mirror of her own, she felt more definite, more visible, more of a presence in the world. She left school with two indifferent A levels, didn't think of university. Her mind was quick, shallow and literal, her character assertive.

She went to a secretarial college – there were still secretaries then – and became competent in shorthand, typing and simple bookkeeping. When the PC came along, she adjusted without difficulty, assimilating successively WordStar, WordPerfect and Microsoft Word. To her second job, in marketing, she brought her spreadsheet skills (Microsoft Excel and Lotus 1-2-3), together with PowerPoint for her presentation packages. Her third job was with a large charity, as an administrator in the fund-raising section. Her mail-merging was beyond reproach; it was indifferent to her whether she used dBase or Access, for she had mastered both. But though she had all the e-skills necessary, her telephone manner was cold and faintly satirical; it was more appropriate, her supervisor noted in her annual review, for someone selling timeshare. She was hurt; she had meant to do some good in the world. She left the charity with excellent references, and took a post with a firm of event organisers. Travel was involved, usually at the back of the plane;

and fourteen-hour days in cities she never got to see. Sometimes she had to think hard: had she been to Geneva? Was Barcelona the place where her travel iron blew up, or was that Dundee?

It was at an event she met Gavin. He was an itinerant software developer whose key card wouldn't work, standing at the reception desk of a hotel in La Défense, entertaining the staff with his sad efforts in Franglais. His tie was in his pocket; his suit hanger, slung over his left shoulder, skewed his jacket away from his shirt, and tugged his shirt away from his skin. She noticed the black chest hairs creeping out of the open top button, and the beads of sweat on his forehead. He seemed the very model of a man. She stood at his elbow and chipped in, sorting out the problem. At the time he seemed grateful. Only later did she realise it was the worst thing she could have done: introducing herself at the moment of his humiliation. He would rather have slept in the corridor than be rescued by some bint wearing a photograph of herself pinned over her left tit. All the same, he asked her to meet him after he'd showered, and have a drink in the bar.

'Well, Colette,' he read her name off her badge. 'Well, Colette, you're not a bad-looking girl.'

Gavin had no sense of humour about himself, and neither did she. So there was a thing, a thing they had in common. He had relatives in Uxbridge, it turned out, and like her he had no interest in getting beyond the hotel bar and into the city. She didn't sleep with him till the final night of the conference, because she didn't want to seem cheap; but she walked back in a daze to her own room, and stared at herself in the full-length mirror, and said, Colette, you're not a bad-looking girl. Her skin was a matt beige. Her beige hair flipped cheekily at chin level, giving her a surrogate smile. Her teeth were sound. Her limbs were straight. Her hips were small. Straight-cut silk trousers covered her tough cyclist's legs. Her bosom was created by a garment with two curved underwires, and boosted by padding which slid into a pocket so you could remove it; but why would anyone want to do that? Without taking her eyes from her own image, she cupped her hands beneath her breasts. Gavin would have the whole of her: all that was hers to give.

They saw a converted flat in Whitton, and thought it might be a good investment. It was leasehold, of course; otherwise, Colette would have done the conveyancing herself, from a DIY guide. As it was, she rang around the solicitors and beat them down to a price, making sure she got their best offers in writing. Once they had moved into the flat, Gavin said, let's split the bills. Kids, he said, were not his priority at this time in his life. She got an IUD fitted, as she didn't trust the Pill; against the workings of nature, some mechanical contrivance seemed called for. Later he would say, you're unnatural, you're cold, I wanted kids but you went off and got this lump of poisoned plastic stuck up you, and you didn't tell me. This was not strictly true; she had cut out an article about the topic from a trade mag passed to her by an ex-colleague who worked for a medical supplies company, and she had put it in the back pocket of his briefcase, where she had thought he might see it.

They got married. People did. It was the fag end of the Thatcher/Major years and people held a wedding to show off. They didn't have friends, so they invited everybody they knew. The wedding took six months to plan. When she woke up on the day, she had an urge to run downstairs, and howl in the streets of Whitton. Instead, she pressed her frock and climbed into it. She was alone in the flat; Gavin was on his stag night, and she wondered what she would do if he didn't turn up; marry herself? The wedding was designed to be exhausting, to wring value from each moment they had paid for. So they could recover, she had booked ten days in the

Seychelles: sea view, balcony, private taxi transfer and fruit in room on arrival.

Gavin turned up just in time, his eyes pouched and his skin grey. After the registry, they went out to a hotel in Berkshire with a trout stream running through the grounds and fishing flies in glass cases on the walls of the bar, and French windows leading on to a terrace. She was photographed against the stone balustrade, with Gavin's little nieces pawing her skirts. They had a marquee, and a band. They had gravadlax with dill sauce, served on black plates, and a chicken dish which tasted, Gavin said, like an airline dinner. The Uxbridge people on both sides came, and never spoke to each other. Gavin kept belching. A niece was sick, luckily not on Colette's dress, which was hired. Her tiara, though, was bought: a special order to fit her narrow skull. Later she didn't know what to do with it. Space was tight in the flat in Whitton, and her drawers were crammed with packets of tights, which she bought by the dozen, and with sachets and scent balls to perfume her knickers. When she reached in among her underwear, the faux pearls of the tiara would roll beneath her fingers, and its gilt lattices and scrolls would remind her that her life was open, unfolding. It seemed mercenary to advertise it in the local paper. Besides, Gavin said, there can't be two people with a head shaped like yours.

The pudding at their wedding breakfast was strawberries and meringue stacked up in a tower, served on frosted-glass platters sprinkled with little green flecks, which proved to be not chopped mint leaves but finely snipped chives. Uxbridge ate it with a stout appetite; after all, they'd already done raw fish. But Colette – once her suspicion was verified, by a tiny taste at the tip of her tongue – had flown out, in her tiara, cornered the duty manager, and told him she proposed to sue the hotel in the small claims court. They paid her off, as she knew they would, being afraid of the publicity; she and

Gavin went back there gratis, for their anniversary dinner, and enjoyed a bottle of house champagne. It was too wet that night to walk by the trout stream: a lowering, misty evening in June. Gavin said it was too hot, and walked out on to the terrace as she was finishing her main course. By then the marriage was over, anyway.

It was no particular sexual incompatibility that had broken up her marriage: Gavin liked it on Sunday mornings, and she had no objection. Neither was there, as she learned later, any particular planetary incompatibility. It was just that the time had come in her relationship with Gavin when, as people said, 'she could see no future in it'.

When she arrived at this point, she bought a large-format softback called *What Your Handwriting Reveals*. She was disappointed to find that your handwriting can't shed any light on your future. It only tells of character, and your present and your past, and her present and her past she was clear about. As for her character, she didn't seem to have any. It was because of her character that she was reduced to going to bookshops.

The following week she returned the handwriting book to the shop. They were having a promotional offer, bring it back if it doesn't thrill. She had to tell the boy behind the counter why, exactly, it didn't; I suppose, she said, after so many years of word processing, I have no handwriting left. Her eyes flickered over him, from his head downwards, to where the counter cut off the view; she was already, she realised, looking for a man she could move on to. 'Can I see the manager?' she asked, and amiably, scratching his barnet, the boy replied, 'You're looking at him.'

'Really?' she said. She had never seen it before: a manager who dressed out of a skip. He gave her back her money, and she browsed the shelves, and picked up a book about tarot cards. 'You'll need a pack to go with that,' the boy said, when she got to the cash desk. 'Otherwise you won't get the idea. There are different sorts, shall I show you? There's Egyptian tarot. There's Shakespeare tarot. Do you like Shakespeare?'

As if, she thought. She was the last customer of the evening. He closed up the shop and they went to the pub. He had a room in a shared flat. In bed he kept pressing her clit with his finger, as if he were inputting a sale on the cash machine: saying, Helen, is that all right for you? She'd given him a wrong name, and she hated it, that he couldn't see through to what she was really called. She'd thought Gavin was useless: but honestly! In the end she faked it, because she was bored and she was getting cramp. The Shakespeare boy said, Helen, that was great for me too.

It was the tarot that started her off. Before that she had been just like everybody, reading her horoscope in the morning paper. She wouldn't have described herself as superstitious or interested in the occult in any way. The next book she bought – from a different bookshop – was *An Encyclopedia of the Psychic Arts*. 'Occult', she discovered, meant hidden. She was beginning to feel that everything of interest was hidden. And none of it in the obvious places; don't, for example, look in trousers.

She had left that original tarot pack in the boy's room, inadvertently. She wondered if he had ever taken it out and looked at the pictures; whether he ever thought of her, a mysterious stranger, a passing Queen of Hearts. She thought of buying another set, but what she read in the handbook baffled and bored her. Seventy-eight cards! Better employ someone qualified to read them for you. She began to visit a woman in Isleworth, but it turned out that her speciality was the crystal ball. The object sat between them on a black velvet cloth; she had expected it to be clear, because that's what they said, crystal clear, but to look into it was like looking into a cloud bank, or into drifting fog. 'The clear ones are glass, dear,' the sensitive explained. 'You won't get anything from those.' She rested her veined hands on the black velvet. 'It's the flaws that are vital,' she said. 'The flaws are what you pay for. You will find some readers who prefer the black mirror. That is an option, of course.' Colette raised her eyebrows.

'Onyx,' the woman said. 'The best are beyond price. The more you look – but you have to know how to look – the more you see stirring in the depths.'

Colette asked straight out, and heard that her crystal ball had set her back five hundred pounds. 'And then only because I have a special friend.' The psychic gained, in Colette's eyes, a deal of prestige. She was avid to part with her twenty pounds for the reading. She drunk in everything the woman said, and when she hit the Isleworth pavement, moss growing between its cracks, she was unable to remember a word of it.

She consulted a palmist a few times, and had her horoscope cast. Then she had Gavin's done. She wasn't sure that his chart was valid, because she couldn't specify the time of his birth. 'What do you want to know that for?' he'd said, when she asked him. She said it was of general interest to her, and he glared at her with extreme suspicion.

'I suppose you don't know, do you?' she said. 'I could ring your mum.'

'I very much doubt,' he'd said, 'that my mother would have retained that piece of useless information, her brain being somewhat overburdened in my opinion with things like where is my plastic washball for my Persil, and what is the latest development in bloody *EastEnders*.'

The astrologer was unfazed by her ignorance. 'Round it up,' he said, 'round it down. Twelve noon is what we use. We always do it for animals.'

'For animals?' she'd said. 'They have their horoscope done, do they?'

'Oh, certainly. It's a valuable service, you see, for the caring owner who has a problem with a pet. Imagine, for instance, if you kept falling off your horse. You'd need to know, is this an ideal pairing? It could be a matter of life or death.'

'And do people know when their horse was born?'

'Frankly, no. That's why we have a strategy to approximate. And as for your partner – if we say noon, that's fine, but we then need latitude and longitude – so where do we imagine hubby first saw the light of day?'

Colette sniffed. 'He won't say.'

'Probably a Scorpio ascendant there. Controls by disinformation. Or could be Pisces. Makes mysteries where none needed. Just joking! Relax and think back for me . . . his mummy must have dropped a hint at some point. Where exactly did the dear chap pop out, into this breathing world scarce half made up?'

'He grew up in Uxbridge. But you know, she might have had him in hospital.'

'So it could have been anywhere along the A40?'

'Could we just say, London?'

'We'll put him on the meridian. Always a wise choice.'

After this incident, she found it difficult to regard Gavin as fully human. He was standardised on zero degrees longitude and twelve noon, like some bucking bronco, or a sad mutt with no pedigree. She did call his mum, one evening when she'd had a half-bottle of wine and was feeling perverse.

'Renee, is that you?' she said.

Renee said, 'How did you get my name?'

'It's me,' she said, and Renee replied, 'I've got replacement windows, and replacement doors. I've got a conservatory and the loft conversion's coming next week. I never give to charity, thank you, and I've planned my holiday for this year, and I had a new kitchen when you were last in my area.'

'It's about Gavin,' she said. 'It's me, Colette. I need to know when he was born.'

'Take my name off your list,' her mother-in-law said. 'And if you must call me, could you not call during my programme? It's one of my few remaining pleasures.' There was a pause, as if she were going to put the receiver down. Then she spoke again. 'Not that I need any others. I've had my suite re-covered. I have a spa bath already. And a case of vintage wine. And a stairlift to help me keep my independence. Have you got that? Are you taking notice? Bugger off.'

Click.

Colette held the phone. Daughter-in-law of fourteen months, spurned by *his* mother. She replaced the receiver, and walked into the kitchen. She stood by the double sink, mastering herself. 'Gavin,' she called, 'do you want peas or green beans?'

There was no answer. She stalked into the sitting room. Gavin, his bare feet on the sofa arm, was reading *What Car?* 'Peas or green beans?' she asked.

No reply. 'Gavin!!!!' she said.

'With wot?'

'Cutlets.'

'What's that?'

'Lamb. Lamb chops.'

'OK,' he said. 'Whatever. Both.'

'You can't.' Her voice shook. 'Two green veg, you can't.'

'Who says?'

'Your mother,' she said; she felt she could say anything, as he never listened.

'When?'

'Just now on the phone.'

'My mother was on the phone?'

'Just now.'

'Bloody amazing.' He shook his head, and flicked over a page.

'Why? Why should it be?'

'Because she's dead.'

'What? Renee?' Colette sat down on the sofa arm: later, when she told the story, she would say, well, at that point, my legs went from under me. But she would never be able to recapture the sudden fright, the weakness that ran through her body, her anger, her indignation, the violent exasperation that possessed her. She said, 'What the hell do you mean, she's dead?'

'It happened this morning. My sis rang. Carole. '

'Is this a joke? I need to know. Is this a joke? Because if it is, Gavin, I'll kneecap you. '

Gavin raised his eyebrows, as if to say, why would it be funny? 'I didn't suggest it was,' she said at once: why wait for him to speak? I asked if it was *your idea* of a joke.'

'God help anybody who made a joke around here.'

Colette laid her hand on her ribcage, behind which something persistently fluttered. She stood up. She walked into the kitchen. She stared at the ceiling. She took a deep breath. She came back. 'Gavin?'

'Mm?'

'She's really dead?'

'Mm.'

She wanted to hit him. 'How?'

'Heart.'

'Oh God! Have you no feeling? You can sit there, going peas or beans—'

'You went that,' he said reasonably.

'Weren't you going to tell me? If I hadn't said, your mother was on the phone—'

Gavin yawned. 'What's the hurry? I'd have told you.'

'You mean you might just have mentioned it? When you got around to it? When would that have been?'

'After the food.'

She gaped at him. He said, with some dignity, 'I can't mention when I'm hungry.'

Colette bunched her fingers into fists, and held them at chest height. She was short of breath, and the flutter inside her chest had subdued to a steady thump. At the same time an uneasy feeling filled her, that anything she could do was inadequate; that she was performing someone else's gestures, perhaps from an equivalent TV moment where news of a sudden death is received. But what are the proper gestures when a ghost's been on the phone? She didn't know. 'Please. Gavin,' she said. 'Put down *What Car?*. Just . . . look at me, will you? Now tell me what happened.'

'Nothing.' He threw the magazine down. 'Nothing happened.'

'But where was she? Was she at home?'

'No. Getting her shopping. In Safeway. Apparently.'

'And?'

Gavin rubbed his forehead. He seemed to be making an honest effort. 'I suppose she was pushing her trolley.'

'Was she on her own?'

'Dunno. Yes.'

'And then?'

'She fell over.'

'She didn't die there, did she? In the aisle?'

'Nah, they got her to the hospital. So no worries about the death certificate.'

'What a relief,' she said grimly.

Carole, it seemed, was proposing to get the bungalow on the market as soon as possible, with Sidgewick & Staff, who for sole agency charged 2 per cent on completion, and promised unlimited colour advertising and national tie-ins. 'There should be a good payout,' he said, 'the place is worth a few quid.'

That was why, he explained, he was reading the new edition of *What Car?*; Renee's will would bring him nearer to what he most coveted in life, which was a Porsche 911.

'Aren't you upset?' she asked him.

He shrugged. 'We've all got to go, haven't we? What's it to you? It's not as if you ever bothered with her.'

'And she lived in a bungalow, Renee?'

'Course she did.' Gavin picked up his magazine and rolled it up in his hand, as if she were a wasp and he were going to swat her. 'We went over for our lunch, that Sunday.'

'No we didn't. We never went.'

'Only because you kept cancelling us.'

It was true. She'd hoped she could keep Renee at arm's length: the wedding reception had proved her to have a coarse joke habit, and slipping false teeth. The teeth weren't all that was false. 'She told me,' she said to Gavin, 'that she had a stairlift installed. Which, if she lived in a bungalow, she couldn't have.'

'When? When did she tell you that?'

'On the phone just now.'

'Hello? Hello? Anyone at home?' Gavin asked. 'Are you ever stupid? I told you she's dead.'

Alerted by the mutiny on her face, he rose from the sofa and slapped her with *What Car?*. She picked up the Yellow Pages and threatened to take out his eye. After he had slunk off to bed, hugging his expectations, she went back into the kitchen and grilled the cutlets. The peas and green beans she fed to the waste disposal; she hated vegetables. She ate the lamb with her fingers, her teeth scraping the bone. Her tongue came out, and licked the last sweetness from the meat. She couldn't work out what was worst, that Renee had answered the phone after she was dead, or that she had answered the phone on purpose to lie to her and tell her to bugger off. She threw the bones down the waste disposal too, and rejoiced as the grinder laboured. She rinsed her fingers and wiped them on a kitchen roll.

In the bedroom, she inspected Gavin, spreadeagled across the available space. He was naked and snoring; his mag, rolled, was thrust under his pillow. That, that, she thought, is how much it means to him, the death of his only mother. She stood frowning down at him; her toe touched something hard and cold. It was a glass tumbler, lolling on its side, melted ice dribbling from its mouth on to the carpet. She picked it up. The breath of spirits hit her nostrils, and made her flinch. She walked into the kitchen and clicked the tumbler down on to the draining board. In the dark, tiny hall, she hauled Gavin's laptop from its case. She lugged it into the sitting room and plugged it into the mains. She copied the files she thought might interest her, and erased his crucial data for tomorrow. In terms of life documentation, Gavin was less than some animal. He routinely misled her: but was it any wonder? What sort of upbringing could he have had, from a woman with false teeth who told lies after she was dead?

She left the machine humming, and went back into the bedroom. She opened the wardrobe and went through Gavin's pockets. The word 'rifled' came to her: 'she rifled through his pockets'. He stirred once or twice in his sleep, reared up, snorted, collapsed back on to the mattress. I could kill him, she thought, as he lies here; or just maim him if I liked. She found a bunch of credit-card receipts in his knicker drawer; her index finger shuffled through them. She found newspaper ads for sex lines: *spicy lesbo chicks!*

She packed a bag. Surely he would wake? Drawers clicked, opening and shutting. She glanced over her shoulder. Gavin stirred, made a sort of whinny, and settled back again into sleep. She reached down to unplug her hairdryer, wrapped the flex around her hand and stood thinking. She was entitled to half the equity in the flat; if he would embrace the car loan, she would continue paying off the wedding. She hesitated for a final moment. Her foot was on the wet patch the ice had left. Automatically, she plucked a tissue from an open box and blotted the carpet. Her fingers squeezed, the paper reduced itself to wet pulp. She walked away, brushing her hands together to jettison it.

Gavin's screensaver had come up. Colette slotted a floppy into his drive, and overwrote his programs. She had heard of women who, before departing, scissored up their husband's clothes. But Gavin's clothes, in their existing state, were punishment enough. She had heard of women who performed castration; but she didn't want to go to jail. No, let's see how he gets on without his bits and bytes, she thought. With one keystroke, she wrecked his operating system.

She went down to the south coast to see a noted psychometrist, Natasha. She didn't know then, of course, that Natasha would figure in her later life. At the time, it was just another hope she grappled with, a hope of making sense of herself; it was just another item in her strained monthly budget.

The flat was two blocks back from the sea. She parked with difficulty and at some distance. She wasted time looking for the street numbers. When she found the right door she rang the bell and spoke into the intercom: 'I'm your eleven thirty.'

Without a word, the psychic buzzed her up; but she thought she had heard a cough, stifling a little laugh. Her cheeks burned. She ran up three flights and as soon as Natasha opened the door she said, 'I'm not late.'

'No, dear. You're my eleven thirty.'

'You really ought to tell your clients where to park.'

The psychic smiled tightly. She was a sharp little bleached-blonde with a big jaw, common as a centrefold. 'What,' she said, 'you think I should exercise my powers and keep a space free?'

'I meant you should send a map.'

Natasha turned to lead the way: tight high bottom in those kind of jeans that act as a corset. She's too old, Colette thought, for denim; shouldn't somebody tell her?

'Sit there,' Natasha said precisely, dipping her false nail.

'The sun's in my eyes,' Colette said.

'Diddums,' said Natasha.

A sad-eyed icon drooped at her, from a cheap gilt frame on the wall; a mist washed up from the sea. She sat, and flipped open her shoulder bag: 'Do you want the cheque now?'

She wrote it. She waited for the offer of a cup of herb tea. It didn't come. She almost had hopes of Natasha; she was nasty, but there was a businesslike briskness about her that she'd never found in any psychic so far.

'Anything to give me?' Natasha said.

She dived into her bag and passed over her mother's wedding ring.

Natasha twirled it around her forefinger. 'Quite a smiley lady.'

'Oh, smiley,' Colette said. 'I concede that.'

She passed over a pair of cuff-links that had belonged to her dad.

'Is that the best you can manage?'

'I don't have anything else of his.'

'Sad,' Natasha said. 'Can't have been much of a relationship, can it? I sense that men don't warm to you, somehow.' She sat back in her chair, her eyes far away. Colette waited, respectfully silent. 'Well, look, I'm not getting much from these.' She jiggled the cuff-links in her hand. 'They're definitely your dad's, are they? The thing is, with cuff-links, with dads, they get them for Christmas and then it's, "Oh, thanks, thanks a bunch, just what I always needed!"'

Colette nodded. 'But what can you do? What can you get, for men?'

'Bottle of Scotch?'

'Yes, but you want something that will last.'

'So he stuffs them in a drawer? Forgets he's got them?'

She wanted to say, *why* do you think men don't warm to me? Instead she opened her bag again. 'My wedding ring,' she said. 'I suppose you didn't think I'd been married?'

Natasha held out a flat, open palm. Colette placed the ring on it. 'Oh dear,' Natasha said. 'Oh dear, oh dear.'

'Don't worry, I've already left.'

'Sometimes you've got to cut your losses,' Natasha agreed. 'Well, sweetie, what else can I tell you?'

'It's possible I might be psychic myself,' Colette said casually. 'Certain, really. I dialled a number and a dead person answered.'

'That's unusual.' Natasha's eyes flitted sideways, in a calculating way. 'Which psychic line offers that service?'

'I wasn't calling a psychic line. I was calling my mother-in-law. It turned out she was dead.'

'So what gave you the idea?'

'No – no, look, you have to understand how it happened. I didn't know she was dead when I rang. I didn't know till afterwards.'

'So she was dead when you called? But you didn't realise?'

'Yes.'

'So she came over from beyond?'

'Yes.'

'What did she say to you?'

'She said she'd got a stairlift. It was a lie.'

'Well, perhaps . . . she's got one in spirit?'

Colette considered. Renee had said there was no comfort she lacked. 'I'm not really bothered about that aspect, about what she said, only that she picked the phone up. That she answered. At first that was what bothered me, about the stairlift – that she didn't even say the truth – but then when I thought about it, her saying anything seemed to be the most surprising – well, you know.' Colette's voice died in her throat. She was not used to speaking her thoughts. Life with Gavin had discouraged her. 'Nothing like that's ever happened to me before, but I think it proves I must have a gift. I'm a bit bored with my job and I wouldn't mind a change. I wondered about this, you know? If there's much money in it.'

Natasha laughed. 'Well, if you think you could stand the pace. You have to train.'

'Oh, do you? It's not enough to be able to do it?'

'Look,' Natasha said, 'I don't want to sound hostile, but isn't it possible that you're being a bit naive? I mean, you've got a good career now, I can see that. So why waste it? You'd need to build up your psychic skills, you can't expect to start cold at your age.'

'I beg your pardon?' Colette said. 'At my age?'

'I started at twelve,' Natasha said. 'You're not telling me you're twelve, are you?' With one hand, she lazily shuffled her cards together. 'Want me to see what I get?' She began to lay out a spread, her nails clicking on the back of each card. 'Look, if you're going to work with higher powers, it will happen. Nothing will stop it. But you'll get the here-and-now sorted, if you'll heed my advice.' She looked up. 'Letter "M" comes to mind.'

Colette thought. 'I don't know anyone of that letter.' She thought, M for Man?

'Someone coming into your life. Not yet. An older bloke. Not too keen on you at first, I must say. '

'But then?'

'All's well that ends well,' Natasha said. 'I suppose.'

She had walked away, disappointed; when she got back to her car, she had been ticketed. After that she had been for crystal healing, and had some reiki sessions. She arranged to meet Gavin in a new bar called Peppermint Plaza. He arrived before her and when she walked in he was sitting on a pale green leather-look banquette, a bottle of Mexican lager planted in front of him, leafing through *Thames Valley Autotrader*.

'Renee's money not come through yet?' she asked. She slid into the seat opposite. 'When it does, you could use some of it to buy me out of the flat.'

'If you think I'm giving up the chance of a decent car, then no way,' said Gavin. 'If I don't get the Porsche this is what I'm getting, I'm getting this Lancia.' He flopped the magazine down on the table. 'There's one here.' He turned the picture round obligingly so it was the right way up for her. 'Recarro seats. Full spec. Seriously speedy.'

'Put it on the market then. The flat. If you can't buy me out.'

'You said that. You said it before. I said, yes. I agree. So don't go on about it. OK?'

There was a silence. Colette looked around. 'Quite nice here. Quiet.'

'Bit girly.'

'That's probably why I like it. Being a girl.'

Her knees touched his, under the table. She tried to pull her chair away, but it was bolted to the floor. Gavin said, 'I want fifty per cent of the bills till the flat's sold.'

'I'll pay half the monthly service charge.' Colette pushed

his magazine back across the table. 'I won't pay half the utilities.'

'What's that, utilities?'

'Gas and electric. Why should I pay to keep you warm?'

'I'll tell you what, you stuffed me with a huge sodding phone bill. You can pay that.'

'It's your phone too.'

'Yeah, but I'm not on it all night, blah-bloody-blah to some bint I've sat next to all day and I'll be seeing again the next morning. And it's not me phoning premium rate lines to what's it called, bloody predictionists, bloody psychic lines at a quid a minute.'

'Actually, sex lines are premium rate too.'

'Oh well, you would know about that, wouldn't you?' Gavin gathered up his car magazine, as if to shield it from her. 'You're not normal.'

She sighed. She couldn't summon up the energy to say, 'I beg your pardon, not normal, what do you mean?' Any abstraction, indirection and allusion was wasted on Gavin, and in fact even the most straightforward form of communication – other than a poke in the eye – was a challenge to his attention span. There hadn't, so far as she'd understood, been any dispute between them about what they did in the bedroom – it had seemed fairly straightforward stuff, though she was fairly ignorant and limited, she supposed, and Gavin, certainly, he was fairly ignorant and limited. But after the marriage is over, maybe that's what men do, they decide it was the sex that was wrong, because it's something they can communicate over a drink, something they can turn into a story, snigger over; it's an explanation they can give themselves, for what would otherwise remain the complete mystery of human relationships. There were other mysteries, which loomed large to her and hardly loomed at all for Gavin: what are we here for, what will happen next? It was no use trying to explain to him that without the fortune tellers she had become afraid to act at all; that she liked to know that things were her fate, that she didn't like life to be arbitrary. It was no use telling him either that she thought she might be psychic herself. The incident of the posthumous phone call, if it had ever sunk into his mind, had been chemically erased, because of the vodka he had drunk the night she moved out; this was lucky for her, because when next day he found his computer trashed he thought he had only himself to blame.

'Don't you want to ask anything?' she asked. 'Like where I'm living?'

'So where are you living, Colette?' he said sarcastically.

'With a friend.'

'Jesus, you've got a friend?'

'But from next week I've arranged a house-share in Twickenham. I'll have to start paying rent, so I need the flat to be sold.'

'All we need is a buyer.'

'No, all we need is a seller.'

'What?'

'Put it on the market.'

'I have. Last week. '

'Oh, for God's sake.' She slammed her glass down. 'Why didn't you just come out and say that?'

'I would if I could get a word in edgewise. Besides, I thought you'd get a tip-off from the spirits. I thought they'd say, a strange man is walking around your bedroom with a steel measure.'

Colette threw herself back in her seat: but it was strangely curved, and pushed her forward again, so her diaphragm was against the table's edge.

'So how much did they suggest?' He told her. 'That's far too low. They must think you're an idiot. And they could be right. Leave it, Gavin, leave it. I'll get on to it tomorrow. I'll phone them myself.'

'They said, realistic price for a quick sale.'

'More likely they've got a mate lined up, who they're selling it on to.'

'That's your trouble.' Gavin scratched his armpit. 'You're paranoid.'

'You don't know what you're talking about. You use words without any idea what they mean. All you know is stupid jargon out of car mags. Recarro seats. Spicy lesbo chicks. That's all you know.'

Gavin turned down his mouth and shrugged. 'So. You want anything?'

'Yes, I want my life back.'

'From the flat.'

'I'll make a list.'

'Anything you want now?'

'The kitchen knives.'

'Why?'

'They're good ones. Japanese. You don't want them. You won't cook.'

'I might want to cut something.'

'Use your teeth.'

He took a pull on his lager. She finished her spritzer.

'If that's all?' she said. She gathered her bag and her jacket. 'I want everything in writing, about the flat. Tell the agents, that all the paperwork must be copied to me. I want full consultation at every point.' She stood up. 'I'll be ringing every two days to check on progress.'

'I'll look forward to that.'

'Not you. The agent. Have you got their card?'

'No. Not on me. Come back and get it.'

Alarm flared inside her. Was he intending to mug her, or rape her?

'Send it to me,' she said.

'I don't have your address.'

'Send it to the office.'

When she got to the door it occurred to her that it might have been his single, clumsy effort at reconciliation. She glanced back. His head was down, and he was leafing through his magazine again. No chance, anyway. She would rather take out her appendix with nail scissors than go back to Gavin.

The encounter, though, had bruised her. Gavin was the first person, she thought, that I was ever really frank and honest with; at home, there wasn't much premium on frankness, and she'd never had a girlfriend she was really close to, not since she was fifteen. She'd opened her heart to him, such as it was. And for what? Probably, when she opened her heart, he hadn't even been listening. The night of Renee's death she had seen him as he truly was: callow and ignorant and not even ashamed of it, not even asking her why she was so panicked, not even appreciating that his mother's death wouldn't, by itself, have affected her like that: but shouldn't it have affected him? Had he even bothered to go to the crematorium, or had he left it all to Carole? When she thought back to that night, which (she now knew) was the last night of her marriage, a peculiar disjointed, unstrung sensation occurred in her head, as if her thoughts and her feelings had been joined together by a zip, and the zip had broken. She had not told Gavin that in the days after she walked out, she had twice dialled Renee's home number, just to see what would happen. What happened was nothing, of course. The phone rang in the empty house: bungalow: whatever.

It put a dent in her belief in her psychic powers. She knew, of course – her recollection was sharp if Gavin's wasn't – that the woman on the phone had at no point actually identified herself. She hadn't said she wasn't Renee, but she hadn't agreed that she was, either. It was just possible that she had misdialled, and that she had been talking to some irate stranger. If pushed, she would have said it was her ma-in-law, but it was true that she didn't know her voice all that well, and the woman had lacked the trademark lisp that was caused by Renee's slipping teeth. Was that significant? It could be. Nothing else of a psychic nature seemed to manifest. She moved into the Twickenham house-share, and discovered that it made her unhappy to live with women younger than herself. She'd never thought of herself as a romantic, God knows, but the way they talked about men was near pornographic, and the way they belched and put their feet on the furniture was like Gavin over again. She didn't have to sleep with them, but that was the only difference. Every morning the kitchen was strewn with Hägen-Dazs tubs, and lager cans, and polystyrene trays from low-fat microwave dinners, with a scraping of something beige and jellified left in the bottom.

So where was she going in life? What was she for? No man with the initial M had come into her life. She was stagnating, and struck by how quickly a temporary situation can become desolating and permanent. Soon she needed her fortune told more than ever. But her regular clairvoyant, the one she trusted most, lived in Brondesbury, which was a long way for her to travel, and kept cats, to which she developed an allergy. She got herself a train timetable, and began to work her way out, each weekend, from the London suburbs to the dormitory towns and verdant conurbations of Berkshire and Surrey. So it came about that one Saturday afternoon in spring, she saw Alison perform in Windsor, at the Victoria Room in the Harte & Garter.

It was a two-day Psychic Extravaganza. She had not pre-booked, but because of her general beigeness and her inoffensive manner, she was good at queue-jumping. She had sat modestly in the third row, her whippy body crouching inside her blouson jacket, her khaki-coloured hair pushed behind her ears. Alison had fingered her right away. The lucky opals flashed fire in her direction. 'I'm getting a broken wedding ring. It's this lady here in beige. Is it you, darling?'

Mutely, Colette held up her hand, the tight gold band intact. She had started wearing it again, she hardly knew why; maybe just to spite Natasha in Hove, to show that a man had warmed to her, at least once.

Impatience crossed Alison's face: then her smile wiped the expression away. 'Yes, I know you still wear his ring. Maybe he thinks of you; maybe you think of him?'

'Only with hatred,' Colette said, and Al said, 'Whatever. But you're on your own for now, darling.' Al had held out her arms to the audience. 'I see images, I can't help it. For a marriage, I see a ring. For a separation, a divorce, I see a ring that's broken. The line of the break is the line of the crack in this young girl's heart.'

There was a murmur of sympathy from the audience. Colette nodded soberly, acknowledging what was said. Natasha had said much the same, when she held the wedding ring, as if in tweezers, between those dodgy false nails of hers. But Natasha had been a spiteful little slag, and the woman on the platform seemed to have no spite in her; Natasha had implied she was too old for new experiences, but Alison spoke as if she had her life before her. She spoke as if her feelings and thoughts could be mended; she imagined popping into the dry-cleaner's, and getting the broken zip replaced, the zip that joined her thoughts to her feelings and joined her up inside.

This was Colette's introduction to the metaphorical side of life. She realised that she hadn't comprehended half that the fortune tellers had said to her. She might as well have stood in the street in Brondesbury ripping up tenners. When they told you something, you were supposed to look at it all ways up; you were supposed to hear it, understand it, feel all around its psychological dimensions. You weren't supposed to fight it, but let the words sink into you. You shouldn't query and quibble and try and beat the psychic out of her convictions; you should listen with your inner ear, and you should accept it, exactly what she said, if the feeling it gave you checked in with your feeling inside. Alison was offering hope and hope was the feeling she wanted to have; hope of redemption from the bathroom bickering of the house-share, and from finding other women's bras stuffed under a sofa cushion when she flopped down after work with the *Evening Standard*: and from the sound of her housemates rutting at dawn.

'Listen,' Alison said. 'What I want to say to you is, don't shed tears. The fact is, you barely started with this man. He didn't know what marriage was. He didn't know how to make an equal relationship. He liked – gadgets, am I right, hi-fi, cars, that stuff, that was what he related to.'

'Oh yes,' Colette chirped up. 'But then wouldn't it be true of most men?' She stopped herself. 'Sorry,' she said.

'True of most men?' Al queried gently. 'I'll give you that. The point is, though, was it true of him? Was it true that at the great highlights of your life, he was thinking about sports seats and sound systems? But look, darling, there is a man for you. A man who will be in your life for years and years to come.' She frowned. 'I want to say . . . oh, you know . . . "for better or worse" – but you've been married, chuck, so you know all that.'

Colette took a deep breath. 'Does he have the initial M?'

'Don't prompt me, dear,' Al said. 'He's not in your life yet, but he's coming into it.'

'So I don't know him now?'

'Not yet.'

Oh good, Colette thought – because she had just done a quick mind-scan of the men she already knew. 'Will I meet him at work?'

Alison closed her eyes. 'Sort of,' she offered. She frowned. 'More through work, than at work. Through work, is how I'd put it. First you'll be sort of colleagues, then it'll get closer. You'll have a, what's the word, a long association. It may take a bit of time to get close. He has to warm to you.' She chuckled. 'His dress sense is a bit lacking, but I expect you'll soon fix that, darling.' Alison smiled around at the audience. 'She'll just have to wait and see. Exciting, isn't it?'

'It is.' Colette nodded. She kept up an inner monologue. It is, it is. I have hope, I have hope. I will get a salary rise – no, not that. I will get a place of my own – no, not that. I must, I had better, I ought to look around for a new job, I ought to shake my life up and open myself to opportunities. But whatever I do, something will happen. I am tired, I am tired of taking care of myself. Something will happen that is out of my hands.

Alison did a few other things that night at the Harte & Garter. She told a depressed-looking woman that she'd be going on a cruise. The woman at once straightened her collapsed spine and revealed in an awestruck voice that she had received a cruise brochure by the morning post, which she had sent for because her silver wedding was coming up shortly, and she thought it was time they exported their happiness somewhere other than the Isle of Wight.

'Well, I want to say to you,' Alison had told her, 'that you will be going on that cruise, yes you will.' Colette marvelled at the way Alison could spend the woman's money. 'And I'll tell you something else; you're going to have a lovely time. You're going to have the time of your life.'

The woman sat up even straighter. 'Oh, thank you, thank you,' she said. She seemed to take on a sort of glow. Colette could see it even though she was four rows away. It encouraged her to think that somebody could hand over a tenner at the door and get so much hope in return. It was cheap, compared to what she was paying in Brondesbury and elsewhere.

After the event, Colette walked to the Riverside Station in the chilly evening air. The sun made a red channel down the centre of the Thames. Swans were bobbing in the milky water near the banks. Over towards Datchet, outside the pub called the Donkey House, some French exchange students were dipping one of their number in the water. She could hear their excited cries; they warmed her heart. She stood on the bridge, and waved to them with a big sweep of her arm, as if she were bringing a light aircraft in to land.

I won't come back tomorrow, she thought. I will, I won't, I will.

The next morning, Sunday, her journey was interrupted by engineering works. She had hoped to be first in the queue but that was not to be. As she stepped out of the station, there was a burst of sunshine. The high street was crammed with coaches. She walked uphill towards the castle and the Harte & Garter. The great Round Tower brooded over the street, and at its feet, like a munching worm, wound a stream of trippers gnawing at burgers.

It was eleven o'clock and the Extravaganza was in full spate. The tables and stands were set up in the hall where the medium had done the demonstration the night before. Spiritual healing was going on in one corner, Kirlian photography in another, and each individual psychic's table, swathed in chenille or fringed silk, bore her stock-in-trade of tarot pack, crystal ball, charms, incense, pendulums and bells: plus a small tape machine so the client could have a record of her consultation. Almost all the psychics were women. There were just two men, lugubrious and neglected; Merlin and Merlyn, according to their name cards. One had on his table a bronze wizard waving a staff, and the other had what appeared to be a shrunken head on a stand. There was no queue at his table. She wandered up. 'What's that?' she mouthed, pointing. It was difficult to make yourself heard; the roar of prediction rose into the air and bounced around in the rafters.

'My spirit guide,' the man said. 'Well, a model of him.'

'Can I touch it?'

'If you must, dear.'

She ran her fingers over the thing. It wasn't skin, but leather, a sort of leather mask bound to a wooden skull. Its brow was encircled by a cord into which were stuck the stumps of quills. 'Oh, I get it,' she said. 'He's a Red Indian.'

'Native American,' the man corrected. 'The actual model is a hundred years old. It was passed on to me by my teacher, who got it from his teacher. Blue Eagle has guided three generations of psychics and healers.'

'It must be hard if you're a bloke. To know what to put on your table. That doesn't look too poncey.'

'Look, do you want a reading, or not?'

'I don't think so,' Colette said. To hear a psychic at all, you would almost have to be cheek to cheek, and she didn't fancy such intimacy with Blue Eagle's mate. 'It's a bit sordid,' she said. 'This head. Off-putting. Why don't you chuck it and get a new model?' She straightened up. She looked around the room. 'Excuse me,' she said, shouting over a client's head to a wizened old bat in a shawl, 'excuse me, but where's the one who did the dem last night? Alison?'

The old woman jerked her thumb. 'Three down. In the corner there. Mind, she knows how to charge. If you hang on till I'm finished here, I can do you psychometry, cards and palms, thirty quid all in.'

'How very unprofessional,' Colette said coldly.

Then she spotted her. A client, beaming, rose from the red leatherette chair, and the queue parted to let her through. Colette saw Alison, very briefly, put her face in her hands: before raising it, smiling, to the next applicant for her services.

Even Sundays bring their ebb and flow – periods of quiet and almost peace, when sleep threatens in the overheated rooms – and then times of such confusion – the sunlight strikes in, sudden and scouring, lighting up the gewgaws on the velvet cloth – and within the space of two heartbeats, the anxiety is palpable, a baby crying, the incense choking, the music whining, more fortune seekers pressing in at the door and backing up those inside against the tables. There is a clatter as a few Egyptian perfume bottles go flying; Mrs Etchells, three tables down, is jawing on about the joys of motherhood; Irina is calming a sobbing adolescent with a broken engagement; the baby, wound up with colic, twisting in the arms of an unseen mother, is preying on her attention as if he were entangled in her gut.

She looked up and saw a woman of her own age, meagrely built, with thin fair hair which lay flat against her skull. Her features were minimal, her figure that of an orphan in a storm. A question jumped into Al's head: how would this play if you were a Victorian, if you were one of those Victorian cheats? She knew all about it; after all, Mrs Etchells, who had trained her, almost went back to those days. In those days the dead manifested in the form of muslin, stained and smelly from the psychic's body cavities. The dead were packed within you, so you coughed or vomited them, or drew them out of your generative organs. They blew trumpets and played portable organs; they moved the furniture; they rapped on the wall, they sang hymns. They offered bouquets to the living, spirit roses bound by scented hands. Sometimes they proffered inconveniently large objects, like a horse. Sometimes they stood at your shoulder, a glowing column made flesh by the eyes of faith. She could see it easily, a picture from the past: herself in a darkened parlour, her superb shoulders rising white out of crimson velvet, and this straight flat creature at her elbow, standing in the half-light: her eyes empty as water, impersonating a spirit form.

'Would you like to come and sit?'

Not fair! the queue said. Not her turn!

'Please be patient,' Alison said sweetly. 'I think someone's trying to come through for this lady, and I daren't keep spirit world waiting.'

The queue fell back, murmuring. She sat down before her, the pallid meek being, like a sacrifice drained of blood. Al searched her for clues. Probably never known the joys of motherhood? Fair bet, with those tits. Oh, wait, didn't I see her last night? Near the front, third row, left of centre, no? Broken wedding ring. Man with the gadgets. Career girl, of sorts. Not much of a career, though. Drifting. Anxious. Pains in her gut. Tension at the back of her neck; a big dead hand squeezing her spine.

On her left, Mrs Etchells was saying, 'Going on hols, are we? I see an aeroplane.' Irina was saying, yes, yes, yes, you are very sad now, but by October zey are coming, four men in a truck, and building your home extension.

Alison held out her hand to Colette. Colette put her hand in it, turned up. The narrow palm was drained of energy, almost corpse-like.

I would have liked that, Al thought, all that Victorian fuss and frippery, the frocks, the spirit pianos, the men with big beards. Was she seeing herself, in a former life, in an earlier and possibly more lucrative career? Had she been famous, perhaps, a household name? Possibly; or possibly it was wish-fulfilment. She supposed she had lived before but she suspected there wasn't much glamour attached to whatever life she'd led. Sometimes when her mind was vacant she had a fleeting vision, low-lit, monochrome, of a line of women hoeing, bending their backs under a mud-coloured sky.

Well now . . . she scrutinised Colette's palm, picking up her magnifying glass. The whole hand was bespattered with crosses, on the major lines and between them. She could see no arches, stars or tridents. There were several worrying islands in the heart line, little vacant plots. Perhaps, she thought, she sleeps with men whose names she doesn't know.

The pale client's voice cut through. She sounded common and sharp. 'You said somebody was coming through for me.'

'Your father. He recently passed into spirit.'

'No.'

'But there's been a passing. I'm getting, six. The number six. About six months back?'

The client looked blank.

'Let me jog your memory,' Alison said. 'I would be talking about Guy Fawkes Night, or maybe the run-up to Christmas. Where they say, only forty shopping days left, that sort of thing.' Her tone was easy; she was used to people not remembering the deaths in their family.

'My uncle died last November. If that's what you mean.'

'Your uncle, not your father?'

'Yes, my uncle. For Christ's sake, I should know.'

'Bear with me,' Alison said easily. 'You don't by any chance have something with you? Something that belonged to your dad?'

'Yes.' She had brought the same props she had given to the psychic in Hove. 'These were his.'

She handed over the cuff-links. Alison cupped them in her left palm, rolled them around with her right forefinger. 'Golf balls. Though he didn't play golf. Still, people don't know what to buy for men, do they?' She tossed them up and caught them again. 'No way,' she said. 'Look, can you accept this? The bloke who owned these was not your dad. He was your uncle.'

'No, it was my uncle that *died.*' The client paused. 'He died in November. My dad died about, I don't know, ages ago—' She put her hand to her mouth. 'Oh,' she said. 'Run it past me again, will you?' Grant her this: she wasn't slow on the uptake.

'Let's just see if we can unknot this,' Al said. 'You say these are your father's cuff-links. I say, no, though they may have belonged to the man you *called* your father. You say your uncle passed last November, and your father passed years ago. But I say, your uncle has been a long time in spirit, but your dad passed in the autumn. Now, are you with me?'

The client nodded.

'You're sure you're with me? I mean, I don't want you to think I'm slandering your mum. But these things happen, in families. Now your uncle's name is—?'

'Mike.'

'Mike, and your dad's – Terry, right? So you think. But the way I see it, Terry's your uncle and Uncle Mike's your dad.'

Silence. The woman shifted in her chair. 'He was always hanging about, Mike, when I was little. Always round at ours.'

'Chez vous,' Al said. 'Well, he would be.'

'It explains a lot. My flat hair, for one thing.'

'Yes, doesn't it?' Alison said. 'When you finally get it sorted out, who's who in your family, it does explain a lot.' She sighed. 'It's a shame your mum's passed, so you can't ask her what was what. Or why. Or anything like that.'

'She wouldn't have told me. Can't you tell me?'

'My guess is, Terry was a quiet type, whereas Uncle Mike,

he was a bit of a boyo. Which was what your mum liked. Impulsive, that's how I'd describe her, if I was pushed. You too, maybe. But only in – not in your general affairs – but only in what we call – er – matters of partnership.'

'What does that mean?'

'It means that when you see a bloke you like you go straight after him.' Like a whippet after a hare, she thought. 'You say to yourself, no, I must do strategy, play it cool, but you don't heed your own advice – you're very much, how shall I say it, bed on the first date. Well, why not? I mean, life's too short.'

'I can't do this, I'm sorry.' The client half rose.

Alison put her hand out. 'It's the shock. About your dad. It takes a bit of getting used to. I wouldn't have broken it to you like that if I didn't think you could take it. And straight talking – I think you can take that too.'

'I can take it,' Colette said. She sat down again.

'You're proud,' Al said softly. 'You won't be bested.'

'That describes me.'

'If Jack and Jill can do it, you can do it.'

'That's true.'

'You don't suffer fools gladly.'

'I don't.'

It was an old Mrs Etchells line; she was probably using it right now, three tables down: 'You don't suffer fools gladly, dear!' As if the client was going to come back at you, 'Fools! I love 'em! Can't get enough! I go out round the streets, me, looking for fools to ask them home to dinner!'

Alison sat back in her chair. 'The way I see you now, you're dissatisfied, restless.'

'Yes.'

'You've reached a place in your life where you don't much want to be.'

'Yes.'

'You're ready and willing to move on.'

'Yes.'

'So do you want to come and work for me?'

'What?'

'Can you type, drive, anything like that? I need a sort of, what do they call it, Girl Friday.'

'This is a bit sudden.'

'Not really. I felt I knew you, when I saw you from the platform last night.'

'The platform?'

'The platform is what we call any kind of stage.'

'Why?'

'I don't know. It's historical, I suppose.'

Colette leaned forward. She locked her fists together between her knees.

Alison said, 'If you come into the front bar in about an hour, we can get a coffee.'

Colette cast a glance at the long queue behind her.

'OK, say an hour and a quarter?'

'What do you do, put up a "closed" sign?'

'No, I just put them on divert. I say, go see Mrs Etchells three tables down.'

'Why? Is she good?'

'Mrs Etchells? *Entre nous*, she's rubbish. But she taught me. I owe her.'

'You're loyal?'

'I hope so.'

'Is that her? Wrinkly old bag with a charm bracelet on? Now I'll tell *you* something. She's not loyal to you.'

She spelled it out: she tried to poach me, tried to catch me as I was looking about for you: cards, crystal and psychometry thrown in, thirty quid.

Alison blushed, a deep crimson blush. 'She said that? Thirty quid?'

'Fancy you not knowing.'

'My mind was somewhere else.' She laughed shakily. '*Voilà*. You've already earned your money, Colette.'

'You know my name?'

'It's that certain something French about you. *Je ne sais quoi*.'

'You speak French?'

'Never till today.'

'You mustn't mind-read me.'

'I would try not to.'

'An hour and a quarter?'

'You could get some fresh air.'

On Windsor Bridge, a young boy was sitting on a bench with his Rottweiler at his feet. He was eating an ice-cream cone and holding another out to the dog. Passers-by, smiling, were collecting to watch. The dog ate with civil, swirling motions of his tongue. Then he crunched the last of his cornet, swarmed up on to the bench and laid his head lovingly on the boy's shoulder. The boy fed him the last of his own ice cream, and the crowd laughed. The dog, encouraged, licked and nibbled the boy's ears, and the crowd went ohh, feech, yuk, how sweet.

The dog jumped down from the bench. Its eyes were steady and its paws huge. For two pins, or the dog equivalent, it would set itself to eat the crowd, worrying each nape and tossing the children like pancakes.

Colette stood and watched until all the crowd had dispersed and she was alone. She crossed the bridge and edged down Eton High Street, impeded by tourists. I am like the dog, she thought. I have an appetite. Is that wrong? My mum had an appetite. I realise it now, how she talked in code all those years. No wonder I never knew what was what and who was who. Not surprising her aunts were always exchanging glances, and saying things like, I wonder where Colette gets her hair from, I wonder where she gets her brains? The man she'd called her father was distinguished by the sort of stupidity that made him squalid. She had a mental picture of him, sprawled before the television scratching his belly: perhaps, when she'd bought him the cuff-links, she'd been hoping to improve him. Her uncle Mike, on the other hand – who was really her father – he was a man whose wallet was always stuffed, hadn't he been round every week, flashing his fivers and saying, here, Angie, get something nice for little Colette? He'd paid, but he hadn't paid enough; he'd paid as an uncle, but not as a dad. I'll sue the bastard, she thought. Then she remembered he was dead.

She went into the Crown & Cushion and got a pineapple juice, which she took into a corner. Every few minutes she checked her watch. Too early, she started back across the bridge.

Alison was sitting in the front room of the Harte & Garter with a cafetière and two cups. She had her back to the door, and Colette paused for a moment, getting a view of her: she's *huge*, she thought, how can she go around like that? As she watched, Alison's plump smooth arm reached for the coffee and poured it into the second cup.

Colette sat down. She crossed her legs. She fixed Alison with a cool stare. 'You don't mind what you say, do you? You could have really upset me, back there.'

'There was a risk.' Alison smiled.

'You think you're a good judge of character.'

'More often than not.'

'And my mum. I mean, for all you know, I could have burst into tears, I could have collapsed.'

Not a real risk, Al thought. At some level, in some recess

of themselves, people know what they know. But the client was determined to have her moment.

'Because what you were saying, really, is that she was having an affair with my uncle under my dad's nose. Which isn't nice, is it? And she let my dad think I was his.'

'I wouldn't call it an affair. It was more of a fling.'

'So what does that make her? A slag.'

Alison put down her coffee cup. 'They say don't speak ill of the dead.' She laughed. 'But why not? They speak ill of you.'

'Do they?' Colette thought of Renee. 'What are they saying?'

'A joke. I was making a joke. I see you think I shouldn't.'

She took from Colette the thimble-sized carton of milk she was fumbling with, flicked up the foil with her nail, tipped the milk into Colette's coffee.

'Black. I take it black.'

'Sorry.'

'Another thing you didn't know.'

'Another.'

'This job you were talking about—' Colette broke off. She narrowed her eyes, and looked speculatively at Al, as if she were a long way off.

Al said, 'Don't frown. You'll stay like that one day. Just ask me what you need to ask.'

'Don't you know?'

'You asked me not to read your mind.'

'You're right. I did. Fair's fair. But can you shut it off like that? Shut it off and then just turn it on when you want it?'

'It's not like that. I don't know how I can explain. It's not like a tap.'

'Is it like a switch?'

'Not like a switch.'

'It's like – I suppose – is it like somebody whispering to you?'

'Yes. More like that. But not exactly whispering. I mean, not in your ear.'

'Not in your ear.' Colette stirred her coffee. Al picked up a paper straw of brown sugar, pinched off the end and dropped it into Colette's cup. 'You need the energy,' she explained. Colette, frowning, continued to stir.

'I have to get back soon,' Al said. 'They're building up in there.'

'So if it's not a switch—'

'About the job – you could sleep on it.'

'And it's not a tap—'

'You could ring me tomorrow.'

'And it's not somebody whispering in your ear—'

'My number's on the leaflet. Have you got my leaflet?'

'Does your spirit guide tell you things?'

'Don't leave it too long.'

'You said he was called Morris. A little bouncing circus clown.'

'Yes.'

'Sounds a pain.'

'He can be. '

'Does he live with you? In your house? I mean, if you call it "live"?'

'You might as well,' Al said. She sounded tired. 'You might as well call it "live", as call it anything.' She pushed herself to her feet. 'It's going to be a long afternoon.'

'Where *do* you live?'

'Wexham.'

'Is that far?'

'Just up into Bucks.'

'How do you get home, do you drive?'

'Train and then a taxi.'

'By the way, I think you must be right. About my family.'

Al looked down at her. 'I sense you're wavering. I mean,

about my offer. It's not like you to be indecisive. More like you to take the plunge.'

'I'm not quite sure what you'd want me to do. I'm used to a job description.'

'We could work one up. If that's what's worrying you. Write your own, why not? You'll soon see what needs to be done.' Alison was rummaging for something in her bag. 'I may not be able to pay as much as your last job. But then, when you've looked at my books, you'll be able to tell me what I can afford. And also, it's a quality of life thing, isn't it? I should think the schedule will be more relaxed than in your last job. You'd have more leisure.' Then she said, as if she were embarrassed, 'You wouldn't get rich out of me. I'm no good for lottery numbers, or anything like that.'

'Can you hang on for a minute?' Colette said. 'I need to know more.'

'They'll be waiting.'

'Make them wait.'

'Yes, but not too long. Or Mrs Etchells will catch them.' Al had found a tube of mints in her bag. She proffered it to Colette. 'Keeps the mind alert,' she said. 'What I need, you see, is someone to keep the diary straight and make sure I don't double-book. Liaise with the management, wherever I'm on the platform. Book hotels. Do the accounts. It would be good to have someone to answer the phone. If I'm with a client, I can't always break off.'

'You don't have an answering machine?'

'Yes, but the clients would rather hear a human voice. Anyway, I'm not very good with electrical things.'

'So how do you do your washing? In a tub?'

'No, the fact is . . .' Alison looked down. She looked harried. 'I can see there's a lot I'm going to have to explain to you,' she said.

The truth was, it emerged, that whatever message Alison

left on her machine was liable to become corrupted. Other messages, quite different ones, would overlay it. Where did they come from? 'There's no simple answer to that,' Alison said. She checked her watch. 'I meant to eat but I've been talking.'

'I'll bring you a sandwich in, shall I?'

'I never eat when I'm reading. It's not professional. Oh well. Do me no harm to be hungry, will it? I'll hardly waste away.' She patted her tummy, smiled miserably. 'Look, about the travelling, I do travel a lot, and I used to drive, but I don't any more. I think if I had a friend with me, I could manage, so we could split it, you see.'

'You need a navigator?'

'It's not so much that.' What Alison needed, she explained – picking again at the sugar straws, opening them and putting them down – was a warm living body beside her, as she drove from town to town, fayre to fayre, and from one Psychic Extravaganza to another. Otherwise, a spirit would come and sit in the passenger seat, and natter on while she tried to negotiate an unfamiliar one-way system. 'Do you know Bracknell? Bracknell's hell. All those roundabouts.'

'What's to stop the spirits from climbing in the back seat instead? Or have you got a two-door?'

Alison looked at her for a long moment. Colette thought she was actually going to answer the question. 'Look, Colette,' she said softly. She had got four straws lined up now, and she moved them about, delicately, with one finger: changing the pattern, shuffling and reshuffling. 'Look, it doesn't matter if you're a bit sceptical. I understand. I'd be sceptical myself. All you need to realise is that it doesn't matter what you think, it doesn't matter what I think – what happens, happens all the same. The only thing is, I don't do tests, I don't do tricks for people to try to prove myself, because I don't need to prove anything. Do you see?'

Colette nodded. Alison raised a finger to a girl who was serving, and pointed to the pot. 'A refill for you,' she explained. 'I can see you're bitter. Why shouldn't you be? Life hasn't treated you well. You've worked hard and had no reward. You've lost your home. And you've lost a lot of your money, haven't you?'

Colette's eyes followed the trail of brown sugar curling across the table; like an initial, trying to form itself. 'You seem to know a lot about me.'

'I laid out a spread for you. After you'd gone.'

'A spread?'

'The tarot cards.'

'I know. Which spread?'

'Basic Romany.'

'Why that?'

'I was in a hurry.'

'And what did you see?'

'I saw myself.'

Al got up and headed back towards the main hall, handing a ten-pound note to a girl as she passed, pointing to the table she had just left. That's far too much, Colette thought, two cafetières, ten pounds, what is she thinking? She felt a flare of indignation, as if it were her own cash that had been spent. She drank all the coffee, so as not to be wasteful, tipping the pot so its muddy grounds shifted. She went to the Ladies, and as she washed her hands she watched herself in the mirror. Maybe no mind-reading in it, she thought. No psychic tricks needed, or information from spirit guides. She did look like a woman who had lost her money: lost her lottery ticket in life, lost her dad and lost her home.

That summer they laughed a lot. They acted as if they were in love, planning for each other treats and nice things to eat, and surprising each other with thoughtful gifts. Alison gave

Colette a voucher for a day spa in Windsor; I won't come, she said cheerfully, I don't want some foul-breathed anorexic lecturing me about my cellulite, but you enjoy yourself, Colette. Colette dropped into Caleys and bought a warm throw, soft mohair and the colour of crushed raspberries; lovely, Al said that evening, just what I need, something to cover me up.

Colette took over most of the driving, finding that she didn't mind it at all. 'Change the car,' she said to Alison, and they went out to a showroom that very afternoon. They picked one because they liked the colour and the upholstery; she imagined herself putting two fingers up to Gavin, and when the salesman tried to talk car-sense they just giggled at each other. 'The truth is, they're all the same these days,' she said loudly. 'I don't know much, but I do know that.'

Al wasn't interested, she just wanted it done with; but when the salesman tried to trap her into a finance deal, she slapped him down smartly. She agreed a delivery date, wrote a cheque; Colette was impressed by her style. When they got home she rummaged through Al's wardrobe and threw out the worst bits of lurex. She tried to smuggle the 'silk' out, in a black bin liner, but Al went after the bag and retrieved it, drawing it out and looping it around her arm. 'Nice try,' she said to Colette. 'But I'm sticking with it, please.'

Colette's education in the psychic trade was brisk and no-nonsense. Al's absurd generosity to the waitress in the coffee shop might represent one side of her nature, but she was businesslike in her own way. She wouldn't be taken for a ride, she knew how to charge out every minute of her time, though her accounts, kept on paper, were a mess. Having been a credulous person so recently, Colette was now cynical and sneery. She wondered how long it would be before Al initiated her into some fraud. She waited and waited. By mid-August she thought, what fraud could there be? Al doesn't have secret wires tapping into people's thoughts. There's no technology in her act. All she does is stand up on stage and make weak jokes. You may say Al's a fake because she has to be, because nobody can do what she claims to do. But there it is; she doesn't make claims, she demonstrates. And when you come down to it she can deliver the goods. If there is a fraud, it's a transparent one; so clear that no one can see it.

Al hadn't even been registered for VAT, when Colette had come on board as her business brain. As for income tax, her allowances were all over the place. Colette had been to the tax office in person. The official she saw admitted to a complete ignorance of a medium's trade; she was poised to take advantage of it. 'What about her clothes,' she said, 'her stage outfits? Her outfits for meeting her clients. She has to look good, it's a professional obligation.'

'Not one we recognise, I'm afraid,' the young woman said.

'Well, you should! As you ought to know, being the size you are yourself, decent clothes in large sizes don't come cheap. She can't get away with the tat you find on the high street. It's got to be specialist shops. Even her bras, well, I don't need to spell it out.'

'I'm afraid it's all dual purpose,' the woman said. 'Underwear, outerwear, whatever, you see it's not just specific to her trade, is it?'

'What? You mean, she could pop to the postbox in it? Do the dusting? In one of her stage outfits?'

'If she liked. I'm trying to envisage – you didn't bring pictures, did you?'

'I'll drop some in.'

'That might be a help. So we could work out what sort of class of item we're dealing with – you see, if it were, well, a barrister's wig, say, or protective clothing, say, boots with steel toecaps, for example . . .'

'So are you telling me they've made special rules about it? For mediums?'

'Well, no, not specifically for – what you say your partner does. I'm just going by the nearest cases I can envisage.' The woman looked restless. 'I suppose you might classify it as show business. Look, I'll pass it up for consideration. Take it under advisement.'

Colette wished – wished very strongly, most sincerely – that she had Al's powers, just for sixty seconds. So that a whisper, a hiss, a flash, so that something would overtake her, some knowledge, insight, some piece of special information, so that she could lean across the desk and tell the woman at the tax office something about her private life, something embarrassing: or something that would make the hair stand up on the back of her neck. For the moment, they agreed to differ. Colette undertook to keep a complete record of Al's expenditure on stage outfits. She lost no time, of course, in computerising their accounts. But the thought nagged at her that a record kept in figures was not quite enough.

Hence her good idea, about writing a book. How hard could it be? Al made tape recordings for her clients, so wasn't it logical, in the larger world, to tape-record Al? Then all she would need to do would be transcribe, edit, tighten up here and there, make some chapter headings . . . her mind moved ahead, to costings, to a layout, a photographer . . . Fleetingly, she thought of the boy in the bookshop, who'd sold her the tarot pack. If I'd been self-employed then, she thought, I could have set those cards against tax. Those days seemed distant now: leaving the boy's bedsit, at 5 a.m. in the rain. Her life with Gavin had receded; she remembered things he had, like his calculator, and his diver's watch, but not necessarily the evil things he had done. She remembered her kitchen, the scales, the knives; but not anything she cooked there. She remembered her bed, and her bed linen; but not sex. I can't keep on losing it, she thought, losing chunks of my life, years at a time. Or who will I be, when I'm old? I should write a book for me, too. I need a proof of some sort, a record of what goes down.

The tape recorder worked well on the whole, though sometimes it sounded as if Alison had a bag over her head; Colette's questions, always, were piercingly clear. But when they played the tapes back, they found that, just as Al had foreseen, other items had intruded. Someone speaking, fast and urgent, in what might be Polish. A twittering, like small birds in a wood. Nightingales, Alison said unexpectedly. Once, a woman's irate voice cut through Alison's mutter: 'Well, you're in for it now. You've started so you may as well finish. It's no use asking for your money back, sunshine. The trade doesn't work that way.'

COLETTE: When you were a child, did you ever suffer a severe blow to the skull?

ALISON: Several . . . Why, didn't you?

FOUR

Click.

COLETTE: It's Tuesday and I'm just – it's ten thirty in the evening and – Al, can you come a bit closer to the mike? I'm just resuming where we left off last night – now, Alison, we've sort of addressed the point about the trivia, haven't we? Still, you might like to put your answer on the tape.

ALISON: I have already explained to you that the reason we get such trivial information from spirit is—

COLETTE: All right, there's no need to sound like a metronome. Monotone. Can't you sound a bit more natural?

ALISON: If the people who've passed – is that OK now?

COLETTE: Go on.

ALISON: —if the people who've passed were to give you messages about angels and, you know, spiritual matters, you'd think it was a bit vague. You wouldn't have any way of checking on them. But if they give you messages about your kitchen units, you can say if they're right or wrong.

COLETTE: So what you're mainly worried about is convincing people?

ALISON: No.

COLETTE: What then?

ALISON: I don't feel I have to convince anybody, personally. It's up to them whether they come to see me. Their choice. There's no compulsion to believe anything they don't want.

Oh, Colette, what's that? Can you hear it?

COLETTE: Just carry on.

ALISON: It's snarling. Somebody's let the dogs out?

COLETTE: What?

ALISON: I can't carry on over this racket.

Click.

Click.

COLETTE: OK, trying again. It's eleven o'clock and we've had a cup of tea—

ALISON: —and a chocolate-chip cookie—

COLETTE: —and we're resuming. We were talking about the whole issue of proof, and I want to ask you, Alison, have you ever been scientifically tested?

ALISON: I've always kept away from that. You see, if you were in a laboratory wired up, it's as good as saying, we think you're some sort of confidence trick. Why should people come through from spirit for other people who don't believe in them? You see, most people, once they've passed, they're not really interested in talking to this side. The effort's too much for them. Even if they wanted to do it, they haven't got the concentration span. You say they give trivial messages, but that's because they're trivial people. You don't get a personality transplant when you're dead. You don't suddenly get a degree in philosophy. They're not interested in helping me out with proof.

COLETTE: On the platform you always say, you've had your gift since you were very small.

ALISON: Yes.

COLETTE (*whispering*): Al, don't do that to me – I need a proper answer on the tape. Yes, you say it, or yes, it's true?

ALISON: I don't generally lie on the platform. Well, only to spare people.

COLETTE: Spare them what?

Pause.

Al?

ALISON: Can you move on?

COLETTE: OK, so you've had this gift—

ALISON: If you call it that.

COLETTE: You've had this ability since you were small. Can you tell us about your childhood?

ALISON: I could. When you were little, did you have a front garden?

COLETTE: Yes.

ALISON: What did you have in it?

COLETTE: Hydrangeas, I think.

ALISON: We had a bath in ours.

When Alison was young she might as well have been a beast in the jungle as a girl growing up outside Aldershot. She and her mum lived in an old terraced house with a lot of banging doors. It faced a busy road, but there was open land at the back. Downstairs there were two rooms, and a lean-to with a flat roof, which was the kitchen. Upstairs were two bedrooms, and a bathroom, which had a bath in it so there was no actual need for the one in the garden. Opposite the bathroom was the steep short staircase that led up to the attic.

Downstairs, the front room was the place where men had

a party. They came and went with bags inside which bottles rattled and chinked. Sometimes her mum would say, better watch ourselves tonight, Gloria, they're bringing spirits in. In the back room, her mum sat smoking and muttering. In the lean-to, she sometimes absently opened cans of carrots or butter beans, or stood staring at the grill pan while something burned on it. The roof leaked, and black mould drew a drippy, wavering line down one corner.

The house was a mess. Bits were continually falling off it. You'd get left with the door handle in your hand, and when somebody put his fist through a window one night it got mended with cardboard and stayed like that. The men were never willing to do hammering or operate with a screwdriver. 'Never do a hand's turn, Gloria!' her mother complained.

As she lay in her little bed at night the doors banged, and sometimes the windows smashed. People came in and out. Sometimes she heard laughing, sometimes scuffling, sometimes raised voices and a steady rhythmic pounding. Sometimes she stayed in her bed till daylight came, sometimes she was called to get up for one reason and another. Some nights she dreamed she could fly; she passed over the ridge tiles, and looked down on the men about their business, skimming over the waste ground, where vans stood with their back doors open, and torchlight snaked through the smoky dark.

Sometimes the men were there in a crowd, sometimes they swarmed off and vanished for days. Sometimes at night just one or two men stayed and went upstairs with her mum. Then next day the bunch of them were back again, tee-heeing beyond the wall at men's private jokes. Behind the house was a scrubby field, with a broken-down caravan on blocks; sometimes there was a light in it. 'Who lives in there?' she asked her mum, and her mum replied, 'What you don't know won't hurt you,' which even at an early age Alison knew was untrue.

Beyond the caravan was a huddle of leaning corrugated sheds, and a line of lock-up garages to which the men had the keys. Two white ponies used to graze in the field, then they didn't. Where have the ponies gone? she asked her mum. Her mum replied, to the knackers, I suppose.

She said, who's Gloria? You keep talking to her. Her mum said, never you mind.

'Where is she?' she said. 'I can't see her. You say, yes, Gloria, no, Gloria, want a cuppa, Gloria? Where is she?'

Her mum said, 'Never mind Gloria, you'll be in kingdom come. Because that's where I'm going to knock you if you keep this up.'

Her mum would never stay in the house if she could help it: pacing, smoking, smoking, pacing. Desperate for a breath of air, she would say, 'Come on, Gloria,' shrug on her coat and flee down the road to the minimart; and because she did not want the trouble of washing or dressing Alison, or having her under her feet whining for sweeties, she would take her up to the top of the house and lock her in the attic. 'She can't come to any harm up there,' she would reason, out loud to Gloria. 'No matches so can't set the house on fire. Too small to climb out the skylight. Nothing sharp up there the like of which she is drawn to, such as knives or pins. There's really no damage she could come to.'

She put an old rug up there for Alison to sit on, when she played with her bricks and animals. 'Quite a little palace,' she said. There was no heating, which again was a safety factor, there being no power points for Alison to put her fingers into. She could have an extra cardy instead. In summer the attic was hot. Midday rays streamed fiercely down, straight from the sky to the dusty rug. They lit up the corner where the little lady used to fade up, all dressed in pink, and call out to Alison in a timid Irish voice.

Alison was perhaps five years old when the little lady first appeared, and in this way she learned how the dead could be helpful and sweet. She had no doubt that the little lady was dead, in every meaningful sense. Her clothes were felt-like and soft to the touch, and her pink cardigan was buttoned right up to the first fold of her chin. 'My name is Mrs McGibbet, darlin',' she said. 'Would you like to have me round and about? I thought you might like to have me with you, round and about.'

Mrs McGibbet's eyes were blue and round and startled. In her cooing voice, she talked about her son, who had passed over before her, met with an accident. They'd never been able to find each other, she said, I never could meet up with Brendan. But sometimes she showed Alison his toys, little miniature cars and tractors, neatly boxed. Once or twice she faded away and left the toys behind. Mum just stubbed her toe on them. It was as if she didn't see them at all.

Mrs McGibbet was always saying, 'I wouldn't want, my darlin', to come between a little girl and her mother. If that were her mother coming up the stairs now, coming up with a heavy tread, no, I wouldn't want to put myself forward at all.' When the door opened she faded away: leaving, sometimes, an old doll collapsed in the corner where she had sat. She chuckled as she fell backwards, into the invisible place behind the wall.

Al's mum forgot to send her to school. 'Good grief,' she said, when the man came round to prosecute her, 'you mean to say she's that age already?'

Even after that, Al was never where she should be. She never had a swimsuit so when it was swimming she was sent home. One of the teachers threatened she'd be made to swim in her knickers next week, but she went home and mentioned it, and one of the men offered to go down there and sort it out. When Al went to school next day she told the teacher, Donnie's coming down; he says he'll push a bottle up your bleeding whatnot, and – I don't think it's very nice, Miss – ram it in till your guts come out your mouf.

After that, on swimming afternoon, she was just sent home again. She never had her rubber-soled shoes for skipping and hopping or her eggs and basin for mixing a cake, her times tables or her poem or her model mosque made out of milk-bottle tops. Sometimes when she came home from school one of the men would stop her in the hall and give her fifty pence. She would run up to the attic and put it away in a secret box she had up there. Her mother would take it off her if she could, so she had to be quick.

One day the men came with a big van. She heard yapping and ran to the window. Three blunt-nosed brindle dogs were being led towards the garages. 'Oh, what are their names?' she cried. Her mother said, 'Don't you go calling their names. Dogs like that, they'll chew your face off. Isn't that right, Gloria?'

She gave them names anyway: Blighto, Harry and Serene. One day Blighto came to the house and bumped against the back door. 'Oh, he's knocking,' Al said. She opened the door though she knew she shouldn't, and tried to give him half her wafer biscuit.

A man came shooting out of nowhere and hauled the dog off her. He kicked it into the yard while he got Alison up off the floor. 'Emmie, sort it!' he yelled, then wrapped his hands in an old jersey of her mum's and went out and pummelled the dog's face, dragging it back to the sheds and twisting its neck as he dragged. He came back in shouting, 'I'll shoot the fucker, I'll strangle that bastard dog.' The man, whose name was Keith, wept when he saw how the dog had ripped at her hairline. He said, Emmie, she ought to go to casualty, that needs stitching. Her mum said she couldn't be sitting in a queue all afternoon.

The man washed her head at the kitchen sink. There wasn't a cloth or a sponge so he put his hand on the back of her neck, pressed her down over the plastic bowl, and slapped the water up at her. It went in her eyes, so the bowl blurred. Her blood went in the bowl but that was all right; it was all right because the bowl itself was red. 'Stay there, darling,' he said, 'just keep still,' and his hand lifted from her nape as he bent to rummage in the cupboard at his feet. Obedient, she bent there; blood came down her nose too and she wondered why that was. She heard the chinking noise as Keith tossed the empties out from under the sink. Em, he said, you not got any disinfectant in here? Give us a rag for Chrissakes, tear up a sheet, I don't know, and her mother said, use your hankie or ain't you got none? In the end her mother came up behind her with the used tea towel and Keith ripped it out of her hand. 'There you go, there you go, there you go,' he kept saying, dabbing away, sighing the words between his teeth. She felt faint with pain. She said, 'Keef, are you my dad?'

He wrung the cloth between his hands. 'What you been telling her, Emmie?'

Her mother said, 'I've not been telling her nothing, you ought to know by now she's a bloody little liar. She says she can hear voices in the wall. She says there are people up in the attic. She's got a screw loose, Gloria says.'

Keith moved: she felt a sudden sick cold at her back, as he pulled away, as his body warmth left her. She reared up, dripping water and dilute pink blood. Keith had crossed the room and pinned her mother up against the wall. 'I told you, Emmie, if I told you once I told you a dozen times, I do not want to hear that name spoken.' And the dozen times, Keith reinforced, by the way he gave her mum a little bounce, raising her by her hair near the scalp and bobbing her down again. 'Gloria's buggered off back to Paddyland,' he said (bounce), that's all (bounce), you bloody (bounce) know about it, do you (bounce) understand (bounce) that, do I bloody (bounce, bounce, bounce, bounce) make myself crystal (bounce) clear? You just (bounce) forget you *ever* (bounce) set eyes.'

'She's all right, is Gloria,' said her mum, 'she can be a good laugh,' and the man said, 'Do you want me to give you a slap? Do you want me to give you a slap and knock your teeth out?'

Alison was interested to see this happen. She had had many kinds of slap, but not that kind. She wiped the water from her eyes, the water and blood, till her vision cleared. But Keith seemed to get tired of it. He let her mother go and her legs went from under her; her body folded and slid down the wall, like the lady in the attic who could fold herself out of sight.

'You look like Mrs McGibbet,' Al said. Her mother twitched, as if her wires had been pulled; she squeaked up from the floor. 'Who's speaking names now?' she said. 'You wallop *her*, Keith, if you don't want names spoken. She's always speaking names.' Then she screamed a new insult that Al had never heard before. 'You poxy little poxer, you got blood on your chin. Where've you got that from? You poxy little poxer.'

Al said, 'Keef, does she mean me?'

Keith wiped his sweating forehead. It made you sweat, bouncing a woman a dozen times by the short hair of her head. 'Yes. No,' he said. 'She means to say poxy little boxer. She can't talk, sweetheart, she don't know who she's talking to, her brain's gone, what she ever had of it.'

'Who's Gloria?' she asked.

Keith made a hissing through his teeth. He tapped one fist into his opposite palm. For a moment she thought he was going to come after her, so she backed up against the sink. The cold edge of it dug into her back; her hair dripped, blood and water, down her T-shirt. Later she would tell Colette, I was never so frightened as then; that was my worst moment, one of the worse ones anyway, that moment when I thought Keef would knock me to kingdom come.

But Keith stepped back. 'Here,' he said. He thrust the tea towel into her hand. 'Keep at it,' he said. 'Keep it clean.'

'Can I stay off school?' she said, and Keith said, yes, she'd better. He gave her a pound note and told her to yell out if she saw a dog loose again.

'And will you come and save me?'

'Somebody'll be about.'

'But I don't want you to strangle it,' she said, with tears in her eyes. 'It's Blighto.'

The next time she recalled seeing Keith was a few months later. It was night, and she should have been in bed as nobody had called her out. But when she heard Keith's name she reached under her mattress for her scissors, which she always kept there in case they should be needed. She clutched them in one hand; with the other she held up the hem of the big nightie that was lent her as a special favour from her mum. When she came scrambling down the stairs, Keith was standing just inside the front door; or at least some legs were, wearing Keith's trousers. He had a blanket over his head. Two men were supporting him. When they took off the blanket she saw that every part of his face looked like fatty mince, oozing blood. ('Oh, this mince is fatty, Gloria!' her mother would say.) She called out to him, 'Keef, that needs stitching!' and one of the men swooped down on her and wrenched the scissors out of her hand. She heard them strike the wall, as the man flung them; looming above her, he pushed her into the back room and slammed the door. Next day a voice beyond the wall said, 'Hear Keef got mashed up last night. Tee-hee. As if he ain't got troubles enough.'

She believed she never saw Keith again, but she might have seen him and just not recognised him; it didn't seem as if he'd have much left, by way of original features. She remembered how, the evening of the dog bite, once her head had stopped bleeding, she had gone out to the garden. She followed the furrows dug by the dog's strong hind legs, as Keith dragged him away from the house, and Blighto twisted to look back. Not until it rained hard did the ruts disappear.

At that time Alison was saving up for a pony. One day she went up to the attic to count her money. 'Ah dear,' said Mrs McGibbet, 'the lady your mother has been up here, darlin', raiding your box that was your own peculiar property. The coins she's tipped into her open purse, and the one single poor note she has tucked away in her brassiere. And not a thing I could do to stop her, my rheumatics being aggravated by the cold and damp, for by the time I was up and out of my corner, she had outstripped me.'

Alison sat down on the floor. 'Mrs McGibbet,' she said, 'can I ask you a question?'

'You surely can. And why should you have to ask if you can ask, I ask myself?'

'Do you know Gloria?'

'Do I know Gloria?' Mrs McGibbet's eyelids fell over her bright blue eyes. 'Ah, you've no business asking.'

'I think I saw her. I think I can see her these days.'

'Gloria is a cheap hoor, what else should she be? I never should have given her the name, for it put ideas in her head that was above her station. Go on the boat then, heedless and headstrong she would go on the boat. Get off at Liverpool with all its attendant vices and then where will she go but via a meat lorry to the dreadful metropolis with its many occasions of sin. End up dead, dead and haunting about in a British army town, in a dirty house with a bath in the front garden, and her own mother a living witness to every hoor's trick that she can contrive.'

After that, when she got fifty pence from the men, she took it straight down the minimart and bought chocolate, which she ate on the way home.

When Alison was eight years old, or maybe nine or ten, she was playing outside one day, a greyish, sticky day in late summer. She was alone, of course: playing horses, neighing occasionally, and progressing at a canter. The rough grass of their back plot was worn in patches, like the pile on the rug that made the attic into a little palace.

Something drew her attention, and she stopped in her paces, and glanced up. She could see men going to and fro from the garages, carrying boxes.

'Hiya!' she said. She waved to them. She was sure they were men she knew.

But then a minute later she thought they were men she didn't know. It was hard to tell. They kept their faces turned away. A sick feeling crept over her.

Silent, faces downcast, the men moved over the tussocky grass. Silent, faces downcast, they passed the boxes. She couldn't judge the distance from herself to them; it was as if the light had grown more thick and dense. She took a step forward, but she knew she should not. Her dirty nails dug into the palms of her hands. Sick came up into her throat. She swallowed it and it burned. Very slowly, she turned her head away. She took one plodding step towards the house. Then another. Air thick as mud clotted around her ankles. She had some idea of what was in the boxes, but as she stepped inside the house it slipped clear from her mind, like a drug slipping from a syringe and deep into a vein.

Her mother was in the lean-to, nattering away to Gloria. 'Excuse me, will you,' she said affably, 'while I just see if this child wants a clip round the ear?' She turned round and glared at her daughter. 'Look at you,' she said. 'Wash your face, you're all running in sweat, you bloody turn me up. I was never like that at your age, I was a neat little thing, I had to be, I wouldn't have made a living if I'd gone about like that. What's the matter with you, you're green, girl, look at yourself in the mirror, have you been stuffing yourself with them Rolos again? If you're going to chuck up, go outside and do it.'

Alison did as she was told and looked at herself in the mirror. She didn't recognise the person she saw there. It was a man, with a check jacket on and a tie skew-whiff; a frowning man with a low hairline and a yellowish face. Then she realised that the door was open, and that the men were piling in behind her. 'Fuck, Emmie, got to wash me hands!' one of them shouted.

She ran. For always, more or less, she was afraid of the men. On the stairs to the attic she doubled up and let brown liquid run out of her mouth. She hoped her mother would think it was the cat, Judy, who was responsible. She toiled on upwards and swung open the door. Mrs McGibbet was sitting, already formed, in her corner. Her stumpy legs in their thick stockings stuck out in front of her, wide apart, as if she had been punched and knocked down. Her eyes were no longer startled, but blank as if their blinds had been drawn.

She did not greet Alison: no 'How's my darlin' girl today?' She just said, in a distracted mutter, 'There's an evil thing you wouldn't want to see at all. There's an evil thing you wouldn't want to see . . .' She faded with rapidity: there was a scrabbling noise beneath the floorboards, and then she was gone.

Mrs McGibbet never came back after that day. She missed

her, but she realised that the old lady was too frightened to return. Al was a child and hadn't got the option of leaving. Now there was no appeal or relief from Gloria and her mum, and the men in the front room. She went out to play at the back as seldom as possible; even the thought of it made thick spit come up into her mouth. Her mother berated her for getting no fresh air. If she was forced to play out – which happened sometimes, with the door locked after her – she made it a rule never to raise her eyes as far as the sheds and the lock-up garages, or the belt of woodland beyond them. She could not shake off the atmosphere of that afternoon, a peculiar suspension, like a breath held: the men's averted faces, the thunderous air, the dying grass, her mother's outgust of tobacco smoke, the yellow face in the mirror where she expected to see her own: the man's need to wash his hands. As for what was in the cardboard boxes, she hoped not to think about it; but sometimes the answer turned up, in dreams.

COLETTE: So . . . are you going to tell me?

ALISON: I might if I was quite sure I knew.

COLETTE: Only 'might'?

ALISON: I don't know if I could speak it out.

COLETTE: Drugs, could it have been? Or didn't they have drugs in those days?

ALISON: God Almighty, of course they had drugs, do you think I come out of the Ark? They've always had drugs.

COLETTE: So?

ALISON: It was a funny district, you see, the army camps all around, these squaddies coming and going, I mean, it was a big area for, well, women like my mum, and the sort of men she knew, there was a lot of illegal gambling, there were women and boys who were on the game, there were all sorts of—

COLETTE: So come on, what do you think was in the boxes?

Pause.

Bits of Gloria?

ALISON: No. Surely not? Keef said she'd gone home to Ireland.

COLETTE: You didn't believe that, did you?

ALISON: I didn't believe it or not believe it.

COLETTE: But she did disappear?

ALISON: Not from our house she didn't. Yes Gloria, no Gloria, have a cuppa Gloria.

COLETTE: I'm quite interested in this because it suggests your mum was mad or something – but let's just keep to the point about the disappearance – was anything reported?

ALISON: I was eight. I didn't know what was reported.

COLETTE: Nothing on TV?

ALISON: I'm not sure we had a TV. Well, yes, we did. Several. I mean, the men used to bring them in under their arms. Just, we never had an aerial. That was us. Two baths. No TV aerial.

COLETTE: Al, why do you make such silly jokes all the time? You do it when you're on the platform. It's not appropriate.

ALISON: Personally, I think the use of humour's very important when you're dealing with the public. It puts them at their ease. Because they're scared, when they come in.

COLETTE: I was never scared. Why do they come if they're scared?

ALISON: Most people have a very low fright threshold. But it doesn't stop them being curious.

COLETTE: They should toughen up.

ALISON: I suppose we all should. (*Sighs.*) Look, Colette –

you come from Uxbridge. Oh, I know you say, Uxbridge not Knightsbridge, but it's a place where you had hydrangeas, right? Well, that's not like where I come from. I suppose if you had a crime in Uxbridge, if you had somebody disappear, the neighbours would notice.

COLETTE: So what are you saying?

ALISON: People went missing all the time, round our way. There was wasteland. There was army land, there was miles of it. There was heathland and just generally these acres where anything . . . could have . . .

COLETTE: Did the police ever come round?

ALISON: The police came round regularly, I mean, there was no surprise in that.

COLETTE: So what did you do?

ALISON: My mother would say, down on the floor. The police would flap the letter box. They'd shout through, is that Mrs Emmeline Cheetham?

COLETTE: Was that her name?

ALISON: Yes, Emmeline. It's nice, isn't it?

COLETTE: I mean Cheetham, that's not your name.

ALISON: I changed it. Think about it.

COLETTE: Oh yes . . . Al, does this mean you might have previous identities?

ALISON: Past lives?

COLETTE: No . . . for God's sake . . . I'm just talking about other names, other names by which you may have been known to the Revenue, I mean you must have worked before you became self-employed, so you must have tax records in the name of Cheetham, with some other district. I wish you'd mentioned this before!

ALISON: I want to go to the loo.

COLETTE: Because I don't think you have any idea how embattled I am. About your tax. And I can do without any complication of this nature.

ALISON: So could you turn the tape off?

COLETTE: Oh, cross your legs, you can hang on for two minutes. Just to get us back on track – we are concluding our conversation about the mysterious boxes Alison saw when she was eight—

ALISON: —or maybe nine, or ten—

COLETTE: —and these boxes were being carried by people she didn't know, men, and towards the back of her house, yes?

ALISON: Yes, towards the back, that's right. Down towards the fields. The open ground. And no, I don't know what was in them. Oh God, Colette, can you switch off? I really need the loo. And Morris is making such a racket. I don't know what was in those boxes, but sometimes I feel as if it's me. Does that make sense to you?

COLETTE: I think the big question is, will it make sense to our reader?

Click.

When Alison was at school, she had to keep 'My Diary'. She was allowed to crayon what she did every day, as well as put words. She put about Keith and his face getting mashed. About the dog Blighto and the drag of his claws in the mud. 'Do we really want to know about this, Alison?' her teacher said.

Her mother was invited in to see the headmaster, but when she lit up he tapped the 'No Smoking' sign perched on top of the typewriter on his desk.

'Yes, I can read,' Emmeline said proudly, as she puffed away.

'I really think,' said he, and her mother said, 'Look, you asked me here, so you've got to put up with it, is that right?' She tapped her ash into his wire in-tray. 'You got a complaint about Alison, is that it?'

'It's not a question of complaint,' the headmaster said.

'Oh, good,' said her mum. 'Because my daughter's as good as gold. So if you had any complaint, it'd be up to you to get it sorted. Otherwise I'd have to get you sorted, wouldn't I?'

'I'm not sure you quite grasp, Mrs Cheetham—'

'I dare say,' Al's mum said. 'We know where your sort get off, smacking little girls' bottoms, I mean, you wouldn't do it otherwise, it's not a man's job, is it?'

'Nothing of that kind—' the headmaster began.

Alison started to cry loudly.

'Shut it,' her mother said casually. 'So I'm just telling you, I don't like people writing to me. I don't like stuff coming through my door. Any more of it, and you'll be picking your teeth out of your typewriter.' She took one last draw on her cigarette, and dropped the stub on the carpet tiles. 'I'm only saying.'

By the time Al was in Mrs Clerides' class, she'd rather not put pen to paper because of the risk that someone else would master the pen and write gibberish in her exercise book. 'Gibberish' was what Mrs Clerides called it, when she got her up to the front of the class and asked her if she were subnormal.

Mrs Clerides read out Al's diary in a disgusted tone. '"Slurp, slurp, yum, yum," said Harry. "Give us some," said Blighto. "No," said Harry, "today it is all for me."'

'It's a dog writing,' Al explained. 'It's Serene. She's the witness. She tells how Harry polished his bowl. When he'd done you could see your face in it.'

'I don't believe I asked you to keep the diary of your pet,' said Mrs C.

'She's not a pet,' Al said. 'Bloody hell, Mrs Clerides, she pays her way, we all have to pay. If you don't work you don't eat.' Then she had gone quiet, thinking, the dogs' work is fighting, but what is the men's? They go about in vans. They say, what game am I in? I am in the entertainment game.

Mrs Clerides slapped her legs. She made her write out something or other, fifty times, maybe a hundred. She couldn't remember what it was. Even when she was writing it she couldn't remember. She had to keep on reminding herself by looking back at the line before.

After that, if she'd got a few words down safely, she preferred to go over them with her blue ballpoint, branding the letters well into the paper: then drawing daisy petals around the 'o's and giving the 'g's little fishy faces. This was dull but it was better to be bored than to risk letting the gibberish in by an unguarded stroke, branching out into white space. It made her look occupied, and as long as she looked occupied she got left alone at the back with the mongols, the dummies and the spastics.

The men said, the bloody little bitch. Is she sorry for what she's done? Because she don't look sorry, stuffing her face wiv sweets like that!

I am, I am, she said; but she couldn't remember what she ought to be sorry for. It had gone woolly in her mind, the way things do when they happen in the night.

The men said, she don't look sorry, Em! It's a wonder nobody's dead. We're going to take her down the back, and teach her a lesson she won't forget.

They didn't say what the lesson was. So after that she always wondered, have I had it? Or is it still to come?

By the time Al was ten, she had begun sleepwalking. She walked in on her mum, rolling on the sofa with a squaddie. The soldier raised his shaven head and roared. Her mother roared too, and her thin legs, blotched with fake tan, stood straight up into the air.

Next day her mum got the squaddie to fix a bolt on the outside of Al's bedroom door. He did it gladly, humming as he worked. You're the first man was ever handy around here, her mum said, is that right, Gloria?

Alison stood behind her bedroom door. She heard the bolt shunt into its bracket, with a small tight thud. The squaddie hummed, happy in his work. 'I wish I was in Dixie, hooray, hooray.' Tap-tap. 'In Dixie Land I'll take my stand . . .' Mum, she said, let us out, I can't breave. She ran to the window. They were walking down the road, laughing, the soldier swigging from a can of lager.

A few nights later she woke suddenly. It was very dark outside, as if they had been able to shut off the street lamp. A number of ill-formed, greasy faces were looking down on her. One of them seemed to be in Dixie, but she couldn't be sure. She closed her eyes. She felt herself lifted up. Then there was nothing, nothing that she remembers.

ALISON: So what puzzles me, and the only thing that makes me think it might have been a dream, was that darkness – because how did they switch the street lamp off?

COLETTE: You slept in the front, did you?

ALISON: Initially in the back, because the front was the bigger bedroom so Mum had it, but then she swapped me, must have been after the dog bite, probably after Keef, I get the impression she didn't want me getting up in the night and looking out over the waste ground, which is possible because . . .

COLETTE: Al, face up to it. You didn't dream it. She had you molested. Probably sold tickets. God knows . . .

ALISON: I think I'd already been – that. What you say. Molested.

COLETTE: Do you?

ALISON: Just not in a group situation.

COLETTE: Alison, you ought to go to the police.

ALISON: It's years—

COLETTE: But some of these men could still be at large!

ALISON: It all gets mixed up in my mind. What happened. How old I was. Whether things happened once or whether they just went on happening – so they all rolled into one, you know.

COLETTE: So did you never tell anybody? Here. Blow your nose.

ALISON: No . . . You see, you don't tell anybody because there's nobody to tell. You try and write it down, you write 'My Diary', but you get your legs slapped. Honestly . . . it doesn't matter now, I don't think about it, it's only once in a while I think about it. I might have dreamed it, I used to dream I was flying. You see, you wipe out in the day what happens in the night. You have to. It's not as if it changed my life. I mean, I've never gone in for sex much. Look at me, who'd want me, it'd need an army. So it's not as if I feel . . . it's not as if I remember . . .

COLETTE: Your mother should have protected you. If she were mine I'd kill her. Don't you sometimes think about it, going over to Aldershot and killing her?

ALISON: She lives in Bracknell now.

COLETTE: Wherever. Why does she live in Bracknell?

ALISON: She went off with a man who had a council house over there, but it never lasted, anyway he went over into spirit and somehow or other she ended up with the tenancy. She wasn't so bad. Isn't. I mean, you have to feel sorry for her. She's the size of a sparrow. In her looks, she's more like your mother than mine. I walked past her once in the street and didn't recognise her. She was always dyeing her hair. It was a different colour every week.

COLETTE: That's no excuse.

ALISON: And it never came out what she intended. Champagne Hi-Life, and she'd end up ginger. Chocolate Mousse, and she'd end up ginger. Same with her pills. She used to swap other people's prescriptions. I couldn't help but feel sorry for her. I wondered how she kept going.

COLETTE: These men – could you still identify them, do you think?

ALISON: Some of them. Maybe. If I saw them in a good light. But they can't arrest them after they're passed.

COLETTE: If they're dead I'm not worried. If they're dead they can't do any more damage.

When Al was twelve or so, she got cheeky. She said to her mum: 'That one last night, what was *his* name then? Or don't you know?'

Her mum tried to slap her around the head but she overbalanced and fell on the floor. Al helped her up.

'Thank you, you're a good girl, Al,' her mum said; and her cheeks burned, because she had never heard that before.

'What you on, Mum?' she asked. 'What you taking?'

Her mum took a lot of Librium and a lot of Bacardi, which does make you fall over. Every week, though, she gave something else a try; it usually worked out, like the hair dye, to have a result she had not foreseen but should have.

Al had to go to the chemist for her mum's prescriptions. 'Are you here again?' said the man behind the counter, and because she was going through her brusque phase she would say, 'It's me or somebody else, what's your opinion?'

'My God,' he said, 'I can't believe she gets through this. Is she selling it on? Come on, you're a bright girl, you must know.'

'She swallows it all,' she said. 'I swear it.'

The man sniggered. 'Swallows, does she? You don't say.'

This remark mocked her; but still, when she left the pharmacy she felt ten feet tall. You're a bright girl, she said to herself. She stared at herself in the next shop window: which was Ash Vale Motor Sport. The window was crammed with all the stuff you need for hacking across country with crappy old cars: sump guards, bull bars, fog lamps, snow chains, and the latest model in a hi-lift jack. Swimming above this equipment was her own face, the face of a bright girl, a good girl too: swimming in the oily glass.

By this time she had spent years pretending she was normal. She was never able to judge what other people knew and what they didn't know. Take Gloria: Gloria had been clear enough to her mother, but not to her. Yet her mother hadn't seen Mrs McGibbet, and she'd almost skated across the attic, putting her foot on one of Brendan's toy cars. And then one day – was it after Keith got mashed, was it after she got her scissors, was it before Harry cleaned his bowl? – one day she'd caught a glimpse of a red-haired lady with false eyelashes, standing at the foot of the stairs. Gloria, she thought, at last; she said, 'Hi, are you all right?' but the woman didn't reply. Another day, as she was coming in at the front door, she had glanced down into the bath, and didn't she see the red-haired lady looking up at her, with her eyelashes half pulled off, and no body attached to her neck?

But that was not possible. They wouldn't just leave a head on full view for passers-by. You kept things under wraps; wasn't that the rule? What else was the rule? Was she, Alison, seeing more or less than she ought? Should she mention it, when she heard a woman sobbing in the wall? When should you shout up and when should you shut up? Was she stupid, or was that other people? And what would she do when she left school?

Tahera was going to do social studies. She didn't know what that was. She and Tahera went shopping on a Saturday, if her mother let her out. Tahera shopped while she watched. Tahera was size six. She was four foot ten, brown and quite spotty. Al herself was not much taller, but she was size eighteen. Tahera said, 'You would be welcome to my cast-offs, but, you know.' She looked Alison up and down, and her tiny nostrils flared.

When she asked her mother for money, her mother said, 'What you want you got to earn, is that right, Gloria? You're not so bad, Al, you've got that lovely complexion, OK, you're fleshy but that's what a lot of men like. You're what we call two handfuls of bubbly fun. Now you didn't ought to hang around with that Indian bint, it puts the punters off, they don't like to think some Patel's after 'em with a Stanley knife.'

'Her name's not Patel.'

'All right, young lady! That's enough from you.' Her mother hurtled across the kitchen in a Librium rage. 'How long d'you expect me to keep you fed and housed, how long, eh? Lie on your back and take it, that's what I had to do. And regular! Not just oh-it's-Thursday-I-don't-feel-like-it. You can forget that caper, Miss! That sort of attitude will get you nowhere. Make it regular, and start charging proper. That's what you've got to do. How else you think you're going to make a living?'

COLETTE: So how did you feel, Alison, when you first knew you had psychic powers?

ALISON: I never . . . I mean, I never really did. There wasn't a moment. How can I put it – I didn't know what I saw, and what I just imagined. It – you see, it's confusing, when the people you grew up with were always coming and going at night. And always with hats on.

COLETTE: Hats?

ALISON: Or their collars pulled up. Disguises. Changing their names. I remember once, I must have been twelve, thirteen, I came in from school and I thought the house was empty for once, I thought, thank Christ for that, I thought, I might make some toast then do a bit of cleaning while they were all gone out. I walked through to the lean-to, and I looked up and this geezer was standing there – not doing anything, just standing there leaning against the sink, and he had a box of matches in his hand. Christ, he was evil-looking! I mean, they all were, but there was something about him, his expression – I can tell you, Colette, he was in a league of his own. He just stared at me and I stared back at him, and I thought I'd seen him before, and you have to make conversation, don't you, even if you feel as if you're going to throw up? So I said, are you the one they call Nick? He said, no, love, I'm a burglar, and I said, go on, you are Nick. He flew into a temper. He rattled the matchbox and it was empty. He threw it down. He went, can't even get a light around here, I'm going to sack the flaming lot of them, they're not worth a bench in hell. He whipped his belt out of his trousers and lashed out at me.

COLETTE: What happened then?

ALISON: I ran out into the street.

COLETTE: Did he follow you?

ALISON: I expect so.

Al was fourteen. Fifteen perhaps. No spots still. She seemed immune to them. She had grown a bit, all ways, up and out. Her tits came around the corner before she did; or that's what one of the men remarked.

She said to her mother, 'Who's my dad?'

Her mother said, 'What you want to know that for?'

'People ought to know who they are.'

Her mother lit another cigarette.

'I bet you don't know,' Al said. 'Why did you bother to have me? I bet you tried to get rid of me, didn't you?'

Her mother exhaled, blowing the smoke down her nose in two disdainful and separate streams. 'We all tried. But you was stuck fast, you silly bitch.'

'You should have gone to the doctor.'

'Doctor?' Her mother's eyes rolled up. 'Listen to her! Doctor! Bloody doctor, they didn't want to know. I was five, six months gone when MacArthur buggered off, and then I'd have shifted you all right, but there wasn't any bloody shifting.'

'MacArthur? Is that my dad?'

'How should I know?' her mother said. 'What you bloody asking me for? What you want to know for anyway? What you don't know can't hurt you. Mind your own bloody business.'

Seeing Gloria's head in the bath was more worrying to her, somehow, than seeing Gloria entire. From the age of eight, nine, ten, she told Colette, she used to see disassembled people lying around, a leg here, an arm there. She couldn't say precisely when it started, or what brought it on. Or whether they were bits of people she knew.

If you could understand what those years were like, she told Colette, you'd think I'm quite a triumph really, the way I keep myself together. When I walk out on stage I love it, when I've got my dress, my hair done, my opals, and my pearls that I wear in the summer. It's for them, for the audience, but it's for me too.

She knew there was this struggle in a woman's life – at least, there had been in her mum's – just to be whole, to be clean, to be tidy, to keep your own teeth in your head: just to have a clean tidy house and not fag ash dropped everywhere and bottle tops underfoot: not to find yourself straying out into the street with no tights on. That's why nowadays she can't bear fluff on the carpet, or a chip in her nail polish; that's why she's a fanatic about depilation, why she's always pestering the dentist about cavities he can't see yet; why she takes two baths a day, sometimes a shower as well; why she puts her special scent on every day. Maybe it's an old-fashioned choice, but it was the first grown-up scent she bought for herself, as soon as she could afford one. Mrs Etchells had remarked at the time, 'Oh, that's lovely, it's your signature perfume.' The house at Aldershot smelled of male farts, stale sheets and something else, not quite identifiable. Her mother said the smell had been there ever since they took the floorboards up: 'Keith and them, you know, that crowd what used to drink down the Phoenix? What did they want to do that for, Gloria? Why did they want to take the floorboards up? Men, honestly! You never know what they'll be up to next.'

Al told Colette, 'One day I saw an eye looking at me. A human eye. It used to roll along the street. One day it followed me to school.'

'What, like, "Mary had a Little Lamb"?'

'Yes, but it felt more like a dog.' Al shivered. 'And then one day, one morning when I was leaving the house . . .'

One day – she was in her school-leaving year – Al came out in the morning and saw a man watching her from the door of the chemist's shop. His hands were plunged into his trouser pockets and he was jiggling an unlit cigarette between his lips.

COLETTE: It wasn't this Nick character? The one in the kitchen, the one who chased you with the belt?

ALISON: No, it wasn't Nick.

COLETTE: But you had seen him before?

ALISON: Yes, yes, I had. But can we switch the tape off, please? Morris is threatening me. He doesn't like me talking about the early days. He doesn't want it recorded.

That same afternoon, she came out of school with Lee Tooley and Catherine Tattersall. Tahera herself was close behind, linking arms with Nicky Scott and Andrea Wossname. Tahera was still rich, small and spotty: and now bespectacled since her dad, she said, had 'read me the riot act'. Catherine had ginger curls and she was the girl who was most far behind in every subject, even further behind than Alison. Lee was Catherine's friend.

Morris was on the other side of the road, leaning against the window of the launderette. His eyes travelled over the girls. She went cold.

He was short, a dwarf nearly, like a jockey, and his legs were bowed like a jockey's. She learned later he'd been more like normal height, at least five foot six, till his legs had been broken: in one of his circus feats, he'd said at first, but later he admitted it was in a gang feud.

'Come on,' she said. 'Come on, Andrea. Hurry up. Come on, Lee.'

Then, because she was cold, she zipped up her jacket, her cherry-red jacket that only just covered her chest. 'Ooh, spastic!' Lee said; because it was not the style to fasten your jacket. The whole group began its shuffling, swaying, sideways procession down the street; there seemed nothing she could do to hurry them. The girls walked with their arms folded, hugging themselves. Lee, in a spirit of mockery, did the same. A radio played somewhere, it was playing an Elton John song. She remembered that. The kids began to sing. She tried, but her mouth was dry.

COLETTE: So was he – I feel I'm a bit in the dark here – this man who was watching you, outside the school: are we talking about Morris? And was he the man with the yellow face?
ALISON: Yes.
COLETTE: The man you saw behind you, through the mirror? The low hairline?
ALISON: His tie not on straight.

Next day, when she came out, he was there again. I'll go on the aggressive, she thought. She nudged Tahera. 'Look at that pervert.'

'Where?'

Alison nodded across the road to where Morris leaned, just as he had the day before. Tahera attracted Nicky Scott's attention by kicking her lightly on the back of her calf. 'Gerroff me, you bloody bhaji,' Nicky bellowed.

'Can you see any pervert?' Tahera asked.

They looked around them. They followed where Alison pointed and then they swivelled their heads from side to side in an exaggerated fashion. Then they turned in circles, crying out, 'Where, where?' – except for Catherine, who hadn't caught on, and just started singing like yesterday. Then they lolled their tongues out and retched, because they confused a perv with a sicko, then they ran off and left her alone in the street.

Morris lurched away from the wall and came limping towards her. He ignored the traffic, and a van must have missed him by inches. He could limp very fast; he seemed to scuttle like some violent crab, and when he reached her he fastened his crab-hand into her arm above the elbow. She flinched and twisted in his grasp, but he held her firmly. Get off me, she was crying, you horrible pervert, but then, as so often, she realised that words were coming out of her mouth but no one could hear them.

After Al's first meeting with Morris, he waited for her most days. 'I'm a gentleman, I am,' he would boast, 'and I am here to escort you. A growing girl like you, you don't want to be out walking the streets on your own. Anything could happen.'

In the early days, he didn't follow her into the house. He seemed nervous about who might be in there. As they turned at the corner of the street he would say, 'Nick bin in?'

She would say no, and he'd say, 'Just as well, never know where you are wiv Nick, if you see Nick you walk the other way, you hear? You don't try any of your tricks round Nick, or he'll upend you, he'll slap you on the soles of your feet till your teeth drop out.' Then he would brighten up: 'What about Aitkenside, you seen Aitkenside?'

She'd say, 'Dunno, what's his other name? Dunno who you mean.'

He'd say, 'Much you don't, oh, very likely. Pikey Pete been round?'

'I told you,' she said, 'I don't know who your friends are or what they're called.'

But Morris sneered at this. 'Not know Pete? The whole country knows him. Wherever there is dealing in dogs they know Pete.'

'I don't deal in dogs.' She remembered the grown-up coldness of her voice.

'Oh, pardon me, I'm sure! You don't deal with any of my mates, is it? You don't deal with 'em in any way, shape or form, is it?' He grumbled under his breath. 'You're not your mother's daughter, I suppose. Not know Pete? Wherever there is dealing in horses, they know Pete.'

When he got to the front gate, he would say, 'Emmie not moved that old bath yet?'

She'd say, 'Have you known my mum a long time?'

He'd say, 'I'll say I have. Known Emmie Cheetham? I'll say I have. Know everybody, me. I know Donnie. I know Pete. Emmie Cheetham? I'll say I have.'

One day she said, 'Morris, are you my dad?'

And he said, 'Dad, me, that's a good one! Did she say so?'

'I think MacArthur's my dad.'

'MacArthur!' he said. He stopped. She stopped too, and looked into his face. He had turned grey: greyer than usual. His voice came out wobbly. 'You can stand there, and say that name?'

'Why not?'

'Cool as a bloody cucumber,' Morris said. He spoke to the air, as if he were talking to an audience. 'Butter wouldn't melt in her mouf.'

They staggered along the street, a pace or two, Morris's hand clamped on her arm. She saw Lee and Catherine going by on the other side of the road. She waved to them to rescue her but they made vomity faces at her and walked on. She didn't know if they could see Morris or not. Under his breath he was muttering, 'MacArthur, she says! Cool as you like.' He stopped and propped himself against the wall with his free hand, his bent fingers spread out. He had a tattoo of a snake running down his arm; now its head, darting across the back of his hand, seemed to gulp, and pulse out its tongue. Morris too made a vomity face, and retched. She was afraid of what might come out of his mouth, so she concentrated on his hand, planted against the brick.

'Speak the name of MacArthur!' He mimicked her voice: '*I think he's my dad.* Suppose he is? Is that how you treat a dad? Is it? Got to hand it to her, she has some cheek, that girl.'

'How?' she said. 'How did I treat him?'

The head pulsed, the snake's tongue flicked out between his spread fingers. 'I'll tell you something about that bugger,' he said. 'I'll tell you something you don't know. MacArthur owes me money. And so if I ever see MacArthur in this neck of the woods, I'll saw him off at the bloody knees. Let the bloody bastard venture, just let him. I'll poke out his *other* eye.'

'Has MacArthur only one eye?'

'Oh, tee-bloody-hee,' Morris said. 'Still, girl, you got paid out. You got a lesson, eh? They taught you what a blade could do.'

'I hope you're not,' she said. 'I hope you're not my dad. I like you worst of anybody. I don't want you anywhere near me. You stink of fags and beer.'

'I bin near you,' Morris said. 'We all have.'

COLETTE: But after that, when Morris came along, you must have known that other people couldn't see him, I mean, you must have realised that you had psychic powers.

ALISON: You see, I was ignorant. I didn't know what a spirit guide was. Until I met Mrs Etchells, I had no idea . . .

COLETTE: We're going to go into that, aren't we? Mrs Etchells?

ALISON: When?

COLETTE: Tonight, if you've got the stamina.

ALISON: Can we eat first?

Click.

Pity Colette, who had to transcribe all this. 'When you're talking about Gloria,' she said, 'I never know if she's alive or dead.'

'No,' Al said. 'Nor me.'

'But it worries me. I need to get it straight – for the book.'

'I'm telling you what I know.'

Was she? Or was she leaving things out? Sparing Colette's feelings, in some way, or testing her memory?

'These awful blokes,' Colette said, 'all these fiends from Aldershot. I keep losing track of their names. Make me a list.'

Alison took a sheet of paper and wrote 'FIENDS FROM ALDERSHOT'.

'Let's see . . . Donnie Aitkenside,' she said.

'The one who said he'd beat up your teacher?'

'Yes . . . well, and rape her, I think he was going to rape her too. There was MacArthur. Morris reckoned MacArthur was worse than most, but I dunno. There was Keith Capstick, that pulled the dog off me. And I thought he was my dad because he did that. But was he? I dunno.'

When she talks about them, Colette thought, she slips away somewhere: to a childhood country, where diction is slipshod. She said, 'Al, are you writing this down?'

'You can see I'm not.'

'You wander off the point. Just make the list.'

Al sucked her pen. 'There was this Pikey character, who was a horse dealer . . . I think he had relatives, cousins, up and down the country, you used to hear him talk about them, they might have come by but I don't really know. And somebody called Bob Fox?'

'Don't ask me! Get it on paper! What did he do, Bob Fox?'

'He tapped on the back window. At my mum's house. He did it to make you jump.'

'What else? He must have done something else?'

'Dunno. Don't think he did. Then there was Nick, of

course. The one with the empty matchbox. In the kitchen. Oh, wait, I remember now. Oh God, yes. I know where I saw him before. We had to go and collect him from the cop shop. They'd picked him up on the street, falling-down drunk. But they didn't want to charge him, they just let him sober up, then they wanted rid of him because he'd put slime on the cell walls.'

'Slime?'

'And they didn't want a heavy cleaning job. He was just lying there sliming everything, you see. He didn't want to come out, so my mum had to go down and get him – they said, the police, they'd found her phone number in his wallet, so they sent a car to fetch her in, then she had to go down the cells. The desk sergeant said, a woman's touch. Tee-hee. He was being sarcastic. He said, he'll be able to go now, won't he, now he's got his bike? My mum said, watch your lip, Little Boy Blue, or I'll fatten it for you. He said, leave that kid here, you can't take her down the cells. And my mum said, what, leave her here, so you can bloody touch her up? So she took me down to get Nick.'

Colette felt faint. 'I wish I'd never started this,' she said.

'He came out on the street and he shouted, can't I get drunk, same as anybody? My mum was trying to calm him down. She says, come back to ours.'

'And did he?'

'I expect. Look, Col, it was a long time ago.'

Colette wanted to ask, what *kind* of slime was it, on the cell walls? But then again, she didn't want to ask.

Click.

COLETTE: OK, so it's eleven thirty—

ALISON: —p.m. that is—

COLETTE: —and we're about to resume—

ALISON: —as I've now had a bottle of Crozes Hermitage

and feel able to continue reminiscing about my teenage years—

COLETTE: Al!

ALISON: —whereas Colette has had a Slimline Tonic and on the basis of this feels she has the courage to switch on the machine—

COLETTE: My uncle used to tickle me.

ALISON: You mean, your dad?

COLETTE: Yes, come to think of it. My dad. It wasn't ordinary tickling—

ALISON: It's all right, take your time—

COLETTE: I mean it was aggressive, stabbing at you with a finger – a man's finger's, you know, it's as thick as that – and I was little, and he knew it hurt me. Oh God, and Gav used to do it. His idea of a joke. Maybe that's why I went and married him. It seemed familiar.

ALISON: Sounds classic to me, marrying a man with the same sense of humour as your father. I hear about it all the time.

COLETTE: I didn't laugh when he did it. It was more – you know, convulsing. As if I were having a fit.

ALISON: That must have been a pretty sight.

COLETTE: He stabbed into me with his finger, between my thin little ribs. It was like – it really was – the way he'd come at me, sticking it out . . . oh, I don't think I can say it . . .

ALISON: It's not like you to be coy.

COLETTE: —as if he was rehearsing me.

ALISON: Giving you a practice for your later life.

Pause.

I suppose that's what dads are for.

Here, do you want a tissue?

COLETTE: Let's get back on track. You need an early night, you've got a client phoning for tarot before her breakfast meeting. Mrs Etchells, you were going to fill me in about Mrs Etchells.

ALISON: You see, I got to the point where I wanted money of my own. I thought, if I saved up, I could get on the train at Ash Vale and just go somewhere, I wouldn't have minded where. So, the way it was, Mrs Etchells got me started. You see, one day I was leaning on her front hedge, bawling my eyes out, because Nicky Scott and Catherine and them – because these girls, my friends, at least they were supposed to be my friends—

COLETTE: Yes?

ALISON: They'd been calling me spastic all afternoon, because in English I'd had this, sort of incident, it was Morris really started it off, he'd come in halfway through English and said oh, William bloody Shakespeare, is it? Bloody Bill Wagstaffe, Bill Crankshaft, I know that cove, *he's* dead he is, or so he claims, and he owes me a fiver. We were doing *Romeo and Juliet* and he said, I seen that Juliet, she's dead, and she's no better than she should be, a right slapper, let me tell you. So then I knew he was lying, because Juliet's a fictional character. But at first, you see, I believed him about things. I didn't know what to believe.

COLETTE: Yes, and?

ALISON: So then he squashed up in the chair next to me, because Nicky Scott and Catherine and all that lot, they weren't bothering with me and they were leaving me to sit on my own. He put his hand on my knee, above my knee really, squeezing, and I couldn't help it, I squealed out. And he was saying, I'll tell you another thing about that Juliet – her mother was at it before she was out of ankle socks, she was no slouch on the couch. Remind you of home, does it, remind you of home sweet home?

And he started pulling my skirt up. And I was trying to pull it down and push his hands away, I was slapping at him but it didn't do any good. And Mr Naysmith said to me, excuse me for intruding on your private reverie, but I don't think I have your undivided attention, Alison. Just then I couldn't stand it and it all came out in a rush, I was crying and swearing and shouting 'Piss off, you perv' and 'Bugger off back where you came from.' So Mr Naysmith looking like thunder came belting down the class towards me, and I shout, keep your filthy pervy hands to yourself. And he got hold of me by the back of my neck. Well, they did. In those days. At my school, anyway. They weren't allowed to cane you but they used to get hold of you in a painful way. And he dragged me off to the headmaster . . . So I got suspended. Excluded, they call it now. For making accusations against Mr Naysmith. You see, I was wailing, he was pulling up my skirt, he was pulling up my skirt. And in those days they didn't have sexual abuse, so nobody believed me, whereas these days nobody would believe him.

COLETTE: So how does this fit in with Mrs Etchells?

ALISON: What?

COLETTE: You said you were leaning on her hedge crying.

ALISON: Yes, that's it, because they'd been tormenting me, you see. I didn't care about getting suspended, it was a relief really, they said they'd be calling my mum in but I knew they wouldn't because the headmaster was too frightened of her. Anyway, Mrs Etchells spotted me and she came running out, she said, leave off, girls, why ever are you tormenting poor Alison like that? And I was surprised, that she knew my name.

COLETTE: And who was Mrs Etchells? I mean, I know she taught you all you know, you've said so several times, but you know, who was she?

ALISON: My gran, or so she said.
COLETTE: What?
Click.

Click.
COLETTE: This is Colette, resuming the session at twelve thirty. Alison, you were telling us about your reunion with your grandmother.
ALISON: Yes, but it wasn't like that, good God, it wasn't like *This is Your Life* and your gran walks in smiling through her bloody tears. I don't know why you put these questions on the tape, Colette. I've just told you how it was.
COLETTE: Oh, for the fifteenth bloody time, it's to have a record—
ALISON: All right, all right, but let me tell it my way, will you? She took me in and made me beans on toast. And do you know it was the first time I ever, I mean, my mum used to get distracted, so the beans and the toast came separate, you'd have your beans at five o'clock and then she'd look at you about ten past and she'd say to you, oh, you didn't get your toast yet, did you? You know when you go to a café, like on the motorway, and they have those big laminated menus with pictures of the food on? I used to wonder what for, I mean, why do they do that, the food doesn't look like that when it comes, it's all huge and coloured in the menus but in real life it's all shrunken up and sick-coloured. Well, the reason they do that, this is what I think, is to help people like my mum, because they don't know what food goes with what. When she'd got some man staying over, one she liked, she'd say, oh, I'm making a big Sunday, by which she meant a big Sunday lunch, but when it came he'd be, what's this, Emmie? I mean,

chicken and cauliflower, with white sauce out of a packet.

COLETTE: And mash?

ALISON: No, that would be later, that would come along at teatime. And she'd go to the corner and get curry, that was her idea of making lunch, she'd say, what you complaining about, I paid for it myself, didn't I?

COLETTE: I really don't want to interrupt your flow—

ALISON: So that's why they have the pictures, to stop people like my mum ordering a fried egg with their chicken. And make sure they assemble all the bits of their meal at the same time.

COLETTE: And Mrs Etchells . . .

ALISON: Made me beans *on* toast. Which made her a winner in my eyes, I mean, I was always hungry then, I think that's why I'm big now.

COLETTE: Just leaving that issue aside for the moment—

ALISON: She said, come in, dear, sit down, tell me all about it. So I did. Because I had nobody to confide in. And I cried a lot, and it all came pouring out. Tahera, Lee. Mr Naysmith. Morris. Everything.

COLETTE: And what did she say?

ALISON: Well, the thing was she seemed to understand. She just sat there nodding. When I'd finished she said, you see, like grandmother like granddaughter. I said what? It's descended to you, she said, my gift, missing out Derek, probably because he was a man. I said, who's Derek, she said, my son Derek. Your dad, darling; well, he could be anyway.

COLETTE: She only said, could be?

ALISON: All I thought was, thank God, so it wasn't Morris. I said, so, if Derek's my dad, and you're my nan, why isn't my name Etchells? She said, because he ran off before your mam could waltz him down the aisle. Not that I blame him there. I said, it's surprising I wasn't drawn to you. She said, you was, in a manner of speaking, because you was always leaning against my hedge with your young friends. And today, she said, I reckon that today, you see, something drew you. You were in trouble, so you came to your nan.

COLETTE: That's quite sad, really. You mean she'd been living down the road all the time?

ALISON: She said she didn't like to interfere. She said, your mam minds her own business, and of course the whole neighbourhood knows what that business is – which was no surprise to me, you know, because I'd understood for quite some time why when a bloke went out he put a tenner on the sideboard.

COLETTE: And so, you and Mrs Etchells, did you become close at this point?

ALISON: I used to go and do little errands for her. Carrying her shopping, because her knees were bad. Running for fags for her, not that she smoked like my mum. I always called her Mrs Etchells, I didn't like to start calling her Nan, I wasn't sure if I ought. I asked my mother about Derek, and she just laughed. She said, she's not on that old story again, is she? Bloody cloud-cuckoo-land.

COLETTE: So she didn't actually confirm it? Or deny it?

ALISON: No. She threw the salt pot at me. So . . . end of that conversation. The way Mrs Etchells told it, Derek and my mum were going to get married, but he took off after he found out what she was like (*laughter*) – probably (*laughter*) – probably she whizzed him up some of her tandoori prawns with tinned spaghetti. Oh God, she has no idea at all about nutrition, that woman. No idea of what constitutes a balanced meal.

COLETTE: Yes, can we get on to how you came to turn professional?

ALISON: When I got towards school-leaving, she said it's time we had a talk, she said, there's advantages and disadvantages to the life—

COLETTE: And did she say what they were, in her opinion?

ALISON: She said, why not use your God-given talent? But then she said, you come in for a great deal of name-calling and disbelief, and I can't pretend that your colleagues in the profession are going to welcome you with open arms – which indeed I did find to be the case, as you know yourself, Colette, to your cost, because you know what they were like when I introduced you as my assistant. She said, of course, you could try to act as if you were normal, and I said I'd give it a try, though it never worked at school. I got a job in a chemist in Farnborough. Temporary sales assistant. It was more temporary than they meant, of course.

COLETTE: What happened?

ALISON: Catherine and Nicky Scott would come in, they hadn't got jobs, they were on the social. When he saw them, Morris would start fiddling around with the contraceptives. Taking them out of their packets and strewing them around. Blowing them up like balloons. Naturally they thought it was me. They thought it was the sort of thing a sixteen-year-old would do, you know, have her mates in and have a laugh. So that was that. Then Mrs Etchells got me a job at a cake shop.

COLETTE: And what happened there?

ALISON: I started eating the cakes.

When Alison decided to change her name, she rang up her mother in Bracknell to ask if she would be offended. Emmie sighed. She sounded frayed and far away. 'I can't think what would be a good name in your sort of work,' she said.

'Where are you?' Alison said. 'You're fading away.'

'In the kitchen,' said Emmie. 'It's the cigs, I can't seem to give up no matter what. Do my voice in.'

'I'm glad I don't smoke,' Alison said. 'It wouldn't be very professional.'

'Huh. Professional,' said Emmie. 'You, a professional. That's a laugh.'

Alison thought, I may as well change the whole thing while I'm about it. I don't have to stick with any part of my old self. She went to a bookshop and bought one of those books for naming babies. 'Congratulations,' said the woman behind the till.

Alison smoothed down the front of her dress. 'I'm not, actually,' she said.

Sonia Hart. Melissa Hart. Susanna Hart. It didn't work. She managed to lose 'Cheetham', but her baptismal name kept sliding back into her life. It was part of her, like Morris was.

Over the next few years she had to get used to life with Morris. When her mum went off to Bracknell she made it clear that she didn't want a daughter trailing after her, so Al got a temporary billet with Mrs Etchells. Morris no longer stopped at the gate. He came inside and exploded the light bulbs, and disarranged Mrs Etchells' china cabinet. 'He is a one!' said Mrs Etchells.

It was only when she got older and moved among a different set of psychics that she realised how vulgar and stupid Morris really was. Other mediums have spirit guides with a bit more about them – dignified impassive medicine men, or ancient Persian sages – but she has this grizzled grinning apparition in a bookmaker's check jacket, and suede shoes with bald toecaps. A typical communication from Sett or Oz or Running Deer would be: 'The way to open the heart is to release yourself from expectation.' But a typical communication from Morris would be: 'Oh, pickled beetroot, I like a nice bit of pickled beetroot. Make a nice sandwich out of pickled beetroot!'

At first she thought that by an effort of will and concentration, she would make him keep his distance. But if she resists Morris, there is a build-up of pressure in her cheekbones and her teeth. There is a crawling feeling, inside her spine, which is like slow torture; sooner or later you have to give in, and listen to what he's saying.

On days when she really needs a break she tries to imagine a big lid, banging down on him. It works for a time. His voice booms, hollow and incomprehensible, inside a huge metal tub. For a while she doesn't have to take any notice of him. Then, little by little, an inch at a time, he begins to raise the lid.

FIVE

It was in the week after Diana's death that Colette felt she got to know Alison properly. It seems another era now, another world: before the millennium, before the Queen's Jubilee, before the Twin Towers burned.

Colette had moved into Al's flat in Wexham, which Alison had described to her as 'the nice part of Slough', though, she added, 'most people don't think Slough has a nice part.'

On the day she moved in, she took a taxi from the station. The driver was young, dark, smiling and spry. He tried to catch her eye through the rear-view mirror, from which dangled a string of prayer beads. Her eyes darted away. She was not prejudiced, but. Inside the cab was an eye-watering reek of air-freshener.

They drove out of town, always uphill. He seemed to know where he was going. Once Slough was left behind, it seemed to her they were travelling to nowhere. The houses ran out. She saw fields, put to no particular use. They were not farms, she supposed. There were not, for instance, crops in the fields. Here and there, a pony grazed. There were structures for the pony to jump over; there were hedgerows. She saw the sprawl of buildings from a hospital, Wexham Park. Some squat quaint cottages fronted the road. For a moment, she worried; did Al live in the country? She had not said anything about the country. But before she could really get her worrying under way, the driver swerved into the gravel drive of a small, neat seventies-built block, set well back from the road. Its shrubberies were clipped and tame; it looked reassuringly suburban. She stepped out. The driver opened the boot and lugged out her two suitcases. She gazed up at the front of the block. Did Al live here, looking out over the road? Or would she face the back? For a moment she struck herself as a figure of pathos. She was a brave young woman on the threshold of a new life. Why is that sad? she wondered. Her eyes fell on the suitcases. That is why; because I can carry all I own. Or the taxi driver can.

She paid him. She asked for a receipt. Her mind was already moving ahead, to Al's accounts, her business expenses. The first thing I shall do, she thought, is bump up her prices. Why should people expect a conversation with the dead for the price of a bottle of wine and a family-size pizza?

The driver ripped a blank off the top of his pad, and offered it to her, bowing. 'Could you fill it in?' she said. 'Signed and dated.'

'Of what amount shall I put?'

'Just the figure on the meter.'

'Home sweet home?'

'I'm visiting a friend.'

He handed back the slip of paper, with an extra blank receipt beneath. Cabman's flirtation; she handed back the blank.

'These flats, two beds?'

'I think so.'

'En suite? How much you've paid for yours?'

Is this what passes for multicultural exchange? she

wondered. Not that she was prejudiced. At least it's to the point. 'I told you, I don't live here.'

He shrugged, smiled. 'You have a business card?'

'No.'

Has Alison got one? Do psychics have cards? She thought, it will be uphill work, dragging her into the business world.

'I can drive you at any time,' the man said. 'Just call this number.'

He passed over his own card. She squinted at it. God, she thought, I'll need glasses soon. Several numbers were crossed out in blue ink and a mobile number written in. 'Mobile phone,' he said. 'You can just try me day or night.'

He left her at the door, drove away. She glanced up again. I hope there's room for me, she thought. I shall have to be very neat. But then, I am. Was Alison looking down, watching her arrive? No, she wouldn't need to look out of the window. If someone arrived she would just know.

Al's flat was at the back, it turned out. She was ready with the door open. 'I thought you'd be waiting,' Colette said.

Alison blushed faintly. 'I have very sharp earsight. I mean, hearing – well, the whole package.' Yet there was nothing sharp about her. Soft and smiling, she seemed to have no edges. She reached out for Colette and pulled her resistant frame against her own. 'I hope you'll be happy. Do you think you can be happy? Come in. It's bigger than you'd think.'

She glanced around the interior. Everything low, squarish, beige. Everything light, safe. 'All the kit's in the hall cupboard,' Al said. 'The crystals and whatnots.'

'Is it OK to keep it in there?'

'It's better in the dark. Tea, coffee?'

Colette asked for a herbal tea. No more meat, she thought, or cakes. She wanted to be pure.

While she was unpacking, Al brought in a green soupy beverage in a white china mug. 'I didn't know how you liked it,' she said, 'so I left the bag in.' She took the cup carefully, her fingertips touching Al's. Al smiled. She clicked the door shut, left her to herself. The bed was made up, a double bed. Big bouncy duvet in a plain cream cover. She turned the duvet back. The sheet was crisply ironed. High standards: good. She'd seen enough squalor. She picked up her washbag. Found herself in Al's bathroom – Al hovering and saying, rather guilty, just push up my things and put yours down – shall I leave you to do that? Another tea?

She stared around. Floris, indeed. Is she rich, or just in need of a great deal of comfort? It's better than we had, she thinks, me and Gavin; she thought of their second-floor conversion, with the clanking and erratic central heating, the sudden icy draughts.

'Come through. Make yourself at home.' There were two sofas, square and tweedy; Al flopped on to one, a stack of glossies beside her, and indicated that Colette should join her. 'I thought you might like to look at my advert.' She picked up one of the magazines. 'Flick through from the back and you'll see me.'

She turned back, past the horoscopes. For once she didn't pause to glance at her own. Why keep a dog and bark yourself? Alison's photograph was a beaming smudge on the page. 'Alison, psychic since birth. Private consultations. Professional and caring. Relationships, business, health. Spiritual guidance.'

'Are people willing to travel to Slough?'

'Once you explain to them it's the nice part. I do telephone consultations, if need be, though if I have the choice I like to look the sitter in the eye.'

'Videophones,' Colette said. 'Can't be long now. It will make all the difference.'

'I can travel to them, if the price is right. I will if I think it's going to be a long-term arrangement. I rely on my regulars, it's where most of my income is. Do you think it's all right, the ad?'

'No. It should be in colour. And bigger. We have to invest.' Above it was an advert for cosmetic surgery, displaying 'before' and 'after' pictures. There was a woman with a sagging jawline who looked, in the second picture, as if she'd been slapped under the chin by a giant. A woman with skin-flaps for breasts had sprouted two vast globules; their nipples stood out like the whistles on a life jacket. Below the pictures . . .

Alison bounced across the sofa towards her, causing the frame to creak. 'Surprisingly sleazy, these journals,' Al said. She laid her long painted nail on an advert for 'Sex Advice', with a number to call after each item. 'Lesbian anal fun. Did you know lesbians had anal fun?'

'No,' Colette said, in a voice as distant as she could manage. Al's scent washed over her in a great wave of sweetness. 'I don't know, I mean, I've never thought. I don't know anything about it.'

'Neither do I,' Al said. Colette thought, *spicy lesbo chicks.* Al patted her shoulder. She froze. 'That was not fun,' Al said. 'That was reassurance.' She dropped her head and her hair slid forward, hiding her smile. 'I just thought we'd get the topic out of the way. So we both know where we stand.'

The room had magnolia walls, corded beige carpet, a coffee table which was simply a low featureless expanse of pale wood. But Al kept her tarot cards in a seagrass basket, wrapped in a yard of scarlet silk, and when she unwrapped it and spilled its length on to the table, it looked as if some bloody incident had occurred.

August. She woke: Al stood in the door of her room. The landing light was on. Colette sat up. 'What time is it? Al? What's the matter, has something happened?'

The light shone through Al's lawn nightdress, illuminating her huge thighs. 'We must get ready,' she said: as if they were catching an early flight.

Al approached and stood by the bed. Colette reached up and took her sleeve. It was a pinch of nothingness between her fingers.

'It's Diana,' Al said. 'Dead.'

Always, Colette would say later, she would remember the shiver that ran through her: like a cold electric current, like an eel.

Al gave a snort of jeering laughter. 'Or as we say, passed.'

'Suicide?'

'Or accident. She won't tell me. Teasing to the last,' Al said. 'Though probably not quite the last. From our point of view.'

Colette jumped out of bed. She pulled her T-shirt down over her thighs. Then she stood and stared at Alison; she didn't know what else to do. Al turned and went downstairs, pausing to turn up the central heating. Colette ran after her.

'I'm sure it will be clearer,' Al said, 'when it actually happens.'

'What do you mean? You mean it hasn't happened yet?' Colette ran a hand through her hair, and it stood up, a pale fuzzy halo. 'Al, we must do something!'

'Like?'

'Warn somebody! Call the police! Telephone the Queen?'

Al raised a hand. 'Quiet, please. She's getting in the car. She's putting on her seat belt – no, no she isn't. They're larking about. Not a care in the world. Why are they going that way? Dear, dear, they're all over the road!'

Alison tumbled to the sofa, moaning and holding her chest. 'No use waiting around,' she said, breaking off, and speaking in a surprisingly normal voice. 'We won't hear from her again for a while.'

'What can I do?' Colette said.

'You can make me some hot milk, and give me two paracetamol.'

Colette went into the kitchen. The fridge breathed out at her a wet cold breath. She spilled the milk as she poured it in the pan, and the gas ring's flame sputtered and licked. She carried it through to Al. 'Oh, the pills, I forgot the pills!'

'Never mind,' Al said.

'No, wait, sit still, I'll get them.'

Al looked at her, faintly reproachful. 'We're now waiting for the emergency services. We're slightly beyond the paracetamol stage.'

Things happen fast, in the lawless country between life and death. Colette wandered up the stairs. She felt *de trop*. Her feet were everywhere: weaving, bony, aimless. What shall I do? Back in her bedroom, she tugged the cover back over her bed, for tidiness. She pulled a sweatshirt on; she sat down on the bed and pinched her thin white legs, looking for cellulite. There was a muffled cry from below, but she didn't think she ought to interfere. I suppose this is where people smoke a cigarette, she thought; but she'd been trying to give up. By and by she stabbed her new PC into life. She had it in mind to prepare a series of invoices that would take advantage of the event. Whatever it was.

Only later, when she thought it over, did she realise that she had never doubted Alison's word. It was true that from Al the news arrived piecemeal, but it was more exciting that way. In time the radio, placed beside her, brought the confirming details. The event, in the real world, had actually taken place; she stopped typing and sat listening. *Lights, a tunnel, impact, lights, a tunnel, black, and then something beyond it: a hiatus, and one final, blinding light.* By dawn, her mood was one of shock and unholy exhilaration, combined with a bubbling self-righteousness; what does she expect, a girl like Diana? There was something so right about it, so *meant*. It had turned out so beautifully badly.

She dived downstairs to check on Alison, who was now rocking herself and groaning. She asked if she wanted the radio, but Al shook her head without speaking. She ran back to catch the latest details. The computer was humming and whirring, making from time to time its little sighs, as if deep within its operating system the princess was gurgling out her story. Colette laid her palm on it, anxious; she was afraid it was overheating. I'll do a shutdown, she thought. When she went downstairs Al seemed entranced, her eyes on some unfolding scene Colette could only imagine. Her milk was untouched, standing beside her with a skin on it. It was a mild night, but her bare feet were blue.

'Why don't you go back to bed, Al? It's Sunday. Nobody's going to call yet.'

'Where's Morris? Still out from last night? Thank God for that.'

You can just imagine the sort of inappropriate joke Morris would be making, at this solemn time. Colette sniggered to herself. She got Alison wrapped up in her dressing gown, and draped over her bulk the raspberry mohair throw. She made a hot-water bottle; she piled a duvet on top of her, but she couldn't stop Al shivering. Over the next hour her face drained of colour. Her eyes seemed to shrink back in her skull. She pitched and tossed and threatened to roll off the sofa. She seemed to be talking, under her breath, to people Colette couldn't see.

Colette's exhilaration turned to fright. She had only known Al a matter of weeks, and now this crisis was thrust upon them. Colette imagined herself trying to heave Al up from the floor, hands under her armpits. It wouldn't work. She'd have to call for an ambulance. What if she had to resuscitate her? Would they get there in time? 'You'd be better off in bed,' she pleaded.

From cold, Al passed into a fever. She pushed off the duvet. The hot-water bottle fell to the carpet with a fat plop. Inside her nightgown, Al shook like a blancmange.

By eight o'clock the phone was ringing. It was the first of Al's regulars, wanting messages. Eyes still half closed, Al levered herself up off the sofa and took the receiver from Colette's hand. Colette hissed at her 'special rate, special rate'. No, Al said, no direct communication yet from the princess, not since the event – but I would expect her to make every effort to come through, once she gathers her wits. If you want an appointment next week I can try to squeeze you in. Fine. Will do. She put the phone down, and at once it rang again. 'Mandy?' She mouthed at Colette, 'Mandy Coughlan from Hove. You know, Natasha.' Yes, she said, and oh, terrible. Mandy spoke. Al said, 'Well, I think in transition, don't you? I shouldn't think at this stage she does, no. Probably not.' Al paused: Mandy talked. Al talked again, her hand absently smoothing her creased nightdress. 'You know how it is when they go over suddenly, they don't know what's happening till somebody puts them right . . . Yes, don't they, hanging around for days. You think Kensington Palace?' She giggled. 'Harvey Nichols, more likely . . . No, OK, so if you hear anything about the funeral, whatever. A bit sick, you know. Not actually vomiting. Hot and cold. Quite a shock for Colette, I can tell you.' Mandy spoke. 'She's my, you know, my whatsit, my new personal assistant . . . Yes, it is good timing, We'll all have quite a week of it, won't we? Need all the help I can get. OK, Mand. Take care. Kiss-kiss. Bye for now.'

She put the phone down. She was sweating. 'Oh sorry, Colette, I said assistant, I should have said partner, I didn't mean to be, you know, patronising to you. Mandy reckons she'll be returning to Kensington Palace, wandering around you know, confused.' She tried to laugh, but it emerged as a little snarl. She put her fingers to her forehead, and they came away dripping. Colette whispered, 'Al, you smell terrible.'

'I know,' she whispered back. 'I'll get in the bath.'

As Al ran the taps, she heard a whistle through the intercom. It was shrill, like a bird call, like a code. Next thing, Morris came crashing in. Usually on a Sunday morning he was tetchy from a hangover, but the news seemed to have bucked him up. He banged on the door, shouting tasteless jokes. 'What's the difference between Princess Di and a roll of carpet? Go on, go on, bet you don't know, do you? What's the difference between—'

She slammed the bolt on. She lowered herself into the bath: lavender oil. She wiped away the stench of death, exfoliating herself for good measure. Morris slipped under the door. He stood leering at her. His yellow face mingled with the steam. When she came out of the bathroom she was scored all over with faint pink lines, but the cuts on her thighs flared darkest, as if she had been whipped with wire.

In the following week Colette learned things about sudden death that she'd never suspected. Al said, what you should understand is this: when people go over, they don't always know they've gone. They have a pain, or the memory of one, and there are people in white, and strange faces that loom up and there's a noise in the background, metal things banging together – as if there were a train wreck going on, but in another country.

Colette said, 'And what are they? These noises.'

'Mrs Etchells says it's the gates of Hell clattering.'

'And do you believe that?'

'There ought to be Hell. But I don't know.'

There are the lights, she said, the noises, the waiting, the loneliness. Everything slips out of focus. They suppose they're in a queue for attention but nobody attends. Sometimes they think they're in a room, sometimes they sense air and space and they think they've been abandoned in a car park. Sometimes they think they're in a corridor, lying on a trolley, and nobody comes. They start to cry, but still nobody comes. You see, she said, they've actually gone over, but they think it's just the NHS.

Sometimes, when famous people pass, their fans-in-spirit are waiting for them. Their fans, and in the case of someone like Diana, their ancestors too; and often those ancestors have something to say, about the way estates have been subdivided, money frittered, their portraits sold at auction. Also, when famous people pass they attract spirit-impostors, just as on this side you have lookalikes and body doubles. This fact, unless kept constantly in mind by a medium, can ruin an evening on the platform, as the tribute bands and the impersonators break through, claiming to be Elvis, Lennon, Glenn Miller. Occasionally some oddball breaks through saying he's Jesus. But I don't know, Al said, there'll be something in his manner – you just know he's not from ancient Palestine. In Mrs Etchells' day, she explained, people still thought they were Napoleon. They were better educated then, she said, they knew dates and battles. Surprisingly, Cleopatra is still popular. 'And I don't like doing Cleopatra because . . .'

'Because you don't do ethnics.'

Al had explained it to her, in delicate language. She didn't work the inner city or places like downtown Slough. 'I'm not a racist, please don't think that, but it just gets too convoluted.' It wasn't just the language barrier, she explained, 'but these people, those races, who think they have more than one life. Which means, of course, more than one family.

Often several families, and I don't know, it just gets—' She closed her eyes tight, and flapped her fingers at her head, as if trying to beat off mosquitoes. She shivered, at the thought of some bangled wrinkly from the Ganges popping up: and she, flailing in time and space, not able to skewer her to the right millennium.

When Colette looked back, from the end of August 1997 to the early summer, when they had met . . . 'It's what you call a steep learning curve,' she said. That the dead can be lonely, that the dead can be confused; all these things were a surprise to Colette, who had only ever spoken to one dead person: who earlier in her life had never given them much thought, except insofar as she had hoped – in some limp sort of way – that the dead were best off where they were. She now understood that Al hadn't been quite straight with her in those first few weeks. There wasn't a necessary tie-up between what she said on the platform and the true state of affairs. Uncomfortable truths were smoothed over, before Al let them out to the public; when she conveyed soothing messages, Colette saw, they came not from the medium but from the saleswoman, from the part of her that saw the value in pleasing people. She had to admire it, grudgingly; it was a knack she had never acquired.

Until the princess died, Colette had not seen the seamy side of the work. Take Morris out of the equation, and it was much like any other business. Al needed a more modern communications system, a better throughput and process flow. She needed a spam-filter for her brain, to screen out unwanted messages from the dead; and if Colette could not provide this, she could at least control how Al managed those messages. She tried to view Al as a project and herself as project manager. It was lucky she'd got such sound experience as a conference organiser, because of course Al was something like a conference in herself. When she moved in with Al, Colette had made a pretty smart exit from her early life – a clean break, she told herself. Nevertheless, she expected old workmates to track her down. She practised in her mind what she'd tell them. I find my new role diverse, rewarding and challenging, she would say. Above all, I like the independence. The personal relationships are a bonus; I'd describe my boss as caring and professional. Do I miss going to the office every day? You must appreciate I never exactly did that; travel was always part of the brief. Think what I haven't got; no slander at the water cooler, no interdepartmental tensions, no sexual harassment, no competitive dressing. I have to be smart, of course, because I'm customer-facing, but it's a real perk to be able to express yourself through your own sense of style. And that encapsulates, more or less, what I feel about my new situation; I've a role that I can sculpt to suit my talents, and no two days are the same.

All this rehearsal was wasted, except upon herself. No one, in fact, did track her down, except Gavin, who called one night wanting to boast about his annual bonus. It was as if she'd ceased to exist.

But after that death-night at the end of August, she couldn't fool herself that her position with Al was just a logical part of her career development. And exactly what was her position with Al? Next day she, Colette, tried to sit her down for a talk, and said, Al, I need you to be straight with me.

Al said, 'It's OK, Col, I've been thinking about it. You're a godsend to me and I don't know what I ever did without you. I never thought I'd get someone to agree to live in, and you can see that, at a time of crisis, twenty-four-hour care is what I need.' Only a half-hour before Al had been bringing up a clear ropy liquid; once again, rank sweat filmed her face. 'I think we should agree new terms, I think you should have a profit share.'

Colette flushed pink up to the roots of her hair. 'I didn't mean money,' she said. 'I didn't mean, be straight with me in that way. I – thank you, Al, I mean it's good to be needed. I know you're not financially dishonest. I wasn't saying that. I only mean I think you're not giving me the full picture about your life. Oh, I know about Morris. *Now* I know, but when I took on the job you didn't tell me I'd be working with some foul-mouthed dwarf spook, you let me find that out. I feel as if I don't want any more nasty shocks. You do see that, surely? I know you mean well. You're sparing my feelings. Like you do with the trade. But you must realise, I'm not the trade. I'm your friend. I'm your partner.'

Alison said, 'What you're asking me is, how do you do it?'

'Yes, that's exactly right. That's what I'm asking you.'

She made Al some ginger tea; and Al talked then about the perfidy of the dead, their partial, penetrative nature, their way of dematerialising and leaving bits of themselves behind, or entangling themselves with your inner organs. She talked about her sharp earsight and voices she heard in the wall. About the dead's propensity to fib and confabulate. Their selfish, trivial outlook. Their general cluelessness.

Colette was not satisfied. She rubbed her eyes, she rubbed her forehead. She stopped and glared, when she saw Alison smiling at her sympathetically. 'Why? Why are you smiling?'

'My friend Cara would say, you're opening your third eye.'

Colette pointed to the space between her brows. 'There is no eye. It's bone.'

'Brain behind it, I hope.'

Colette said angrily, 'It's not that I disbelieve in you. Well, I do. I have to believe in what you do, because I see you doing it, I see and hear you, but how *can* I believe it, when it's against the laws of nature?'

'Oh, those,' Al said. 'Are you sure we have them any more? I think it's a bit of a free-for-all these days.'

They had arranged, on the Saturday of the princess's funeral, to do an evening event in the Midlands, a major fayre in an area where psychic fayres were just establishing themselves. Mandy Coughlan said on the phone to Al, 'It would be a shame to cancel, sweetie. You can take a sick bag in the car if you're still feeling queasy. Because you know if you pull out they'll charge you full price for the stall, and some amateur from up the M6 will be straight in there, quick-sticks. So if you're feeling up to it? Good girl. Do you think Mrs Etchells is going?'

'Oh yes. She loved Diana. She'll be expecting a contact.'

'Joys of motherhood,' Mandy said. 'Of course. Perhaps Di will come through and let her know if she was up the duff. But how will Mrs Etchells get up to Nottingham? Will there be trains, or will they be cancelled out of respect? You're not far away – maybe you could give her a lift.'

Al dropped her voice. 'I'm not being professionally divisive, Mandy, but there are certain issues around Mrs Etchells – undercutting on tarot readings, slashing prices without prior consultation, trying to lure other people's clients – Colette heard her doing it.'

'Oh yes. This person Colette. Whoever is she, Al? Where did you find her? Is she psychic?'

'God, no. She's a client. And before that she was a client of yours.'

'Really? When did we meet?'

'Last year sometime. She came down to Hove with some cuff-links. She was trying to find out who her father was.'

'And who was he?'

'Her uncle.'

'Oh, one of those. I can't put a face to her.' Mandy sounded impatient. 'So is she mad with me, or something?'

'No. I don't think so. Though she is quite sceptical. In patches.'

Al said her polite goodbyes. She put the phone down and stood looking at it. Did I do the right thing, when I took on Colette? Mandy didn't seem keen. Have I been impulsive, and is it an impulse I will regret? She almost called Mandy back, to seek further advice. Mandy knows what's what, she's been through the mill, thrown out a lover at midnight and his whole troop after him, some dead Druid who'd moved in with the bloke, and a whole bunch of Celtic spirits more used to life in a cave than life in Hove. Out they go with their bloody cauldrons and their spears, Lug and Trog and Glug; and out goes Psychic Simon with his rotting Y-fronts dropped out of a first-floor window, his Morfesa the Great Teacher statue chucked in the gutter with its wand snapped off, and his last quarter's invoice file tossed like a Frisbee in the direction of the sea: and several unbanked cheques rendered illegible and useless, speared by Mandy's stiletto heel.

That was how it usually went, when you were unguarded enough to get into a relationship with a colleague. It wasn't a question of personal compatibility between the two of you; it was a question of the baggage you trailed, your entourage, whether they'd fight and lay waste to each other, thrashing with their vestigial limbs and snapping with their stumps of teeth. Al's hand moved to the phone and away again; she didn't want Colette to overhear, so she talked to Mandy in her mind. I know it's bad when you go out with someone in our line, but some people say it's worse to get into a thing with a punter—

A thing?

Not a thing, not a sex thing. But a relationship, you can't deny that. If she's going to live with you, it's a relationship. God knows you need somebody to talk to, but—

But how can you talk to the trade?

Yes, that's the trouble, isn't it? How can they understand what you go through? How can they understand anything? You try to explain but the more you try the less you succeed.

They haven't got the language, have they? Don't tell me, sweetheart. They haven't got the range.

You say something perfectly obvious and they look at you as if you're mad. You tell them again, but by then it sounds mad to you. You lose your confidence, if you have to keep going over and over it.

And yet you're paying the rent. Mortgage, whatever. It's fine as long as everything's humming along sweetly, but the first cross word you have, they start casting it up, throwing it in your face, oh, you're taking advantage of me because you've got all these people I can't see, how do you know this stuff about me, you're opening my mail – I mean, why should you need to open their bloody mail? As if you can't see straight through to what they are. I tell you, Al, I went out with a punter once, I let him move in and it was murder. I saw within the week he was just trying to use me. Fill in my pools coupon. Pick me something at Plumpton.

Yes, I've explained it to Col, I told her straight off, I'm no good for lottery numbers.

And what did she say?

I think she could understand it. I mean, she's a numerate woman. I think she understands the limitations.

Oh, she says that *now*. But honestly, when you let them move in, they're like leeches, they're like – whatever, whatever it is that's at you twenty-four hours a day. Actually my mum said as much. She warned me, well, she tried to warn me, but you don't take any notice, do you? Did you know I was born the night that Kennedy was shot? Well, that dates me! (Mandy, in Al's mind, laughed shakily.) No point trying to keep secrets from you, Al! The point is, my mum – you know she was like me, Natasha, Psychic to the Stars, and my grandma was Natasha, Psychic to the Tsars – this man she was with then, when I was born, he said, didn't you know anything about it, doll? Couldn't you of – oh, he was ignorant in his speech – couldn't you of prevented it? My mum said, what do you want me to do, ring up the White House, with my feet up in stirrups and this withered old nun shouting in my ear Push, Mother, push?

Nun? Alison was surprised. Are you a Catholic, Mandy?

No, Russian Orthodox. But you know what I mean, don't you? About a relationship with the laity. They expect too much.

I know they do. But Mandy, I need someone, someone with me. A friend.

Of course you do. Mandy's voice softened. A friend. A live-in friend. I'm not judgemental. God knows. Takes all sorts. Live and let live. Who am I to moralise? Oh, Al, you can tell me. We go back, you and me. You want a little love in your life, yes you do, you do.

Mandy, do you know the pleasures of lesbian anal sex? No. Nor me. Nor any other pleasures. With Morris around I really need some sort of fanny guard. You know what they do, don't you? The guides, while you're asleep? Creepy creepy. Creak at the door, then a hand on the duvet, a hairy paw tugging the sheet. I know you thought Lug and Glug tried it on, though you say you had been taking Nytol so were a bit confused at being woken and you suspect it may well have been Simon, judging by the smell. It's difficult to say, isn't it? What kind of violation. Spirit or not spirit. Especially if your boyfriend has a small one. I am fairly confident that Morris, when it comes down to it, he can't – not with me, anyway. But what gets to me is all this back-alley masculinity, all this beer and belching and scratching your belly, billiards and darts and minor acts of criminal damage,

I get tired of being exposed to it all the time, and it was fine for you, I know you kicked out the Druid and Lug and Glug, but they were Psychic Simon's, and Morris is mine. And somehow I suppose, what it is, with Colette as my partner – with Colette as my *business* partner – I was hoping – oh, let me say it – I was aspiring – I want a way out of Aldershot, out of my childhood, away from my mother, some way to upscale, to move into the affluent world of the Berkshire or Surrey commuter, the world of the businessman, the entrepreneur: to imagine how the rich and clever die. To imagine how it is, if you're senior in IT and your system crashes: or the finance director, when your last shekel is spent: or in charge of Human Resources, when you lose your claim to have any.

When she was packing for their trip to Nottingham, Colette came in. Al was wearing just a T-shirt, bending over the case. For the first time, Colette saw the backs of her thighs. 'Christ,' she said. 'Did you do that?'

'Me?'

'Like Di? Did you cut yourself?'

Alison turned back to her packing. She was perplexed. It had never occurred to her that she might have inflicted the damage herself. Perhaps I did, she thought, and I've just forgotten; there is so much I've forgotten, so much that has slipped away from me. It was a long time since she'd given much thought to the scars. They flared, in a hot bath, and the skin around them itched in hot weather. She avoided seeing them, which was not difficult if she avoided mirrors. But now, she thought, Colette will always be noticing them. I had better have a story because she will want answers.

She fingered her damaged flesh; the skin felt dead and

distant. She remembered Morris saying, we showed you what a blade could do! For the first time she thought, oh, I see now, that was what they taught me; that was the lesson I had.

SIX

As they drove north, Colette said to Alison, 'When you were a little girl, did you ever think you were a princess?'

'Me? God, no.'

'What did you think then?'

'I thought I was a freak.'

And now? The question hung in the air. It was the day of Diana's funeral, and the road was almost empty. Al had slept badly. Beyond the bedroom wall of the flat in Wexham, Colette had heard her muttering, and heard the deep groan of her mattress as she turned over and over in bed. She had been downstairs at seven thirty, standing in the kitchen: bundled into her dressing gown, her hair straggling out of its rollers. 'We may as well get on the road,' she said. 'Get ahead of the coffin.'

By ten thirty crowds were assembling on the bridges over the M1, waiting for the dead woman to pass by on her way to her ancestral burial ground just off Junction 15A. The police were lining the route as if waiting for disaster, drawn up in phalanxes of motorcycles and cordons of watching vans. It was a bright, cool morning – perfect September weather.

''S'funny,' Colette said. 'It's only a fortnight ago – those pictures of her in the boat with Dodi, in her bikini. And we were all saying, what a slapper.'

Al opened the glove box and ferreted out a chocolate biscuit.

'That's the emergency KitKat,' Colette protested.

'This is an emergency. I couldn't eat my breakfast.' She ate the chocolate morosely, finger by finger. 'If Gavin had been the Prince of Wales,' she said, 'do you think you'd have tried harder with your marriage?'

'Definitely.'

Colette's eyes were on the road; in the passenger seat Alison twisted over her shoulder to look at Morris in the back, kicking his short legs and singing a medley of patriotic songs. As they passed beneath a bridge policemen's faces peered down at them, pink sweating ovals above the sick glow of high-viz jackets. Stubble-headed boys – the type who, in normal times, heave a concrete block through your windscreen – now jabbed the mild air with bunches of carnations. A ragged bed sheet, grey-white, drifted down into their view. It was scrawled in crimson capitals, as if in virgin's blood: DIANA, QUEEN OF OUR HEARTS. 'You'd think they'd show more respect,' Alison said. 'Not flap about with their old bed linen.'

'Dirty linen,' Colette said. 'She washed her dirty linen . . . It comes back on you in the end.' They sped a mile or two in silence. 'I mean, it's not as if it's exactly a surprise. You didn't expect it to last, did you? Not as if she was exactly stable. If she'd been in real life, she'd have been just the sort of slut who'd end up with her arms and legs in left-luggage lockers and her head in a bin bag in Walthamstow.'

'Shh!' Al said. 'She might be listening. She's not gone yet, you know. Not as far as I – as far as we're concerned.'

'Do you think you might get a message from Dodi? No, I forget, you don't do ethnics, do you?'

At each bridge they glanced up. The crowds thickened. As they crossed the border into Northamptonshire, a leather-jacketed man was waving the Stars and Stripes. The hitch-hikers lurking by the slip roads had tied black bands around their sleeves. Alison hummed along with Morris, who was doing 'Land of Our Fathers'. She struggled to find loyalty within herself: loyalty, compassion, something other than mere fatigue at the thought of the trouble Diana was going to cause her. 'Of course,' she said, 'she was against land-mines.'

'That doesn't seem much to be against,' Colette said. 'Not exactly sticking your neck out, is it? Not like being against . . . dolphins.'

Silence within the car: except that Morris, in the back, had progressed to 'Roll Out the Barrel'. A helicopter whirled overhead, monitoring the near-empty road. 'We're much too early,' Colette said. 'Our room won't be ready. Do you want to stop for a wee? Or a proper breakfast? Could you manage a fry-up?'

Al thought, when I was awake in the night, I was so cold. Being cold makes you feel sick; or does feeling sick make you cold? Nothing to be hoped for from days like these, except nausea, cramps, shortness of breath, acceleration of the pulse, gooseflesh, and a leaden tinge to the skin.

Colette said, 'Five miles, shall I pull in? Make your mind up, yes or no?'

Morris at once stopped singing and began agitating for his comfort stop. He showed an unhealthy interest in gents' toilets: when he swarmed back into the car after a break at a service area, you could catch the whiff of piss and floral disinfectant from the crêpe soles of his shoes. He liked to creep around the parked cars, pulling off hubcaps and bowling them like hoops among the feet of their returning owners. He would double up with laughter as the punters stood jaw-dropped at the sight of the metal discs, spinning of their own volition, clattering to rest amid the overspill of polystyrene from the litter bins. Sometimes he would go into the shop and pull the newspapers from their racks, tossing top-shelf magazines into the wire baskets of respectable dads queuing with their families for giant packs of crisps. He would plunge his paw into the pick'n'mix sweets and stuff his bulging jaw. He would snatch from the shelves of travellers' supplies a tartan box of choc-chip shortbread or traditional motorway fudge; then munching, spitting, denouncing it as ladies' pap, he would head for the HGV park, for the café where men's men swigged from mugs of strong tea. He hoped, always, to see somebody he knew, Aitkenside or Bob Fox or even bloody MacArthur, 'though if I see MacArthur,' he'd say, 'the ruddy swindler'll wish he'd never been born, I'll creep up on his blind side and twist his head off.' He would sneak around the parked-up rigs, bouncing himself on the bumper bars to snap off windscreen wipers; through the gaps in frilled curtains, he would peep in at the private interiors where tattooed drivers snored against flowered cushions, where hands rubbed lonely crotches: ooh, sissy-boy, Morris would jeer, and sometimes a man stirred from his doze and jolted awake, thinking for a moment that he had seen a yellow face staring in at him, lips drawn back in a grimace to show yellow fangs, like those of an ape behind toughened glass. I was dreaming, the man would tell himself: I was dreaming, what brought that on?

Truth was, he longed for a friend; it was no life, holed up with a bunch of women, always squawking and making leaflets. 'Oh, what shall we have,' he mimicked, 'shall we have a flower, a rose is nice, a dove of peace is nice, shall we have a dove of peace with a flower in its mouf?' Then would come Colette's higher, flatter voice, 'Beak, Alison, a beak's what birds have.' Then Alison, 'It doesn't sound so nice, bill's nicer, doesn't a dove have a bill?' and Colette's grudging, 'You could be right.' Bill's nice, is it? he would jeer, from his perch on the back of the sofa: 'bill's nice, you should see the bloody bills I've mounted up, I could tell you about bills, Aitkenside owes me a pony, bloody Bill Wagstaffe, he owes me, I'll give him Swan of bloody Avon, I put him on a florin at Doncaster only to oblige, goo-on, he says, goo-on, I'll give you 'alf, Morris, he says if she romps home, romp, did she bloody romp, she ran like the clappers out of hell, dropped dead two hours after in her trailer but san-fairy-ann, what's that to me, and where's my fiver? Then he's explainin', ooh, Morris, the trouble is I'm dead, the trouble is there's a steward's inquiry, the trouble is my pocket got frayed, the trouble is it must of fallen out me pocket of me pantaloons and bloody Kyd snapped it up, I say, then you get after Kyd and break his legs or I will, he says, the trouble is he's dead he ain't got no legs, I says, William old son, don't come that wiv me, break him where 'is legs would be.

When he thought of the debts he had incurred, of the injuries done and what was rightfully owed him, he would run after Alison, agitated: after his hostess, his missus. Al would be in the kitchen making a toasted sarnie. He was eager to press on her the weight of his injustices, but she would say to him, get away, Morris, get your fingers out of that low-fat Cheddar. He wanted a man's life, men's company, and he would creep around the lorry park waving, gesturing, looking for his mates, making the secret signal that men make to other men, to say they want a chinwag and a smoke, to say they're lonely, to say they want company but they're not *like that.* Bloody Wagstaffe were like that, if you ask me, he would tell Alison, but she would say, who? Him in pantaloons, he'd say. Come on, I wasn't born yesterday, anybody showing his legs like that 'as got to be of the fairy persuasion. And again she'd say, who?, dabbing up a shaving of cheese with her finger, and he'd say, Wagstaffe, he's bloody famous, you must have heard of him, he's coining it, he's got his name in bloody lights and what do I get? Not even me stake money back. Not even me florin.

So in the caff at the lorry park he would roll between the tables, saying, ''scuse me, mate, 'scuse me, mate' (because he wanted to be polite) 'have you seen Aitkenside around here? Cos Aitkenside he used to drive a forty-two tonner, and he 'ad this belly dancer tattooed on his back, he got it when he were in Egypt, he were in the forces, he were stationed overseas, Aitkenside. And he's a mermaid on his thigh, not that I seen his thigh, I'm not of that persuasion don't get me wrong.' But much as he tried to engage them, much as he thrust his face into theirs, much as he interposed between them and their All Day Breakfasts, so much did they ignore him, freeze him, give him the elbow and the old heave-ho. So he would wander out, disconsolate, into the open air, sucking up from between his fingers a sausage he had snatched, call this a sausage, it's not what I call a sausage, bleeding Yankee Doodle pap, how can you have a sausage wiv no skin? And around the tankers and the trucks he would slide on his crêpe-soled feet, calling, 'Aitkenside, MacArthur, are you there, lads?'

For in truth he intended to cripple them but after he had crippled them he meant to make his peace. For they were dead too and in the halls of the dead they were in different halls. And in the lorry parks of the dead they had not coincided yet. He would rub his chin, contemplating his sins. Then slide among the trucks, scrambling up to unhook tarpaulins, dragging up the crinkled covers to see what was stowed beneath. Once eyes looked back at him, and those eyes were alive. Once eyes looked back at him and those eyes were dead, swivelled up in their sockets and hard like yellow marbles. When he saw eyes he hooked back the tarp double-quick. Unless the cable had zinged out of his hand. That could happen.

And them silly tarts who was now in the Ladies titivating, he would think of them with contempt: ooh, Colette, do you want a gherkin with your toastie? I'll give you gherkin, gel, he would think. But then if he had dallied too long among the men, if he thought they might drive off without him, his heart would hammer at his dried ribs: wait for me! And he would sprint back to the public area, as far as sprint was in him, his legs being, as they were, multiply fractured and badly set: he would sprint back and swish in – bloody central locking! – through the air vent, roll into the back seat and collapse there, puffing, panting, wrenching off his shoes, and Colette – the stringy one – would complain, what's that smell? It came to his own nostrils, faintly: petrol and onions and hot dead feet.

If his owners were still in the Ladies, he would not sit alone and wait for them. He would insinuate himself into other cars, loosening the straps of baby seats, wrenching the heads off the furry animals that dangled from the back windows: spinning the furry dice. But then, when he had done all the mischief he could think of, he would sit on the ground, alone, and let people run over him. He would chew his lip, and he would sing softly to himself:

Hitler has only got one ball,
Hitler has only got one ball,
His mother, bit off the other,
But Capstick has no balls at all.

The missus don't like it when I sing that, he would mutter to himself. She don't like reminding, I suppose. Thinking of the old Aldershot days, he'd sniffle a little. Course she don't like reminding, course she don't. He looked up. The women were approaching, his missus rolling towards him, her pal skipping and yattering and twirling her car keys. Just in time, he slid into the back seat.

Alison's spine tensed as he settled himself, and Colette's nostrils twitched. Morris laughed to himself: she thinks she don't see me, but in time she'll see me, she thinks she don't hear me but she'll come to hear, she don't know if she smells me, she hopes she don't, but she don't want to think it's herself. Morris lifted himself in his seat and discharged a cabbagy blast. Colette swung them through the EXIT sign. A flag flew at half-mast over the Travelodge.

At Junction 23, a lorry carrying bales of straw cut in ahead of them. The wisps blew back towards them, back down the empty grey road, back towards the south. The morning clouded up, the sky assumed a glacial shimmer. The sun skulked behind a cloud, smirking. As they turned off the M1 on to the A52, the bells pealed out to mark the end of the National Silence. Curtains were drawn in the Nottingham suburbs. 'That's nice,' Alison said. 'It's respectful. It's old-fashioned.'

'Don't be stupid,' Colette said. 'It's to keep the sun out, so they can see the TV.'

They pulled into the hotel car park, and Colette jumped out. A spirit woman slid into her place in the driver's seat. She was little, old and poor, and she seemed overwhelmed to find herself behind the wheel of a car, dabbing her hands at the indicators, saying, ee, this is a novelty, do you peddle it, Miss? Excuse me, excuse me, she said, do you know Maureen Harrison? Only I'm looking for Maureen Harrison.

No, Al said kindly, but I'll tell you if I bump into her.

Because Maureen Harrison were friends with me, the little

woman said, aye, she were an' all. A complaining note entered her voice, faint and nostalgic, like the moon through mist. Maureen Harrison were me friend, you know, and I've been searching this thirty year. Excuse me, excuse me, Miss, have you seen Maureen Harrison?

Al climbed out. 'That's Mandy's car, she's early too.' She looked around. 'There's Merlin. And there's Merlyn with a y, dear God, I see his old van has got another bash.' She nodded towards a shiny new people carrier. 'That's those white witches from Egham.'

Colette lugged the bags out of the boot. Alison frowned. 'I've been meaning to say something. I think we should go shopping for you, if you've no objection. I don't feel a nylon holdall gives quite the right message.'

'It's designer!' Colette bellowed. 'Nylon holdall? I've been all around Europe with this. I've been in club class.'

'Well, it doesn't look designer. It looks like market stall.'

They checked in, squabbling. Their room was a box on the second floor, overlooking the green paladins which received the back-door rubbish. Morris strolled around making himself at home, sticking his fingers with impunity into the electrical sockets. There was a tapping from beyond the wall, and Alison said, 'That'll be Raven, practising his Celtic Sex Magic.'

'What happened to Mrs Etchells, did she get a lift in the end?'

'Silvana went for her. But she's asked to be dropped off at some bed and breakfast in Beeston.'

'Feeling the pinch, is she? Good. Cheating old bat.'

'Oh, I think she does all right, she does a lot of postal readings. She's got regulars going back years. No, it's just she finds a hotel impersonal, she says, she prefers a family home. You know what she's like. She reads the teacups and leaves her flyer. She tries to sign up the landlady. Sometimes they let her stop for nothing.'

Colette pulled a sheaf of Al's new leaflets out of their box. They had chosen lavender, and a form of wording that declared her to be 'One of the most acclaimed psychics working in Britain today'. Al had objected, modestly, but Colette said, what do you want me to put? 'Alison Hart, Slightly Famous Along the A4'?

The schedule was this: a fayre this evening, Saturday, to be followed next day by a grand fayre, where a group of them would have their forty-minute slots on the platform; meanwhile, whoever was not on stage could carry on with private readings in the side rooms.

The venue was an old primary school, the marks of violence still chipped into its red brick. As Al stepped inside she shuddered. She said, 'As you know, my schooldays weren't what you call happy.'

She put a smile on her face, and lolloped among the trestles, beaming from side to side as her colleagues set out their stalls. 'Hi, Angel. Hi, Cara, how are you? This is Colette, my new assistant and working partner.'

Cara, setting down her Norse Wisdom Sticks, lifted her sunny little face. 'Hi, Alison. I see you've not lost any weight.'

Mrs Etchells staggered in, a box of baubles in her arms: 'Oh, what a journey! What a day after the night before!'

'You got a toyboy, Mrs Etchells?' Cara asked, giving Al a wink.

'If you must know, I was up all night with the princess. Silvana, love, help me dress my table, would you?'

Silvana, raising her pencilled brows and hissing between her teeth, dumped down their carrier bags and unfurled Mrs Etchells' fringed crimson cloth into air laden already with the smell from oil burners. 'Personally,' she said, 'I never heard a squeak from Di. Mrs Etchells reckons she was with her, talking about the joys of motherhood.'

'Imagine that,' Mandy said.

'So this is your assistant, Alison?' Silvana ran her eyes over Colette; then ran them over Alison, with insulting slowness, as if they had to feel their way over a large surface area. They hate it, Al thought, they hate it; because I've got Colette, they think I'm coining it.

'I thought. You know,' she said. 'A bit of help with the, with the secretarial, the bookkeeping, the driving, you know. Lonely on the road.'

'Yes, isn't it?' Silvana said. 'Mind you, if you wanted company on the motorway you could have run over to Aldershot and collected your granny, instead of leaving it to me. This your new flyer?' She picked it up and held it close to her eyes; psychics don't wear glasses. 'Mm,' she said. 'Did you do this, Colette? Very nice.'

'I shall be setting up a website for Alison,' Colette said.

Silvana tossed the leaflet down on Mrs Etchells' table, and passed her hands around Colette to feel her aura. 'Oh dear,' she said, and moved away.

Seven o'clock. The scheduled finish was at eight, but tonight they would be lucky to get them out by half past; the caretaker was already banging about, kicking his vacuum cleaner up and down the corridor. But what could you do with the punters – lever them, sodden and sobbing, into the streets? There was hardly one customer who had not mentioned Di; many broke down and cried, putting their elbows on the trestles, edging up the lucky pisky figurines and the brass finger-cymbals so they could sob their hearts out in comfort. I identified with her, she was like a friend to me. Yes, yes, yes, Al would say, like her you are drawn to suffering, oh yes, I am, I am, that's me. You like to have a good time, oh yes, I have always loved dancing. I think of those two boys, I would have had two boys, except the last one was a girl.

Diana was Cancer like me, I was born under Cancer, it means you are like a crab, inside your shell you are squidgy, I think that's where her nickname came from, don't you? I never thought of that, Al said, but you could be right. I think they made her a scrapegoat. I dreamt of her last night, appearing to me in the form of a bird.

There was something gluttonous in their grief, something gloating. Al let them sob, agreeing with them and feeding them their lines, sometimes making little there-there noises; her eyes travelled from side to side, to see who was conspiring against her; Colette stalked between the tables, listening in. I must tell her not to do that, Al thought; or at least, not to do it so conspicuously. As she passed, ill will trailed after her; let them not cold-shoulder me, Al prayed.

For it was usual among the psychics to pass clients to each other, to work in little rings and clusters, trading off their specialities, their weaknesses and strengths: well, darling, I'm not a medium personally, but you see Eve there, in the corner, just give her a little wave, tell her I've recommended you. They pass notes to each other, table to table – titbits gleaned, snippets of personal information with which to impress the clients. And if for some reason you're not on the inside track, you can get disrecommended, you can get forced out. It's a cold world when your colleagues turn their backs. 'Yes, yes, yes,' she sighed, patting the mottled palms she had just read. 'It will all work out for the best. And I'm sure young Harry will look more like his daddy as time goes by.' The woman wrote her a cheque for three services – palms, crystal and general clairvoyance – and as she detached it a final fat tear rolled out of her eye and splashed on her bank sort code.

As the woman rose, a new prospect hesitated in passing: 'Do you do Vedic palmistry, or ordinary?'

'Just ordinary, I'm afraid,' Alison said. The woman sneered

and moved on. Alison began, 'You could try Silvana over there—' but she checked herself. Silvana, after all, was a fraud; her mother used to manage a newsagent in Farnborough, a fact at odds with her claim to be a Romany whose family origins were lost in the mists of occult tradition. Sometimes the punters would ask, 'What's the difference between a clairaudient and an aura reader, a wotsit and a thing?' and Alison would say, 'No great difference, my dear, it's not the instrument you choose that matters, it's not the method, it's not the technique, it's your attunement to a higher reality.' But what she really wanted to do was lean across the table and say, you know what's the difference, the difference between them and me? Most of them can't do it, and I can. And the difference shows, she tells herself, not just in results, but in attitude, in deportment, in some essential seriousness. Her tarot cards, unused so far today, sat at her right hand, burning through their wrap of scarlet satin: priestess, lover and fool. She had never touched them with a hand that was soiled, or opened them to the air without opening her heart; whereas Silvana will light a fag between customers, and Merlin and Merlyn will send out for cheeseburgers if there's a lull. It isn't right to smoke and eat in front of clients, to blow smoke at them over your crystals. It's this she must teach Colette, that a casual approach won't do: you don't shove your stuff in a nylon holdall and wrap your rose quartz in your knickers. You don't carry your kit around in a cardboard box that used to contain a dozen bottles of lavatory cleaner, you don't clear up at the end of a fayre by bundling your bits and pieces into a supermarket carrier bag. And you control your face, your expression, every moment you're awake. She had sometimes noticed an unguarded expression on a colleague's face, as the departing client turned away – a compound of deep weariness and boredom, as the lines of professional alertness faded and the face fell into its customary avaricious folds. She had made up her mind, in the early days, that the client would not like to see this expression, and so she had invented a smile, complicit and wistful, which she kept cemented to her face between readings; it was there now.

Meanwhile, Colette moved scornfully on her trajectory, helpfully clearing an ashtray or righting an upturned Hobbit; anything to allow herself to lean in close and listen. She eavesdropped on Cara, Cara with her cropped head, her pointy ears, her butterfly tattoo: your aura's like your bar code, think of it that way. So your husband's first wife, could that be the blonde I'm seeing? I sense that you are a person of great hidden drive and force of will.

'Would you like a cuppa from the machine, Mrs Etchells?' Colette called, but Al's grandmama waved her away: 'Have you known the joys of motherhood, dear? Only I'm seeing a little boy in your palm.'

'A girl, actually,' said her client.

'It may be a girl I'm seeing. Now, dear, and I don't want you to take this the wrong way, and I don't want to alarm you, but I want you to look out for a little accident that could happen to her, nothing serious, I'm not seeing a hospital bed; it's more as if, as if she might just fall over and cut her knee.'

'She's twenty-three,' said the woman coldly.

'Oh, I see.' Mrs Etchells tittered. 'You must have been very young, dear, when you knew the joys of motherhood. And just the one, is it? No little brothers or sisters? You didn't want, or you couldn't have? Am I seeing a little op, at all?'

'Well, if you can call it little.'

'Oh, I always call an op little. I never say a big op. It doesn't do to upset people.'

You daft old beggar, Colette says to herself. What is this 'joy', what is this word and what does it mean? The psychics say, you're not going to find joy in the external world, you've got to go looking for it inside, *dear.* Even Alison goes along with the theory, when she's in public mode; privately, back in Wexham, she often looks as if it's a hopeless task. Rummaging in your heart for *joy* – may as well go through the bins for it. Where's God, she had said to Al, where's God in all this? and Al had said, Morris says he's never seen God, He doesn't get out much. But he says he's seen the devil, he says he's on first-name terms with him, he claims he beat him at darts once.

And you believe that? Colette asked her, and Al said, No, Morris, he drinks too much and his eyesight's gone, his hand shakes, he can barely hit the board.

For Saturday night the hotel had put on a late buffet for the psychic party: crinkled chicken legs stained the colour of old walnut, a wheel-sized quiche with a thick cardboard base. There was a cold pasta salad and a bowl of complicated-looking greenery which Colette turned, without enthusiasm, with the utensils provided. Raven sat with his desert boots on a coffee table, rolling one of his special cigarettes. 'The thing is, have you got *The Grimoire of Anciara St Remy*? Only it's got forty spells, with detailed diagrams and conjuring charts.'

'You selling it?' Silvana asked.

'No, but . . .'

'But you're on commission for it, am I right?'

Oh, they're such cynics, Colette thought. She had imagined that when psychics got together they'd talk about – well, things of the psyche; that they would share at least a little of their bemusement and daily fear, the fear that – if she could judge by Alison – was the price of success. But now, a little way into their association, she understood that all they talked about was money. They tried to sell things to each other; they compared their rates; they tried to hear of new stratagems – 'believe me, it's the new aromatherapy,' Gemma was saying – and to learn about new tricks and fiddles that they could try out. They came to swap jargon, pick up the latest terms: and *why* do they look so ridiculous? Why all these crystal pendant earrings swinging from withered lobes, why the shrunken busts exposed in daylight, the fringes, the beading, the headscarves, the wraps, the patchwork and the shawls? In their room – just time, before the buffet, to freshen up – she'd said to Alison, 'You criticise my holdall – but have you seen your friends, have you seen the state of them?'

Alison's silk, the length of apricot polyester, lay folded on the bed, ready to be draped next day; in private life she flinches at its touch – oh yes, she has admitted she does – but somehow it's necessary, she will claim, as part of her public persona. With the silk around her studio portrait, she loses the sensation that she is shrinking inside her own skin. It blunts her sensitivity, in a way that is welcome to her; it is an extra, synthetic skin she has grown, to compensate for the skins the work strips away.

But now Colette moved around the room, grumbling. 'Why does everything have to be so tacky? That fairground stuff. They can't think it impresses anybody. I mean, when you see Silvana, you don't say, ooh look, here comes a Gypsy Princess, you say, here comes a withered old slapper with a streak of fake tan down the side of her neck.'

'It's – I don't know,' Al said. 'It's to make it, like a game.'

Colette stared. 'But it's their job. A job's not a game.'

'I agree, I agree completely, there's just no need these days to dress up as if you were in a circus. But then again, I don't think mediums should wear trainers either.'

'Who's wearing trainers?'

'Cara. Under her robes.' Al looked perplexed, and stood up to take off a layer or two. 'I never know what to wear myself, these days.' Suit your outfit to the audience, to the town, had always been her watchword. A touch of Jaeger – their clothes don't fit her, but she can have an accessory – feels eternally right in Guildford – whereas down the road in Woking they'd mistrust you if you weren't in some way mismatched and uncoordinated. Each town on her loop had its requirements, and when you head up the country, you mustn't expect sophistication; the further north you go, the more the psychics' outfits tend to suggest hot Mediterranean blood, or the mysterious East, and today maybe it's she who's got it wrong, because at the fayre she had the feeling of being devalued, marked down in some way . . . that woman who wanted Vedic palmistry . . . Colette had told her she wouldn't go wrong with a little cashmere cardigan, preferably black. But of course there was no *little* cardigan that would meet Al's need, only something like a Bedouin tent, something capacious and hot, and as she peeled this garment off, her scent came with it, and wafted through the room; the whiff of royal mortification was suppressed now, but she had told Colette, do alert me, I shan't take offence, if you catch a hint of anything from the sepulchre.

'What can I go down in?' she asked. Colette passed her a silk top, which had been carefully pressed and wrapped in tissue for its journey. Her eye fell on the holdall, with her own stuff still rolled up inside it. Maybe Al's right, she thought. Maybe I'm too old for a casual safari look – she caught her own eye in the mirror, as she stood behind Alison to unfasten the clasp of her pearls. As Al's assistant, could she possibly benefit from tax allowances on her appearance? It was an issue she'd not yet thrashed out with the Revenue; I'm working on it, she said to herself.

'You know this book we're doing?' Al was hauling her bosoms into conformity; they were trying to escape from her bra, and she eased them back with little shoves and pinches. 'Is it OK to mention it on the platform? Advertise it?'

'It's early days,' Colette said.

'How long do you think it will take?'

'How long's a piece of string?'

It depended, Colette said, on how much nonsense continued to appear on their tapes. Alison insisted on listening to them all through, at maximum volume; behind the hissing, behind whatever foreign-language garbage she could hear up front, there were sometimes startled wails and whistles, which she said were old souls; I owe it to them to listen, she said, if they're trying so hard to come through. Sometimes they found the tape running, when neither of them had switched it on. Colette was inclined to blame Morris; speaking of which, where—

'At the pub.'

'Are they open tonight?'

'Morris will find one that is.'

'I suppose. Anyway, the men wouldn't stand for it, would they? Shutting the pubs because of Di.'

'All he has to do is follow Merlin and Merlyn. They could find a drink in . . .' Al flapped her sleeves. She tried to think of the name of a Muslim country, but a name didn't readily spring to her lips. 'Do you know Merlin's done a book called *Master of Thoth*? And Merlyn with a y, he's done *Casebook of a Psychic Detective*?'

'That's a point. Have you thought about working for the police?'

Alison didn't answer; she stared through the mirror, her finger tracing the ridge her bra made under the thin silk. In time, she shook her head.

'Only it would give you some sort of, what do you call it, accreditation.'

'Why would I need that?'

'As publicity.'

'Yes. I suppose so. But no.'

'You mean, no you won't do it?' Silence. 'You don't ever want to make yourself useful to society?'

'Come on, let's go down before there's no food left.'

At nine thirty Silvana, complaining and darting venomous looks at Al, was parted from her glass of red and persuaded to take Mrs Etchells back to her lodgings. Once she had been coaxed to it, she stood jangling her car keys. 'Come on,' she said, 'I want to get back by ten for the funeral highlights.'

'They'll repeat them,' Gemma said, and Colette muttered, shouldn't wonder if we have reruns all next Christmas, but Silvana said, 'No, it won't be the same, I want to watch them live.'

Raven sniggered. Mrs Etchells levered herself to the vertical and brushed coleslaw from her skirt. 'Thank you for your caring spirit,' she said, 'or I wouldn't have slept in a bed tonight, they'd have locked the front door. Condemned to walk the streets of Beeston. Friendless.'

'I don't know why you don't just stop here like everybody else,' Cara said. 'It can't cost much more than you're paying.'

Colette smiled; she had negotiated a group rate for Al, just as if she were a company.

'Thank you, but I couldn't,' Mrs Etchells said. 'I value the personal touch.'

'What, like locking you out?' Colette said. 'And whatever you think,' she said to Silvana, 'Aldershot is not close to Slough. Whereas you, you're just down the road.'

'When I joined this profession,' Silvana said, 'it would have been unthinkable to refuse aid to someone who'd helped you develop. Let alone your own grandmother.'

She swept out; as Mrs Etchells shambled after her, a chicken bone fell from some fold in her garments, and lay on the carpet. Colette turned to Alison, whispering, 'What does she mean, help you develop?'

Cara heard. 'I see Colette's not one of us,' she said.

Mandy Coughlan said, 'Training, it's just what we call training. You sit, you see. In a circle.'

'Anyone could do that. You don't need to be trained for that.'

'No, a – Alison, tell her. A development circle. Then you find out if you've got the knack. You see if anybody comes through. The others help you. It's a tricky time.'

'Of course, it's only for the mediums,' Gemma said. 'For example, if you're just psychometry, palms, crystal healing, general clairvoyance, aura cleansing, feng shui, tarot, I Ching, then you don't need to sit. Not in a circle.'

'So how do you know if you can do it?'

Gemma said, 'Well, darling, you have a feeling for it,' but Mandy flashed her pale blue eyes and said, 'General client satisfaction.'

'You mean they don't come wanting their money back?'

'I've never had an instance,' Mandy said. 'Not even you, Colette. Though you don't seem backward at coming forward. If you don't mind my saying so.'

Al said, 'Look, Colette's new to this, she's only asking, she doesn't mean to upset anybody. I think the thing is, Colette, possibly what you don't quite see is that we're all – we're all worn to a frazzle, we've all lost sleep over this Di business, it's not just me – we're on the end of our nerves.'

'Make or break time,' Raven said. 'I mean, if any of us could give her the opening, just, you know, be there for her, just let her express anything that's uppermost in her mind, about those final moments . . .' His voice died away, and he stared at the wall.

'I think they murdered her,' Colette said. 'The royals. If she'd lived, she'd have only brought them into further disrepute.'

'But it was her time,' Gemma said, 'it was her time, and she was called away.'

'She was a bit thick, wasn't she?' Cara said. 'She didn't get any exams at school.'

'Oh, be fair now,' Alison said. 'I read she got a cup for being kind to her guinea pig.'

'That's not an exam, though, is it? Did you—'

'What,' Al said, 'me have a guinea pig? Christ, no, my mum would have barbecued it. We didn't have pets. We had dogs. But not pets.'

'No,' Cara said, her brow crinkling, 'I meant, did you get any exams, Al?'

'I tried. They entered me. I turned up. I had a pencil and everything. But there'd always be some sort of disturbance in the hall.'

Gemma said, 'I was barred from biology for labelling a drawing in obscene terms. But I didn't do it myself. I don't think I even knew half those words.'

There was a murmur of fellow feeling. Alison said, 'Colette didn't have those problems, she's got exams, I need somebody brighter than me in my life.' Her voice rattled on . . . Colette, my working partner . . . my partner, not assistant: she broke off, and laughed uncertainly.

Raven said, 'Do you know that for every person on this side, there's thirty-three on the other?'

'Really?' Gemma said. 'Thirty-three airside, for every one earthside?'

Colette thought, in that case, I'm backing the dead.

* * *

Merlin and Merlyn came back from the pub: boring on with men's talk. I use Transit Forecaster, I find it invaluable, oh yes, I can run it on my old Amstrad, what's the point of pouring money into the pockets of Bill Gates? Colette leaned over to put him right on the matter, but Merlyn caught her by the arm and said 'Have you read *The Truth About Exodus*? Basically it's how they found this bit of the Bible written on a pyramid, inscribed on the side. And how contrary to popular belief the Egyptians actually, they actually paid the Israelis to leave. And they used the money for making the Ark of the Covenant. Jesus was an Egyptian, they've found scrolls, he was actually of pharaoh descent. And it's why they walk round and round at Mecca. Like they used to walk round the Great Pyramid.'

'Oh, did they? I see,' Colette said. 'Well, you've put me right, there, Merlyn, I always did wonder.'

'*Mountain K2, Search for the Gods*, that's another good one. *The Lost Book of Enki*. That's the one you've got to get. He's this god from the planet Nibiru. You see, they were from space, and they needed gold from the earth to enrich the dying atmosphere of their planet, so they saw that it was on earth, gold was, so they needed somebody to mine it for them, so they therefore created man . . .'

Al's eyes were distant; she was back at school, back in the exam hall. Hazel Leigh opposite, working her red ponytail round and round in her fingers till it was like a twist of barley sugar . . . and peppermints, you were allowed to suck peppermints, you weren't allowed much, not a fag: when Bryan lit up Miss Adshead was down the hall like a laser beam.

All during the maths paper there was a man chattering in her ear. It wasn't Morris, she knew it was not by his accent, and his whole general tone and bearing, by what he was talking about, and by how he was weeping: for Morris could not weep. The man, the spirit, he was talking just below the threshold, retching and sobbing. The questions were algebra; she filled in a few disordered letters, a, b, x, z. When she reached question 5 the man began to break through. He said, look for my cousin John Joseph, tell our Jo that my hands are bound with wire. In spirit, even now, he had a terrible pain where the bones of his feet used to be, and that's what he relied on her to pass on to his cousin, the knowledge of this pain: tell our Jo, tell him it was that bastard that drives the Escort with the rusty wing, that cunt that always has a cold, him . . . and when in the end the crushing of the rifle butts and the men's boots seemed to drive her own feet through the scuffed vinyl tiles of the exam room, she had let the letters freely intermingle on the page, so that when Miss Adshead came to flick her paper into the pile there was nothing on it but thin pen scrawls, like the traces and loops of the wire with which the hands of this total stranger had been bound.

'Alison?' She jumped. Mandy had taken her by the wrist; she was shaking her, bringing her back to the present. 'You all right, Al?' Over her shoulder she said, 'Cara, go get her a stiff drink and a chicken leg. Al? Are you back with us, love? Is she pestering you? The princess?'

'No,' Al said. 'It's paramilitaries.'

'Oh, them,' Gemma said. 'They can be shocking.'

'I get Cossacks,' Mandy said. 'Apologising for, you know. What they used to do. Cleaving. Slashing. Scourging peasants to death. Terrible.'

'What's Cossacks?' Cara said, and Mandy said, 'They are a very unpleasant kind of mounted police.'

Raven said, 'I never get anything like that. I have led various pacific lives. That's why I'm so karmically adjusted.'

Al roused herself. She rubbed the wounds on her wrists. Live in the present moment, she told herself. Nottingham. September. Funeral Night. Ten minutes to ten. 'Time for bed, Col,' she said.

'We're not watching the highlights?'

'We can watch them upstairs.' She pushed herself up from the sofa. Her feet seemed unable to support her. An effort of will saw her limp across the room, but she had wobbled as she took the weight on her feet, and her skirt flicked a wine glass from a low table, sent it spinning away from her, the liquid flying across the room and splashing red down the paintwork. It flew with such force it looked as if someone had flung it, a fact that did not escape the women; though it escaped Raven, who was slumped in his chair, and hardly twitched as the glass smashed.

There was a silence. Into it, Cara said, 'Whoops-a-daisy.'

Alison turned her head over her shoulder, and looked back, her face blank; did I do that? She stood, her head swivelled, too weary to move back to attend to the accident.

'I'll get it,' Mandy said, hopping up, crouching neatly over the shards and splinters. Gemma turned her large cowlike eyes on Al and said, 'All in, poor love,' and Silvana, walking back in at that moment, tut-tutted at them: 'What's this, Alison? Breaking up the happy home?'

'This is the fact,' Al said. She was rocking to and fro on the bed – she was trying to rub her feet, but finding the rest of her body got in the way. 'I feel used. All the time I feel used. I'm put up on stage for them to see me. I have to experience for them the things they don't dare.' With a little moan, she gripped her ankle, and rolled backwards. 'I'm like, I'm like some form of . . . muckraker. No, I don't mean that. I mean I'm in there, in the pockets of their dirty minds. I'm up to my elbows, I'm like—'

'A sewage worker?' Colette suggested.

'Yes! Because the clients won't do their own dirty work. They want it contracted out. They write me a cheque for thirty quid and expect me to clean their drains. You say help the police. I'll tell you why I don't help the police. First cos I hate the police. Then because, do you know where it gets you?'

'Al, I take it back. You don't have to help the police.'

'That's not the point. I have to tell you why not. You have to know.'

'I don't have to.'

'You do. Or you'll keep coming back to it again and again. Make yourself useful, Alison. Make yourself socially useful.'

'I won't. I'll never mention it.'

'You will. You're that type, Colette, you can't help mentioning and mentioning things. I'm not getting at you. I'm not criticising. But you do mention, you are, Colette, you are, one of the world's great mentioners.' Al uncurled herself with a whimper, and fell back on the bed. 'Can you find my brandy?'

'You've had too much already.'

Alison moaned. Colette added generously, 'It's not your fault. We should have stopped for an early lunch. Or I could easily have brought you in a sandwich. I did offer.'

'I can't eat when I'm sitting. The cards won't work if you smudge them.'

'No, you've said that before.'

'Not cheeseburgers. I don't agree with it.'

'Nor me. It's disgusting.'

'You get fingerprints on your crystals.'

'It's hard to see how you could help it.'

'Don't you ever drink too much, Col?'

'No, I hardly ever do.'

'Don't you ever, ever? Didn't you ever, ever, make a mistake?'

'Yes. Not that kind, though.'

Then Al's wrath seemed to deflate. Her body collapsed too, back on to the hotel bed, as if hot air were leaking from a balloon. 'I do want that brandy,' she said, quietly and humbly.

She stretched out her legs. Over her own rolling contours she saw a distant view of feet. They lolled outwards as she watched: dead man's joints. 'Christ,' she said: and screwed up her face. The cousin of John Joseph was back, and talking in her ear: I don't want the hospital to take my legs off; I'd rather be dead out there in the field and buried, than alive with no legs.

She lay whimpering up at the dim ceiling, until Colette sighed and rose. 'OK. I'll get you a drink. But you'd do better with an aspirin and some peppermint foot lotion.' She tripped into the bathroom and took from the shelf above the wash-basin a plastic tumbler in a polythene shroud. Her nails punctured it; like a human membrane, it adhered, it had to be drawn away, and when she rubbed her fingertips together to discard it, and held up the tumbler, she felt against her face a bottled breath, something second-hand and not entirely clean, something breathing up at her from the interior of the glass.

She screwed open the brandy bottle and poured two fingers. Al had rolled herself up in the duvet. Her plump pink feet stuck out of the end. They did look hot, swollen. Mischievously, Colette took hold of a toe and waggled it. 'This little piggy went to market—'

Alison bellowed, in someone else's voice, 'In the name of Bloody Christ!'

'Sorr-ee!' Colette sang.

Alison's arm fought its way out of her wrappings, and her fingers took a grip on the tumbler, buckling its sides. She wriggled so that her shoulders were propped against the headboard, and swallowed half her drink in the first gulp. 'Listen, Colette. Shall I tell you about the police? Shall I tell you? Why I won't have anything to do with them?'

'You're clearly going to,' Colette said. 'Look, wait a minute. Just hold on . . .'

Al began, 'You know Merlyn?'

'Wait,' Colette said. 'We should get it on tape.'

'OK. But hurry up.'

Alison swallowed the rest of her drink. At once her face flushed. Her head was tipped back, her shiny dark hair spilling over the pillows. 'So are you fixing it?'

'Yes, just a minute – OK.'

Click.

COLETTE: So, it's 6 September 1997, 10.33 p.m., Alison is telling me—

ALISON: You know Merlyn, Merlyn with a y? He says he's a psychic detective. He says he's helped police forces all over the south-east. He says they call him in regularly. And you know where Merlyn lives? He lives in a trailer home.

COLETTE: So?

ALISON: So that's where it gets you, helping the police. He doesn't even have a proper lavatory.

COLETTE: How tragic.

ALISON: You say that, Miss Sneery, but you wouldn't like it. He lives outside Aylesbury. And do you know what it's like, when you help the police?

Al's eyes closed. She thought of reliving – over and over – the last few seconds of a strangled child. She thought of drowning in a car under the waters of the canal, she thought of waking in a shallow grave. She slept for a moment and woke in her duvet, wrapped in it like a sausage in its roll; she pushed up and out, fighting for space and air, and she remembered why she couldn't breathe – it was because she was dead, because she was buried. She thought, I can't think about it any more, I'm at the end of, the end of my – and she released her breath with a great gasp: she heard *click*.

Colette was at her side, her voice nervous, oh God, Al, bending over her now: Colette's breath was against her face, polythene breath, not unpleasant but not quite natural. 'Al, is it your heart?'

She felt Colette's tiny, bony hand sliding under her head, lifting it. As Colette's wrist and forearm took the weight, she felt a sudden sense of release. She gasped, sighed, as if she were newborn. Her eyes snapped open: 'Switch on the tape again.'

Breakfast time. Colette was down early. Listening to Alison while the tape ran – Alison crying like a child, talking in a child's voice, replying to spirit questions Colette could not hear – she had found her own hand creeping towards the brandy bottle. A shot had stiffened her spine, but the effect didn't last. She felt cold and pale now, colder and paler than ever, and she nearly threw up when she came into the breakfast room and saw Merlyn and Merlin stirring a ladle around in a vat of baked beans.

'You look as if you've been up all night,' Gemma said, picking at the horns of a croissant.

'I'm fine,' Colette snapped. She looked around; she couldn't very well take a table by herself, and she didn't want to sit with the boys. She pointed imperiously to the coffee pot on its hotplate, and the waitress hurried across with it. 'Black is fine.'

'Are you lactose-intolerant?' Gemma asked her. 'Soya milk is very good.'

'I prefer black.'

'Where's Alison?'

'Doing her hair.'

'I'd have thought that would have been your job.'

'I'm her business partner, not her maid.'

Gemma turned the corners of her mouth down. She nudged Cara conspiratorially, but Cara was unfolding the papers to see the funeral pictures. Mandy Coughlan came in. Her eyes were red-rimmed and her lips compressed. 'Another one who's had a bad night,' Gemma said. 'Princess?'

'Morris,' Mandy said. She rummaged bad-temperedly at the breakfast buffet and slammed a banana down on to the table. 'I've passed the whole night under psychic attack.'

'Tea or coffee?' the waitress said.

'Got any rat poison?' Mandy said. 'I wish I'd had some last night for that little bastard Morris. You know, I pity Alison, I really do, I wouldn't be in her shoes for any money. But can't she get him under control? I'd hardly got into bed before he was there trying to pull the duvet off me.'

'He always did fancy you,' Cara said, flapping the newspaper. 'Ooh, look at poor little Prince Harry. Look at his liddle face, bless him.'

'Pulling and tugging till nearly three o'clock. I thought he'd gone, I got out of bed to go to the loo, and he just jumped out from behind the curtains and put his filthy paw right up my nightie.'

'Yeah, he does that,' Colette said. 'Hides behind the curtains. Alison says she finds it very annoying.'

Alison winced in a moment later, looking green.

'Oh, poor love,' Mandy breathed. 'Look at her.'

'I see you didn't manage to do anything with your hair after all,' Cara said sympathetically.

'At least she doesn't look like a bloody pixie,' Colette snapped.

'Tea, coffee?' the waitress said.

Al pulled her chair well out from the table and sat down heavily. 'I'll get changed later,' she said, by way of explaining herself. 'I was sick in the night.'

'Too much of that red,' Gemma said. 'You were sozzled when you went up.'

'Too much of everything,' Al said. Her eyes, dull and downcast, rested on the dish of corn flakes Colette had placed before her. Mechanically, she picked up a spoon.

'That's nice,' Gemma said. 'She gets your cereal for you. Even though she's not your maid, she says.'

'Could you just shut up?' Colette enquired. 'Could you just give her a minute's peace and let her get something inside her?'

'Mandy—'Alison began.

Mandy waved a hand. 'Nugh about it,' she said, her mouth full of muesli. 'Id nig. Nobbel self.'

'But I do blame myself,' Al insisted.

Mandy swallowed. She flapped a hand, as if she were drying her nail varnish. 'We can talk about it another time. We can stay in separate hotels, if we have to.'

'I hope it won't come to that.'

'You look done up,' Mandy said. 'I feel for you, Al, I really do.'

'We were up talking till late, me and Colette. And other people came through, that I used to know when I was a kid. And you know I said paramilitaries were tormenting me? The thing is, they broke through and smashed up my feet. I had to take two Distalgesic. By dawn I was just dropping off to sleep. Then Morris came in. He yanked out the pillow from under my head and started boasting in my ear.'

'Boasting?' Gemma said.

'What he'd done with Mandy. Sorry, Mandy. It's not that – I mean, I didn't believe him or anything.'

'If he were mine,' Gemma said, 'I'd get him exorcised.'

Cara shook her head. 'You could control, Morris, you know, if you were to approach him with unconditional love.'

Colette said, 'Could you manage a tomato juice, Alison?'

Alison shook her head, and put down her spoon. 'I suppose we're in for another day of the princess.'

'Another day, another dollar,' Merlin said.

'Snivel, bloody snivel,' Al said. 'Do they ever think what it's like for us? Down I go, whoosh. Plunged head first into their shit. Like a lavatory brush.'

'Well, it's a living, Al,' Mandy Coughlan said, but Cara, startled, dropped her knife on the *Mail*'s Full-Colour Tribute, and smeared butter on the Prince of Wales.

Last night, Saturday, the first card Al had laid down was the page of hearts: significator of her pale companion, the emblem of the woman who appeared in the cards at the Harte & Garter, Windsor, on the morning when Colette first came into her line of vision. White hair, pale eyes, red-rimmed like the eyes of some small scurrying pet you ought to be kind to.

She looked up, at the woman, the client, who was sitting there sniffling. The reading Al was getting was close to home, it was for herself, not for the client before her. You can't control the cards; they will only give the messages they want to give. Here's the king of spades, reversed: probably, what was his name . . . Gavin. Colette is aching for a man to come into her life. Night-times, she can feel it, in the flat at Wexham, the slow drag of desire beyond the plasterboard wall. Colette's busy little fingers, seeking solitary pleasure . . . What turn of fate brought Colette my way? Did I take up with her for my own advantage, for an advantage not yet revealed even to me: for some purpose that is working itself out? She pushed the thought away, along with any guilt that attended it. I can't help what I do. I have to live. I have to protect myself. And if it's at her expense . . . so what if it is? What's Colette to me? If Mandy Coughlan offered her a better prospect I wouldn't see her for dust, she'd have her stuff rolled up in that holdall of hers and she'd be on the next train to Brighton and Hove. At least, I hope she would. I hope she wouldn't steal my car.

Diana is the queen of hearts; every time the card turns up in a spread, this week and next, she will signify the princess, and the clients' grief will draw the card time and time again from the depth of the pack. Already the first sightings of her have been reported, peeping over the shoulder of her ancestor Charles I in a portrait at St James's Palace. Some people who have seen the apparition say that she is wearing a dress the colour of blood. All agree that she is wearing her tiara. If you look hard you will see her face in fountains, in raindrops, in the puddles on service-station forecourts. Diana is a water sign, which means she's the psychic type. She's just the type that lingers and drips, who waxes and wanes, breathes in and out her tides: who, by the slow accretion of tears, brings ceilings down and wears a path into stone.

When Alison had seen Colette's horoscope (cast by Merlyn as a favour) she had quailed. 'Really?' she'd said. 'Don't tell me, Merlyn. I don't want to know.' Farking air signs, Merlyn had said, what can you bloody do? He had felt for Alison's hand with his damp Pisces palm.

Sunday morning: she gave readings in a side room, tense, waiting to go on the platform at 2 p.m. From her clients, through the morning, it was more of the same. Diana, she had her problems, I have my problems too. I reckon she had her choice of men, but she was a bad picker. After an hour of it, a feeling of mutiny rose inside her. Mutiny on the Bounty, was the phrase that came into her head. She put her elbows on the table, leaned towards the punter and said, 'Prince Charles, you think he was a bad pick? So you'd have known better, eh? You'd have turned him down, would you?'

The client shrank back in her chair. A moment, and the

little poor woman sat there again, in the client's lap: 'Excuse me, Miss, have you seen Maureen Harrison? I've been seeking Maureen for thirty year.'

About lunchtime she sneaked out for a sandwich. She and Gemma split a pack of tuna and cucumber. 'If I had your problems with the Irish,' Gemma said, 'I'd be straight on the phone to Ian Paisley. We all have our crosses to bear, and mine personally tend to be derived from my ninth life, when I went on crusade. So any upheaval east of Cyprus, and frankly, Al, I'm tossed.' A sliver of cucumber fell out of her sandwich, a sliding green shadow on her white paper plate. She speared it artfully and popped it into her mouth.

'It's not just the Irish,' Al said. 'With me, it's everybody really.'

'I used to know Silvana, in that life. Course, she was on the other side. A Saracen warrior. Impaled her prisoners.'

'I thought that was Romanians,' Al said. 'It just goes to show.'

'You were never a vampire, were you? No, you're too nice.'

'I've seen a few today.'

'Yes, Di's brought them out. You can't miss them, can you?' But Gemma did not say what signs she looked for in a vampire. She balled up her paper napkin and dropped it on her plate.

Two twenty. She was on the platform. It was question time: 'Could I get in touch with Diana if I used a Ouija board?'

'I wouldn't advise it, darling.'

'My gran used to do it.'

And where's your gran now?

She didn't say it: not aloud. She thought: that's the last thing we need, Amateur Night, Diana pulled about and puzzled by a thousand rolling wine glasses. The young girls in the audience bounced up and down in their seats, not knowing what a Ouija board was – being the current generation, they didn't wait to be told, they yipped at her and whistled and shouted out.

'It's just an old parlour game,' she explained. 'It's not a thing any serious practitioner would do. You put out the letters and a glass rolls around and spells out words. Spells out names, you know, or phrases that you think mean something.'

'I've heard it can be quite dangerous,' a woman said. 'Dabbling in that sort of thing.'

'Oh, yes, dabbling,' Al said. It made her smile, the way the punters used it as a technical term. 'Yes, you don't want to go dabbling. Because you have to consider who would come through. There are some spirits that are, I'm not being rude now, but they are on a very low level. They're only drifting about earthside because they've got nothing better to do. They're like those kids you see on sink estates hanging about parked cars – you don't know if they're going to break in and drive them away or just slash the tyres and scratch the paintwork. But why find out? Just don't go there! Now those sort of kids, you wouldn't ask them in your house, would you? Well, that's what you're doing if you mess about with a Ouija board.'

She looked down at her hands. The lucky opals were occluded, steamy, as if their surfaces were secreting. There are things you need to know about the dead, she wanted to say. Things you really ought to know. For instance, it's no good trying to enlist them for any good cause you have in mind, world peace or whatever. Because they'll only bugger you about. They're not reliable. They'll pull the rug from under you. They don't become decent people just because they're dead. People are right to be afraid of ghosts. If you get people who are bad in life – I mean, cruel people, dangerous people – why do you think they're going to be any better after they're dead?

But she would never speak it. Never. Never utter the word 'death', if she could help it. And even though they needed frightening, even though they deserved frightening, she would never, when she was with her clients, slip a hint or tip a wink about the true nature of the place beyond black.

At teatime, when the event was over and they went down in the lift with their bags, Colette said, 'Well now!'

'Well now what?'

'Your little outburst at breakfast! The less said about that, the better.'

Al looked sideways at her. Now that they were alone together, and with the drive home before them, Colette was obviously about to say a great deal.

As they stood at the desk, checking out, Mandy came up behind them. 'All right, Al? Feeling better?'

'I'll be OK, Mandy. And look, I really want to apologise about Morris last night—'

'Forget it. Could happen to any of us.'

'You know what Cara said, about unconditional love. I suppose she's right. But it's hard to love Morris.'

'I don't think that trying to love him would get you anywhere. You've just got to get clever about him. I don't suppose there's anyone new on the horizon, is there?'

'Not that I can see.'

'It's just that around about our age, you do sometimes get a second chance – well, you know yourself how it is with men, they leave you for a younger model. Now I've known some psychics who, frankly, they find it devastating when their guide walks out, but for others, let me say, it's a blessed relief – you get a fresh start, with a new guide, and before you know where you are your trade's taken an upturn and you feel twenty years younger.' She took Al's hand. Her pink-frosted nails caressed the opals. 'Alison, can I speak frankly to you? As one of your oldest friends? You've got to get off the Wheel of Fear. On to the Wheel of Freedom.'

Al pushed her hair back, smiling bravely. 'It sounds a bit too athletic for me.'

'Enlightenment proceeds level by level. You know that. If I had to take a guess, I'd say that thinking was at the source of your problems. Too much thinking. Take the pressure off, Al. Open your heart.'

'Thanks. I know you mean well, Mandy.'

Colette turned from the desk, credit-card slip between her fingers, fumbling with the strap of her bag. The nail of Mandy's forefinger dug her in the ribs. Startled, Colette looked up into her face. Her mouth was set in a grim pink line. She's quite old, Colette thought; her neck's going.

'Look after Al,' Mandy said. 'Al is very gifted and very special, and you'll have to answer to me for it if you let her talent bring her to grief.'

In the car park Colette strode briskly ahead with her holdall. Alison was dragging her case – one of the wheels had come off – and she was still limping, in pain from her smashed-up feet. She knew she should call Colette back to help her. But it seemed more suitable to suffer; I ought to suffer, she thought. Though I am not sure why.

'The amount you take away!' Colette said. 'For one night.'

'It's not that I pack too much,' Al said meekly, 'it's that my clothes are bigger.'

She didn't want a row, not just at this minute. There was a quivering in her abdomen which she knew meant that someone was trying to break through from spirit. Her pulse was leaping. Once again she felt nauseated, and as if she wanted to belch. Sorry, Diana, she said, I just had to get that wind up, and Colette said – well, she said nothing, really, but Al could see she was annoyed about being told off by Mandy. 'She was only advising you,' she said. 'She didn't mean any harm. Me and Mand, we go back a long way.'

'Put your seat belt on,' Colette said. 'I'm hoping to get home before dark. You'll need to stop somewhere to eat, I suppose.'

'Fucking will,' Morris said, dropping himself into the rear seat. 'Here, don't drive off yet, wait till we get settled.'

'We?' Al said. She swivelled in her seat; was there a thickening of the air, a ripple and disturbance, a perturbation below the level of her senses? A smell of rot and blight? Morris was in wonderful spirits, chortling and bouncing. 'Here's Donald Aitkenside hitching a ride, Donnie what I've been trying to meet up wiv. You know Donnie, don't you? Course you do! Donnie and me, we go back a long way. Donnie knew MacArthur. You remember MacArthur, from the old days? And here's young Dean. Don't know Dean, do you? Dean's new at this game, he don't know nobody, well, he knows Donnie, but he don't know the army crowd nor any of that lot from the old fight game. Dean, meet the missus. That? That's the missus's pal. Like a length o' string, ain't she? Would you? No, not me, no chance, I like a bit of meat on their bones.' He laughed, raucously. 'Tell you what, gel, tell you what, stop off south of Leicester somewhere, and we might meet up with Pikey Pete. For Pikey Pete,' he told Dean, 'he is such a man, if he's down on his luck you'll see him picking fag ends off the road, but let him have a win on the dogs and he will see you and slot a cigar in your top pocket, he's that generous.'

'Should we pull in south of Leicester?' Al asked.

Colette was irritated. 'That's no distance.'

'Look, it's not worth antagonising him.'

'Morris?'

'Of course, Morris. Colette, you know the tape, you know those men that were coming through?'

'Paramilitaries?'

'No. Forget them. I mean the other men, the fiends, the fiends I used to know.'

'Can we please not talk about it? Not while I'm driving.'

The services were quiet, winding down after the weekend trade; though it had been an odd sort of weekend, of course, because of Di. The fiends swarmed out of the back of the car, yipping and squeaking. Inside the building, Al wandered around the food court, an anxious expression on her face. She lifted the lid of a mock-rustic tureen and gazed into the soup, and picked up filled rolls and tugged at their cling film, turning them up to look at them end on. 'What's in this one, do you think?' she said. The film was misty, as if the lettuce had been breathing out.

'For God's sake sit down,' Colette said. 'I'll bring you some pizza.'

When she came back, edging among the tables with her tray, she saw that Al had taken out her tarot cards.

She was amazed. 'Not here!' she said.

'I just have to—'

The cards' scarlet wrappings flowed over the table, and puddled in Colette's lap as she sat down. Alison drew out one card. She held it for a moment, flipped it over. She didn't speak, but laid it down on top of the pack.

'What is it?'

It was the Tower. Lightning strikes. The masonry of the tower is blasted away. Flames shoot out of the brickwork. Debris is thrown into space. The occupants hurtle towards earth, their legs scissoring and their arms outflung. The ground rushes up at them.

'Eat your pizza,' Colette said, 'before it goes all flabby.'

'I don't want it.' The Tower, she thought, it's my least favourite. The Death card I can handle. I don't like the Tower. The Tower means—

Colette saw with alarm that Al's eyes had slipped out of focus; as if Al were a baby whom she were desperate to placate, whose mouth she was desperate to fill, she grabbed the plastic fork and plunged it into the pizza. 'Look, Al. Try a bit of this.'

The fork buckled against the crust; Al snapped back, smiled, took the fork from her hand. 'It may not be so bad,' she said. Her voice was small and tight. 'Here, Col, let me. When you get the Tower it means your world blows up. Generally. But it can have a, you know, quite a *small* meaning. Oh, blast this thing.'

'Pick it up in your fingers,' Colette advised.

'Wrap my cards up, then.'

Colette shrank; she was afraid to touch them.

'It's all right. They won't bite. They know you. They know you're my partner.'

Hastily, Colette bundled them into their red wrappings.

'That's right. Just drop them in my bag.'

'What came over you?'

'I don't know. I just had to see. It gets you that way sometimes.' Al bit into a piece of raw-looking green pepper, and chewed it for a while. 'Colette, there's something you ought to know. About last night.'

'Your baby voice,' Colette said. 'Talking to nobody. That made me laugh. But then I thought at one point you were having a heart attack.'

'I don't think there's anything wrong with my heart.'

Colette looked meaningfully at her pizza slice.

'Well, yes,' Alison said. 'But that's not going to finish me off. Nobody perishes of a pizza slice. Think of all those millions of Italians, running round quite healthy.'

'It was a horrible weekend.'

'What did you expect?'

'I don't know,' Colette said. 'I didn't have any expectations. That card – what do you mean by a *small* meaning?'

'It can be a warning that the structure you're in won't contain you any more. Whether it's your job, or your love life, or whatever it is. You've outgrown it. It's not safe to stay put. The Tower is a house, you know. So it can mean just that. Move on.'

'What, leave Wexham?'

'Why not? It's a nice little flat but I've got no roots there.'

'Where would you like to move?'

'Somewhere clean. Somewhere new. A house that nobody's lived in before. Could we do that?'

'New build is a good investment.' Colette put down her coffee cup. 'I'll look into it.'

'I thought – well, listen, Colette, I'm sure you're as tired of Morris as I am. I don't know if he'd ever agree to, you know, take his pension – I think Mandy was being a bit optimistic there. But our lives would be easier, wouldn't they, if his friends didn't come round?'

'His friends?' Colette said blankly.

Oh, Jesus, Al said to herself, it's all uphill work.

'He's beginning to meet up with his friends,' she explained. 'I don't know why he feels the need, but it seems he does. There's one called Don Aitkenside. I remember him. He had a mermaid on his thigh. And this Dean, now, he's new to me, but I don't like the sound of him. He was in the back of the car just now. Spotty kid. Got a police record.'

'Really?' Colette's flesh crawled. 'In the back?'

'With Morris and Don.' Al pushed her plate away. 'And now Morris is off looking for this gypsy.'

'Gypsy? But there won't be room!'

Alison just looked at her sadly. 'They don't take up room, in the usual way,' she said.

'No. Of course not. It's the way you talk about them.'

'I can't think how else to talk. I only have the usual words.'

'Of course you do, but it makes me think – I mean, it makes me think they're ordinary blokes, except I can't see them.'

'I hope they're not. Not ordinary. I mean, I hope the standard is better than that.'

'You never knew Gavin.'

'Did he smell?'

Colette hesitated. She wanted to be fair. 'Not more than he could help.'

'He'd take a bath, would he?'

'Oh yes, a shower.'

'And he wouldn't, sort of, undo his clothes and take out private bits of himself in public?'

'No!'

'And if he saw a little girl on the street, he wouldn't turn round and make comments about her? Like, look at it waggle its little arse?'

'You frighten me, Al,' Colette said coldly.

I know, Al thought. Why mention it now?

'You have a very peculiar imagination. How can you think I would marry a man like that?'

'You might not know. Till you'd tied the knot. You might have had a nasty surprise.'

'I wouldn't have been married to that kind of a man. Not for an instant.'

'But he had magazines, did he?'

'I never looked at them.'

'It's on the Internet, these days.'

Colette thought, I should have searched his systems. But those were early days, as far as technology went. People weren't sophisticated, like they are now.

'He used to call hotlines,' she admitted. 'Once I myself, just out of curiosity—'

'Did you? What happened?'

'They kept you hanging on for ages. Just messing you about, basically, while you were running up a bill. I put the phone down. I thought, what will it be? Just some woman pretending to come. Moaning, I suppose.'

'You could do that for yourself,' Al said.

'Precisely.'

'If we moved, we might be able to lose them. I suppose Morris will stick, but I'd like to shake off his friends.'

'Wouldn't they come after us?'

'We'd go somewhere they don't know.'

'Don't they have maps?'

'I don't think they do. I think it's more like . . . they're more like dogs. They have to pick up the scent.'

In the Ladies, she watched her own face in the mirror, as she washed her hands. Colette must be coaxed towards a house move, she must be made to see the sense. Yet she must not be terrified too much. Last night the tape had frightened her, but how could that have been prevented? It was a shock to me too, she said to herself. If Morris has caught up with Aitkenside, can Capstick be far behind? Will he be bringing home MacArthur, and lodging him in the bread bin, or in her dressing-table drawer? Will she sit down to breakfast one day and find Pikey Pete lurking under the lid of the butter dish? Will she get a sudden fright, as Bob Fox taps at the window?

Move on, she thought: it might baffle them for a bit. Even a temporary bewilderment could keep them off your back. It might cause them to disperse, lose each other again in those vast tracts the dead inhabit.

'Oi, oi, oi oi!' Morris called, yelling right in her ear. 'Bob's your uncle!'

'Is he?' she said, surprised. 'Bob Fox? I always wanted a relative.'

'Blimey, Emmie,' Morris said, 'is she simple, or what?'

That night, when they got home Morris crept in with them; the others, his friends, seemed to have melted away, somewhere in Bedfordshire between Junctions 9 and 10. To check for them, she lifted the carpet in the boot of the car, peered into the cold metal well; no one was there, and when she dragged out her case she found it was no heavier than it had been when she packed it. So far so good. To keep them out permanently – that would be another matter. Once inside she was solicitous to Colette, recommending a hot bath and the *Coronation Street* omnibus edition. 'If it's on,' Colette said. All she could summon up was funeral coverage. 'For God's sake. I wish they'd give it a rest. They've buried her now. She's not going to get up again.' She slumped on the sofa with a bowl of breakfast cereal. 'We ought to get a satellite dish.'

'We can when we move.'

'Or cable. Whatever.'

She's resilient, Al thought, as she climbed the stairs: or maybe she's just forgetful? At the services back in Leicestershire, Colette had turned the shade of porridge, when it was broken to her about the menagerie riding in the back seat of the car. But now she was her usual self, carping away, always with some petty grievance. You couldn't say her colour had come back, because she never had any colour; but when she was frightened, Al had noticed, she sucked her lips inwards so that they seemed almost to disappear; at the same time, her eyes seemed to shrink back in her skull, so that you noticed their pink rims even more.

In her own room, Al sank down on to the bed. Hers was the master bedroom; Colette, when she moved in, had squeezed into what even the estate agent, when he'd sold the flat to Al, had the grace to describe as a *small* double. It was a good thing she had few clothes and no possessions; or, to put it as Colette did, a capsule wardrobe and a minimalist philosophy.

Al sighed; she stretched her cramped limbs, checking out her body for spirit aches and pains. Some entity was tweaking her left knee, some desolate soul was trying to hold her hand; not now, kids, she said, give me a break. I need, she thought, to give Colette more of a stake in life. Get her name on the house deeds. Give her more reason to stick around, so she's less inclined to take off in a sulk or on a whim, or under the pressure of unnatural events. For we all have our limits; though she's brave – brave with the true-blue staunchness of those who lack imagination. I could, she thought, go downstairs and tell her face to face how much I appreciate her; I could, as it were, pin a medal on her, 'Order of Diana' (deceased). She levered herself upright. But her resolution failed. No, she thought; as soon as I see her she'll irritate me, sitting sideways with her legs flung over the arm of the chair, swinging her feet in her little beige ankle socks. Why doesn't she get slippers? You can get quite acceptable kinds of slippers these days. Moccasins, something like that. Then there will be a bowl half full of milk, on the floor by her chair, with a few malted flakes bobbing in it. Why does she drop her spoon into the bowl, when she decides she's finished, so that driblets of milk shoot out on to the carpet? And why should such small things work one up to an extreme level of agitation? Before I lived with Colette, she thought, I believed I was easy to live with, I thought I would be happy if people didn't actually vomit on the carpet, or bring home friends who did. I thought it was quite good to have a carpet, even. I thought of myself as quite a placid person. Probably I was mistaken.

She took the tape recorder out of its bag and set it up on her bedside table. She kept the volume low, whizzing the tape backwards to find last night.

MORRIS: Run out for five Woodbine, would you? Thanks, Bob, you're a scholar and a gentleman. (*Eructation.*) Blimey. I should never 'ave 'ad that cheese an' onion pie.

AITKENSIDE: Cheese an' onion? Christ, I 'ad that once, it was at the races, remember that time we went up to Redcar?

MORRIS: Ooh, yer, do I? And Pikey had his motorbike with the sidecar? Redcar, sidecar, we was laughing about that!

AITKENSIDE: Bloody crucified me, that pie. Repeating on me for three bloody weeks.

MORRIS: 'Ere, Dean, they don't make pies like that these days. I remember Pikey Pete, he kept saying, fanks, Donnie, fanks for the memory. Oh, he were a right laugh! 'Ere, Bob, are you going for them fags?

AITKENSIDE: They don't make Woodbine no more.

MORRIS: What, they don't make Woodies? Why not? Why don't they?

AITKENSIDE: And you can't buy five. You've got to buy ten these days.

MORRIS: What, buy ten, and not even Woodies?

BOY'S VOICE: Where've you been, Uncle Morris?

MORRIS: Dead. That's where I bloody been.

BOY'S VOICE: Have we got to stay dead, Uncle Morris?

MORRIS: Well, it's up to you, Dean lad, if you can find some way to bloody recycle yourself you get on and do it, san-fairy-ann, no skin off my blooming nose. If you've got the contacts, you bloody use 'em. I give a hundred pounds, one hundred nicker in notes to a

> bloke I met that said he could get me restarted. I said to him, I don't want borning in bloody wogland, you hear what I'm saying, I don't want to come back as some nig, and he swore he could get me born in Brighton, or Hove which is near as dammit, born in Brighton and free, white and twenty-one. Well, not twenty-one, but nar what I mean. And I thought, not bad, Brighton's near the course, and when I'm a tiddler I'll be getting the sea air and all, grow up strong and healthy, besides I always had mates in Brighton, show me the bloke wiv no mates in Brighton and I'll show you a tosser. Anyway, he took my readies and he scarpered. Left me high and dry, dead.

Alison switched off the tape. It's so humiliating, she thought, so crushing and shameful to have Morris in your life and to have lived with him all these years. She put her arms across her body, rocked herself gently. Brighton, well, naturally. Brighton and Hove. The sea air, the horse racing. If only she'd thought about it earlier . . . that was why he was trying to get inside Mandy, back at the hotel. That was why he kept her up all night, pawing and pulling at her – not because he wanted sex, but because he was plotting to be born, to be carried inside some unknowing hostess . . . the filthy, dirty little sneak. She could imagine him, in Mandy's hotel room, whining, slobbering, abasing himself by crawling across the carpet, slithering towards her on his chin with his pitiful haunches in the air: born me, born me! Dear God, it didn't bear thinking about.

And clearly – at least it was clear to her now – it wouldn't be the first time Morris had tried it on. She well remembered Mandy's pregnancy test, was it last year? She'd been on the phone that very night, I was feeling strange, Al, really queasy, well, I don't know what made me but I went out to the chemist, I tested my wee and the line's gone blue. Al, I blame myself, I must have been extremely careless.

In Mandy's mind the solution was straightforward; she had it done away with. So that was the end of Morris and his hundred pounds. For months afterwards she would say, whenever they met, do you know I'm baffled about that episode, I can't think who or where – I think it must have been when we went to that café-bar in Northampton, somebody must have spiked my drink. They'd blamed Raven – though not to his face; as Mandy said, you didn't want to push it, because if Raven denied it categorically, that would more or less mean it must have been Merlin or Merlyn.

Those speculations were hard enough and distasteful; she admired the way Mandy faced them, the putative fathers, at every psychic fayre, her chin tilted up, her eyes cold and knowing. But she'd be sick to her stomach if she knew what Al was thinking now. I won't tell her, she decided. She's been a good friend to me over the years and she doesn't deserve that. I'll keep Morris under control, somehow, when I'm in her vicinity; God knows how, though. A million pounds wouldn't be enough, it wouldn't be enough of a bribe to make you carry Morris or any of his friends. Imagine your trips to the ante-natal clinic. Imagine what they'd say at your playgroup.

She clicked the tape back on. I have to make myself do it, she thought, I have to listen right through: see if I get any insight, any grip on other furtive schemes that Morris might come up with.

MORRIS: So what ciggies *can* I 'ave?
DEAN: You can have a roll-up, Uncle Morris.
UNKNOWN VOICE: Can we have a bit of respect, please? We're here on a funeral.
DEAN (*timid*): It is all right if I call you Uncle Morris . . . ?

UNKNOWN VOICE #2: . . . this sceptred isle . . . this precious stone set in the silver sea . . .
AITKENSIDE: Oi oi oi oi! It's Wagstaffe!
MORRIS: Mended the bloody hole in your bloody pantaloons, yet, Wagstaffe?
WAGSTAFFE: There's rosemary, that's for remembrance.
Click.

She recognised voices from her childhood; she heard the clink of beer bottles, and the military rattle, as bone clicked into joint. They were reassembling themselves, the old crew: root and branch, arm and leg. Only Wagstaffe seemed baffled to be there; and the unknown person who had called for respect.

She remembered the night, long ago in Aldershot, when the street light shone on her bed. She remembered the afternoon when she had come into the house and seen a man's face looking through the mirror, where her own face ought to be.

She thought, I should phone my mum. If they're breaking through like this, she ought to be tipped off. At her age, a shock could kill her.

She had to scrabble through an old address book to find Emmie's number in Bracknell. A man answered. 'Who is that?' she asked, and he said, 'Who's asking?'

'Don't come that with me, matey,' she said, in Aitkenside's voice.

The man dropped the receiver.

She waited. A static crackle filled her ear. A moment later her mother spoke. 'Who's that?'

'It's me. Alison.' She added, she couldn't think why, 'It's me, your little girl.'

'What do you want?' her mother said. 'Bothering me, after all this time.'

'Who's that you've got there, in your house?'

'Nobody,' her mother said.

'I thought I knew his voice. Is it Keith Capstick? Is it Bob Fox?'

'What are you talking about? I don't know what somebody's been telling you. There's some filthy tongues about, you should know better. You'd think they'd mind their own bloody business.'

'I only want to know who answered the phone.'

'I answered it. God Almighty, Alison, you always were a bit soft.'

'A man answered.'

'What man?'

'Mum, don't encourage them. If they come round you don't let them in.'

'Who?'

'MacArthur. Aitkenside. That old crowd.'

'Must be dead, I should think,' her mother said. 'I haven't heard them names in years. Bloody Bill Wagstaffe, weren't he a friend of theirs? That Morris, and all. And there was that gypsy fella, dealt in horses, what did they call him? Yes, I reckon they must all be dead by now. I wouldn't mind it if they did come round. They was a laugh.'

'Mum, don't let them in. If they come knocking, don't answer.'

'Aitkenside, he was a GBH driver.'

'HGV.'

'That's the one. Always got a wodge in his wallet. Used to do favours, you know. Drop off loads, this and that, he'd say one stiff more or less it don't hardly make no difference to the weight. This gypsy fella, Pete they called him, now he had a trailer.'

'Mum, if they turn up, any of them, you let me know. You've got my number.'

'I might have it written down somewhere.'

'I'll give it you again.'

She did so. Emmie waited till she finished and said, 'I haven't got a pencil.'

Al sighed. 'You go and get one.'

She heard the receiver drop. A buzzing filled the line; like flies around a dustbin. When Emmie returned she said, 'Found up my eyebrow pencil. That was a good idea, wasn't it?'

She repeated the number.

Emmie said, 'Wagstaffe always had a pen. You could rely on him for that.'

'Have you got it now?'

'No.'

'Why not, Mum?'

'I haven't got a paper.'

'Haven't you got anything you can write on? You must have a writing pad.'

'Oh, la-di-da.'

'Go and get a bit of toilet paper.'

'All right. Don't get shirty.'

She could hear Emmie singing, as she moved away, 'I wish I was in Dixie, hooray, hooray . . .'; then, again, the buzzing occupied the line. She thought, the men came into the bedroom and looked down at me as I lay in my little bed. They took me out of the house by night, into the thick belt of birch trees and dead bracken beyond the pony field. There on the ground they operated on me, took out my will and put in their own.

'Hello?' Emmie said. 'That you, Al? I got the toilet paper, you can tell me again now. Oops, hang on, me pencil's rolled off.' There was a grunt of effort.

Alison was almost sure she could hear a man, complaining in the background.

'OK, I got it now. Fire away.'

Once again, she gave her number. She felt exhausted.

'Now tell me again,' her mother said. 'What have I got to ring you, when and if what?'

'If any of them come round. Any of that old crowd.'

'Oh yes. Aitkenside. Well, I should hear 'is lorry, I should think.'

'That's right. But he might not be driving a lorry any more.'

'What's happened to it?'

'I don't know. I'm just saying, he might not. He might just turn up. If anybody comes knocking at your window—'

'Bob Fox, he always used to knock on the window. Come around the back and knock on the window and give me a fright.' Emmie laughed. '"Caught you that time," he'd say.'

'Yes, so . . . you ring me.'

'Keith Capstick,' her mother said. 'He were another. Keef, you used to call him, couldn't say your tee-haitchs, you was a stupid little bugger. Keef Catsick. Course, you didn't know any better. Oh, it used to make him mad, though. Keef Catsick. He caught you many a slap.'

'Did he?'

'He used to say, I'll skin the hide off her, I'll knock her to kingdom come. Course, if it weren't for Keith, that dog would have had your throat out. What did you want to let him in for?'

'I don't know. I don't remember, now. I expect I wanted a pet.'

'Pet? They weren't pets. Fighting dogs, them. Not as if you hadn't been told. Not as if you hadn't been told a dozen times and Keith give you the back of his hand to drive it through your skull. Not that he did succeeded, did he? What did you want to open the back door for? You was all over Keith after that, after he pulled the dog off you. Couldn't make enough of him. Used to call him Daddy.'

'Yes, I remember.'

'He said, that's worse than Catsick, her calling me Daddy, I don't want to be her daddy, I'll throttle the little fucker if she don't leave off.' Emmie chuckled. 'He would too. He'd throttled a few, in his time, Keith.'

There was a pause.

Al put her hand to her throat. She spoke. 'I see. And you'd like to meet up with Keith again, would you? A laugh, was he? Always got a wodge in his wallet?'

'No, that was Aitkenside,' her mother said. 'God help you, girl, you never could keep anything straight in your head. I don't know if I'd recognise Keith if he come round here today. Not after that fight he had, he was that mangled I don't know if I'd know him. I remember that fight, I see it as if it were yesterday – old Mac with the patch over his eye socket, and me embarrassed, not knowing where to look. We didn't know where to put our loyalties, you see? Not in this house we didn't. Morris said he was putting a fiver on Keith, he said I'll back a man with no balls over a man with one eye. He had a fiver on Keith, oh, he was mad with him, the way he went down. I remember they said, after, that MacArthur must have had a blade in his fist. Still, you'd know, wouldn't you? You'd know about blades, you little madam. By Christ, did I wallop you, when I found you with those wotsits in your pocket.'

Al said, 'I want to stop you, Mum.'

'What?'

'I want to stop you and rewind you.'

She thought, they took out my will and they paid my mother in notes for the privilege. She took the money and she put it in that old cracked vase that she used to keep on the top shelf of the cupboard to the left of the chimney breast.

Her mum said, 'Al, you still there? I was thinking, you never do know, Keith might have got his face fixed up. They can do wonders these days, can't they? He might have got his appearance changed. Funny, that. He could be living round the corner. And we'd never know.'

Another pause. 'Alison?'

'Yes . . . Are you still taking pills, Mum?'

'On and off.'

'You see your doctor?'

'Every week.'

'You been in the hospital at all?'

'They closed it.'

'You all right for money?'

'I get by.'

What else to say? Nothing, really. Emmie said, 'I miss Aldershot. I wish I'd never moved here. There's nobody here worth talking to. They're a miserable lot. Never had a laugh since I moved.'

'Maybe you should get out more.'

'Maybe I should. Nobody to go with, that's the trouble. Still, they say there's no going back in life.' After a longer pause, just as Al was about to say goodbye, her mother asked, 'How are you then? Busy?'

'Yes. Busy week.'

'Would be. With the princess. Shame, innit? I always think we had a lot in common, me and her. All these blokes, and then you get the rough end of it. Do you reckon she'd have been all right with Dido?'

'I don't know. I haven't an idea.'

'Never one for the boys, were you? I reckon you got put off it.'

'Do you? How?'

'Oh, you know.'

'No, I don't,' she was starting to say, 'I don't know, but I very much want to know, I find this enlightening, you've told me quite a few things I—' But Emmie said, 'Got to go. The gas is running out,' and put the phone down.

Al dropped the handset on the duvet cover. She lowered her head to her knees. Pulses beat; in her neck, in her temples, at the end of her fingers. She felt a pricking in the palms of her hands. Galloping high blood pressure, she thought. Too much pizza. She felt a low, seeping fury, as if something inside her had broken and was leaking black blood into her mouth.

I need to be with Colette, she thought. I need her for protection. I need to sit with her and watch the TV, whatever she's watching, whatever she's watching will be all right. I want to be normal. I want to be normal for half an hour, just enjoying the funeral highlights; before Morris starts up again.

She opened the bedroom door and stepped out into the small square hall. The sitting-room door was closed but raucous laughter was rocking the room where Colette, she knew, kicked up her heels in her little socks. To avoid hearing the tape, Colette had turned the TV volume up. That was natural, very natural. She thought of tapping on the door. But no, no, let her enjoy. She turned away. At once Diana manifested: a blink in the hall mirror, a twinkle. Within a moment she had become a definite pinkish glow.

She was wearing her wedding dress, and it hung on her now; she was gaunt, and it looked crumpled and worn, as if dragged through the halls of the hereafter, where the housekeeping, understandably, is never of the best. She had pinned some of her press cuttings to her skirts; they lifted, in some other-worldly breeze, and flapped. She consulted them, lifting her skirts and peering; but, in Alison's opinion, her eyes seemed to cross.

'Give my love to my boys,' Diana said. 'My boys, I'm sure you know who I mean.'

Al wouldn't prompt her: you must never, in that fashion,

give way to the dead. They will tease you and urge you, they will suggest and flatter; you mustn't take their bait. If they want to speak, let them speak for themselves.

Diana stamped her foot. 'You do know their names,' she accused. 'You oiky little greasespot, you're just being hideous. Oh, fuckerama! Whatever are they called?'

It takes them that way, sometimes, the people who have passed: memory lapses, an early detachment. It's a mercy, really. It's wrong to call them back, after they want to go. They're not like Morris and Co. – fighting to get back, playing tricks and scheming to get reborn: leaning on the doorbell, knocking at the window, crawling inside your lungs and billowing out on your breath.

Diana dropped her eyes. They rolled, under her blue lids. Her painted lips fumbled for names. 'It's on the tip of my tongue,' she said. 'Anyway, whatever. You tell them, because you know. Give my love to . . . Kingy. And the other kid. Kingy and Thingy.' There was a sickly glow behind her now, like the glow from a fire in a chemical factory. She's going, Al thought, she's melting away to nothing, to poisoned ash in the wind. 'So,' the princess said, 'my love to them, my love to you, my good woman. And my love to him – to – wait a minute.' She picked up her skirts, and puzzled over a fan of the press cuttings, whipping them aside in her search for the name she wanted. 'So many words,' she moaned, then giggled. The hem of her wedding gown slipped from her fingers. 'No use, lost it. Love to all of you! Why don't you just bog off now and let me get some privacy.'

The princess faded. Al implored her silently, Di, don't go. The room was cold. With a click, the tape switched itself on.

WAGSTAFFE: This sceptred isle . . .
MORRIS: My sceptred—

Colette yelled, 'Al, are you playing that tape again?'

'Not on purpose, it just switched itself—'

'—because I don't think I can face it.'

'You don't want it for the book?'

'God, no. We can't put that stuff in the book!'

'So what shall I do with it?'

WAGSTAFFE: This other Eden—
MORRIS: My sceptred arse.

Colette called, 'Wipe it.'

SEVEN

At Admiral Drive there were these house types: the Collingwood, the Frobisher, the Beatty, the Mountbatten, the Rodney and the Hawkyns. Colette, initially, was unimpressed. The site was ragged grassland, half of it turned over already by the diggers.

'Why is it called Admiral Drive?'

The woman in the sales caravan said, 'We theme all our developments nautically, you know?'

She wore a name badge and a bright orange skirt and jersey, like a supermarket cashier. 'Awful uniform,' Colette said. 'Wouldn't navy be more appropriate?'

'We'll be glad of it,' the woman said, 'once the building starts. Orange stands out against the landscape. We'll have to wear helmets when we go out there. It'll be mud up to your knees. Like a battlefield.' One of nature's saleswomen, Colette thought. 'What I'm saying is,' the woman added, 'it's really much better to buy off-plan.'

Colette picked up a fistful of brochures from the desk, banged them end on to tidy them and dropped them into her bag. 'Can I help you there at all?' the woman said. She looked aggrieved at the loss of her leaflets. 'How many beds were you looking at?'

'I don't know. Three?'

'Here you are then. The Beatty?'

Colette was puzzled by the woman, who turned most of her statements into questions. It must be what they do in Surrey, she decided; they must have had it twinned with Australia.

She opened the brochure for the Beatty and took it to the light.

'Are these the actual room sizes, Suzi?'

'Oh no. It's for information purposes only?'

'So it's information, but it's wrong?'

'It's guidelines?'

'So the rooms could be bigger than this?'

'Probably not.'

'But they could be smaller?'

'Some contraction could occur.'

'We aren't midgets, you know? What are the four-beds like? We could merge the rooms, or something.'

'At this stage, subject to building regulations, some redesign is possible?' Suzi said. 'Extra costs may be incurred?'

'You'd charge for walls you didn't put up?'

'Any alteration to the basic plan may be subject to extra costs,' Suzi said, 'but I don't say it will. Might you be interested in the Frobisher at all? It comes with a spacious utility area?'

'Wait a minute,' Colette said. 'Wait a minute, I'll get my friend.' She skipped out of the sales caravan and across the hardstanding to where the car was parked. The builders had put up a flagpole to dignify their sales area, and Alison was watching their emblem sailing in the wind. Colette swung open the car door. 'Al, you'd better come in. The Frobisher comes with a spacious utility area. So I'm told.'

Al released her seat belt and stepped out. Her knees were stiff after the short drive down into Surrey. Colette had said, new-built appeals, but I need time to do my research. You have to go back beyond paint finishes and colour schemes, back beyond bricks and mortar, look at the ground we'll be standing on. It isn't just a place to live. It's an investment. We need to maximise the profit. We need to think long term. After all, she said, you appear to have no pension plans in place.

'Don't be silly,' Al had said. 'How could I retire?'

Now she stood looking about her. She sensed the underscape, shuddering as it waited to be ripped. Builders' machines stood ready, their maws crusted with soil, waiting for Monday morning. Violence hung in the air, like the smell of explosive. Birds had flown. Foxes had abandoned their lairs. The bones of mice and voles were mulched into mud, and she sensed the minute snapping of frail necks and the grinding into paste of muscle and fur. Through the soles of her shoes she felt gashed worms turning, twisting and repairing themselves. She looked up, to the grassland that remained. The site was framed by a belt of conifers, like a baffle wall; you could not guess what lay beyond it. In the middle distance was a belt of young birch trees. She could see a ditch running with water. Towards the main road to Guildford, she could see a hedge, a miscarried foetus dug in beneath it. She could see ghost horses, huddled in the shadow of a wall. It was an indifferent place; no better nor worse than most others.

Colette said briskly, 'Is something upsetting you?'

'No.'

'Was there something here before?'

'Nothing. Just the country.'

'Come in the caravan. Talk to Suzi.'

Al caught the scent of standing water; the ditch, a pond,

a sludgy canal, widening into a basin which reflected faces looking down at her from the sky: sneering. The dead don't ascend, or descend, so properly speaking they can neither leer down at you from the treetops nor grumble and toss beneath your feet; but they can give the appearance of it, if it takes them that way.

She followed Colette and heaved herself into the caravan; the metal steps were flimsy; each tread, under her weight, bowed a little and came snapping back.

'This is my friend,' Colette said.

'Oh, hello?' Suzi said. She looked as if she meant to say, we discourage friends. For a few minutes she left them alone. She took out a duster and passed it over her model drawer fronts and cupboard doors, clicking them backwards and forwards on their swivel-jointed display stand with a sound like the gnashing of giant dentures. She blew some dust off her carpet samples, and found a spot of something disagreeable on her stack of vinyl tiles, which she worked at by spitting on it and then scrubbing at it with her fingernail.

'You could offer us a coffee?' Colette said. 'We're not time-wasters.'

'Some people make a hobby of it. Driving around the new developments on a Sunday afternoon, comparing prices? With their friends?'

I never got this far with Gavin, Colette thought. She tried to imagine the life they might have had, if they'd been planning to have a family. She would have said to him, what kitchen do you want? And he'd have said, wot's the choice? And when she pointed to the model drawer fronts and cupboards, he'd have said, are they kitchens? And when she had said yes, he'd have said, wotever.

But here was Alison, studying the details of the Frobisher; behaving just like a normal purchaser. Suzi had put her duster away and, her back still turned, was edging towards the counter by degrees. Al looked up. 'It's tiny, Col. You can't do anything with these rooms, they're just dog kennels.' She handed the leaflet back to the woman. 'No thank you,' she said. 'Have you got anything bigger?' She rolled her eyes and said to Colette, 'Story of my life, eh?'

Suzi enquired, 'Which lady is the purchaser?'

'We are both the purchaser.'

Suzi turned away and snatched up the coffee pot from its hotplate. 'Coffee? Milk and sugar?' She turned, the pot held defensively before her, and gave them a wide smile. 'Certainly,' she said. 'Oh, yes, of course. We don't discriminate. Far from it. Far on the other side. We've been away for a training day. We are enthused to play our part to enhance the diversity of the community. The very special kind of community that's created wherever you find a Galleon Home?'

Colette said, 'What do you mean, far on the other side?'

'I mean, no discrimination at all?'

Al said, 'No sugar, thanks.'

'But you don't get a bonus? I mean, if we were lesbians? Which by the way we aren't? Would you get extra commission?'

Just then a normal couple came up the steps. 'Hello?' Suzi called to them, with a warmth that almost scared them down again. 'Coffee?' she sang. A few drips from the poised pot leaked on to the plans of the Frobisher, and widened like a fresh faecal stain.

Alison turned away. Her cheeks were plum-coloured. Colette followed her. 'Ignore her. This is Surrey. They don't get many gays and they're easily upset.'

She thought, if I *were* a lesbian, I hope I'd get a woman who wasn't so bulky.

'Could we come back later?' Alison asked. 'When there are houses here?

Suzi said coldly, 'Half of these plots are under offer.'

Colette took her back to the car and laid the facts before her. This is prime building land, she said. She consulted the literature and read it out. Convenient transport links and first-class health and leisure facilities.

'But there's aren't,' Al said. 'It's a field. There's nothing here. No facilities of any sort.'

'You have to imagine them.'

'It's not even on a map, is it?'

'They'll redraw the map, in time.'

She touched Colette's arm, conciliatory. 'No, what I mean is, I like it. I'd like to live nowhere. How long would it be before we could move in?'

'About nine months, I should think.'

Alison was silent. She had given Colette a free hand in the choice of site. Just nowhere near my old house, she had said. Nowhere near Aldershot. Nowhere near a racecourse, a dog track, an army camp, a dockyard, a lorry park nor a clinic for special diseases. Nowhere near a sidings or a depot, a customs shed or a warehouse; not near an outdoor market nor an indoor market nor a sweatshop nor a body shop nor a bookies. Colette had said, I thought you might have a psychic way of choosing – for instance, you'd get the map and swing a pendulum over it. God, no, Alison said, if I did that we'd probably end up in the sea.

'Nine months,' she said. 'I was hoping to do it quicker.'

She had thought of Dean and Aitkenside and whoever, wondered what would happen if Morris brought them home and they got dug in at Wexham. She imagined them hanging around the communal grounds and making their presence felt: tipping over the bins and scratching the residents' cars. Her neighbours didn't know the nature of her trade; she had been able to keep it from them. But she imagined them talking behind her back. She imagined the residents' meeting, which they held every six months. It was at best a rancorous affair: who moves furniture late at night, how did the stair carpet get frayed? She imagined them muttering, talking about her, levelling spiteful but unspecific accusations. Then she would be tempted to apologise; worse, tempted to try to explain.

'Well, there it is,' Colette signed. 'If you want new-build, I don't think we can do it any quicker. Not unless we buy something that nobody else wants.'

Alison swivelled in her seat. 'We could do that, couldn't we? We don't have to want what everybody else wants?'

'Fine. If you're prepared to settle for some peculiar little house next to a rubbish dump. Or a plot next to a main road, with all the traffic noise day and night.'

'No, we wouldn't want that.'

'Alison, should we give it up for today? You're just not in the mood, are you? It's like dealing with a five-year-old.'

'Sorry. It's Morris.'

'Tell him to go to the pub.'

'I have. But he says there isn't a pub. He keeps going on about his mates. I think he's met up with another one. I can't get the name. Oh, wait. Hush, Col, he's coming through now.'

Morris came through, loud, clear, indignant. 'What, are we going to come and live in the middle of a field? I'm not living here.'

Al said, 'Wait. He just said something interesting.' She paused, her hand held above her abdomen, as if she were tuning him in. 'All right,' she said, 'if you're going to be like that, you know what you can do. See if you can find a better home to go to. Not you, Col, I'm talking to Morris. What makes you think I want you moving in anyway? I don't need you. I've had it up to here! Bugger off!'

She shouted the last phrase, staring through the windscreen. Colette said, 'Shh! Keep it down!' She checked over her shoulder that no one was watching them.

Al smiled. 'I'll tell you what, Colette, I'll tell you what we should do. Go back in there, and tell that woman to put us down for the biggest house she's got.'

Colette placed a small holding deposit and they returned two days later. Suzi was on duty, but it was a weekday morning and the caravan was empty.

'Hello again. So you're not working ladies?' Suzi enquired. Her eyes skittered over them, sharp as scissors.

'Self-employed,' Colette said.

'Oh, I see. Both of you?'

'Yes, is that a problem?'

Suzi took a deep breath. Once again a smile spread over her face. 'No problem at all? But you will be wanting our package of personally tailored mortgage advice and assistance?'

'No thank you.'

Suzi spread out the site map. 'The Collingwood,' she said, 'is very unique, on this site we shall only be erecting three. Being exclusive, it is in a preferential situation, here on top of the hill? We don't have a computer-generated image as of this moment, because we're waiting for the computer to generate it. But if you can imagine the Rodney? With an extra bedroom en suite?'

'But what will it look like on the outside?'

'If you'll excuse me?' Suzi got on the phone. 'Those two ladies?' she said. 'That I mentioned? Yes, those ones. Wanting to know about the Collingwood, the exterior elevations? Like the Rodney? Different gob-ons? Yes. Mmm. Just ordinary, really. No, not to look at them. Bye-eee.' She turned back to Colette. 'Now, if you can imagine?' She passed her forefinger over the sales leaflet. 'For the Rodney you have this band of decorative plasterwork with the nautical knots motif, but with the Collingwood you will get extra portholes?'

'Instead of windows?'

'Oh no, they will just be decorative.'

'They won't open?'

'I'll check that for you, shall I?' She picked up the phone again. 'Hi there! Yes, fine. My ladies – yes, those ones – want to know, do the portholes open? That's on the Collingwood?'

The answer took some time to find. A voice in Al's ear said, did you know Capstick was at sea? He was in the merchant navy before he got taken on as a bouncer.

'Colette,' she said. She put her hand on Colette's hand. 'I think Morris has met Keef Catsick.'

'No?' Suzi said. 'No! Really? You too? In Dorking? Well, there must be a plague of them. What can you do? Live and let live, that's what I say. Yes. Will do. Bye-ee.'

She clicked the phone down and turned away politely, believing she was witnessing a moment of lesbian intimacy.

Colette said, 'Keith who?'

Alison took her hand away. 'No, it's all right. It's nothing.' Her knuckles looked skinned and darkly bruised. The lucky opals had congealed in their settings, dull and matt like healing scabs.

Al thought that you couldn't bargain with a housebuilder, but Colette showed her that you can. Even when they had agreed a basic price, three thousand below Suzi's target, she kept on pushing, pushing, pushing, until Suzi felt sick and hot and she began to capitulate to Colette's demands: for Colette made it clear that until she was dealt with, and dealt with in a way satisfactory to herself, she would keep away any other potential customers: which she did, by darting her head at them as they climbed the steps and fixing them with her pale glare; by snapping 'Do you mind, Suzi is busy with me?' When Suzi's phone rang, Colette picked it up and said, 'Yes? No, she can't. Call back.' When Suzi yearned after lost prospects as they stumbled down the steps, following them with her eyes, Colette zipped her bag, stood up and said, 'I could come back when you're more fully staffed – say next Saturday afternoon?' Suzi grew frantic then, as she saw her commission seeping away. She became accommodating and flexible. When Suzi agreed to upgrade to a power-shower en suite to bed two, Colette signed up for fitted wardrobes. When Colette hesitated over a double oven, Suzi offered to make it a multifunction model including microwave. When Colette – after prolonged deliberation – gave the nod to brass switch-plates throughout, Suzi was so relieved she threw in a carriage lamp free. And when Colette – after stabbing at her calculator buttons and gnawing her lip – opted for wood-style flooring to kitchen and utility, Suzi, sweating inside her orange skin, agreed to turf the back garden at Galleon's expense.

Meanwhile, Alison had plummeted down on the click-'n'fix korner-group seating. I can afford it, she thought, I can probably afford it. Business was booming, thanks in part to Colette's efficiency and bright ideas. There was no shortage of clients; and it was just as Colette said, one must invest, one must invest against leaner times. Morris sat in the corner, picking at the carpet tiles, trying to lift one. He looked like a toddler, absorbed, his short legs and pot belly thrust out, his tongue between his teeth.

She watched Colette negotiating, small rigid hand chopping the air. At last she got the nod, and limped out to the car after her. Colette jumped into the driving seat, whipped out her calculator again, and held it up so that Al could see the display.

Al turned away. 'Tell me in words,' she said. Morris leaned forward and poked her in the shoulder. Here's the lads coming, he shouted. Here's the cheeky chappies. Knew you'd find me, knew you would, that's the spirit.

'You could take more of an interest,' Colette snapped. 'I've probably saved us ten k.'

'I know. I just can't read the panel. The light's in my eyes.'

'Plain ceilings or Artex?' Colette said. Her voice rose to a squeak, imitating Suzi. 'They think you'll give them money to stop them making plaster swirls.'

'I expect it's harder to make plaster smooth.'

'That's what *she* said! I said, smooth should be standard! Silly bitch. I wouldn't pay her in washers.'

Aitkenside said, we can't live here. There's no bleeding accommodation.

Dean said, Morris, are we going camping? I went camping once.

Morris said, how was it, mate?

Dean said, it were crap.

Aitkenside said, call it a porthole and it don't bleeding open? Won't do for Keef, you know, it won't do for Keef.

'Brilliant,' Al said. 'Couldn't be better. What won't do for Keith will do just fine for me.' She put out her hand and squeezed Colette's cold bony fingers.

That summer, the birch trees were cut down and the last birds flew away. Their song was replaced by the roaring of road drills, the beeping of the JCBs backing up, the cursing of hod carriers and the cries of the wounded, and scrubland gave way to a gashed landscape of trenches and moats, of mud chutes and standing pools of yellow water; which within a year, in its turn, gave way to the violent emerald of new turf, the Sunday-morning roar of mowers and strimmers, the tinkling of the ice-cream vans, the trundling of gas barbecues over paving and the stench of searing meat.

The flat in Wexham had sold to the first people who saw

it. Alison wondered, will they sense something – Morris glugging inside the hot-water tank, or murmuring in the drains? But they seemed delighted, and offered the full asking price.

'It seems so unfair,' Colette said. 'When our flat in Whitton wouldn't sell. Not even when we dropped the price.'

She and Gavin had sacked Sidgewick's, tried another agent; still no takers. Eventually, they had agreed Gavin should stay there, and buy her out by instalments. 'We have hopes the arrangement will be persuasive to Mrs Waynflete,' his solicitor had written, 'as we understand she is now living with a partner.' Colette had scrawled over the letter, 'Not *that* sort of partner!!!' It was just for her own satisfaction that she wrote it; it was no business of Gavin's, she thought, what kind of partnership she was in now.

On the day they moved from Wexham, Morris was fuming and snarled in a corner. 'How can I move,' he said, 'when I have given out this as my address? How will Nick find me, how will my old mates know where to come?' When the men came to take the pine dresser away, he lay on top of it to make it heavy. He infiltrated Al's mattress and infused his spirit sulks among the fibres, so that it bucked and rippled in the men's hands, and they almost dropped it in alarm. When the men slammed the tailgate and vaulted into the driver's cab, they found their whole windscreen had been spattered with something green, viscid and dripping. 'What kind of pigeons do you have around here?' they said. 'Vultures?'

As the Collingwood was Galleon's top-of-the-range model, it had more gob-ons than any other house type on the development, more twiddles and teases, more gables and spindles; but most of them, Colette predicted, would fall off within the first six months. Down the hill they were still building, and yellow machines picked and pecked at the soil, their stiff bending necks strangely articulated, like the necks of prototype dinosaurs. Trucks jolted up with glue-on timbers of plastic oak, bound together in bundles like kindling. Swearing men in woolly hats unloaded paper-thin panels of false brickwork, which they pinned to the raw building blocks; they disembarked stick-on anchor motifs, and panels of faux pargeting with dolphin and mermaid designs. The beeping, roaring and drilling began promptly at seven, each morning. Inside the house there were a few mistakes, like a couple of the internal doors being hung the wrong way round, and the Adam-style fireplace being off-centre. Nothing, Al said, that really affected your quality of life. Colette wanted to keep rowing with the builders till she got compensation, but Al said, let it go, what does it matter, just close the door on it. Colette said, I would but the frame's warped.

The day their kitchen ceiling fell in, she strode off to the sales caravan, where Suzi was still selling off the last remaining units. She made a scene; punters fled back to their cars, thinking they'd had a lucky escape. But when she left Suzi and began splashing uphill, picking her way between stacked paving slabs and lengths of piping, she found that she was shaking. The Collingwood stood at the top of a rise; its portholes stared out over the neighbours, like blind eyes.

Is this my life now? she thought. How will I ever meet a man? At Wexham there were one or two young bachelors she used to glimpse down by the bins. One had never met her eye and only grunted when she greeted him. The other was Gavin to the life and went about swinging his car keys around his forefinger; the sight of him had almost made her nostalgic. But the men who had moved into Admiral Drive were married with two kids. They were computer programmers, systems analysts. They drove people carriers like square little houses on wheels. They wore jackets with flaps and zips that their wives chose for them from mail-order catalogues. Already the postman could be seen, ploughing across the furrows carrying flat boxes containing these jackets, and splattered white vans bounced over the ruts, delivering gobbons for their home computers. At weekends they were outside, wearing their jackets, constructing playhouses and climbing frames of primary-coloured plastic. They were hardly men at all, not men as Colette knew them; they were dutiful emasculates, squat and waddling under their burden of mortgage debt, and she despised them with an impartial, all-embracing spite. Sometimes she stood at her bedroom window, as the men drove away in the mornings, each edging his square-nosed vehicle cautiously into the muddy track; she watched them and hoped they got into a pile-up on the M3, each folding neatly, fatally, into the back of the vehicle in front. She wanted to see their widows sitting in the road, daubing themselves with mud, wailing.

The Collingwood still smelled of paint. As she let herself in at the front door, kicking off her shoes, it caught in her throat and mingled with the taste of salt and phlegm. She went upstairs to her own room – bed two, 15′ x 14′, with en suite shower – and slammed the door, and sat down on the bed. Her little shoulders shook, she pressed her knees together; she clenched her fists and pressed them into her skull. She cried quite loudly, thinking that Al might hear. If Al opened the bedroom door she would throw something at her, she decided – not anything like a bottle, something like a cushion – but there wasn't a cushion. I could throw a pillow, she thought, but you can't throw a pillow hard. I could throw a book, but there isn't a book. She looked around her, dazed, frustrated, eyes filmed and brimming, looking for something to throw.

But it was a useless effort. Al wasn't coming, not to comfort her: nor for any other purpose. She was, Colette knew, selectively deaf. She listened into spirits and to the voice of her own self-pity, carrying messages to her from her childhood. She listened to her clients, as much as was needful to get money out of them. But she didn't listen to her closest associate and personal assistant, the one who got up with her when she had nightmares, the friend who boiled the kettle in the wan dawn: oh no. She had no time for the person who had taken her at her word and given up her career in event management, no time for the one who drove her up and down the country without a word of complaint and carried her heavy suitcase when the bloody wheels fell off. Oh no. Who carried her case full of her huge fat clothes – even though she had a bad back.

Colette cried until two red tracks were scored into her cheeks, and she got hiccups. She began to feel ashamed. Every lurch of her diaphragm added to her indignity. She was afraid that Alison, after her deafness, might now choose to hear.

Downstairs, Al had her tarot pack fanned out before her. The cards were face down, and when Colette appeared in the doorway she was idly sliding them in a rightward direction, over the pristine surface of their new dining table.

'What are you doing? You're cheating.'

'Mm? It's not a game.'

'But you're fixing it, you're shoving them back into the pack! With your finger! You are!'

'It's called Washing the Cards,' Al said. 'Have you been crying?'

Colette sat down in front of her. 'Do me a reading.'

'Oh, you have been crying. You have *so*.'

Colette said nothing.

'What can I do to help?'

'I'd rather not talk about it.'

'So I should make general conversation?'

'If you like.'

'I can't. You start.'

'Did you have any more thoughts about the garden?'

'Yes. I like it as it is.'

'What, just turf?'

'For the moment.'

'I thought we could have a pond.'

'No, the children. The neighbours' children.'

'What about them?'

'Cut the pack.'

Colette did it.

'Children can drown in two inches of water.'

'Aren't they ingenious?'

'Cut again. Left hand.'

'I could get some quotes for landscaping.'

'Don't you like grass?'

'It needs cutting.'

'Can't you do it?'

'Not with my back.'

'Your back? You never mentioned it.'

'You never gave me the chance.'

'Cut again. Left hand, Colette, left hand. Well, I can't do it. I've got a bad back too.'

'Really? When did that originate?'

'When I was a child.'

I was dragged, Alison thought, over the rough ground.

'I'd have thought it would have been better.'

'Why?'

'I thought time was a great healer.'

'Not of backs.'

Colette's hand hovered. 'Choose one,' Al said. 'One hand of seven. Seven cards. Hand them to me.' She laid down the cards. 'And your back, Colette?'

'What?'

'The problem. Where it began?'

'Brussels.'

'Really?'

'I was carrying fold-up tables.'

'That's a pity.'

'Why?'

'You've spoiled my mental picture. I thought that perhaps Gavin had put you in some unorthodox sexual position.'

'How could you have a picture? You don't know Gavin.'

'I wasn't picturing his face.' Alison began to turn the cards. The lucky opals were flashing their green glints. Alison said, 'The Chariot, reversed.'

'So what do you want me to do? About the garden?'

'Nine of swords. Oh dear.'

'We could take it in turns to mow it.'

'I've never worked a mower.'

'Anyway, with your weight. You might have a stroke.'

'Wheel of Fortune, reversed.'

'When you first met me, in Windsor, you said I was going to meet a man. Through work, you said.'

'I don't think I committed to a time scheme, did I?'

'But how can I meet a man through work? I don't have any work except yours. I'm not going out with Raven, or one of those freaks.'

l fluttered her hand over the cards. 'This is heavy on the major arcana, as you see. The Chariot, reversed, I'm not sure I like to think of wheels turning backwards . . . Did you send Gavin a change-of-address card?'

'Yes.'

'Why?'

'As a precaution.'

'Sorry?'

'Something might come for me. For forwarding. A letter. A package.'

'A package? What would be in it?'

Al heard tapping, tapping, at the sliding glass doors of the patio. Fear jolted through her; she thought, Bob Fox. But it was only Morris, trapped in the garden; beyond the glass, she could see his mouth moving. She lowered her eyes, turned a card. 'The Hermit reversed.'

'Bugger,' Colette said. 'I think you were reversing them on purpose, when you were messing about. *Washing* them.'

'What a strange hand! All those swords, blades.' Al looked up. 'Unless it's just about the lawnmower. That would make some sense, wouldn't it?'

'No use asking me. You're the expert.'

'Colette . . . Col . . . don't cry now.'

Colette put her elbows on the table, her head on her hands, and howled away. 'I ask you to do a reading for me and it's about bloody garden machinery. I don't think you have any consideration for me at all. Day in, day out, I am doing your VAT. We never go anywhere. We never do anything nice. I don't think you have any respect for my professional skills whatsoever, and all I have to listen to is you rabbiting on to dead people I can't see.'

Alison said gently, 'I'm sorry if it seems as if I don't appreciate you. I do remember, I know what my life was like when I was alone. I do remember and I value everything you do.'

'Oh, stop it. *Burbling* like that. Being professional.'

'I'm trying to be nice. I'm just trying—'

'That's what I mean. Being nice. Being professional. It's all the same to you. You're the most insincere person I know. It's no use pretending to me. I'm too close. I know what goes on. You're rotten. You're a horrible person. You're not even normal.'

There was a silence. Alison picked up the cards, dabbing each one with a damp fingertip. After a time she said, 'I don't expect you to mow the lawn.'

Silence.

'Honest, Col, I don't.'

Silence.

'Can I be professional for a moment?'

Silence.

'The Hermit, reversed, suggests that your energy could be put to better use.'

Colette sniffed. 'So what shall we do?'

'You could ring up a gardening service. Get a quote. For, let's say, a fortnightly cut through the summer.' She added, smiling, 'I expect they'd send a man.'

A thought about the garden had gone through her head: it will be nice for the dogs. Her smile faded. She pushed the thought violently away, seeing in her mind the waste ground behind her mother's house at Aldershot.

Colette had taken on the task of contacting Al's regular clients, to let them know about the house-move. She made a pretty lilac-coloured card, with the new details, which they handed out to contacts at their next big psychic fayre. In return they got cards back. 'You'll want a bit of Goddess Power, I expect,' said a nice woman in a ragged pullover, as she unloaded her kit from her beat-up old van. 'You'll want to come into alignment with the Path.' When they saw her next she was wearing a hairpiece and a push-up bra, charging forty pounds and calling herself Siobhan, Palms and Clairvoyance.

'Shall I come up and do your feng shui?' Mandy Coughlan asked. 'It's nice that you're nearer to Hove.'

Cara rolled her eyes. 'You're not still offering feng shui? And are you getting any uptake? I'm training as a vastu consultant. It's five thousand years old. This demon falls to earth, right? And you have to see which way his head comes down and where his feet are pointing. Then you can draw a mandala. Then you know which way the house should go.'

'It's a bit late,' Al said. 'It's finished and we've moved in.'

'No, but it can still apply. You can fit your existing property into the grid. That's advanced, though. I've not got up to that yet.'

'Well, come round when you have,' Al said.

Al said, I don't want the neighbours to know what we do. Wherever I've lived I've kept away from the neighbours, I don't want this lot around asking me to read their tea bags. I don't want them turning up on our doorstep saying, you know what you told me, it hasn't come true yet, can I have my money back? I don't want them watching me and commenting on me. I want to be private.

The development progressed piecemeal, the houses at the fringes going up before the middle was filled in. They would look over to the opposite ridge, against the screen of pines, and see the householders running out into the streets, or where the streets would be, fleeing from gas leaks, floods and falling masonry. Colette made tea for their next-door neighbours from the Beatty, when their kitchen ceiling came down in its turn; Al was busy with a client. 'Are you sisters?' Michelle asked, standing in the kitchen and jiggling an infant up and down on her hip.

Colette's eyes grew wide. 'Sisters? No.'

'There, Evan,' she said to her husband. 'Told you they couldn't be. We thought perhaps one of you wasn't staying. We thought perhaps she was helping the other one settle in.'

Colette said, 'Are those boys or girls?'

'One of each.'

'Oh. But which is which?'

'You work at home?' Evan asked. 'A contractor?'

'Yes.' He was waiting. She said, flustered, 'I'm in communications,'

'BT?'

'No.'

'It's so confusing now,' Michelle said. 'All these different tariffs you can go on. What's the cheapest for phoning my nan in Australia?'

'That's not my side of it,' Colette said.

'And what does your – your friend – do?'

'Forecasting,' Colette said. For a moment, she began to enjoy herself.

'Met Office, eh?' Evan said. 'Bracknell, aren't they? Bloody murder, getting on to the M3. Bet you didn't know that till you moved in, eh? Three-mile tailback every morning. Should have done your research, eh?'

Both infants began to squall. The grown-ups watched as a workman came out of the Beatty, damp to his knees, carrying a bucket. 'I'll sue those fuckers,' Evan said.

Later, Colette said to Al, 'How could he ever have imagined we were sisters? I would have thought half-sisters, at the most. And even that would be stretching a point.'

'People aren't very observant,' Alison said kindly. 'So you mustn't be insulted, Colette.'

Colette didn't tell Alison that the neighbours thought she worked for the Met Office. Word spread, around the estate, and the neighbours would call out to her. 'No joke, you know, this rain! Can't you do better than this?' Or simply, with a wave and a grin, 'Oi! I see you got it wrong again.'

'I seem to be a personality around here,' Al said. 'I don't know why.'

Colette said, 'I should think it's because you're fat.'

As Easter approached, Michelle popped her head over the fence and asked Al what she should pack for their holiday in Spain. 'I'm sorry,' Al said, aghast, 'I simply wouldn't be able to forecast anything like that.'

'Yes, but unofficially,' Michelle coaxed. 'You must know.'

'Off the record,' Evan said, wheedling.

Colette ran her eyes over Michelle. Was she pregnant again, or just letting herself go? 'Cover up, would be my advice,' she said.

The weather affects the motorway as it affects the sea. The traffic has its rising tides. The road surface glistens with a pearly sheen, or heaves its black wet deeps. They find themselves at distant service stations as dawn breaks, where yellow light spills out into an oily dimness and a line of huddled birds watches them from above. On the M40 near High Wycombe, a kestrel glides on the updraught, swoops to pluck small squealing creatures from the rough grass of the margins. Magpies toddle among the roadkill.

They travel: Orpington, Sevenoaks, Chertsey, Runnymede, Reigate and Sutton. They strike out east of the Thames barrier, where travellers' encampments huddle beneath tower blocks and seagulls cry over the flood plains, where the smell of sewage is carried on the cutting wind. There are floodlights and bunkers, gravel pits and pallet yards, junctions where traffic cones cluster. There are featureless hangars with 'To Let' signs pinned to them, tyres spun away into shabby fields. Colette puts her foot down; they pass vehicles mounted on the backs of vehicles, locked in oily copulation. They pass housing developments just like theirs – 'Look, portholes,' Al says – their dormers and their Juliet balconies staring out over low hills made of compacted London waste. They pass Xmas tree farms and puppy farms, barnyards piled with scrap. Pictures of salivating dogs are hung on wire fences, so that those who don't read English get the point. Crosswinds rock them, cables lash across a fast sky. Colette's radio is tuned to traffic reports – trouble at Trellick Tower, an insurmountable blockage afflicting the Kingston bypass. Al's mind drifts, across the central reservation. She sees the walls of warehouses shining silver like the tinny armour of the tarot knights. She sees incinerators, oil-storage tankers, gas holders, electricity substations. Haulage yards. Portakabins, underpasses, subways and walkways. Industrial parks and science parks and retail parks.

The world beyond the glass is the world of masculine action. Everything she sees is what a man has built. But at each turn-off, each junction, women are waiting to know their fate. They are looking deep inside themselves, into their private hearts, where the foetus forms and buds, where the shape forms inside the crystal, where fingernails click softly at the backs of the cards, and pictures flutter upwards, towards the air: Justice, Temperance, the Sun, the Moon, the World.

At the motorway services, there are cameras pointing, watching the queues for fish and chips and tepid jellified cheesecake. Outside there are notices affixed to poles, warning of hawkers, peddlers, itinerant sellers and illegal traders. There are none that warn against the loose, travelling dead. There are cameras guarding the exits, but none that register the entrances of Pikey Pete.

'You don't know what will trigger them,' Al says. 'There's a whole pack of them, you see. Accumulating. It worries me. I'm not saying it doesn't worry me. The only thing is, the only good thing – Morris doesn't bring them home. They fade away somewhere, before we turn into Admiral Drive. He doesn't like it, you see. Says it's not a proper home. He doesn't like the garden.'

They were coming back from Suffolk; or somewhere, at any rate, where people still had an appetite, because they were behind a van that said 'Wright's Famous Pies, Savouries,

Confectionery'. 'Look at that,' Al said, and read it out, laughing. At once she thought, why did I do that? I could kick myself. They claim they're hungry now.

Morris gripped the passenger seat and rocked it, saying, 'I could murder a Famous Pie.' Said Pikey Pete, 'You can't beat a Savoury.' Said young Dean, with his customary politeness, 'I'll have a Confectionery, please.'

Colette said, 'Is that headrest rocking again? Or is it you fidgeting? God, I'm starving, I'm going to pull in at Clacket Lane.'

When Colette was at home she lived on vitamin pills and ginseng. She was a vegetarian except for bacon and skinless chicken breasts. On the road they ate what they could get, when they could get it. They dined in the theme pubs of Billericay and Egham. In Virginia Water they ate nachos and in Broxbourne they ate fat pillows of dough which the baker called Belgian Buns. In lay-bys they ate leaking seafood sandwiches, and when spring came, in the pedestrianised zones of small Thameside towns they sat on benches with warm Cornish pasties, nibbling daintily around the frills. They ate broccoli and three-cheese bake straight from the cash and carry, and wholesaler's quiche Lorraine with sinewy nuggets of ham as pink as a scalded baby, and KrispyKrum Chickettes, and lemon mousse that reminded them of the kind of foam that you clean carpets with. 'I have to have something sweet,' Alison said. 'I have to keep my energy levels up.' She added, 'Some people think it's glamorous having psychic powers. They're dead wrong.' Colette thought, it's hard enough keeping her tidy, never mind glamorous. She served her time with Al, in the shopping precincts of small towns, standing outside fitting rooms the size of sentry boxes, with curtains that never pulled straight across. There were creaks and sighs from the other sentry boxes; the thin smell of desperation and self-hatred hung in the air. Colette had made a vow to take her upmarket, but Al was uncomfortable in posh shops. She did have some pride, though. Whatever she bought, she decanted into a carrier bag from a shop that catered to normal-sized women.

'I have to keep body and mind receptive and quiet,' she said. 'If carrying a bit of flesh is the price I have to pay, so be it. I can't tune into spirit if I'm bouncing around in an aerobics class.'

Morris said, 'Have you seen MacArthur, he is a mate of mine and Keef Capstick, he is a mate of Keef's too. Have you seen MacArthur, he is a mate of mine and he wears a knitted weskit. Have you seen MacArthur, he has only one eye, have you seen him, he has one earlobe ripped off, a sailor ripped it off in a fracas, that's what he tells people. How did he lose his eye? Well, that's another story. He blames that on a sailor too, but round here, we know he's lying.' And Morris gave a dirty laugh.

When spring came, the gardening service sent a man. A truck dropped him, and his mower, then rattled off. Colette went to the door to administer him. No use waiting for Al to do it.

'It's only I don't know how to start it?' he said. He stood pushing a finger under his woolly hat; as if, Colette thought, he were making some sort of secret sign to her.

She stared at him. 'You don't know how to start the mower?'

He said, 'What do I look like, in this hat?'

'I can't imagine,' she said.

'Do you think I look like a brickie?'

'I couldn't say.'

'You can see 'em all over the place, they're building walls.' He pointed. 'Down there.'

'You're soaked through,' Colette said, noticing this.

The man said, 'No, it's not up to much, is it, this cardigan, parka, jacket? I could do with a fleece.'

'A fleece wouldn't keep the rain out.'

'I could get a plastic, a plastic to put over it.'

'Whatever you think best,' Colette said coldly.

The man trudged away. Colette shut the door.

Ten minutes later the doorbell rang. The man had pulled his hat over his eyes. He was standing on the doormat, dripping under the porch. 'So, starting it? Could you?'

Colette's eyes swept him, up and down. She saw with disgust that his toes were poking out of his shoes, waggling the cracked leather up and down. 'Are you sure you're qualified for this job?'

The man shook his head. 'I've not been trained on a mower,' he said.

'Why did they send you?'

'I suppose they thought you could train me on it.'

'And why would they think that?'

'Well, you look a lovely girl.'

'Don't try it on,' Colette said. 'I'm ringing your manager.' She slammed the door. Al came to the head of the stairs. She had been having a lie-down, after seeing a bereaved client. 'Col?'

'Yes?'

'Was that a man?' Her voice was vague, sleepy.

'It was the gardening service. He was crap. He couldn't start the mower.'

'So what happened?'

'So I told him to bugger off and I'm ringing them to complain.'

'What sort of man was he?'

'An idiot.'

'Young, old?'

'I don't know. I didn't look. He was wet. He had a hat on.'

* * *

In summer, they drove through countryside perfumed by the noxious vapours of pesticides and herbicides, and by the sweet cloud that lay over the golden fields of oilseed rape. Their eyes streamed, their throats dried and tightened; Al groped in her bag for antiseptic lozenges. Autumn: she saw the full moon snared in the netting of a football field, caught there bulging, its face bruised. When a traffic snarl-up brought them to a halt, she noticed the trudging shopper with her grocery bags, leaning into the wind. She noticed the rotted wood of a balcony, London brick weeping soot, winter mould on a stack of garden chairs. A curve in the road, a pause at traffic lights, brings you close to another life, to an office window where a man leans on a filing cabinet in a crumpled shirt, as close as some man you know: while a van backs into the road, you halt, you are detained, and the pause makes you intimate with a man stroking his bald head, framed in the lighted cavity of his garage beneath the up-and-over door.

At journey's end comes the struggle with randomly arriving trivia, zinging through the ether. You are going to get a new sofa. You are a very tenacious person. Morris is supposed to act as a sort of doorman, ushering the spirits and making them queue up, threatening them so they don't all talk at once. But he seemed to have fallen into a prolonged sulk, since they moved to Admiral Drive. Nothing suited him, and he left her to be teased and tormented by Diana imitators, by Elvis imitators, by the petty dead purveying misinformation, working tricks and setting riddles. From her audiences, the same old questions: for example, is there sex in spirit world?

She would answer, giggling, 'There's an elderly lady I know who's very psychic, and I'll tell you what she says: she says, there's a tremendous amount of love in spirit world, but there's none of that funny stuff.'

It would get a laugh. The audience would relax. They didn't really suppose there could be an answer to this question. But once when they got home, Colette had said, 'Well, is there sex in spirit world? I don't want to know what Mrs Etchells says, I want to know what you say.'

'Mostly, they don't have body parts,' Al said. 'Not as such. There are exceptions. There are some really low spirits that are, well, just genitals, really. The others, they just . . . they like to watch us doing it.'

'Then we can't provide them with much entertainment,' Colette said.

Winter: from the passenger seat Al turns her face towards the lit windows of a school. Children's drawings are pinned up, facing away from her: she sees the backs of triangular angels, with pointing frosted wings. Weeks after Christmas, into the new year, the cardboard stars still hang against the glass, and polyester snowflakes fall drily, harmlessly down the inside of the panes. Winter and another spring. On the A12 towards Ipswich the lamps overhead burst into flower, their capsules splitting: they snap open like seed pods, and from their metal cups the rays of light burst out against the sky.

One day in early spring Alison looked out over the garden, and saw Morris squatting in the far corner, crying: or pretending to. Morris's complaint about the garden was that, when you looked out of the window, all you could see was turf and fence: and him.

They had paid extra for a plot backing south. But that first summer the light beat in through the French windows, and they were forced to hang voile panels to protect themselves. Morris spent his time sequestered in these drapes, swathed in them; he did not care for the light of the sun or the unshaded moon. After the idiot from the gardening service, they had bought their own mower, and Colette, complaining, had trimmed the lawn; but I'm not grubbing about in flower beds, she said, I'm not planting things. Al was embarrassed at first, when the neighbours stopped her and offered her magazine articles about garden planning, and recommended certain television programmes with celebrity horticulturalists, which they felt sure she would enjoy. They think we're letting the side down, she thought; as well as being sexual deviants, we don't have a pond or even decking. Morris complained there was no cover for his nefarious activities. His mates, he said, were jeering at him, crying, 'Hup! Hup! Hup! Morris on parade! By the left quick march, by the right quick march . . . Fall out, Morrr-iisss, report for special fucking kitchen duties and licking ladies' shoes.'

Al sneered at him. 'I don't want you in my kitchen.' No chance, she thought; not among our hygienic granite-look worktops. There is no crack or corner and there is no place to hide in our stainless-steel double oven; not without the risk of being cooked. At her mum's house in Aldershot the sink had an old-style wooden draining board, reeking, mouldy, sodden to the touch. For Morris, after he passed, it had been his natural home. He insinuated himself through the spongy fibres and lay there breathing wetly, puffing through his mouth and snorting through his nose.

When this first happened she couldn't bear to do the washing-up. After she had left it for three days in a row her mother had said, I'll have you, young lady, and came after her with a plastic clothes line. Emmie couldn't decide whether to lash her, or tie her up, or hang her: and while she was deciding, she wobbled and fell over. Alison sighed and stepped over her. She took one end of the clothes line and drew it through her mother's half-closed hand until Emmie yielded the last foot, the last inch. Then she took it outside and hung it back, between the hook driven into the brickwork and the sloping post that was sunk into the grass.

It was twilight, a moon rising over Aldershot. The line was not taut, and her amateurish, womanly knots slipped away from their anchors. Some spirits fluttered down on to the line, and fluttered away again, squawking, when it dipped and swayed under their feet. She threw a stone after them, jeering. She was only a girl then.

At first, Morris had mocked the new house. 'This is posh, innit? You're doing very well out of me, ducks.' Then he threatened her. 'I can take you over, you cheeky bitch. I can have you away airside. I can chew you up and spit you out. I'll come for you one night and the next day all they'll find is your torn knickers. Don't think I've not done it before.'

'Who?' she said. 'Who have you taken over?'

'Gloria, for one. Remember her? Tart with red hair.'

'But you were earthside then, Morris. Anybody can do it with knives and hatchets but what can you do with your spirit hands? Your memory's going. You're forgetting what's what. You've been kicking around too long.' She spoke to him roughly, man to man, as Aitkenside might: 'You're fading, mate. Fading fast.'

Then he began to coax her. 'We want to go back to Wexham. It was a nice area in Wexham. We liked going down Slough, we liked it there because we could go down the dog track, where the dog track used to be. We liked it because you could go out fighting, but here there ain't the possibility of fighting. There ain't a bit of land where you can set up a cockfight. Young Dean enjoys nicking cars, but you can't nick 'em, these buggers have all got alarms and Dean don't do alarms, he's only a kid and he ain't got trained on alarms yet. Donnie Aitkenside, he says we'll never meet up with MacArthur if we stay around these parts. He says, we'll never get Keef Capstick to stick around, Keef he likes a bit of a rough-house and the chance of a ruckus.' Morris's voice rose, he began to wheedle and whine. 'Suppose I got a parcel? Where'm I going to keep me parcel?'

'What kind of parcel?' Al asked him.

'Suppose I got a consignment? Supposing I got a package? Supposing I had to keep guard on a few packing cases or a few crates. To help out me mates. You never know when your mate is going to come to you and say, Morris, Morris old son, can you keep an eye on these for me, ask me no questions and I'll tell you no lies?'

'You? You don't know anything but lies.'

'And if that happens, where am I going to keep 'em? Answer me that, girl.'

Alison told him, 'You'll just have to say no, won't you?', and Morris said, 'Say no, say no? Is that a way to treat a mate of yours? If old string bean asked you, keep this package for me, would you refuse her, would you say, Colette, me old mate, no can do?'

'I might.'

'But what if Nick asked you? What if old Nick himself was to come to you with a proposition, what if he was to say, cut you in on this, my friend, trust me and I'll see you right, what if he was to say, least said soonest mended, what if he was to say, I'd regard it as a special favour?'

'What's Nick to me? I wouldn't cross the road for him.'

'Because Nick, he don't ask you, he tells you. Because Nick, he hangs you from a tree and shoots off your kneecaps, I've seen it done. Because you don't say no to Nick or if you do you're bloody crippled. I seen him personally poke out a man's eye with a pencil. Where 'is eye would be.'

'Is that what happened to MacArthur? You said he only had one eye.'

A jeering, incredulous look spread over Morris's face.

'Don't play the innocent wiv me,' he said. 'You evil baggage. You know bloody fine how his eye got took out.' He headed, grumbling, for the French windows and wrapped his head in the curtain. 'Tries it on wiv me, plays the innocent, fucking 'ell it won't wash. Tell it to Dean, try it on some kid and see if it will wash wiv him, it won't wash wiv me. I was there, girl. You claim my memory's gone. Nothing wrong with mine, I'm telling you. Could be something wrong with yours. I don't bloody forget his eye springing out. You don't forget a thing like that.'

He looked frightened, she thought. Going up to bed, she hesitated outside Colette's room, bed two with en suite shower. She would have liked to say, I am lonely sometimes, and – the brute fact is – I want human company. Was Colette human? Just about. She felt a yawning inside her, an unfilled space of loss, as if a door in her solar plexus were opening on an empty room, or a stage waiting for a play to begin.

The day Morris said he was going, she could hardly wait to tell people the news. 'He's been called away,' she said. 'Isn't that great?' Smiles kept breaking out. She felt as if she were fizzing inside.

'Oh, that's wonderful,' Mandy said on the phone. 'I mean, it's good news for all of us, Al. Merlin said he was at the limit of his tolerance, and so did Merlyn. Your Morris had a really nasty way with him, he upset me dreadfully that night of Di's funeral. I never felt clean afterwards. Well, you don't, do you?'

'You don't think it's a trick?' Al said, but Mandy reassured her. 'It's his time, Al. He's pulled towards the light. He can't resist, I bet you. It's time he broke out of that cycle of criminality and self-destructive behaviour. He'll be moving upwards. You'll see.'

Colette was in the kitchen making decaffeinated coffee. Al

told her, Morris is leaving. He's been called away. Colette raised her eyebrows and said, 'Called away by who?'

'I don't know, but he says he's going on a course. I talked to Mandy, she says it means he's moving to a higher level. '

Colette stood waiting for the kettle to boil, her fingers tapping. 'Does that mean he won't be bothering us in the future?'

'He swears he's leaving today.'

'And it's like, a residential course, is it?'

'I suppose.'

'And how long is it? Will he be coming back?'

'I think it takes as long as it takes. I can't believe he'll come back to the Woking area. Spirits don't generally go backwards. I've never heard of that happening. When he's moved towards the light he'll be free to—' She stopped, perplexed. 'Whatever they do,' she said finally. 'Melt. Disperse.'

The kettle clicked itself off. 'And all those other people he talks about – Dean, and those others we get in the back of the car – will they be melting too?'

'I don't know about Dean. He doesn't seemed very evolved. But yes, I think, it's Morris who attracts them, not me, so if he goes they'll all go. You see, it might be the end of Morris as we know him. It had to happen one day.

'Then what? What will it be like?'

'Well, it'll be – silent. We'll have some peace, I can get a night's sleep.'

Colette said, 'Could you move, please, so I can get to the fridge? You won't be giving up the business, will you?'

'If I gave up, how would I make a living?'

'I just want the milk. Thanks. But what will you do for a spirit guide?'

'Another one could turn up any day. Or I could borrow yours.'

Colette almost dropped the milk carton. 'Mine?'

'Didn't I tell you?'

Colette looked horrified. 'But who is he?'

'It's a she. Maureen Harrison, her name is.'

Colette poured her milk all over the granite-style work surface, and stood watching it stupidly as it dripped. 'Who's that? I don't know her. I don't know anyone of that name.'

'No, you wouldn't. She passed before you were born. In fact, it took me a while to locate her, but her poor old friend kept calling around, asking for her. So I thought I'd do a good action, link them up together. OK, I should have told you! I should have mentioned it. But what's your problem? She won't make any difference to you. Look, relax, she's not doing you any harm, she's just one of those grannies who lose the buttons off their cardigans.'

'But can she see me? Is she looking at me now?'

'Maureen,' Al said softly. 'You around, love?'

From a cupboard came the chink of a teacup. 'There,' Al said.

'Can she see me in my room at night?'

Alison crossed the kitchen and began to mop up the spilled milk. 'Go and sit down, Colette, you've had a shock. I'll make you another cup.'

She boiled the kettle again. Decaf's not much use for a shock. She stood looking out over the empty garden. When Morris actually goes, she thought, we'll have champagne. Colette called out to know where Maureen Harrison came from, and when Al called back, somewhere up north, she sounded shocked, as if it would have been more natural to have a spirit guide from Uxbridge: Al couldn't help smiling to herself. Look on the bright side, she said, bringing the coffee through; she'd put out some chocolate biscuits, as the beginning of her celebration. Look on the bright side, you might have been lumbered with a Tibetan. She imagined the Collingwood, ringing with temple bells.

There was an unusual calm in their sitting room. She stared hard at the voile panels, but Morris's form was not bulking them out, nor was he lying, stretched, along the hem. No Aitkenside, no Dean, no Pikey. She sat down. 'Here we are,' she said, beaming. 'Just the two of us.' She heard a moaning, a scraping, a metallic rattle; then the flap of the letter box, as Morris made his exit.

EIGHT

As the millennium approached, their trade declined. It was nothing personal, no misstep in Colette's business plan. All the psychics called up to grouch about it. It was as if their clients had put their personal curiosity on pause: as if they had been caught up in some general intake of breath. The new age was celebrated at Admiral Drive with fireworks, released by careful fathers from the raw back plots. The children's play area, the natural site for the fiesta, had been fenced off, and KEEP OUT notices erected.

The local free sheet said Japanese knotweed had been found. 'Is that a good thing?' Michelle asked, over the back fence. 'I mean, are they conserving it?'

'No, I think it's noxious,' Al said. She went inside, worried. I hope it's not my fault, she thought. Had Morris pissed on the plot, on his way out of her life?

Some people didn't buy into the knotweed theory. They said the problem was an unexploded bomb, left over from the last war – whenever that was. Evan leaned over the fence and said, 'Have you heard about that bloke over Reading way, Lower Earley? On a new estate like this? He kept noticing his paint was blistering. His drains filled up with black sludge. One day he was digging in his vegetable plot, and he saw something wriggling on his spade. He thought, hell, what's this?'

'And what was it?' Colette asked. Sometimes she found Evan entrancing.

'It was a heap of white worms,' he said. 'Where you've got white worms you've got radioactivity. That's the only thing you need to know about white worms.'

'So what did he do?'

'Called in the council,' Evan said.

'If it were me I'd call in the army.'

'Of course it's a cover-up. They denied everything. Poor beggar's boarded the place up and cut his losses.'

'So what caused it?'

'Secret underground nuclear explosion,' Evan said. 'Stands to reason.'

At Admiral Drive a few people phoned the local environmental health department, putting questions about the play area, but officials would only admit to some sort of blockage, some sort of seepage, some sort of contamination the nature of which they were unable as yet to confirm. They insisted that the white worm problem was confined to the Reading area, and that none of them had made their way to Woking. Meanwhile, the infants remained shut out of paradise. They roared with temper when they saw the swings and the slide, and rattled the railings. Their mothers dragged them uphill, towards their Frobishers and Mountbattens, out of harm's way. Nobody wanted news of the problem to leak, in case it affected their house prices. The populace was restless and transient, and already the first 'For Sale' signs were going up, as footloose young couples tried their luck in a rising market.

New Year's Eve was cold at Admiral Drive, and the skies were bright. The planes didn't fall out of them, and there was no flood or epidemic – none, anyway, affecting the south-east of England. The clients gave a listless, apathetic sigh and – just for a month or two – accepted their lives as they were. By spring, trade was creeping back.

'They're coming to take samples from the drains,' Michelle told Alison.

'Who are?'

'Drain officials,' Michelle said fearfully.

After Morris left, their life was like a holiday. For the first time in years Alison went to bed knowing she wouldn't be tossed out of it in the small hours. She could have a leisurely late-night bath without a hairy hand pulling out the plug, or Morris's snake tattoo rising beneath the rose-scented bubbles. She slept through the night and woke refreshed, ready for what the day might bring. She blossomed, her plumped-out skin refining itself, the violet shadows vanishing from beneath her eyes. 'I don't know when I've felt so well,' she said.

Colette slept through the nights too, but she looked just the same.

They began to talk about booking a last-minute holiday, a break in the sun. Morris on an aircraft had been impossible, Al said. When she was checking in, he would jump on her luggage, so that it weighed heavy and she was surcharged. He would flash his knuckledusters as they walked through the metal detector, causing the security staff to stop and search her. If they made it as far as the plane, he would lock himself in the lavatory, or hide in some vulnerable person's sick bag, and come up – BOOM!! – into their face when they opened it. On the way to Madeira once, he had caused a cardiac arrest.

'You don't have to worry about that any more,' Colette said. 'Where would you like to go?'

'Dunno,' Al said. Then: 'Somewhere with ruins. Or where

they sing opera. It's night, and you hold candles, and they sing in an arena, an amphitheatre. Or they perform plays wearing masks. If I were an opera singer I'd be quite alluring. Nobody would think I was overweight.'

Colette had been thinking in terms of sex with a Greek waiter. There was no reason, on the face of it, why Alison's cultural yearnings and her sexual ones shouldn't be fulfilled within five hundred yards of each other. But she pictured her hot-eyed beau, circling their table on the terrace: his sighs, his raised pulse, his fiery breath, his thoughts running ahead: is it worth it, because I'll have to pay a mate of mine to sleep with the fat girl?

'Besides,' Al said, 'it would be nice to have somebody with me. I went to Cyprus with Mandy but I never saw her, she was in and out of bed with somebody new every night. I found it quite squalid. Oh, I love Mandy, don't get me wrong. People should enjoy themselves, if they can.'

'It just happens you can't,' Colette said.

It didn't matter what she said to Al, she reasoned. Even if she didn't speak out loud, Al would pull the thoughts out of her head; so she would know anyway.

Alison had withdrawn into a hurt silence; so they never got the holiday. A month on, she mentioned it again, timidly, but Colette snapped at her, 'I don't want to go anywhere with ruins. I want to drink too much and dance on the table. Why do you think this is all I want to do, live with you and drive you to sodding Oxted for a Celtic Mystery Convention? I spend my sodding life on the M25, with you throwing up in the passenger seat.'

Alison said timidly, 'I'm not sick much, since Morris went.' She tried to imagine Colette dancing on a table. She could only conjure a harsh tango on the blonde wood of the coffee table, Colette's spine arched, her chicken-skin armpits exposed as if for a bite. She heard a buzz in her ear; the meek little woman came through, saying, 'scuse me, 'scuse me, have you seen Maureen Harrison?

'Look in the kitchen,' Al said. 'I think she's behind the fridge.'

When 9/11 came, Colette was watching daytime TV. She called Alison through. Al rested her hands on the back of the sofa. She looked without surprise as the Twin Towers crumbled, as the burning bodies plunged through the air. Alison watched till the news looped itself around again and the same pictures were played. Then she left the room without comment. You feel as if you should say something, but you don't know what it is. You can't say you foresaw it; yet you can't say no one foresaw it. The whole world has drawn this card.

Merlyn rang up later that day. 'Hello,' she said. 'How's you? Seen the news?'

'Awful,' Merlyn said, and she said, 'Yes, awful. And how's Merlin?'

'No idea,' he said.

'Not seen him on the circuit?'

'I'm quitting that.'

'Really? You're going to build up the psychic detective work?'

Or psychic security services, she thought. You could certainly offer them. You could stand at airports and X-ray people's intentions. 'No, nothing like that,' Merlyn said. He sounded remarkably buoyant. 'I'm thinking of becoming a life coach. I'm writing a book. A new one. *Self-Heal through Success*. It's using the ancient wisdom traditions for health, wealth and happiness. Believe the world owes you: that's what I say.'

Alison excused herself, put the receiver down and went

into the kitchen to get an orange. When she came back, she wedged the receiver under her chin while she peeled it. You don't want to waste your time, Merlyn was saying, with these young girls and grandmas. Here we are in the heartland of the hi-tech boom. Affluence is as natural as breathing. Each morning when you rise you stretch out your arms and say, 'I possess the universe.'

'Merlyn, why are you telling me this?'

'I was hoping you'd buy a franchise. You're very inspirational, Alison.'

'You'd have to talk to Colette. She makes the business decisions.'

'Oh, does she?' said Merlyn. 'Let me tell you now, and I'll tell you for free, you alone are responsible for your health and your wealth. You cannot delegate what is at the core of your being. Remember the universal law – you get what you think you deserve.'

Peel fell on the carpet, fragrant and curly. 'Really?' she said. 'Not much then, in my case.'

'Alison, I'm disappointed by your negativity. I may have to put the phone down, before it contaminates my day.'

'OK,' she said, and Merlyn said, 'No, don't go . . . I'd hoped – oh well. I was thinking along the lines of a partnership. Well, there you are. I've said it. What do you think?'

'A business partnership?'

'Any kind you like.'

She thought, he thinks I'm stupid, just because I'm fat; because I'm fat, he thinks I'm desperate.

'No.'

'Would you be more specific?'

'More specific than no?'

'I value feedback. I can take it on the chin.'

The trouble is, she thought, you don't have a chin. Merlyn was running to fat, and his damp grey skin seemed to sweat out, in public, the private moisture contained within the shell of his trailer home. She looked, in imagination, into his chocolate-coloured eyes, and saw how his pastel shirt stretched over his belly.

'I couldn't,' she said. 'You're overweight.'

'Well, pardonnez-moi,' Merlyn said. 'Look who's talking.'

'Yes, I know, me too. But I don't like the way your shirt buttons are bursting off. I hate sewing, I'm no good with a needle.'

'You can get staplers,' Merlyn said nastily. 'You can get dedicated staplers nowadays. Anyway, who told you that I would require you to sew on my shirt buttons?'

'I thought you might.'

'And you are seriously giving me this as a reason why you are turning down my offer of a business arrangement?'

'But I thought you were offering something else.'

'*Who knows?*' Merlyn said. 'That's the technical term, I believe, that people use when advertising. "For friendship, and *who knows?*"'

'But in your case, what you want is my money in your bank, and who knows? Come on, Merlyn! You just think I'm an easy touch. And by the way, it's no good ringing up Mandy – Natasha, I mean – or any of the girls. They all don't like you, for the reasons I don't like you.' She paused. No, that's unfair, she thought. There is a particular reason I don't like Merlyn. 'It's your tiepin,' she said. 'I don't like the sight of a tiepin. I always think it's dangerous.'

'I see,' Merlyn said. 'Or rather, I don't, I don't at all.'

She sighed. 'I'm not sure I can account for it myself. Goes back to a past life, I suppose.'

'Oh, come on,' Merlyn sneered. 'Martyred with a tiepin? In antiquity they didn't have tiepins. Brooches, I grant you.'

'Maybe it was me who did the martyring,' she said. 'I don't know, Merlyn. Look, good luck with your book. I hope you do get all that wealth. I do really. If you deserve it, of course. And I'm sure you do. Whatever. Whatever you think. When you leave your mobile home for Beverly Hills, let us have your new address.'

Colette came in five minutes later, with the shopping. 'Do you want a fudge double-choc brownie?' she asked.

Al said, 'Merlyn phoned. He's doing a new book.'

'Oh yes?' Colette said. 'You do like these yogurts, don't you?'

'Are they high-fat?' Al said happily. Colette turned the pot about in her fingers, frowning. 'They must be,' Al said, 'if I like them. By the way, Merlyn asked me to go and live with him.'

Colette continued stacking the fridge. 'Your chops are past their sell-by,' she said. She hurled them in the bin and said, '*What?* In his trailer?'

'I said no.'

'Who the fuck does he think he is?'

'He propositioned me,' Al said. She wiped her hand down her skirt. 'What about our book, Colette? Will it ever be finished?'

Colette had accumulated a little pile of printouts, upstairs; she guarded it, locking it in her wardrobe – a precaution which Al found touching. The tapes still gave them trouble. Sometimes they would find their last session had been replaced entirely by gibberish. Sometimes their conversation was overlain by squeaks, scrapes and coughs, as if a winter audience were tuning up for a symphony concert.

COLETTE: So, do you regard it as a gift or more as a – what's the opposite of a gift?

ALISON: Unsolicited goods. A burden. An infliction.

COLETTE: Is that your answer?

ALISON: No. I was just telling you some expressions.

COLETTE: So . . . ?

ALISON: Look, I just am this way. I can't imagine anything else. If I'd had somebody around me with more sense when I was training, instead of Mrs Etchells, I might have had a better life.

COLETTE: So it could be different?

ALISON: Yes. Given a more evolved guide.

COLETTE: You seem to be doing OK without Morris.

ALISON: I told you I would.

COLETTE After all, you've said yourself, a lot of it is psychology.

ALISON: When you say 'psychology', you're calling it cheating.

COLETTE: What would you call it?

ALISON: You don't call Sherlock Holmes cheating! Look, if you get knowledge, you have to use it however it comes.

COLETTE: But I'd rather think, in a way – let me finish – I'd rather think you were cheating, if I had your welfare at heart, because a lot of people who hear voices, they get diagnosed and put in hospital.

ALISON: Not so much now. Because of cutbacks, you know? There are people who walk around believing all sorts of things. You see them on the streets.

COLETTE: Yes, but that's just a policy. That doesn't make them sane.

ALISON: I make a living, you see. That's the difference between me and the people who are mad. They don't call you mad, if you're making a living.

Sometimes Colette would leave the tape running without telling Al. There was some obscure idea in her mind that she might need a witness. That if she had a record she could make Al stick to any bargains she made; or that, in an unwary moment while she was out of the house, Al might record something incriminating. Though she didn't know what her crime might be.

COLETTE: My project for the new millennium is to manage you more efficiently. I'm going to set you monthly targets. It's time for blue-skies thinking. There's no reason why you shouldn't be at least ten per cent more productive. You're sleeping through the night now, aren't you? And possibly I could handle a more proactive role. I could pick up the overflow clients. Just the ones who require fortune telling. After all, you can't really tell the future, can you? The cards don't know it.

ALISON: Most people don't want to know about the future. They just want to know about the present. They want to be told they're doing all right.

COLETTE: Nobody ever told me I was doing all right. When I used to go to Brondesbury, and places.

ALISON: You didn't feel helped, you didn't feel you'd had any emotional guidance?

COLETTE: No.

ALISON: When I think back to those days, I think you were trying to believe too much. People can't believe everything at once. They have to work up to it.

COLETTE: Gavin thought it was all a fraud. But then Gavin was stupid.

ALISON: You know, you still talk about him a lot.

COLETTE: I don't. I never talk about him.

ALISON: Mm.

COLETTE: Never.

'So OK, OK,' Al said. 'If you want to learn. What do you want to try first, cards or palms? Palms? OK.'

But after five minutes, Colette said, 'I can't see the lines, Al. I think my eyes are going.' Al said nothing. 'I might get contacts. I'm not having glasses.'

'You can use a magnifying glass, the punters don't mind. In fact, they think they're getting more for their money.'

They tried again. 'Don't try to tell my future,' Al said. 'Leave that aside for now. Take my left hand. That's where my character is written. The capacities I was born with. You can see all my potential, waiting to come out. Your job is to alert me to it.'

Colette held her hand tentatively, as if she found it disagreeable. She glanced down at it, and up at Alison again. 'Come on,' Al said. 'You know my character. Or you say you do. You're always talking about my character. And you know about my potential. You've just made me a business plan.'

I don't know, Colette said, even when I look through a magnifier I can't make sense of it.

We'll have a go with the cards then, Al said. As you know there are seventy-eight to learn plus all the meaningful combinations, so you'll have a lot of homework. You know the basics, you must have picked that up by now. Clubs rule the fire signs – you know the signs, don't you? Hearts rule water, diamonds earth; Colette said, diamonds earth, that's easy to remember. But why do spades rule air? Al said, in the tarot, spades are swords. Think of them cutting through the air. Clubs are wands. Diamonds are pentacles. Hearts are cups.

Colette's hands were clumsy when she shuffled; pictures cascaded from the pack, and she gave herself paper-cuts, as if the cards were nipping her. Al taught her to lay out a consequences spread and a Celtic cross. She turned the major arcana face up so she could learn them one by one. But Colette couldn't get the idea. She was diligent and conscientious but when she saw the cards she couldn't see beyond the pictures on them. A crayfish is crawling out of a pond: why? A man in a silly hat stands on the brink of a precipice. He carries his possessions in a bundle and a dog is nipping at his thigh. Where is he going? Why doesn't he feel the teeth? A woman is forcing open the jaws of a lion. She seems happy with life. There is a collusive buzz in the air.

Al said, 'What does it convey to you? No, don't look at me for an answer. Close your eyes. How do you feel?'

'I don't feel anything,' Colette said. 'How should I feel?'

'When I work with the tarot, I generally feel as if the top of my head has been taken off with a tin-opener.'

Colette threw down the cards. I'll stick to my side of the business, she said. Al said, that would be very wise. She couldn't explain to Colette how it felt to read for a client: even if it was just psychology. You start out, you start talking, you don't know what you're going to say. You don't even know your way to the end of the sentence. You don't know anything. Then suddenly you do know. You have to walk blind. And you walk slap into the truth.

In the new millennium Colette intended to lever her away from low-rent venues, where there are recycling bins in the car parks, crisps ground into the carpet, strip lighting. She wanted to see her in big well-furbished auditoria with proper sound and lighting crews. She detested the public nature of public halls, where tipsy comics played on Saturday night and gusts of dirty laughter hung in the air. She loathed the worn grubby chairs, stained with beer and worse; hated the thought of Al attuning to spirit in some broom cupboard, very often with a tin bucket and a string mop for company. She said, I don't like it down there by the Gymnastics Club, by the Snooker Centre. I don't like the types you get. I want to get down to the south coast where they have some lovely restored theatres, gilt and red plush, where you can fill the stalls and the royal circle, fill the balcony right to the back.

At Admiral Drive the early bulbs pushed through, points of light in the lush grass. The brick of the Mountbatten and the Frobisher was still raw, the tiled roofs slicked by April rain. Al was right when she said that the people down the hill would have a problem with damp. Their turf squelched beneath their feet, and a swampish swelling and bubbling lifted their patios. At night the security lights flittered, as if all the neighbours were creeping from house to house stealing each other's games consoles and DVD players.

Gavin never called, though his monthly payment for his share of the flat in Whitton continued to arrive in her bank account. Then one day, when she and Al were shopping in Farnham, they ran straight into him; they were coming out of Elphicks department store, and he was going in.

'What are you doing in Farnham?' she said, shocked.

Gavin said, 'It's a free country.'

It was just the sort of inane reply he always used to make when you asked him why he was doing anything, or why he was wherever he was. It was the kind of reply that reminded her why she had been right to leave him. He couldn't have done much better if he'd premeditated it for a week.

Al's glance took him in. When Colette turned to introduce her, she was already backing away. 'I'll just be . . .' she said, and melted in the direction of cosmetics and perfume. Tactfully, she averted her eyes, and stood spraying herself with one scent and then another, to distract herself from tuning into what they were saying.

'That her? Your friend?' Gavin said. 'Christ, she's a size, isn't she? That the best you could do?'

'She's a remarkably sound businesswoman,' Colette said, 'and a very kind and thoughtful employer.'

'And you live with her?'

'We have a lovely new house.'

'But why do you have to live in?'

'Because she needs me. She works twenty-four/seven.'

'Nobody does that.'

'She does. But you wouldn't understand.'

'I always thought you were a bit of a lezzie, Col. I'd have thought so when I first saw you, only you came down the bar, that hotel, where was it, France, you walked straight up to me with your tongue hanging out. So I thought, could be wrong on this one.'

She turned her back and walked away from him. He called, 'Colette . . .' She turned. He said, 'We could meet up for a drink, sometime. Not her, though. She can't come.'

Her mouth opened – she stared at him – a lifetime of insults swallowed, insults swallowed and digested, gushed up from deep inside her and jammed in her throat. She hauled in her breath, her hands formed claws; but the only words which came out were, 'Get stuffed.' As she dived back into the store, she caught sight of herself in a mirror, her skin mottled with wrath and her eyes popping, and for the first time she understood why when she was at school they had called her Monster.

The following week, in Walton-on-Thames, they got into a parking dispute with a man in a multi-storey. Two cars nosing for the same space; it was just one of those crude suburban flare-ups, which men easily forget but which make women cry and shake for hours. Nine times out of ten, in these spats, Al would put her restraining hand on Colette's hand, as it tightened on the wheel, and say, forget it, let him have what he wants, it doesn't matter. But this time, she whizzed down her window and asked the man, 'What's your name?'

He swore at her. She was inured to bad language from the

fiends; but why should you expect it from such a man, from an Admiral Drive sort of man, from a mail-order-jacket sort of man, a let's-get-out-the-barbecue sort of man?

She said to him, 'Stop, stop, stop! You should have more on your mind than cursing women in car parks. Go straight home and boost your life insurance. Clean up your computer and wipe off those kiddie pictures, that's not the sort of thing you want to leave behind you. Ring up your GP. Ask for an early appointment and don't take no for an answer. Tell them, left lung. They can do a lot these days, you know. If they catch these things before they spread.'

She whizzed up the window again. The man mouthed something; his car squealed away. Colette slotted them neatly into the disputed space. She glanced sideways at Al. She didn't dare question her. They were running late, of course; they did need the space. She said to Al, testing her, 'I wish I had done that.' Al didn't answer.

When they got home that night and they had poured a drink, she said, 'Al, the man in the car park . . .'

'Oh, yes,' Al said. 'Of course, I was just guessing.' She added, 'About the pornography.'

These days when they travelled there was blissful silence from the back of the car. Didcot and Abingdon, Blewbury and Goring: Shinfield, Wonersh, Long Ditton and Lightwater. They knew the lives they glimpsed on the road were lives more ordinary than theirs. They saw an ironing board in a lean-to, waiting for its garment. A grandma at a bus stop, stooping to slot a biscuit into a child's open mouth. Dirty pigeons hanging in the trees. A lamp shining behind a black hedge. Underpasses dropping away, lit by dim bulbs: Otford, Limpsfield, New Eltham and Blackfen. They tried to avoid the high streets and shopping malls of the denatured towns, because of the bewildered dead clustered among the skips outside the burger bars, clutching door keys in their hands, or queuing with their lunch boxes where the gates of small factories once stood, where machines once whirred and chugged behind sooty panes of old glass. There are thousands of them out there, so pathetic and lame-brained that they can't cross the road to get where they're going, dithering on the kerbs of new arterial roads and bypasses, as the vehicles swish by: congregating under railway arches and under the stairwells of multi-storey car parks, thickening the air at the entrance to underground stations. If they brush up against Alison they follow her home, and start pestering her the first chance they get. They elbow her in the ribs with questions, always questions: but never the right ones. Always, where's my pension book, has the number 64 gone, are we having a fry-up this morning? Never, am I dead? When she puts them right on that, they want to go over how it happened, trying to glean some sense out of it, trying to throw a slippery bridge over the gap between time and eternity. 'I had just plugged in the iron,' a woman would say, 'and I was just starting on the left sleeve of Jim's blue-striped shirt . . . of his . . . our Jim . . . of his stripes . . .' And her voice will grow faint with bafflement, until Alison explains to her, puts her in the picture, and, 'Oh, I see now,' she will say, quite equably, and then, 'I get it. These things happen, don't they? So I'll not take up your time any further, I'm very much obliged. No thanks, I've my own tea waiting for me when I get home . . . I wouldn't want to cut into your evening . . .'

And so she passes, her voice fading until she melts into the wall. Even the ones who went over with plenty of warning liked to recall their last hours on the ward, dwelling in a leisurely fashion on which of their family showed up for the deathbed and which of them left it too late and got stuck in traffic. They wanted Alison to put tributes in the newspaper for them: 'Thanks, sincerely meant, to the staff at St Bernard's' – and she promised she would, for I'll do anything, she would say, that will make them lie down, wait quietly and waft to their next abode; instead of making themselves at home in mine. They will finish their ramblings with, 'Well, that's all from me for now' and 'Hoping this finds you well' and 'Let me have your family news soon': sometimes with a quiet, stoical, 'I ought to go now.' Sometimes when they bob back, with a cheery 'Hello, it's me', they are claiming to be Queen Victoria, or their own older sister, or a woman who lived next door to them before they were born. It's not intentional fraud, it's more that a mingling and mincing and mixing of personality goes on, the fusing of personal memory with the collective. You see, she'd explain to Colette, you and me, when we come back, we could manifest as one person. Because these last years, we've shared a lot. You could come back as my mum. I could come over, thirty years from now, to some psychic standing on a stage somewhere, and claim I was my own dad. Not that I know who my dad is, but I will one day, perhaps after I've passed.

But Colette would say, panicked for a moment, stampeded into belief, what if I die? Al, what shall I do, what shall I do if I die?

Al would say to her, keep your wits about you. Don't start crying. Don't speak to anybody. Don't eat anything. Keep saying your name over and over. Close your eyes and look for the light. If somebody says, follow me, ask to see their ID. When you see the light, move towards it. Keep your bag clamped to your body, where your body would be. Don't open your bag, and remember the last thing you should do is pull out a map, however lost you feel. If anybody asks you for money ignore them, push past. Just keep moving towards the light. Don't make eye contact. Don't let anyone stop you. If somebody points out there's paint on your coat or bird droppings in your hair, just keep motoring, don't pause, don't look left or right. If a woman approaches you with some snotty-nosed kid, kick her out of the way. It sounds harsh, but it's for your own safety. Keep moving. Move towards the light.

And if I lose it? Colette would say. What if I lose the light and I'm wandering around in a fog, with all these people trying to snatch my purse and my mobile? You can always come home, Alison would tell her. You know your home now, Admiral Drive. I'll be here to explain it all to you and put you on the right path so that you can manage the next bit, and then when I come over in the fullness of time we can get together and have a coffee and maybe share a house again if we think it will work out.

But what if you go before me, Colette would say, what if we go together, what if we're on the M25 and a wind blows up and what if it's a mighty wind and we're blown into the path of a lorry?

Alison would sigh and say, Colette, Colette, we all get there in the end. Look at Morris! We end up in the next world raw, indignant, baffled or furious, and ignorant, all of us: but we get sent on courses. Our spirits move, given time, to a higher level, where everything becomes clear. Or so people tell me, anyway. Hauntings can persist for centuries, for sure: but why wouldn't they? People have no sense of urgency, airside.

Inside the Collingwood the air was serene. Weekly, Colette polished the crystal ball. You had to wash it in vinegar and water and rub it up with a chamois. Al said, the tools of the trade are what keep you on track. They focus the mind and direct the energy. But they have no magic in themselves. Power is contained in domestic objects, in the familiar items you handle every day. You can look into the side of an aluminium pan and see a face that's not your own. You can see a movement on the inside of an empty glass.

The days, months, blurred into one. The venues offered a

thousand grannies with buttons missing; a thousand hands raised. Why are we here? Why must we suffer? Why must children suffer? Why does God mistreat us? Can you bend spoons?

Smiling, Al said to her questioner, 'I should give it a go, shouldn't I? Give me something to do in the kitchen. Stop me raiding the fridge.'

The truth was – though she never admitted it to anyone – that she had once tried it. She was against party tricks, and generally against showing off and being wasteful, and wrecking your cutlery seemed to come under those heads. But one day at Admiral Drive the urge overcame her. Colette was out: all well and good. She tiptoed into the kitchen and slid out a drawer. It snagged, bounced back. The potato masher had rolled forward spitefully and was catching its rim on the front of the unit. Unusually irritated, she slid in her hand, dragged the utensil out and threw it across the kitchen. Now she was in the mood for spoon-bending, she wasn't to be thwarted.

Her hand jumped for the knives. She picked one out, a blunt round-edged table knife. She ran her fingers around the blade. She put it down. Picked up a soup spoon. She knew how to do this. She held it loosely, fingers caressing its neck, her will flowing from her spinal column sweetly into the pads of her fingers. She closed her eyes. She felt a slight humming behind them. Her breathing deepened. She relaxed. Then her eyes snapped open. She looked down. The spoon, unaltered, smiled up at her; and suddenly she understood it, she understood the essence of spoonhood. Bending it wasn't the point, any more. The point was that she would never feel the same about cutlery. Something stirred deep in her memory, as if she had been cross-wired, as if some old source of feeling had been tapped. She laid the spoon to rest, reverently, snug inside a fellow spoon. As she closed the drawer her eye caught the glint of the paring knife – a more worthwhile blade. She thought, I understand the nature of it. I understand the nature of spoon and knife.

Later, Colette picked up the potato masher from where it had fallen. 'It's bent,' she said.

'That's all right. I did it.'

'Oh. You're sure?'

'Just a little experiment.'

'I thought for a minute it must be Morris come back.' Colette hesitated. 'You would tell me, wouldn't you?'

But truly, there was no sign of him. Al sometimes wondered how he was doing on his course. It must be that he's going to a higher level, she reasoned, you wouldn't get sent on a course to go to a lower level.

'No, not even Morris,' Colette said, when she mentioned it. If Morris were on a lower level, he'd be no good, he'd not even scrape up to standard as an ordinary spirit, let alone get employed anywhere as a guide. He'd be just an agglomeration of meaninglessness, a clump of cells rolling around through the netherworld.

'Colette,' she said, 'when you're sweeping, have a look at the vacuum-cleaner bag from time to time. If you find any big lumps you can't account for, check it out with me, OK?'

Colette said, 'I don't think that sifting through the vacuum-cleaner bag was in my job description.'

'Well, write it in, there's a good girl,' Al said.

There are some spirits, she knew, who are willing to sink: who are so tenacious of existence that they will assume any form, however debased, ridiculous and filthy. That was why Al, unlike her mother, made sure to keep a clean house. She thought that she and Colette, between them, could keep down the lower sort, who drift in dust-rolls under beds, and make streaks and fingerprints on window panes. They cloud mirrors, and sometimes vanish with a chortle: leaving the mirror clear and unkind. They clump in hairbrushes, and when you comb them out, you think, can this thin grey frizz be mine?

Sometimes, when Alison came into a room, she thought the furniture had shifted slightly; but no doubt that was Colette, pushing it around as she cleaned. Her own boundaries seemed invisible, uncertain. Her core temperature tended to fluctuate, but there was nothing new in that. Her extremities drifted, in time and space. Sometimes she thought an hour, an afternoon, a day had gone missing. Less and less did she want to go out; her clients emailed her, the phone rang less often; Colette, who was restless, could always be persuaded to shop for them. It was the house's silence that entranced her, lulled her. Her daydreams and night dreams ran together. She thought she saw two cars, trucks really, parked outside the Collingwood; it was dark, Colette was in bed, she pulled her coat around her shoulders and went outside.

The carriage lamp flared into life, and the thump of a hi-fi came from a Hawkyns. There was no one around. She looked into the cab of one truck and it was empty. The cab of the other was empty too, but in the back there was a grey blanket tied with twine, covering something irregular and lumpy.

She shivered, and went back inside. When she woke the next morning the trucks had gone.

She wondered about them; whose were they? Had they not looked a bit old-fashioned? She wasn't good on makes of cars, but there was something about their lines that suggested her childhood. 'Colette,' she said, 'when you're at Sainsbury's, you wouldn't pick up a car magazine? One of those with lots and lots of pictures of every car anyone might want?' She thought, at least I could exclude all modern makes.

Colette said, 'Are you winding me up?'

'What?' she said.

'Gavin!'

'There you are! I told you that you're always talking about him.'

Later, she was sorry for upsetting Colette. I meant no harm, she said to herself, I just didn't think. As for the trucks, they were spirit vehicles, probably, but whose? Sometimes she rose in the night to look down, from the landing porthole, over Admiral Drive. Around the children's playground, warning lamps shone from deep holes in the ground. Great pipes, like troglodyte dwellings, lay gaping at the landscape; the moon's single eye stared down at them.

Colette would find her, standing by the porthole, tense and cold. She would find her and draw her back to bed; her touch was like a spirit touch, her face hollow, her feet noiseless. By day or night, Colette's aura remained patchy, wispy. When she was out and Alison found traces of her about the house – a discarded shoe, a bangle, one of her elastic hairbands – she thought, whoever is she, and how did she get here? Did I invite her? If so, why did I do that? She thought about Gloria and Mrs McGibbet. She wondered if Colette might disappear one day, just as suddenly as they did, fading into nothingness and leaving behind only snatches of conversation, a faint heat-trace on the air.

They had been given a breathing space. Time to reconsider. To pause. To re-evaluate. They could see middle age ahead of them. Forty is the new thirty, Colette said. Fifty is the new forty. Senescence is the new juvenility, Alzheimer's is the new acne. Sometimes they would sit over a bottle of wine and talk about their future. But it was difficult for them to plan in the way other people did. Colette felt that maybe Al was withholding information, information about the future that she could very well part with. Her questions about this life and the next were by no means resolved in a way that satisfied her; and she was always thinking of new ones. But what can you do? You have to make an accommodation. You have to accept certain givens. You can't waste time every day worrying about the theory of your life, you have to get on with the practice. Maybe I'll get into Kabbalah, Al said. That seems to be the thing now. Colette said, maybe I'll get into gardening. We could have some shrubs, now Morris isn't here to hide behind them. Michelle and Evan keep hinting we should do something at the back. Get some flags laid, at least.

'They keep talking to me about the weather,' Al said. 'I don't know why.'

'Just being English, I suppose,' Colette said innocently. She sat brooding over the Yellow Pages. 'I might ring up a gardening service. But not the one that sent that idiot last time, the one who couldn't start the mower.'

'Do the next-doors still think we're lesbians?'

'I expect so.' Colette added, 'I hope it spoils their enjoyment of their property.'

She rang up the gardening service. A few flags, so less grass to mow, she thought. Her imagination didn't stretch beyond an alleviation of her weekly routine. She made sure it didn't. If she allowed herself to think about her life as a whole she felt an emptiness, an insufficiency: as if her plate had been taken away before she'd finished eating.

Meanwhile, Evan leaned on the fence, watching her mow. She wondered if he was wearing an expression of lechery, but when she turned, it was actually an expression of sympathy. 'I sometimes think, AstroTurf?' he said. 'Don't you? They're bringing in an auto-mower, one you pre-programme. But I suppose it'll be a while before they hit the shops.'

His own plot was scuffed up and worn bald by the skirmishing of his two older brats. Colette was amazed at the speed with which they had grown. She remembered Michelle jiggling them on a hip; now they were out at all hours, scavenging and savaging, leaving scorched earth behind them, like child soldiers in an African war. Inside the house, Michelle was training up another one; when they had the French windows open, you could hear its stifled wails and roars.

'What you need there is a shed,' Evan said. 'Stop you needing to get your mower out of the garage and walk it round the side.'

'I'm going to hire a man,' Colette said. 'It didn't work out before, but I'm trying somebody different. Going to do some planting.'

'There it is,' Evan said. 'You need a man for some things, you see.'

Colette banged into the house. 'Evan says we need a man.'

'Oh, surely not,' Alison said. 'Or not any man we know.'

'He also says we need a shed.'

Alison looked surprised, a little hesitant. She frowned. 'A shed? I suppose that'll be all right,' she said.

On Sunday they went down the A322 to a shed supplier. Alison wandered around looking at the different kinds. There were some like Regency arbours, and some like miniaturised Tudor houses, and some with cupolas and arabesque cornicing. There was one that reminded her of a Shinto shrine; Cara would probably go for that, she thought. Mandy would want the one with the onion dome. She liked the Swiss chalets, with little porches. She imagined hanging gingham curtains. I could go in there, she thought, shrunk (in thought-form) to a small size. I could have a doll's teaset and little cakes with pastel fondant icing and candied fruit on top.

Colette said, 'We were hoping, my friend and I, to buy a shed.'

'Nowadays,' the man advised, 'we call them garden buildings.'

'OK, a garden building,' Al said. 'Yes, that would be nice.'

'We only need something basic,' Colette said. 'What sort of price are we looking at?'

'Oh,' said the man, 'before we discuss price, let's study your needs.'

Alison pointed to a sort of cricket pavilion. 'What if our need were that one?'

'Yes, the Grace Road,' the man said. 'An excellent choice where space is no object.' He thumbed his lists. 'Let me tell you what that comes in at.'

Colette peered over his shoulder. 'Good God,' Colette said. 'Don't be silly, Al. We don't want that.'

The man ushered them to a revolving summerhouse. 'This is nice,' he said, 'for a lady. You can envisage yourself, as the day closes, sitting with your face turned to the west, a cooling drink in hand.'

'Give over!' Colette said. 'All we want is a place to keep the mower.'

'But what about your other essential equipment? What about your barbecue? And what about your winter storage? Tables, waterproof covers for tables, parasols, waterproof covers for parasols—'

'Garage,' said Colette.

'I see,' the man said. 'So forcing you to park your car in the open, exposing it to the elements and the risk of theft?'

'We've got neighbourhood watch.'

'Yes,' Alison said. 'We all watch each other, and report each other's movements.'

She thought of the spirit trucks, and the mound beneath the blanket: she imagined the nature of it.

'Neighbourhood watch? I wish you joy of it! In my opinion, householders should be armed. We in the Bisley area are run ragged by opportunistic thieves and every type of intruder. Police Constable Delingbole gave us a lecture on home security.'

'Can we get on?' Colette said. 'I've set aside this afternoon for buying a shed, and I want to get it sorted, we still have to get our food shopping.'

Alison saw her dreams of dolls' teatime fading. Come to think of it, had she ever had a doll? She followed the salesman towards a small log cabin. 'We call this one "Old Smokey",' he said. 'It takes its inspiration, the designers claim, from railway buildings in the golden days of the Old West.'

Colette turned her back, and stalked away in the direction of the honest working sheds. Just as Alison was about to follow her, she thought she saw something move, inside Old Smokey. For a second she saw a face, looking out at her. Bugger, she thought, a haunted shed. But it was nobody she knew. She trailed after Colette, thinking, we're not going to get anything nice, we're just going to get one of these titchy sheds that anybody could have. What if I lay on the ground and said, it's my money, I want one of those cream-painted Shaker-style ones with a porch?

She caught up with them. Colette must be in an exceptionally nice mood today, because she hadn't struck the salesman. 'Pent or apex?' he demanded.

Colette said, 'It's no good trying to blind me with science. The pent are the ones with a sloping roof, and the apex are the ones with pointy roofs. That's obvious.'

'I can do you a Sissinghurst. Wooden garden workshop, twelve by ten, double door and eight fixed glass windows, delivery date normally one month, but we could be flexible on that. £699.99, on the road price.'

'You've got a nerve,' Colette said.

Alison said, 'Did you see somebody, Colette? Inside Old Smokey?'

The salesman said, 'That will be a customer, madam.'

'He didn't look like a customer.'

'Nor do I,' Colette said. 'That's obvious. Are you going to sell me something, or shall I drive up to Nottcutts on the A30?'

Al pitied the man; like her, he had his job to do, and part of his job was to stimulate the customer's imagination. 'Don't worry,' she said, 'we'll have one from you. Honest. If you can just point us to the kind my friend wants.'

'I've lost my bearings here,' the man said. 'I confess to a certain amount of total bafflement. Which of you ladies is the purchaser?'

'Oh, let's not go through that again,' Colette groaned. 'Al, you take over.' She walked away, giggling, between the ornamental wheelbarrow planters, the cast-iron conservatory frogs and the roughcast buddhas. Her thin shoulders twitched.

'Will you sell one to me?' Al asked. She smiled her sweetest smile. 'What about that one?'

'What, the Balmoral?' the man sneered. 'Eight by ten pent with single pitch roof? Well, that seems like a decision made, at last. Thank you, madam, it seems we've found something to suit you. The only problem is, as I could have told you if you'd let me get a word in edgewise, it's the end of the range.'

'That's OK,' Al said. 'I'm not bothered about whether it's in fashion.

'No,' the man said, 'what I'm saying to you is this, it would be futile, at this stage in the season, for me to ask the manufacturer to supply.'

'But what about this one? The one standing here?' Al tapped its walls. 'You could send it right away, couldn't you?'

The man turned away. He needed to struggle with his temper. His grandad had come through in spirit, and was sitting on the Balmoral's roof – its pent – ruminatively working his way through a bag of sweets. When the man spoke, Grandad flapped his tongue out, with a melting humbug on the end of it. 'Excuse me, madam—'

'Go ahead.'

'—are you asking me and my colleagues to dismantle that garden building and supervise its immediate transport, for a price of some four hundred pounds plus VAT plus our normal service charge? While the World Cup's on?'

'Well, what else are you going to do with it?' Colette came up to rejoin them, her hands thrust deep in the pockets of her jeans. 'You planning to leave it there till it falls down by itself?' Her foot scuffed the ground, kicked out casually at a concrete otter with its concrete pup. 'If you don't sell it now, mate, you never will. So come on, look sharp. Whistle up your crew and let's get on with the job.'

'What about your hardstanding?' the man said. 'I don't suppose you've given a thought to your hardstanding. Have you?'

As they walked back to the car, Colette said, 'You know, I really think, when men talk, it's worse than when they don't.'

Alison looked at her narrowly, sideways. She waited for more.

'Gavin never said much. He'd say nothing for such a long time that you wanted to lean over and poke your finger in him to see if he was dead. I used to say, tell me your thoughts, Gavin. You must have thoughts. You remember when we met him, in Farnham?'

Alison nodded. She had smelled, trailing after Gavin, the reek of a past life: an old tweed collar rancid with hair oil. His aura was oatmeal, grey: it was as tough as old rope.

'Well . . .' Colette said. She flicked her remote to open the car doors. 'I wonder what he was doing in Farnham.'

'Having a run-out?'

'He could shop in Twickenham.'

'Change of scene?'

'Or Richmond.' Colette chewed her pale lip. 'I wonder what he wanted in Elphicks? Because when you think, he gets all he needs at car shops.'

'Perhaps he wanted a new shirt.'

'He has a wardrobe full of shirts. He has fifty shirts. He must have. I used to pay a woman to iron them. Why did *I* pay? He seemed to think, if I didn't want to do it myself, I ought to pay. When I look back now, I can't for one minute imagine what was going through my head, when I agreed to that.'

'Still,' Al said. She eased herself into her seat. 'Some years have passed. Since you were together. They might be – I don't know – frayed? His neck might have grown.'

'Oh yes,' Colette said. 'He looks porky, all right. But he never did up his top button. So. Anyway. Plenty of shirts.'

'But a new tie? Socks, underpants?' She felt shy; she'd never lived with a man.

'Knickers?' Colette said. 'Car shops every time. Halfords. Velour for the proles, but leather for Gavin, top spec. They stock them in six-packs, shouldn't wonder. Or else he buys them mail order from a rescue service.'

'A rescue service?'

'You know. AA. RAC. National Breakdown.'

'I know. But I didn't think Gavin would need rescuing.'

'Oh, he just likes to have a badge and a personal number.'

'Have I got a personal number?'

'You are in all the major motoring organisations, Alison.'

'Belt-and-braces approach?'

'If you like.' Colette swung them out of the shed sellers'

compound, carelessly scattering a party of parents and children who were clustering about the hot-dog stand. 'That's done their arteries a favour,' Colette said. 'Yes, you have several, but you don't need to know them.'

'Perhaps I do,' Al said. 'In case anything happened to you.'

'Why?' Colette was alarmed. 'Are you seeing something?'

'No, no, nothing like that. Colette, don't drive us off the road!'

Colette corrected their course. Their hearts were beating fast. The lucky opals had paled on Alison's fists. You see, she thought. That's how accidents happen. There was a silence.

'I don't really like secrets,' Alison said.

'Bloody hell!' Colette said. 'It's only a few digits.' She relented. 'I'll show you where I keep them. On the computer. Which file.'

Her heart sank. Why had she said that? She'd just bought an elegant little laptop, silver and pleasingly feminine. She could perch it on her knees and work in bed. But when Al loomed up with a cup of coffee for her, the keyboard started chattering and scrambled itself.

'So what about when you lived with Gavin, did he tell you his personal number?'

Colette tilted up her chin. 'He kept it secret. He kept it where I couldn't access it.'

'That seems a bit unnecessary,' Alison said, thinking, now you know how it feels, my girl.

'He wouldn't put me on joint membership. I think he was ashamed to phone them up and mention my car. It was all I could afford, at the time. I used to say, what's your problem, Gavin? It gets me from A to B.'

Alison thought, if I were a great enthusiast for motoring, and somebody said, 'It gets me from A to B,' I think I would sneak up on them and smash their skull in with a spanner

– or whatever's good to smash skulls in, that you keep in the back of a car.

'We'd have rows,' Colette said. 'He thought I should have a better car. Something flash. He thought I should run up debts.'

Debt and dishonour, Al thought. Oh dear. Oh dear and damnation. If somebody said to me, 'What's your problem?' in that tone of voice, I would probably wait till they were snoring and drive a hot needle through their tongue.

'And as it worked out, I was putting so much into the household – his ironing, and so on – I went through a whole winter without cover. Anything could have happened. I could have broken down in the middle of nowhere.'

'On a lonely road at night.'

'Exactly.'

'On a lonely motorway.'

'Yes! You stop on the hard shoulder, if you get out – Jesus,' Colette slapped the wheel, 'they just drive into you.'

'Or suppose a man stopped to help you. Could you trust him?'

'A stranger?'

'He would be. On a lonely road at night. He wouldn't be anyone you knew.'

'You're advised to stay put and lock your doors. Don't even put your window down.'

'By the rescue services? Is that what they say?'

'It's what the police say! Alison, you drove yourself around, didn't you? Before me? You must know.'

She said, 'I try to imagine.'

For think of the perils. Men who wait for you to break down just so they can come and kill you. Men hovering, monitoring the junctions. How would you know a sick car, to follow it? Presumably, smoke would come out of it. She herself, in her driving days, had never thought of such disasters: she sang as she drove, and her engine sang in tune. At the least whine, stutter or hiccup, she sent it her love and prayers, then stuffed it in the garage. She supposed they were fleecing her, at the garage: but that's the way it goes.

She thought, when me and Colette bought the car, soon after we got together, it was quite easy, a good afternoon out, but now we can't even buy a Balmoral without Colette nearly driving us off the road, and me thinking of ways to stave her skull in. It shows how our relationship's come on.

Colette careered them to a halt in the Collingwood's drive, and the handbrake groaned as she hauled at it. 'Bugger,' she said. 'We should have food-shopped.'

'Never mind.'

'You see, Gavin, he didn't care if I was raped, or anything.'

'You could have been drugged with date-rape drugs, and taken away by a man who made you live in a shed. Sorry. Garden building.'

'Don't laugh at me, Al.'

'Look, the man back there asked us a question. Have we given a thought to our hardstanding?'

'Yes! Yes! Of course! I got a man out of the local paper. But I got three quotes!'

'That's OK then. Let's go in. Come on, Colette. It's OK, sweetheart. We can have a cheese omelette. I'll make it. We can go back. We can shop later. For God's sake, they're open till ten.'

Colette walked into the house and her eyes roamed everywhere. 'We'll have to replace that stair carpet,' she said, 'in under a year.'

'You think so?'

'The pile's completely flattened.'

'I could avoid wearing it, if I jumped down the last three steps.'

'No, you might put your back out. But it seems a shame. Only been here two minutes.'

'Three years. Four.'

'Still. All those marks rubbed along the walls. Do you know you leave a mark? Wherever your shoulders touch it, and your big hips. You smear everything, Al. Even if you're eating an orange you slime it all down the wall. It's a disgrace. I'm ashamed to live here.'

'At the mercy of shed merchants,' Al said. 'Ah dear, ah dear, ah dear.'

At first she didn't recognise who was speaking and then she realised it was Mrs McGibbet. She urged Colette towards the kitchen by slow degrees and consoled her with a microwaved sponge pudding, with hot jam and double cream. 'You seriously think I'm going to eat this?' Colette asked: then gulped it down like a hungry dog.

They went to bed all tucked up safe that night. But she dreamt of snapping jaws, and temporary wooden structures. Of Blighto, Harry and Serene.

NINE

It was about 2 a.m.; Colette woke in darkness to the screeching of garden birds. She lay suffering under her duvet, till birdsong was replaced by the long swish of waves against a shingle beach. Then came some twitters, scrapes and squeaks. What's it called? Oh yes, rainforest. She thought, what is rainforest anyway? We never had it when I was at school.

She sat up, grabbed her pillow and beat it. Beyond the wall the croaking and chirping continued, the cheeping of strange night fowl, the rustling of the undergrowth. She lay back again, stared at the ceiling: where the ceiling would be. The jungle, she thought, that's what we had; but they don't call it the jungle now. A green snake looped down from a branch and smiled into her face. It unravelled itself, falling, falling . . . she slept again. A need to urinate woke her. Al's sodding relaxation tapes had reached the Waterfall track.

She stood up, dazed, passing her hand over her hair to flatten it. Now she could see the outlines of the furniture; the light behind the curtains was brilliant. She crept into her en suite and relieved herself. On her way back to bed she pulled aside the curtain. A full moon silvered the Balmoral, and frosted its pent.

There was a man on the lawn. He was walking around it in circles, as if under an enchantment. She pulled back, dropped the curtain. She had seen him before, perhaps in a dream.

She lay down again. The Waterfall track was finished, and had given way to the music of dolphins and whales. In the cradle of the deep she swayed, slept, and slept more deeply still.

It was 5 a.m. when Al came down. Her guts were churning; this happened. She could eat quite an ordinary meal, but her insides would say, no-no, not for you. She raised the kitchen blind, and while her bicarb fizzed in a glass at her elbow she looked out over the larch-lap fences swathed in pearly light. Something moved, a shadow against the lawn. In the distance, a milk float hummed, and nearer at hand an early businessman slammed with a metallic clatter his garage's Georgian door.

Alison unlocked the kitchen door and stepped out. The morning was fresh and damp. From across the estate a car alarm whooped and yodelled. The man on the lawn was young, and had a dark stubble and a bluish pallor. He wore a woolly hat pulled down over his brow. His big trainers bruised his footprints into the dew. He saw Alison, but hardly checked his stride, simply raising two fingers to his forehead in acknowledgement.

What's your name? she asked him silently.

There was no reply.

It's all right, you can tell Al, don't be shy. The creature smiled shyly and continued to circle.

She thought, you can go under a false name if you like. Just as long as I have something to call you by, to make our life together possible. She thought, look at him, look at him!

Why can't I get a spirit guide with some dress sense?

Yet there was something humble in his manner that she liked. She stood shivering, waiting for him to communicate. A train rattled away in the distance, up from Hampshire, London-bound. She noticed how it gently shook the morning; the light broke up around her, flaking into creamy fragments edged with gold, then settling again. The sun was creeping around the edge of a Rodney. She blinked, and the lawn was empty.

Colette, pouring her orange juice at eight thirty, said, 'Al, you cannot have two pieces of toast.'

Colette was making her diet; it was her new hobby.

'One?'

'Yes, one. With a scrape – no more than a scrape, mind – of low-fat spread.'

'And a scrape of jam?'

'No. Jam will play havoc with your metabolism.' She sipped her orange juice. 'I dreamt there was a man on the lawn.'

'Did you?' Alison frowned, holding the lid of the bread bin before her like a shield. 'On the lawn? Last night? What was he like?'

'Dunno,' Colette said. 'I almost came and woke you.'

'In your dream?'

'Yes. No. I think I was dreaming that I was awake.'

'That's common,' Al said. 'Those sorts of dreams, people who are sensitives have them all the time.' She thought, I dreamt there were trucks outside the house, and a blanket in the back of one, and under that blanket, what? In my dream I came inside and lay down again, and dreamt again, within my dream; I dreamt of an animal, tight and trembling inside its skin, quivering with lust as it wolfed human meat from a bowl. She said, I wonder if you're becoming a sensitive, Colette? She didn't say it aloud. Colette said, 'When

I agreed to one slice of bread, I meant one normal-sized one, not one slice two inches thick.'

'Ah. Then you should have said.'

'Be reasonable.' Colette crossed the kitchen and barged into her. 'I'll show you what you can have. Give me that bread knife.'

Al's fingers yielded it: unwillingly. She and the bread knife were friends.

It was gardening day. The new contractors had brought plans and costed out the decking. They were going to build a water feature; it would be more like a small fountain than a pond. By the time Colette had beaten down their estimate by a few hundred pounds, she had forgotten all about her disturbed night, and her mood, like the day, was sunny.

As the men were leaving, Michelle beckoned her to the fence. 'Glad to see you're doing something with it, at last. It was a bit of an eyesore, lying all bare like that. By the way . . . I don't know if I should mention . . . when Evan got up this morning he saw a man in your garden. Evan thought he was trying the shed door.'

'Oh. Anyone we know?'

'Evan had never seen him before. He rang your doorbell.'

'Who, the man?'

'No, Evan. You must have been in the land of dreams, both of you. Evan said, they're not hearing me. He said, all right for some.'

'The advantages,' Colette said, 'of the child-free lifestyle.'

'Evan said, they've got no lock on their side gate. And them two women alone.'

'I'll get a lock,' Colette snapped. 'And seeing as the blessed gate is all of five feet high, and anybody but a midget could vault over it, I'll get some barbed wire on top, shall I?'

'Now that would be unsightly,' Michelle said. 'No, what

you should do, come to our next meeting with community policing and get some advice. This is a big time of year for shed crime. Police Constable Delingbole gave us a talk on it.'

'I'm sorry I missed that,' Colette said. 'Anyway, the shed's empty. All the stuff's still locked in the garage, waiting for me to move it. By the way, has Evan found any of those white worms?'

'What?' Michelle said. 'White worms? Yuk. Are they in your garden?'

'No, they're in Reading,' Colette said. 'At the last sighting. A man was digging in his garden and there they were on the end of his spade, huge writhing clusters of them. Did Constable Wossname not mention it?'

Michelle shook her head. She looked as if she might throw up.

'I can't think why he didn't. It's been in all the papers. The poor man's had to board his property up. Now he's asking for an investigation. Thing with worms is, they travel under ground, they'll be heading out in search of a food source, and of course being radioactive they won't hang about, they'll be scorching along like buggery. Excuse my language, but being the police he ought to have warned you really.'

'Oh God,' Michelle said. 'Evan didn't mention it either. Didn't want to scare me, I suppose. What can we do? Shall I ring the council?'

'You ask for pest control, I think. And then they come out with very fine mesh nets, and fence all around your garden with them.'

'Are you having them?'

'Oh yes. Same time as we get the decking, to save digging up twice near the house.'

'Do you have to pay?'

''Fraid so. But it's worth it, wouldn't you say?'

* * *

She went back into the house and said, 'Al, I've told Michelle that gross poisoned worms are going to come and eat her kiddiewinks.'

Al looked up, frowning, from her tarot spread. 'Why did you do that?'

'Just to see her shit herself.' Then she remembered. 'By the way, that dream I had, it wasn't a dream. When Evan got up this morning he saw some bloke messing around near the shed.'

Alison laid the cards down. Her situation, she saw, needed a rethink. I'll have that rethink, she decided, when Colette goes out.

In the kitchen, out of Colette's earshot, the breakfast dishes were chinking together; a little spirit woman was pushing them around on the worktop, wanting to help, wanting to wash up for them but not knowing how. 'Excuse me, excuse me,' she was saying, 'have you seen Maureen Harrison?'

Honestly, Al thought. A spirit guide is wasted on Colette. I ought to take time out and lay hold of Maureen Harrison and send her zinging to the next stage, out of Colette's way, and then grab her poor little friend and catapult her after. It would be doing them a favour, in the long run. But she imagined their frail flesh shrinking inside the baggy sleeves of their cardigans (where their cardigans would be) as her strong psychic grip fell on their arms; she imagined the old pair weeping and struggling, snapping their feeble bones under her hand. Muscular tactics were seldom of use, she had found, when you needed to send a spirit over. You call it firm action and you think it's for their own good, but they don't think so. She knows psychics who will call in a clergyman at the least excuse. But that's like sending the bailiffs in: it shames them. It's like dosing them with a laxative when they can't get to their commode.

The telephone rang. Al lifted the receiver and said loudly,

'Hello, and how's Natasha this fine morning? And the Tsars? Good, good.' She dropped her voice confidingly. 'Hi, Mandy, how are you, love?' She smirked to herself: who needs caller display? Colette, that's who. She saw Colette scowl at her: as if she were taking some mean advantage. When Colette left the room she said to Mandy, 'Guess what? I thought Colette had seen a spirit.'

'And had she?'

'It seems not. It looks like it was a burglar.'

'Oh dear, anything taken?'

'No, he didn't get in. Just walked about outside.'

'Why did she think he was a spirit?'

'It was last night. She thought she was dreaming. It was me who thought it was a spirit. When she said, I saw a man outside by moonlight, I thought I'd got a new guide.'

'No sign of Morris coming back?'

'None, thankfully.'

'I'll drink to that.'

Only I have nightmares, Al wanted to say: but who doesn't, in our trade?

'So did you ring the police?' Mandy said. 'Because it's awful down here on the coast. Your teeth aren't safe in your head.'

'No, I didn't bother. There's nothing to tell them. I think I saw him myself. He didn't look harmful. If it was the same man. Unless there are different men wandering around our garden. Which is possible, of course.'

'Don't take any chances,' Mandy said. 'Anyway, Al, I won't take up your morning, let's cut to the chase. There's a new psychic supplier opened down in Cornwall, and they've got a very keen price list with some special introductory offers. Also, for a limited period they're doing free postage and packaging. Cara put me on to them. She's got some excellent runes and she says they're going down very well with her regulars. You want a change, don't you, from time to time? A change is as good as a rest.'

Alison scribbled down the details. 'OK,' she said, 'I'll pass it on to Colette. You're a good mate, Mand. I wish I saw more of you.'

'Drive down,' Mandy said. 'We'll have a girls' night out.'

'I couldn't. I don't drive any more.'

'How hard can it be? Cut across to Dorking, then straight down the A24—'

'I've lost confidence. Behind the wheel.'

'Let me know what time you're leaving, and I'll chant for you.'

'I couldn't. I couldn't stay out overnight. I couldn't leave Colette.'

'Chrissake! Get in the car and do it, Al! She doesn't own you.'

'She says what toast I can have.'

'What?'

'How thick a slice. I can't have butter. Not any. It's awful.'

'God, she's such a bossy little madam!'

'But she's very efficient. She's great with the VAT. I couldn't do it, you see. So I have to put up with her.'

'Have you heard of accountants?' Mandy said scathingly. 'What do you think an accountant is for? Toss your bloody receipts in a brown envelope and stuff them in the postbox at the end of the quarter. That's what I do.'

'She'd be so hurt,' Al said. 'She's got so little in her life, really. She has this ex with a nasty aura, I only got a glimpse of it but it churns your stomach. She needs me, you see. She needs some love.'

'She needs a slap!' Mandy said. 'And if I hear any more of this toast business, I'll whizz up there to Woking and give it her myself.'

* * *

Over the course of the day, it became clear to Al's sharp eye that they had a guest in the shed. Something or someone was lurking; presumably it was the young lad in the hat. Perhaps, she thought, I should take something to defend myself, in case he turns nasty. Hesitating in the kitchen, she had at last picked up the bacon scissors. The blades fitted snugly into her palm, and the bright orange handles looked playfully robust, in a rough-and-tumble sort of way; it was much the sort of weapon you'd choose to break up a fight in a primary school playground. If anybody sees me, she thought, they'll just assume that I'm about some tricky little garden operation; that I'm notching a stem, nipping a bud, cutting a bloom, except there isn't one to cut, we're not up to flowers yet.

When she opened the shed door, she braced herself for the young man to rush at her, try to push past. It might be the best thing, she thought, if he did. I ought to step back and let him go, if it comes to that. Except that if someone's been in my outbuilding I'd like to know why.

The shed was in gloom, its small window spattered, as if it had been raining mud. In the corner was a mournful bundle which barely stirred, let alone made a dash for it. The boy was drawn into a foetal position, arms around his knees; his eyes travelled upwards, and stuck when they reached her right hand.

'I'm not going to hurt you,' she said. She peered down at him, perplexed. 'Shall I make you a cup of tea?'

He had been living rough at the garden centre, the young man said. 'I saw you with your friend, blonde-haired lady, innit? You were looking at the Grace Road.'

'That's right,' Al said.

'Thanks for this tea, by the way, this is good tea. Then after that you looked at Old Smokey, but you gave it the thumbs down. You gave it the old heave-ho.'

As Al leaned back against the wall of the new shed, it shivered slightly, swayed. Not the most solid structure, she thought. 'That's where you were,' she said, 'when I spotted you. You were hanging about inside Old Smokey.'

'I thought you saw me.' His head drooped. 'You didn't say hello.'

'I didn't know you, how could I?' She didn't say, I thought you were in spectral form.

'Any more of this tea?'

'Wait a minute.'

Alison took the mug from him. She inched open the door of the Balmoral, and peeped out to make sure there was no one in the neighbouring gardens, before she made a dash for the house. She couldn't rule out, of course, being seen by spectators from an upper window. She thought, I've a perfect right to walk across my own lawn, from my own shed, with a china mug in my hand. But she found herself scuttling, head down.

She scurried into the kitchen and slammed the back door after her. She ran to the kettle and slammed down the switch. She rummaged in a cupboard. Better make him a flask, she thought. Can't be running across the lawn, bent double, every time he wants a hot drink.

The flask was at the back of the cupboard, bottom shelf, skidding shyly from her fingertips into the corner. She had to bend deeply to fish it out. The blood rushed to her head and thumped at the back of her nose. As she straightened up, her head swam. She thought, he's my visitor. I can have a visitor, if I want, I suppose?

His mug was on the draining board, marked with grimy fingerprints. He can make do with the top of the flask for his cup, she thought. I'll take him some kitchen roll to wipe it round with. She tore some off, waiting impatiently for the kettle. Sugar, she thought, diving into a cupboard.

I expect he'll want lots of sugar, tramps always do.

When she got back, Mart – that was his name, he said – was crouching in the corner away from the light. 'I thought somebody might look through that window,' he said, 'while you was away.'

'I've been as quick as I could. Here.'

He shook as he held the cup. She put her hand round his to steady it as she poured. 'You not having one?' he said.

'I'll have mine inside later.' She said gently, 'You'd better not come inside. My friend wouldn't like it.'

'I used to live in the Far Pavilions,' he said. 'I lived there nice for two nights. Then they chased me out. They thought I was off the premises but I looped back and broke into Old Smokey. I was just hanging about wondering what I should do next, then I saw you. And later I saw your shed go. So I followed it.'

'Where did you live before that?'

'Dunno. One time I slept on me mate's floor. But his floor got took up. They came from the council. The rat officer.'

'That was unlucky. People say – Evan, the man next door, he says – that you're never more than three feet from a rat in Britain today. Or is it two feet?' She frowned. 'So when the floor was taken up, was that when you went to the garden centre?'

'No, next I went in the park under the bandstand. With Pinto. My mate. Whose floor got took up. We used to go down Sheerwater, they had a drop-in centre. One day we get there and they've put steel shutters up. They said, it's just a policy, don't take it to heart.'

Mart wore a khaki jacket with lots of pockets, and beneath it a sweatshirt that was once a colour, and stained cotton trousers with some rips in them. Alison thought, I've seen worse things, in the silence of the night.

'Look,' she said, 'don't misunderstand me, I have no right

to ask you questions, but if you're going to be in my garden for much more of today I would like to know if you're violent, or on drugs.'

Mart lurched sideways. Though he was young, his joints creaked and snapped. Al saw that he had been sitting on a rucksack. It was a flat one, with very little in it. Perhaps he was trying to hatch something, she thought; some possessions. She felt a rush of pity; her face flushed. It's not an easy life in a shed.

'You feeling all right?' Mart asked her. Out of his rucksack he took a collection of pill bottles and passed them to her one by one.

'Oh, but these are from the chemist,' she said. 'So that's all right.' She peered at the label. 'My mum used to have these. And these, too, I think.' She unscrewed the cap and put a finger in, swizzling the capsules around. 'I recognise the colour. I don't think she liked those ones.'

'Those are nice rings you've got,' he said.

'They're my lucky opals.'

'That's where I went wrong,' Mart said. 'No luck.'

As she passed him the bottles back, she noticed that the surface of the stones had turned a sulky, resistant blue. Stuff you, she thought, I'm not going to be told what to do by a bunch of opals. Mart stowed the bottles carefully in his rucksack.

'So,' she said, 'have you been in hospital recently?'

'You know, here and there,' Mart said. 'On and off. As and when. I was going to be in a policy, but then they never.'

'What policy was that?'

Mart struggled. 'A policy, it's like . . . it's either like, shutting down, or it's like, admissions, or it's . . . removals. You go to another place. But not with a removal van. Because you haven't anything to put in one.'

'So when you – when they, when they get a new policy, you get moved to somewhere else?'

'More or less,' Mart said. 'But they didn't get one, or I wasn't in for it, I don't know if they put me down for it under another name, but I didn't get moved, so I just went, after a bit I just went.'

'And this drop-in centre, is it still closed?'

'Dunno,' Mart said. 'I couldn't go to Sheerwater on the off chance, with shoes like mine.'

She looked at his feet and thought, I see what you mean. She said, 'I could drive you. That would save you wearing your shoes out any more. But my friend's gone out in our car. So if you could just hide here till she comes back?'

'I dunno,' Mart said. 'Could I have a sandwich?'

'Yes,' she said. She added bitterly, 'There's plenty of bread.'

Back in the kitchen, she thought, I see it all. Mother scooped into hospital at the last minute, the foetal heart monitor banging away like the bells of hell. Mama unregistered, unweighed, unloved, innocent of antenatal care and turning up at the hospital because she believes – God love her – that her cramping needs relief: then sweat-streaked, panicked and amazed, she is crying out so hard for a glass of water that by the time they give it her, she prefers a glass of water to her newborn child. She would have sold him, new as he was, in his skin. She would have sold him to the midwives for an early relief from her thirst.

What can I give him? Alison wonders. What would he enjoy? Poor little bugger. You see somebody like that and say, well, his mother must have loved him: but in his case, no. She took out a cold chicken from the fridge and turned it out from its jellied, splintering foil. It was half used, half stripped. She washed her hands, opened a drawer, picked out a sharp little knife and worked away, shearing tender fragments from the carcass. Close to the bone, the meat was tender. So was the child Mart himself, picked out of the womb; as he was carried away, his legs kicked, the blood on his torso staled and dried.

And then the foster-mother. Who stuck for a year or two. Till a policy moved him on to the next. I wish I'd had a foster-mother, Al thought. If I'd just been given a break till I was two or three, I might have turned out normal, instead of my brain all cross-wired so I'm forced to know the biographies of strangers. And pity them.

By the time she'd thought all this, she was grilling bacon. As she whipped the rashers over with the tongs, she thought, why am I doing this? God knows. I feel sorry for the bloke. Homeless and down on his luck.

She made towering, toasted sandwiches, oiled with mayonnaise, garnished with cucumber, cherry tomatoes and hard-boiled eggs. She made twice as many as one homeless mad person could possibly consume. She made what she anticipated would be the very best plate of sandwiches Mart had ever seen in his life.

He ate them without comment, except for saying, 'Not very good bacon, this. You ought to get that kind that is made by the Prince of Wales.'

Sometimes he said, 'Aren't you having one?' but she knew he hoped she wasn't, and she said, 'I'll have mine later.' She glanced at her watch. 'Is that the time? I've got a telephone client.'

'I used to have a watch,' Mart said. 'But Police Constable Delingbole stamped on it.' He looked up at her from the corner and begged, 'Don't be long.'

Lucky that Colette had gone to Guildford! Al could count on her to be away for some hours – in that time she could give the boy some advice and twenty quid, and set him on his way. Colette had things to do – pop into the occult shop on White Lion Walk with some flyers, etc. – but mainly she would be going shopping, trawling around the House of Fraser for that elusive perfect lip-shade, and getting her hair cut into a white pudding-bowl shape. Colette's hair never seemed to grow, not so that you noticed, yet she felt some sort of social obligation to have it trimmed and tweaked every six weeks. When she came home she would stand before the mirror and rage at the stylist, but it never looked any different – not that Alison could see.

Her telephone consultation ran the full hour, and after it Al was so hungry that she had to grab a bowl of corn flakes, standing up in the kitchen. A feeling, something like fellow feeling, was hauling her back in the direction of Mart; she hated to think of him shrinking from the light, crouching on the hard floor.

'First I was a white-liner,' Mart said. 'That's where you paint lines on the road, excellent daily rate and no previous experience required. A truck picked us up every morning at the bandstand and took us to where we were lining that day. You see, Pinto was with me. He got bored of it. I didn't get bored of it, I liked it. But Pinto, he started painting little islands in the road, then he said, go on, go on, let's do a box junction. It took us an hour. But when they saw it, they weren't all that keen. They said, you're off the job, mate, and the ganger said, come here while I give you a smack with this shovel.' Mart rubbed his head, his eyes distant. 'But then they said, we'll give you another chance, you can go on roadworks. We got put on human traffic light. Twirling a sign, STOP–GO. But the motorists wouldn't observe me. Stop and go when they fucking well liked. So the boss says, lads, you're not in sync. He says that's your big problem that you've got. You're twirling, but you're not twirling in sync. So I got took off that job.'

'And then?'

Al had been to the garage to fetch them two folding garden chairs. She didn't feel she could keep standing, with her back to the shed wall and Mart crouching at her feet. It was natural for Mart to want to tell his life story, his career history, just to reassure her that he wasn't an axe murderer; not that anything he had told her had actually reassured her of that, but she thought, I would have a feeling, my skin would prickle and I'd know.

'So, and then . . .' Mart said. He frowned.

'Don't worry,' Al said. 'You don't have to tell me if you don't want.'

All Mart's jobs seemed to have involved hanging about in public places. For a while he was a car-park attendant, but they said he didn't attend it enough. He was a park patroller, selling tickets for the attractions. 'But some little lads knocked me down and robbed my tickets and threw them in the pond.'

'Didn't the hospital give you any help? When you got out?'

'You see, I came through the net,' Mart said. 'I'm an outloop. I'm on a list, but I'm not computerate yet. I think, the list I was on, I think they lost it.'

More than likely, Al thought. I dare say, when I was a kid, people put me on a list. I expect they made a list of bruises, that sort of thing, noticeable marks. But it never came to anything. I guess that list got put in a file; I guess that file got left in a drawer; 'I'd like to know,' she said, 'how you got in trouble with the police.'

Mart said, 'I was at the zone. I was near the scene. I had to be somewhere. Somebody had to be there. Police Constable Delingbole beat the shit out of me.'

'Mart, ought you to be taking your pills? What time do you have them?'

'You see, we got some stickers and we put them on people's cars, that were parked. We waited till we saw them leave and then we came with the stickers and put NO PARKING BY ORDER on their windscreen. Then we hid in the bushes. When they came back we jumped out and fined them a fine.'

'Did they pay?'

'No way. One geezer got on his mobile. Delingbole was round like a shot.'

'And where were you?'

'Back in the bushes. He didn't catch us that day. It was a good idea, but it caused a description of us to be made and put in the local paper. *Have you seen this distinctively attired man?'*

'But you're not. I wouldn't call you distinctive.'

'You didn't see the hat I had in those days.'

'No. That's true.'

'By the time I came round your place, I'd got a different hat. I was down on the building site, sometimes they give us tea. I said to this Paddy, look, mate, can I have your hat? Because it's been in the paper about mine. He says, sure, I says, I'll buy it off you, he says, no, you're all right, I've another one at home, a yellow one. So when I came for mowing your garden, I said to your friend, does this hat make me look like a brickie? Because it belonged to a brickie. And she said, I'd take you for a brickie anywhere.'

'So you've met Colette,' Alison said. 'I see. You're the bloke from the gardening service.'

'Yes.' Mart gnawed his lip. 'And that was another job that didn't last. How about some more tea?'

Alison hurried across the garden. Michelle's kids were home from their nursery; she could hear their wailing, and the air was loud with their mother's threats and curses. She brought out another flask, with a mug for herself, and a packet of chocolate digestives, which Colette allowed her to keep in for nervous clients, who liked to crumble and nibble.

This time she made sure she got some; she held the packet on her lap, and offered them to Mart one by one. 'Missus,' he said, 'have you ever been described in the paper?'

She said, 'I have, actually. In the *Windsor Express*.' She'd had three dozen photocopies made. *Attractive, full-figured psychic, Alison Hart.* She'd sent one to her mum, but her mum never said anything. She'd sent them out to her friends, but they'd never said anything either. She had plenty of press cuttings now, of course: but none of them mentioned her appearance. They skirt around it, she thought. She had shown the *Windsor Express* cutting to Colette. Colette had sniggered.

'You were lucky,' Mart said. 'Windsor, you see. That's outside Delingbole's area.'

'I've never had any time for the police,' she said. I suppose I should have called them, when I was a kid. I suppose I could have laid charges. But I was brought up to be scared of a uniform. She remembered them shouting through the letter box: '*Mrs Emmeline Cheetham?*' She thought, why didn't my mum get one of her boyfriends to nail it shut? It isn't as if we had any letters.

Just as Al had finished cleaning the kitchen and tidying away signs of Mart's lunch, Colette came in with a handful of carrier bags, and in a state of outrage. 'I was putting the car away,' she said. 'Somebody's swiped our garden chairs! How did that happen? It must have been that man in the night. But how did he get in the garage? There's no sign of forced entry!'

'You sound like Constable Delingbole,' Alison said.

'Been talking to Michelle, have you? I can tell you, I wish I'd been a bit more wide awake this morning. I should have rung the police as soon as I spotted him. I blame myself.'

'Yes, do,' Alison said, in such a commiserating tone that Colette didn't notice.

'Oh well. I'll claim it on the insurance. What have you had to eat while I've been out?'

'Just some corn flakes. And a bit of salad.'

'Really?' Colette swung open the fridge door. 'Really and truly?' She frowned. 'Where's the rest of the chicken?'

'There wasn't much left, I threw it out. And the bread.'

Colette looked knowing. 'Oh yes?' She lifted the lid of the butter dish. Her eyes swept the worktops, looking for evidence – crumbs, or a slight smearing of the surface. She crossed the kitchen, wrenched open the dishwasher and peered inside; but Al had already washed the grill pan and dishes, and put everything back where it should be. 'Fair enough,' she said grudgingly. 'You know, maybe that bloke down at Bisley was right. If they can get into the garage, they could certainly get into the shed. Maybe it wasn't the best idea. I won't move anything in yet. Till we see. If there's any recurrence, in the neighbourhood. Because I've laid out quite a lot. On forks, and so on.'

'Forks?' Alison said.

'Forks, spades. Hoes. Et cetera.'

'Oh. Right.'

Al thought, she's in such a state of self-reproach that she's forgotten to count the bacon rashers. Or even check the biscuit tin.

'Mart,' Al said, 'do you hear voices? I mean, inside your head? What's it like when you hear them?'

'My hands sweat,' Mart said. 'And my eyes go small in my head.'

'What do they say?'

Mart looked at her cunningly. 'They say, we want tea.'

'I don't mean to intrude, but do you find the pills help?'

'Not really. They just make you thirsty.'

'You know you can't stay here,' Al said.

'Could I just for tonight, missus?'

He calls me missus, she thought, when he wants to be extra-pitiful. 'Don't you have a blanket? I mean, I thought if you'd been sleeping rough you'd at least have a blanket, a sleeping bag. Look, I'll sneak something out.'

'And a flask refill,' said Mart. 'And a dinner, please.'

'I don't see how I can do that.'

She felt ill already – she'd gone all day on a bowl of cereal and a few biscuits. If she were to bring out her low-fat turkey strips and vegetable rice to Mart, he would eat it in two swoops, and then she'd probably faint or something – plus, Colette would say, Al, why are you going into the garden with your ready meal?

'Suppose I give you some money,' she said. 'The supermarket's still open.'

'I'm barred.'

'Really? You could go to the garage shop.'

'Barred there, too. And the off-licence, or else I could get crisps. They shout, sod off, you filthy gyppo.'

'You're not! A gyppo.'

'I tried to get a wash with the hose at the garage, but they chased me out. They said, come round here again and we'll run you over. They said I was disgusting the customers and taking their trade away. I blame Delingbole. I'm barred out of everywhere.'

Anger swarmed up from her empty belly. It was unexpected and unfamiliar, and it created a hot glow behind her ribs. 'Here,' she said. 'Take this, go down the kebab van, I'm sure they'll serve anybody. Don't set off the security lights when you come back.'

While Mart was away, and Colette was watching *EastEnders*, she crept out with a spare duvet and two pillows. She tossed them into the Balmoral, and sped back to the house. The microwave was pinging. She ate in the kitchen, standing once again. I am refused bread in my own house, she thought. I am refused a slice of bread.

For a day or two, Mart came and went by night. 'If Colette sees you, you're stuffed,' she said. 'Unfortunately, I can't predict her comings and goings, she's a real fidget these days, always banging in and out. You'll have to take your chances. Evan next door leaves at eight sharp. Don't let him see you. Half past nine, Michelle takes the kids to nursery. Keep your head down. Post comes at ten, keep out of the postman's way. The middle of the day's not too bad. By three o'clock it gets busy again.'

Mart began again, on the story of how PC Delingbole stamped on his watch.

'I'll lend you one of mine,' she said.

'I don't want your neighbours to see me,' Mart said. 'Or they'll think I'm after their kids. Pinto and me, when we lived down Byfleet, some blokes came kicking on the door, shouting, paedos out!'

'Why did they think you were paedophiles?'

'Dunno. Pinto said, it's the way you look, the way you go around, your toes coming out of your shoes, and that hat you have. But that was when I still had my other hat.'

'So what happened then? After they kicked the door?'

'Pinto called the police!'

'Did they come?'

'Oh, yes. They came in a patrol car. But then they saw it was me.'

'And then?'

A slow smile crept over Mart's face. '"Drive on, Constable Delingbole!"'

She went through her jewellery box for spare watches, and discarded the diamanté ones, which were for on stage. I'd better buy him one, she thought, just a cheap one. And some shoes, I'd have to ask his size. Maybe if he had new shoes he'd move on, before Colette noticed. She had to keep diverting Colette, attracting her attention to spectacles at the front of the house, and chatting to distract her whenever she went into the kitchen. He'll have to be gone, she thought, before she decides to implement any shed security, because as soon as she goes down there she'll see signs of occupation; she imagined the screaming Colette jabbing with her garden fork, and the panic-stricken visitor impaled on its tines.

'Do you think we'd get a bed in here?' Mart asked, when she took him down his flask.

Al said, 'Maybe a futon,' but then she could have bitten her tongue.

'I should of thought to bring a sunlounger, from the garden centre,' Mart said. 'I know!' He struck his hat with the flat of his hand. 'A hammock! That would do me.'

'Mart,' she said, 'are you sure you haven't got a criminal record? Because I couldn't be responsible, I couldn't take a chance, I'd have to tell somebody, you see. You'd have to go.'

'My dad beat my head in with a piece of pipe,' Mart said. 'Does that count?'

'No,' she said. 'You're the victim. That doesn't count.' Severe blows to the skull, she thought. Colette thinks they're very significant. She asked me about them once, on tape. I didn't know why, at the time. I realise now that she thought they might have been the beginning of my abnormality.

'Though it was my stepdad, you know? I always thought it was my dad but my mum said not. No, she said, he's your step.'

'How many stepdads did you have?'

'A few.'

'Me too.'

It was a warm day; they were sitting on the garden chairs, the door propped open slightly to give them some air. 'Good thing we went for one with a window that opens,' Al said. 'Or you'd be stifled.'

'But then again, not,' Mart said. 'For reasons of them surveying me, peeking in and tipping off the Big D.'

'But then again, not,' she agreed. 'I thought of getting curtains, at one time.'

One of the next-door children darted out of the playhouse, shrieking. Al stood up and watched her scoot across the lawn, skid to a halt and sink her teeth into her brother's calf. 'Ouch!' Al said; she winced as if she had felt the wound herself.

'Mummy, Mummy!' the infant yelled. Mart banged the shed door and dropped on all fours. Michelle's voice rang out from the kitchen: 'I'm coming out there, by God I am, and there'll be slaps all round.'

'Get down,' Mart pulled her skirt. 'Don't let her see you.'

'Bite him,' Michelle roared, 'and I'll bloody bite you.'

They knelt on the floor together. Mart was trembling. Al felt she ought to pray. 'Oh Jesus!' Mart said. Tears sprang out of his eyes. He lurched into her. She supported his weight. Sagging against her, he was made of bones and dustbin scraps; his flesh breathed the odour of well-rotted manure. 'There, there,' she murmured. She patted his hat. Michelle shot across the scabby turf, the baby on her arm and her teeth bared.

Colette answered her mobile phone, and a voice said, 'Guess who?'

She guessed at once. What other man would be phoning her? 'Haven't seen you since we ran into you coming out of Elphicks.'

'What?' Gavin said. He sounded dumbstruck; as if she had cursed him.

'The shop,' she said. 'In Farnham. That Saturday?'

'Out of *what*?'

'Elphicks. Why do you have such trouble, Gavin, with the ordinary names of things?'

A pause. Gavin said uneasily, 'You mean that's what it's called? That department store?'

'Yes.'

'Why didn't you say so?'

She said, 'God give me strength.' Then, 'Perhaps you should end this call and we could start again?'

'If you like,' Gavin said. 'OK.' His line went dead. She waited. Her phone buzzed. 'Gavin? Hello?'

'Colette? It's me,' he said.

'What a nice surprise.'

'Is it OK to talk to you now?'

'Yes.'

'Were you busy, or something?'

'Let's just forget you called me before. Let's just have another go, and I won't mention where I last saw you.'

'If that's what you want,' Gavin said airily. His tone showed he thought her capricious in the extreme. 'But why couldn't you talk, was it because *she* was around? You know, fat girl?'

'If you mean Alison, she's out. She's gone for a walk.' Even as Colette said it, it sounded unlikely to her; but that was what Alison had said she was doing.

'So you can talk?'

'Look, Gavin, what do you want?'

'Just checking up on you. Seeing how you're doing.'

'Fine. I'm fine. And how are you doing?' Really, she thought, I'm losing patience with this.

He said, 'I'm seeing somebody. I thought you should know.'

'It's no concern of mine, Gavin.'

But she thought, how odd of him to get it right for once; I may not need to know, but I want to know, of course I want to know. I want her CV, her salary details, and a recent full-length photograph, with her body measurements written on the back, so that I can work out what she's got that's so much better than me.

'What's her name?'

'Zoë.'

'That won't last. Far too classy for you. Is it serious?' It must be, she thought, or he wouldn't be telling me. 'Where did you meet her? Is she in IT?' She must be, of course. Who else did he meet?

'Actually,' he said, 'she's a model.'

'Really?' Colette's voice was cold. She almost said, a model what?

She stood up. 'Look, I can see Alison coming back. I have to go.'

She cut off the call. Alison was lumbering up the hill. Colette stood watching her, the phone still in her hand. Why's she wearing that big coat? Her temperature control must be shot again. She says it's spirits but I bet it's just an early menopause. Look at her! The size of her! Fat girl!

When Al came in Colette was standing in the hall waiting for her. Her face was savage. 'I suppose it's something, that you're taking a bit of exercise!'

Alison nodded. She was out of breath.

'You were practically on your knees, by the time you got halfway up the hill – you should have seen yourself! How far have you waddled, about a mile? You'll have to be sprinting that distance, with weights attached to you, before you see any improvement! Look at you, puffing and sweating!'

Obedient, Al glanced at herself in the hall mirror. There

was a flicker of movement: that's Mart, she thought, scooting out of the side gate.

Alison went into the kitchen, and out of the back door. She unbuttoned her coat and – listening out all the time for Colette – disentangled herself from the two supermarket carrier bags that were swinging like saddlebags at her sides. She placed her surreptitious groceries behind the wheelie bin, came in, and shrugged off the coat.

It's like being a reverse shoplifter, she thought. You get to the checkout with your trolley and you pay for everything; then, when you get outside, you open your coat and start concealing the bags about your person. People stare at you, but you stare back. If they asked you why you were doing it, what would you say? You can't think of a single good reason, except that you want to do a good action.

It had come to this; either she ate, or Mart did. I'll have to explain to him, she thought. How Colette checks up on me all the time. How she controls the groceries. How she shouted, the day you came, when she finally stocktaked the fridge and realised two eggs were missing. How she accused me of eating them boiled and made me ashamed, even though I never ate them, you did. How she supervises every minute of my day. How I can't just go freelance shopping. How, if I took the car, she'd want to know where. And if I drove off by myself, she'd want to know why.

She thought, on Friday at Sainsbury's they have twenty-four-hour opening. So I could sneak out when she was asleep. Not ordinary asleep, that wouldn't do. I'd have to get her drunk. She imagined herself wedging a plastic funnel into Colette's open throat, and pouring Chardonnay through it. I could take the car, she thought, if backing it out of the drive wouldn't wake her. Probably that would only work if

I drugged her. Beat her into insensibility. Come here, she thought: would you like a slap with this shovel?

But really, he must be gone by the weekend. I'll tell him. Even if she doesn't form the ambition to rehome the forks and the hoes, those water-feature people will be around again early next week.

She locked the back door. She crossed the kitchen, stood at the sink and downed a glass of water. All quiet on the shed front; the door was closed, the ground undisturbed. She refilled her glass. Quick, quick, she thought, before she comes in and says tap water can kill you, quick, before she says drinking too fast is a notorious cause of death in the obese.

She was aware that the Collingwood was silent.

She went into the hall. 'Colette?'

No answer. But from above she heard a bleating, a little trail of bleating that grew louder as she followed it upstairs.

She stood outside Colette's door. She is lying on her bed sobbing, she thought. But why? Can she have regretted what she said to me, about my personal fatness? Has a lifetime of tactlessness flashed before her eyes? This didn't seem likely. Colette didn't think she was tactless. She thought she was right.

Whatever, Al thought. Now is my opportunity. While her emotions are detaining her, I will just sneak down the garden and distribute my haul to Mart. Or, as he's gone out, I will leave it inside his door, for him to find as a happy surprise when he returns.

Yesterday she had brought him three oranges. He had not been impressed when she had explained that she could get away with oranges, by claiming to have juiced them. He had hinted that he preferred a steak, but she couldn't see her way to setting up cooking facilities. So he was getting tinned tuna, that sort of thing. She hoped he would appreciate that tins were extremely heavy.

She creaked down the stairs, away from Colette and her grief: whatever that was. At the foot of the stairs, she saw herself, unavoidably, in the glass. Her face looked as pink as a ham. She thought, I could have got him sliced cold meat, I bet that would have been lighter, though of course it being warm weather he'd have to eat it all the same day. At least, this way, I've built him up a little store that he can put in his rucksack, when he leaves.

She opened the back door, tottered out, reached behind the wheelie bin. The bags had gone. Mart must have darted back, crouching low, and swooped them up on his way in. In which case I hope he's got strong teeth, she thought, as I didn't buy him a can-opener.

By close of day, Colette had not come down; but all it will take, Al thought, is a casual glance from her bedroom window, as Mart flits across the lawn by moonlight. Why don't I just give him some money to set him on his way? I can't afford more than, say, a hundred pounds, or Colette will want to know where I drew it out and what I spent it on. She will be quite pleasant about it, knowing I have the right, but she'll be curious all the same . . .

When it was almost dark, she stepped out of the sliding doors.

'Alison? Is that you?' Michelle was waving.

Who else did she think it was? Reluctantly, she moved towards the fence.

'Lean over,' Michelle said. 'I want to whisper to you. Have you heard about this plague of rabbit deaths?'

She shook her head.

'It's very strange, you see. Not that I have any time

personally for rabbits, I wouldn't have any pets near my kids because they spread all sorts of toxicosis. But these little ones at the nursery, they're crying their eyes out. They go down the garden to feed it and it's keeled over in its hutch with a horrible trickle of black blood coming out of its mouth.'

I suppose, Al thought, me keeping Mart in the shed, it's like being a kid again, doing things behind people's backs, stealing food, all that stuff I used to do; running to the corner with any money I got. It's a game really, it's like that dolls' tea party I wanted. We have a lot in common, she thought, me and Mart, it's like having a little brother. She had noticed that Mart was always falling over; that was because of his medication. She thought, my mum, too, she was always falling over.

'So what do the vets say?' she asked Michelle.

'They just say, oh, rabbits, what do you expect? They try to put it on what they've been eating, a bad diet. They blame you, don't they, the owner? That's how they get around it. Evan says personally he has no time for rabbits either, but it's very worrying, in the light of what's going down with the playground. And the vets denying it, you see. He wonders if they know something we don't.'

Oh dear, she said. They ought to hold post-mortems, maybe. She couldn't think what else to say. Got to go, she said; as she limped away from the fence, Michelle called, will the warm weather last till the weekend?

By eight o'clock Al was beginning to feel very hungry. Colette didn't show any sign of coming down and supervising her dinner. She crept upstairs to listen. More and more, this evening reminded her of her youth. The need to tiptoe, listen at doors: sighs and groans from other rooms. 'Colette?' she called softly. 'I need you to do my calories.'

No reply. She eased the door open. 'Colette?'

'Go and eat yourself to death,' Colette said. 'What do I care?'

She was lying face down on the bed. She looked very flat. She looked very out of it. Alison drew the door closed, in a manner so quiet that she hoped it showed her complete respect for Colette's state of mind: so quiet that it offered condolences.

She crept down the garden. The moon had not yet turned the corner above the Jellicoe at the curve of the road, and she wasn't clear where she was putting her feet. She felt she ought to knock; but that's ridiculous, she thought, knock at your own shed?

She inched open the door. Mart was sitting in the dark. He had a torch, and batteries, but they were the wrong size: something else for my shopping list, she thought. She could have fixed him up with a candle, but she didn't trust him not to start a fire.

'Get your shopping?'

'No,' he said. 'What shopping? I'm ravenous in here. Fainting.'

'I'm giving you fifty quid,' Al said. 'Sneak off into Knaphill, will you, and get a takeaway Chinese? Get me a set menu for two, and whatever you want for yourself. Keep the change.'

When Mart left, diving low under the light sensors, she tried to make herself comfortable in the canvas garden chair. The earth was cooling, beneath their hardstanding; she lifted her feet and tried to tuck them beneath her, but the chair threatened to overbalance; she had to sit up straight, metal digging into her back, and plant her feet back on the ground. She thought, I wonder what happened to the shopping?

When Mart came back they sat companionably, licking

spare ribs and tossing down the bones. 'You've got to take the cartons away,' she said. 'Do you understand that? You mustn't put them in our wheelie bin. Or Colette will see them. You have to be gone soon. The garden design will be coming. They'll probably, say, take down that shed, it's an eyesore.' She chewed thoughtfully on a sweet-and-sour prawn. 'I knew we should get a better one.'

'It's late,' Mart said, consulting his new watch. 'You ought to go in.'

'Oh, just so you can finish everything off by yourself!'

'I'm more hungry than you,' Mart said, and she thought, that's true. So in she went. Up to bed. All quiet from Colette's room. She didn't dream, for once; or not of being hungry.

It couldn't last, of course. Previously there had been an element of camouflage about Mart, his dirty clothes blending into the earth-tones of the gardens, but you noticed his feet now, in the big clean navy-and-white shoes, seeming to come around the corner before him.

When he saw Colette approaching, he slammed the door of the shed and wedged his rucksack against it; but Colette defeated him with one push. Her yodel of alarm drove him back against the wall; Al galumphed down the garden, shouting, 'Don't hit him! Don't call the police, he's not dangerous.'

Mart laughed, when Colette said she had seen him on the lawn. 'I bet you thought I was from space, didn't you? You said, oops, there goes an extraterrestrial! Or did you think I was a brickie from off the building site?'

'I didn't form any opinion,' Colette said.

'She thought she was dreaming,' Al said.

'Alison, I'll deal with this, please.'

'In fact, my troubles started with an alien encounter,' Mart said. 'Aliens give you a headache, did you know that? Plus they make you fall over. When you've seen an alien, it's like somebody's drilled your middle out.' He made a gesture – a gouge and a twist – like someone plunging a corer into an apple. 'Pinto,' he said, 'when we was white-lining up near St Albans, he got taken up bodily into an alien craft. Female aliens come and pulled off his overalls and palpitated his body all over.'

'He was dreaming,' Colette said.

Al thought, she doesn't know how lucky we are, we could have been playing host to Pinto as well.

'He wasn't asleep,' Mart said. 'He was carried off. The proof of it is, when he got back, he took his shirt off and they'd erased his tattoo.'

'You can't stay here any longer,' Colette said. 'I hope that's perfectly clear to you?'

'A shed wouldn't do for everybody,' Mart conceded. 'But it'll do nicely for me. Less bugs in a shed.'

'I should have thought there'd be more. Though I'm sure you'll find that it's perfectly clean.'

'Not crawling bugs. Listening bugs.'

'Don't be silly. Who'd want to listen to you? You're a vagrant.'

'And there's cameras everywhere these days,' Mart said. 'Blokes watching you out of control towers. You can't go anywhere without somebody knows about it. You get post from people that don't know you, how do you do that? Even I get post, and I don't have an address. Constable Delingbole says, I've got your number, mate.' He added, under his breath, 'His is written on him.'

'I expect you out of here within ten minutes,' Colette said. 'I am going back to the house and I shall be counting. Then, whatever you say, Alison, I shall call the police and have you removed.'

Al thought, I wonder if Delingbole is real, or in a dream?

Then she thought, yes, of course he's real, Michelle knows him, doesn't she? He gave a talk on shed crime. She wouldn't have dreamt that.

It was some hours before Colette was speaking to her again. There were interactions, chance meetings; at one point Colette had to hand her the telephone to take a call from a client, and later they arrived in the utility room at the same time, with two baskets of washing, and stood saying coldly, after you, no, after you.

But the Collingwood wasn't big enough to keep up a feud.

'What do you want me to say?' she demanded. 'That I won't keep a vagrant again? Well, I won't, if you feel that strongly about it. Jesus! It isn't as if there was any harm done.'

'No thanks to you.'

'Let's not start again,' she said.

'I don't think you realise the kind of people who are out there.'

'No, I'm too good,' Al muttered. 'You don't realise half the evil that is in the world,' she told herself under her breath.

Colette said, 'I saw Michelle earlier. She says, guard your shopping.'

'What?'

'In the boot of the car. In case it vanishes while you're unlocking the front door. Don't leave the boot lid open. There's been a spate of grocery theft.'

'I don't go shopping by myself, do I?'

Colette said, 'Stop muttering like that.'

'Truce?' she said. 'Peace talks? Cup of tea?'

Colette did not answer but she took it as a yes, standing at the sink filling the kettle, looking down the garden towards the now-deserted Balmoral. Colette had accused her of harbouring Mart, but not of actually feeding him; not of actually buying supplies and smuggling them in. She had not actually slapped her, but she had screamed in her face, asked her if she was insane, and if it was her intention to bring into the neighbourhood a gang of robbers, child molesters, terrorists and would-be murderers. I don't know, she'd said, I don't think so, I didn't have an intention, I just wanted to do a good action, I suppose I didn't think, I just felt sorry for him, because he's got nowhere to go and so he has to go in a shed. 'Sometimes,' Colette said, 'I think you're retarded as well as fat.'

But that's not true, Al thought. Surely not? She knows I'm not stupid. I might be temporarily muddled by the ingress of memory, some seepage from my early life. I feel I was kept in a shed. I feel I was chased there, that I ran in the shed for refuge and hiding place, I feel I was then knocked to the floor, because in the shed someone was waiting for me, a dark shape rising up from the corner, and as I didn't have my scissors on me at the time I couldn't even snip him. I feel that, soon afterwards, I was temporarily inconvenienced by someone putting a lock on the door; and I lay bleeding, alone, on newspapers, in the dark.

She couldn't see the past clearly; only an outline, a black bulk against black air. She couldn't see the present; it was muddled by the force of the scene Colette had made, the scene which was still banging around inside her skull. But she could see the future. She'll be forcing me out for walks, hanging weights – this is what she threatens – on my wrists and ankles. She might drive alongside me, in the car, monitoring me, but probably only at first. She won't want to spare the time from sending out invoices, billing people for predictions I have made and spirits I have raised: To Your Uncle Bob, 10 minutes' conversation, £150 plus VAT. So perhaps she won't drive alongside me, she'll just drive me out of the house. And I'll have nowhere to go. Perhaps I, too, can take refuge in someone's outbuilding. First I can go by the supermarket and get a sandwich and a bun, then I can eat them sitting on a bench somewhere, or if it's wet and I can't get into a shed I could go to the park and crawl under the bandstand. It's easy to see how it happens, really, how a person turns destitute.

'So who's stealing the shopping?' she asked: thinking, it could soon be me.

'Illegal immigrants, Evan says.'

'In Woking?'

'Oh, they get everywhere,' Colette said. 'Asylum seekers, you know. The council is taking the benches out of the park, so that no one can sleep on them. Still, we've had our warning, haven't we? With the shed.'

She drank the tea Alison had made her, leaning against the work surface as if she were in a station buffet. I moved him on smartly, she thought, he knew better than to mess with me, one look at me and he knew I wasn't a soft touch. She felt hungry. It would have been easy enough to dip into the clients' biscuit tin, when Al wasn't looking; but she denied herself. Michelle had said that their wheelie bin had been crammed with takeaway cartons, and she now realised the homeless person must have been responsible for these. Food is over, as far as I'm concerned, she thought. Pictures of Zoë were gnawing at her brain, like rats in a cage with no door.

TEN

That summer, black slime came up through the drains of a Frobisher just down the hill. There was a heatwave, with temperatures creeping towards the upper nineties. Animals crawled into the shade. Children turned lobster red inside their playsuits. Fragile citizens bought charcoal masks to protect against the excess ozone. Sales of ice cream and lager doubled, as did sales of cold and flu remedies. The lawns at Admiral Drive baked until they cracked, and the grass turned to patchy straw. Colette's water feature had to be turned off: as all water features were turned off, by order. Fountains dried, reservoirs dwindled. Hospitals filled. The elderly expired. A plague of psychic shows broke out on TV, crawling all over the schedules.

Colette sat watching them with a sullen expression, denouncing the transparent cheating, the collusion, the simple-mindedness of the studio audiences. It's totally irresponsible, she said, to encourage people to think that's the way you go about dealing with the dead. In the days when she and first Al got together, the days when the princess passed, the punters squirmed when they were fingered; they twitched in their seats, desperate to foist the message on to the person next to them or the person in front or just behind. But now, when they came to a dem, the TV shows had tuned up their expectations, they couldn't wait for their messages. When a sensitive asked, 'Who's got a Mike in spirit world?' fifty hands would shoot into the air. They yelled, cheered, embraced each other, made faces for the camera even though there wasn't one. They shouted, 'Oh my Gahhd!' when a message came through, and burst into grating sobs and doggy howls.

I find it exhausting, Al said, just to watch. And I couldn't do television myself, she said. If I were there in the studio something would malfunction. The picture would blank out. The network would go down. Then they'd sue me.

And you're too fat for television, Colette said.

To think I used to blame so much on Morris! Al said. If the light bulbs started flickering I'd shout, 'Oi, Morris!' and if the washing machine overflowed I would just give him a piece of my mind. But even now, your computer goes on the blink whenever I come near it, and we're still not getting anywhere with the recordings, are we? The machine plays back tapes that aren't even in it, we get material coming through from the year before last. All the tapes are speaking on top of each other, it's like a compost heap.

And you're too fat, Colette said.

So I think it's my electromagnetic field, I think it's hostile to modern technology.

They had got all the satellite channels, because Alison liked to home-shop; she often felt shy when she was out, and she complained that people looked at her in a funny way, as if they knew what she did for a living. 'It's not shameful,' she said. 'Not like being a sex worker.' Still, it was a comfort to be able to buy some chunky gold chains and glittery earrings, low-taste stuff she could wear on stage. Once when they switched on their TV, Cara's pixie face appeared on screen;

another time, Mandy's sharp foxy features bobbed up. Colette said, 'Natasha, huh! She doesn't look a bit Russian.'

'She's not.'

'They could have made her up to look Russian, that's all I'm saying.'

When the credits came at the end of the show, the producers put a disclaimer notice on the screen, to say that the programme was 'for entertainment purposes only'. Colette snorted and stabbed the off-switch. 'You should tell them straight, at your next dem. Tell them what it's really like in spirit world. Why do you have to be so soft on them? Tell them what Morris used to do to you.' She sniggered. 'I'd like to see their faces then. I'd like to see Mandy's face, when she's on camera and Morris puts his hand up her skirt. I'd like to see them burbling on about the world beyond, if Morris came back and he was in one of his moods.'

'Don't say that,' Al begged. 'Don't say you'd like to see Morris.' She had never been able to teach her the art of self-censorship; never been able to make her understand how simple and literal-minded the organisers of spirit world could be. You had to guard the words that came out of your mouth and even the words as they formed up in your mind. Wasn't that simple enough? Sometimes she thought Colette couldn't be such a slow learner. Surely she was doing it on purpose, tormenting her?

Gavin rang. He asked for Colette and she passed the phone over without speaking to him. She hung about, overhearing; though proximity wasn't really necessary to her. She could tune into Gavin any time she liked, but the thought tired her. Quite clearly she heard him say, 'How's the fat lesbian?'

Colette said, 'I've told you, Alison is not a lesbian. In fact, there are several men in her life.'

'Who?' Gavin demanded.

'Let me see.' Colette paused. 'There's Donnie. There's Keith . . . she and Keith go way back.'

Al stood in the doorway. 'Colette . . . don't.'

Colette gestured to her angrily to go away.

Don't make a joke out of the fiends, Al pleaded: but not out loud. She turned and left the room. You should know better, Colette, but how can you know better? You believe and you half believe, that's the trouble with you. You want the frisson and you want the money, but you don't want to alter your dumb view of the world. She heard Colette say to Gavin, 'There's Dean. Dean really fancies me. But he's quite young.'

'What do they do, these blokes?' Gavin said. 'Are they fortune tellers as well?'

'There's Mart,' she said. 'Oh, and our neighbour, Evan. Plenty of men in our lives, you see.'

'You're carrying on with a neighbour?' Gavin said. 'Married, is he?'

'That's my business.'

Colette had that fizzing, crawling feeling you get when you're lying. When she heard what was coming out of her mouth she was frightened. It was quite natural that she should want to put the best face on things, with Gavin, but stop, stop, she said to herself, Donnie and Keith aren't real and Evan is a wanker and Mart lives in the shed. Or used to.

'Fair dos,' Gavin said. 'I mean, I can't see anybody leaving his wife and kids for you, Colette, but then I've no right to an opinion, have I?'

'Damn right you haven't.'

'No, you see who you like,' he said – still, she thought, with that lordly air, as if he were giving her permission. 'Look, what I called about – they've been having a bit of a shake-out at work. They've let me go.'

'I see. When did this happen, this shake-out?'

'Three months back.'

'You could have said.'

'Yes, but I thought I'd get fixed up. I called a few people.'

'And they were out, were they? In a meeting? On holiday this week?'

'There's a downturn, you know?'

'I don't think it's a downturn. I think they've finally rumbled you, Gavin.'

'No, it's happening everywhere, all the big consultancies are shedding.'

'So how are you managing? Money must be tight?'

'It's just a cash-flow problem.'

'I'm sure Zoë can help you out.'

He seemed to hesitate – so that Colette said sharply, 'She is still with you, I suppose?'

'Oh yes, she's very loyal. I mean, she's not the sort of girl to chuck you if you had a temporary setback.'

'Not like me, eh? I'd be out of there like a shot.'

'So I have to ask you about the payments, for the flat. I have to cut down my outgoings. Just till I get sorted.'

'So is there a downturn in the modelling business too? Or is she in hock for her tit lift and her bum suction? Oh, it's all right, Gavin, I can afford to carry you for a while. Alison and I are doing really, really well.'

'Yeah, it's all over the TV, psychic shows.'

'Yes, but that's fraud. We're not fraud. And we're not dependent on the whims of schedulers, thank you.' Something touched her, a small hand on her sleeve: compunction. 'So how are you,' she said, 'apart from poor? How's your car running?'

There was a short silence. 'I have to go,' Gavin said. 'Zoë wants me.'

'Probably some bit of her fallen off,' Colette said. 'Bye-ee.'

As she put down the phone she chuckled. Gavin had always lived in anticipation of his next salary cheque, and with his credit cards charged up to their limit. He'll be wanting a loan soon, she said to herself. She sang out to Alison, 'Guess what? Gavin's got the boot.' But Al was on the other line.

Mandy said, 'It's time we started offering something to the punters that they can't get from satellite TV. It's all very well, but who's making money out of it? Not us, for sure. It's three hours hanging about in a back room with a plate of stale biscuits, an hour in make-up with some snooty cow drawing your eyebrows in the wrong place, and then when you see yourself you're edited down to the blink of an eye and you're supposed to be bloody grateful.'

'I thought it would be glamorous,' Al said wistfully. 'Colette says I can't go on because of my size, but I thought it would be nice for you.'

'In my view,' Mandy said, 'we have to reinstate the personal touch. Silvana's been advertising psychic hen parties, and she's getting a very good response. You need to be able to provide one reader to about every six ladies, so I said I'd see if you were willing.'

'Be a change, wouldn't it?'

'That's what I think. A change for the guests, too. It's a bit more upmarket than going on the razz and sicking up vodka outside some club. What with date-rape drugs, all that, you wouldn't want to venture out.'

'No men,' Al suggested. 'We don't want Raven droning about ley lines.'

'Definitely no men. That's what they've come to get away from.'

'And we're not including Mrs Etchells, are we? We don't want her twittering on about the joys of motherhood.'

'Or telling them they need a little op. No, definitely no

Mrs E. I'll sign you up, Al. You know those people in Cornwall, those new suppliers? They offer party packs, sort of goody bags for the clients to take away, mini-sizes of aromatic oils, three-pack of incense sticks, candle in tin, you know the sort of thing, presented in a velvet-look pouch. We can put a mark-up on them and sell them to the party organiser and we can bring along our own stocks of angel cards and spiritual CDs. Gemma's got a cash-and-carry card so we could supply the champagne and party snacks. Ideally we'll make it an evening of pampering and relaxation, as well as prediction. We can give nutritional advice – perhaps not you, Al – and we need somebody to do massage and reflexology. Silvana does reiki, doesn't she? And Cara's got this new therapy she's going in for, I forget what they call it. Anyway, you rub their feet and it brings back memories of life pre-birth.'

'Really?' Al said. 'Have you tried it, Mandy?'

'Mm. Quite intriguing. Peaceful.'

'What was it like?'

'Darkness. Sort of swishing.'

She thought, I wouldn't like to have access to my thoughts before I was born. An image came to her of her mother, patiently fishing for her with a knitting needle.

'Anything else? Besides swishing?'

'Yes. Now you mention it. I think I got reverted to my past life. The closing moments, you know. Bloody great hoof coming down on my head. I could hear my own skull cracking.'

At the hen parties, through the summer evenings, Colette sat in other women's kitchens, perched on a stool, frowning as she inputted data into her palmtop organiser. She was cool and neat in her little beige skirts and tiny T-shirts, an inch of flat midriff showing, as fashion decreed. She sat with legs crossed, a sandalled foot swinging, as she squared up Alison's autumn schedule and calculated her expenses. When the sensitives in their floaty scarves slid away for a break, when they leaned against the fridge and tried to engage her in conversation, she would give them her flat-eyed stare, and with an irritated twitch of her lips go back to her sums. When they were called back to the party, she would take a long breath, finding herself alone, and look about her. They were working some upmarket locations, Weybridge, Chobham, and there were state-of-the-art kitchen fittings for her to admire: granite worktops like dark mirrors, and brushed steel in which she saw, faintly, her slight and wavering form as she crossed the room to pour herself a glass of San Pellegrino. When the door opened, New Age music wafted towards her, and dreamy half-clad girls, slippery with aromatic oils, drifted past and sometimes offered her a carrot baton or a bite of sushi.

'Ironic,' she said to Al. 'You lot, giving advice on love and marriage. There's not an intact relationship between you.'

She heard the psychics muttering about her presence, heard herself referred to by Silvana as 'that hanger-on'. She knew Silvana was jealous, because she herself couldn't afford a manager. She pictured herself hitting back: I'm really the core to the heart of this enterprise. You ask my ex, Gavin. I keep him, these days. I've made this business boom. I have many skills and talents. I could tell the punters what's going to happen in their love lives. You don't need psychic powers.

Alison came into the kitchen looking hot. 'I'm just slipping out. Tell the clients I'll be ten minutes. Or shift some of mine over to Cara.'

'Certainly.' Colette opened the chart on which she kept track of the evening's proceedings.

'Skiving off, eh?' Gemma said, following Alison into the kitchen. 'I'm needing some matches, the moon candles keep going out.' She cast her eyes around. 'There's nothing that needs lighting, is there, in a house like this? And they don't smoke. Or claim they don't.'

Colette opened her bag, and took out a box. She rattled it, looking smug. 'Don't,' said Al, flinching. They stared at her. 'I don't know,' she said. 'I just don't like people rattling a box of matches. It reminds me of something.'

'You were probably burned at the stake,' Gemma said. 'In a previous existence. You were probably a Cathar.'

'When were they?' Colette said.

Gemma frowned. 'It's medieval,' she said.

'Then I don't think they had matches.'

Gemma flounced out. 'It's a presence in there,' Al said, 'blowing out the candles. Cara tried to get it in a corner, but we don't want to be frightening the punters. I'm just popping over the road, because there's a bunch of grannies standing by the hedge.'

'Where?' Colette went to the window.

'Spirit grannies. Great-grannies. Great-greats.'

'What do they want?'

'Just to say hello. Congratulations. To have a look at the decor. You know how it is.'

'You're too soft,' Colette said. 'Let the grannies stand there, and you get back to your clients.'

'I have to explain to them,' Al said, 'that they're not wanted. I have to put it so as not to cause pain.'

As she went out towards the lift, the little woman followed her, saying, 'Excuse me, Miss, have you seen Maureen Harrison?'

'You again?' Al said. 'Haven't you found her yet? Stick around, ducks, follow us home.'

Gemma came back into the kitchen with a girl leaning on her shoulder: pin-thin, teetering on high heels, wailing and dripping tears. 'Get up, Colette,' she said, 'this is Charlotte, our hostess, let Charlotte sit down.'

Colette vacated her stool, Charlotte hopped on to it; it wasn't the sort of stool you could sink on to. Her bleating continued, and when Gemma tried to hug her she squealed, 'No, no,' and beat her away with little flapping motions of her hands. 'He just texted her,' Gemma said. 'The bastard. It's off.'

Hens filled the doorway; their mouths were ajar. 'Come on back, ladies,' Silvana urged, 'don't all crowd around, let her get over the shock.'

'Christ,' Colette said. 'She's the bride?'

Cara pushed the hens aside. She looked little and fierce. 'Text him back, Charlotte.'

'Can you pre-text?' Gemma asked. 'Is that possible? Would you know, Colette? If she made it look as if she sent a message before he sent his, then she could be the one to call it off.'

'Yes, do that,' Cara urged. 'Your self-esteem's at stake here. Pretend you never got it.'

'Now look, darling,' Gemma squatted on the ground before Charlotte. Charlotte keened and flapped at her, but Gemma took her hands and squeezed them tight. 'Now look, you think the world has stopped turning, but it hasn't. You've had a shock but you'll get over it. This is your lowest ebb and now the only way is up.'

'That filthy scumbag,' wailed the girl.

'That's the spirit,' Gemma said. 'You've got to put it behind you, sweetheart.'

'Not till she's billed him,' Colette said. 'Surely. I mean, there'll be deposits. On the venue. And the honeymoon, air tickets paid for. Unless she goes anyway, with a girlfriend.'

'At least she's got to text and ask him why,' Cara said. 'Or she'll never achieve closure.'

'That's right,' Gemma said. 'You've got to move on. I mean, if you've had bad luck in your life, what's the use of brooding?'

'I disagree,' Colette said. 'It wasn't bad luck. It was bad judgement.'

'Will you shut it?' Gemma said.

'There's no point in her moving on until she's sure she's learned something from it.'

She glanced up. Alison was wedged in the doorway. 'Actually, I agree with Colette,' she said. 'Just on this occasion. You have to think about the past. You ought to. You can work out where it went wrong. There must have been warning signs.'

'There, there,' Gemma said. She patted the girl's bare bronzed shoulder. Charlotte sniffed, and whispered something; Gemma said, 'Witchcraft, oh no!' But Charlotte continued to insist, blowing her nose on a piece of kitchen roll that Al handed to her; until at last Gemma whispered back, 'I do know someone in Godalming. If you really want to make him impotent.'

'I expect that will cost you,' Colette said. She thought, I wonder, if I went in for it, could I get a trade discount? That would be one in the eye for Zoë. She said, 'Some girls in your position would go the direct route. What do you need a witch for, when you could go round there with a carving knife? More permanent, isn't it?'

She remembered her own moments of temptation, the night she left Gavin. I can be reckless, she thought, at second-hand.

'You'd go to jail,' Gemma said severely. 'Don't listen, sweetheart. What do they say? Revenge is a dish best eaten cold?'

Al moaned and clasped a hand to her belly. She made a dash for the kitchen sink, but it was too late. 'Oh, that's all I bloody need,' said the bride-to-be. She jumped from her stool to fetch a mop and bucket.

Afterwards, Colette said, 'I told you prawns were dodgy

in weather like this. But you can't curb your appetite, can you? Now you've embarrassed yourself.'

'It wasn't the prawns.' Hunched in the passenger seat, Al sounded snuffly and depressed. 'Prawns are protein, besides.'

'Yes,' Colette said patiently, 'but you can't have the extra protein *and* the carbohydrates *and* the fat, Al, something has to give. It's a simple enough principle to get into your head, I've explained it a dozen times.'

'It was when you rattled the matches,' Al said. 'That's when I started feeling sick.'

'That doesn't make any sense at all,' Colette said. She sighed. 'But I've ceased expecting sense from you. How can you be frightened of a box of matches?'

Between the bride's sudden jilting and Al's sudden vomit, the hen party had broken up early. It was not quite dark when they let themselves into the Collingwood. The air had cooled, and the cats of Admiral Drive tiptoed along the garden fences, their eyes shining. In the hall, Al put her hand on Colette's arm. 'Listen.'

From the sitting room came two gruff male voices, rising and falling in amicable conversation.

'A tape's playing,' she said. 'Listen. Is that Aitkenside?'

Colette raised her eyebrows. She flung open the double doors from the hall; though as they were glass, the gesture was superfluous. No one was within; and all she could hear, from the machine on the table, was a faint hiss and twitter that could have been the machine's own workings. 'We ought to get some more sophisticated recording equipment,' she said. 'I'm sure it must be possible to cut out these blips and twitters.'

'Shh,' Alison said. 'Oh dear, Colette.'

AITKENSIDE: Here, Morris, you don't get a good gherkin these days. Not like you used to get. Where would you go for a good gherkin?

MORRIS: You don't get a good pickled onion. You don't get a good pickled onion like we used to get after the war.

'It's Morris.'

'If you say so.'

'Can't you hear him? Maybe his course is finished. But he shouldn't be back.' Al turned to Colette, tears in her eyes. 'He should have moved on, higher. That's what happens. That's what always happens.'

'I don't know.' Colette threw her bag down. 'You said yourself, you get these cross-recordings from the year before last. Maybe it's old.'

'Maybe.'

'What's he saying? Is he threatening you?'

'No, he's talking about pickles.'

AITKENSIDE: You don't get a mutton pie. Whatever happened to mutton? You never see it.

MORRIS: When you go on the station for a samwidge you can't get ham, you can't get a sheet of pink ham and some hot mustard like you used to get, they want to go stuffing it with all this green stuff, lettuce, and lettuce is for girls.

AITKENSIDE: It's all wog food, pansy food, you can't get a nice pickled egg like you used to get.

MORRIS: Could have some fun with a pickled egg, see a pickled egg and Bob Fox he would start up without fail, Pass it round, lads, he'd say, and when MacArthur comes in you just drop it on the table, say, aye aye, MacArthur, have you lost something, old son? I seen MacArthur turn pale, I seen him nearly drop in his tracks—

AITKENSIDE: I seen him clap his hand to his empty socket—

MORRIS: And Bob Fox cool as you like take up his fork and stab the little fucker then squeeze it up in his fingers—

AITKENSIDE: —all wobbling—

MORRIS: —and take a bite. Tee-hee. I wonder what happened to Bob Fox?

AITKENSIDE: Used to knock on the window, didn't he? Tap-tap, tap-tap. That was Bob.

Towards dawn Colette came down and found Al standing in the kitchen. The cutlery drawer was open, and Al was staring down into it.

'Al?' she said softly. She saw with distaste that Al had not bothered to tie up her housecoat; it flapped back at either side to show her round belly and shadowy triangle of pubic hair. She looked up, registered Colette and slowly, as if half-asleep, pulled the thin cotton gown across her; it fell open again as her fingers fumbled for the ties.

'What are you looking for?' Colette said.

'A spoon.'

'There's a drawerful of spoons!'

'No, a particular spoon,' Al insisted. 'Or perhaps a fork. A fork would do.'

'I should have known you'd be down here, eating.'

'I feel I've done something, Colette. Something terrible. But I don't know what.'

'If you must eat something, you're allowed a slice of cheese.' Colette opened the door of the dishwasher and began to take out yesterday's crockery. 'Done something terrible? What sort of thing?'

Alison picked out a spoon. 'This one.'

'Not corn flakes, please! Unless you want to undo all the good work. Why don't you go back to bed?'

'I will,' Al said, without conviction. She moved away, the

spoon still in her hand, then turned, and handed it to Colette. 'I can't think what I did,' she said. 'I can't quite place it.'

A shaft of rosy sunlight lay across the window ledge, and an engine purred as an early Beatty backed out of his garage. 'Cover yourself up, Al,' Colette said. 'Oh, come here, let me . . .' She took hold of the housecoat, wrapped it across Al, and tied a firm double bow. 'You don't look well. Do you want me to cancel your morning clients?'

'No. Let them be.'

'I'll bring you some green tea at eight thirty.'

Al moved slowly towards the stairs. 'I can't wait.'

Colette opened the cutlery drawer and slotted the spoon among its fellows. She brooded. She's probably hungry, considering she sicked up all the party snacks. Which she shouldn't have been eating anyway. Maybe I should have let her have some cereal. But who is this diet for? It's not for my sake. It's for her sake. Without me behind her, she goes right off the rails.

She stacked some saucers into the cupboard, tip-tap, tip-tap. Did Al have to look so naked? But fat people do. Laid open to the morning shadows, Al's white belly had seemed like an offering, something yielded up; a sacrifice. The sight had embarrassed Colette. Colette disliked her for it.

The summer heat took its toll on Al. In the week that followed, she lay awake through the nights. In the heat of the day her thighs chafed when she walked, and her feet brimmed over the straps of her sandals. 'Stop moaning!' Colette said. 'We're all suffering.'

'Sometimes,' Al said, 'I have a sort of creeping sensation. Do you get that?'

'Where?'

'It runs down my spine. My fingers tingle. And bits of me go cold.'

'In this weather?'

'Yes. It's like, my feet won't walk properly. I want to go one way, and they want to go a different way. I'm supposed to come home, but my feet don't want to.' She paused. 'It's hard to explain it. I feel as if I might fall.'

'Probably multiple sclerosis,' Colette said. She was flicking through *Slimming* magazine. 'You ought to get tested.'

Al booked herself in at the health centre. When she rang up, the receptionist demanded to know what was the matter with her, and when Al explained carefully, my feet go different ways, she heard the woman sharing the news with her colleagues.

The woman's voice boomed down the phone, 'Do you want me to put you in as an emergency?'

'No, I can wait.'

'It's just, you need to be sure you don't wander off,' the woman said. There were cackles in the background: screeches. I could ill-wish them, Al said, but I won't, on this occasion. She thought, are there occasions when I have ill-wished?

'I can fit you in Thursday,' the woman said. 'You won't get lost on the way here?'

'My manager will drive me,' Al said. 'By the way, if I were you I should cancel your holiday. I know you'll lose your deposit, but what's a lost deposit compared to being kidnapped by Islamic terrorists and spending several months in leg-irons in a tin shack in the desert?'

When Thursday came, Colette did drive her, of course. 'You don't have to wait with me,' Al said.

'Of course I do.'

'If you leave me your moby, I could call a cab to take me home. You could go to the post office and post off my spells. There's one going airmail that needs to be weighed.'

'Do you really think I'd leave you, Alison? To get bad news by yourself? Surely you think more of me than that?' Colette sniffed. 'I feel devalued. I feel betrayed.'

'Oh dear,' Al said. 'Too many of those psychic hens. It's bringing your emotions out.'

'You don't realise,' Colette said. 'You don't understand how Gavin let me down. I know what it's like, you see. I wouldn't do it to someone else.'

'There you go again. You're always taking about Gavin these days.'

'I am not. I never mention him.'

When they got into reception, Al scrutinised the practice staff behind their glass screens. She couldn't see the one who had laughed at her. Maybe I shouldn't have said anything, but when I saw she was booked on a Nile Cruise I just couldn't resist. It's not, it's really not, as if I wished her any ill. I only told her.

'This is interesting,' she said, looking around. It was just like the doctors' waiting room that the punters always described: people sneezing and coughing on you, and a long, long wait. I'm never ill, she thought, so I don't know, first-hand. I'm ailing, of course. But not in ways doctors can cure. At least, I've assumed not.

They waited, side by side on stacking chairs, and Colette talked about her self-esteem, her lack of it, her lonely life. Her voice quavered. Al thought, poor Colette, it's the times we live in. If she can't be in a psychic show, she fancies her chances on a true-confession show. She pictured Gavin, stumbling over the cables, drawn from dark into dazzling light, from the dark of his own obtuse nature into the dazzling light of pale accusing eyes. She heard the audience groaning, hissing; saw Gavin tried, convicted, hung by the neck. It came to her that Gavin had been hanged, in his former life as a poacher. That's why, she thought, in this life, he never does up the top button on his shirt. She closed her eyes. She could smell shit, farmyard manure. Gavin was standing with a noose around his neck. He wore sideburns, and his expression was despondent. Someone was bashing a tin drum. The crowd was small but keen. And she? She was enjoying her day off. A woman was selling mutton pies. She had just bought two.

'Wake up, Al,' Colette said. 'They're calling your number! Shall I come in with you?'

'No.' Al gave Colette a shove in the chest, which dropped her back in her chair. 'Look after my bag,' she said, throwing it into her lap.

When she walked in, her hand – the palm burning and slightly greasy from her second pie – was still outstretched. For a moment the doctor seemed to think he was expected to shake it. He looked outraged at the familiarity, then he remembered his communication skills. 'Miss Hart!' he said, with a smile that showed his teeth. 'Sit ye down, sit ye down. And how are you today?'

He's been on a course, she thought. Like Morris. There was a stained coffee mug by his elbow, bearing the logo of a popular pharmaceutical company. 'I take it you're here about your weight?' he said.

'Oh no,' she said. 'I can't help my weight, I'm afraid.'

'Huh. I've heard that a time or two,' the doctor said. 'Let me tell you, if I had a pound for every woman who sat in that chair and told me about her slow metabolism, I'd be a rich man now.'

Not that riches would help you, Al thought. Not with a liver like yours. Slowly, with a lingering regret, she pulled out her gaze from his viscera and focused on his Adam's apple. 'I have tinglings down my arms,' she said. 'And my feet: when I try to go home, my feet take me somewhere else. My fingers twitch, and the muscles in my hands. Sometimes I can't use my knife and fork.'

'And so . . . ?' said the doctor.

'So I use a spoon.'

'You're not giving me much to go on,' the doctor said. 'Have you tried eating with your fingers?'

It was his little joke, she saw. I will bear it, she thought. I won't abuse my powers by foreseeing about him. I'll just be calm, and try and be ordinary. 'Look, I'll tell you what my friend thinks.' She put Colette's theory to him.

'You women!' the doctor exclaimed. 'You all think you've got multiple sclerosis! It beats me why you're all so keen to be in wheelchairs. Shoes off, please, and step on these scales.'

Al tried to ease her feet out of her sandals. They were stuck, the straps embedded in her flesh. 'Sorry, sorry,' she said, bending down to unbuckle them, peel the leather away.

'Come on, come on,' the doctor said. 'There are people waiting out there.'

She kicked away her shoes and stepped on the scales. She stared at the paint on the wall, and then, nerving herself, she glanced down. She couldn't see past herself, to read the figure.

'Oh dear, oh dear,' the doctor said. 'Get the nurse to test your wee. You're probably diabetic. I suppose we ought to get your cholesterol checked, though I don't know why we bother. Be cheaper to send a patrol officer to confiscate your crisps and beer. When did you last have a blood pressure check?'

She shrugged. 'Sit here,' he said. 'Never mind your shoes, we haven't time for that, you can get back into your shoes when you get outside. Roll up your sleeve.'

Al touched her own warm skin. She was wearing a short-sleeved T-shirt. She hardly liked to draw attention to it. 'It is rolled up,' she whispered.

The doctor clasped a band around her arm. His other hand began to pump. 'Oh dear, oh dear. At this level I would always treat.' He shot a glance upward, at her face. 'Thyroid's probably shot, come to that.' He turned away and tapped his keyboard. He said, 'We don't seem to have seen you before.'

'That would be right.'

'You're not registered with two doctors, are you? Because I should have expected a person in your state to be in here twice a week. You're not moonlighting? Signed up with another practice? Because if you are, I warn you, the system will catch up with you. You can't pull that stunt.'

Her head began hurting. The doctor typed. Al fingered her scalp, as if feeling for the lumpy thread of an old scar. I got that somewhere in my past lives, she thought, when I was a labourer in the fields. Years passed like that, back bent, head down. A lifetime, two, three, four. I suppose there's always a call for labourers.

'Now I'm going to try you on these,' the doctor said. 'These are for your blood pressure. Book in with the nurse for a three-month check. These are for your thyroid. One a day. Just one, mind. No point you doubling the dose, Miss – er – Hart – because all that will do is ensure your total endocrine collapse takes place sooner than scheduled. Here you are.'

'Shall I come back?' she asked. 'To see you personally? Though not too often?'

'See how it goes,' the doctor said, nodding and sucking his lip. But he was not nodding to her in particular. He was already thinking of the next patient, and as he wiped her from the screen, he erased her from his mind, and a well-drilled cheeriness overtook him. 'Oh yes,' he said, rubbing his forehead, 'Wait, Miss Hart – not depressed at all, are you? We can do a lot for that, you know.'

When Colette saw Al shuffling down the passage into the waiting area, trying to keep her unbuckled sandals on her feet, she threw down her magazine, drew her feet from the table, and leapt up, balancing sweetly like a member of a dance troupe. It's nice to be lighter! she thought; Al's diet was working, though not for Al. 'Well? So have you got MS?'

'I dunno,' Al said.

'What do you mean, Al, you *don't know*? You went in there with a specific question, and I should think you could come out with an answer, yes or bloody no.'

'It wasn't that simple,' Al said.

'What was the doctor like?'

'He was bald and nasty.'

'I see,' Colette said. 'Fasten your shoes.'

Al bent at the waist: where her waist would be. 'I can't reach,' she said pitifully. By the reception desk, she put one foot on a vacant chair, and bent over. A receptionist tapped the glass. Tap-tap, tap-tap. Startled, Al wobbled; her body trembled; Colette leaned against her, to prop her upright. 'Let's go,' Al said, limping faster. When they reached the car she opened the door, plopped her right foot on the door sill, and fastened her sandal.

'Just get in,' Colette said. 'In this heat, doing up the other foot will kill you.'

Al heaved herself into her seat, scooping up her left shoe with her toe. 'I could have made him a prediction,' she said, 'but I didn't. He says it could be my thyroid.'

'Did he give you a diet plan?'

Al slammed the passenger door. She tried to worm her swollen foot into her shoe. 'I'm like an Ugly Sister,' she said. She took out a Cologne tissue and fumbled with the sachet. 'Ninety-six degrees is too much, in England.'

'Give it here.' Colette snatched the sachet and ripped it open.

'And for some reason, the neighbours seem to think I'm responsible.'

Colette smirked.

Al mopped her forehead. 'That doctor, I could see straight through him. His liver's beyond saving. So I didn't mention it.'

'Why not?'

'No point. I wanted to do a good action.'

Colette said, 'Oh, give over!'

They came to a halt in the drive of number twelve. 'You don't understand,' Al said. 'I wanted to do a good action but I never seem to manage it. It's not enough just to be nice. It's not enough, just to ignore it when people put you down. It's not enough to be – forbearing. You have to do a good action.'

'Why?'

'To stop Morris coming back.'

'And what makes you think he will?'

'The tape. Him and Aitkenside, talking about pickles. My feet and hands tingling.'

'You didn't say this was work-related! So we've been through this for nothing?'

'You haven't been through anything. It's only me had to listen to that stinky old soak criticising my weight.'

'It can stand criticism.'

'And though I could have made him a prediction, I didn't. A good action means – I know you don't understand, so shut up now, Colette, you might learn something. A good action might mean that you sacrificed yourself. Or that you gave your money away.'

'Where did you get this stuff?' Colette said. 'Out of RE at school?'

'I never had religious education,' Alison said. 'Not after I was thirteen. I was always made to stand in the corridor. That lesson, it would tend to lead to Morris and people trying to materialise. So I got sent out. I don't seem to feel the lack of it. I know the difference between right and wrong. I'm sure I always did.'

'Will you stop this drivel?' Colette said, wailing. 'You never think of me, do you?! You don't seem to realise how I'm fixed! Gavin's going out with a supermodel!'

A week passed. Al had got her prescriptions. Her heart now beat slowly, thump, thump, like a lead weight swinging in space. The change was not disagreeable; she felt slower, though, as if her every action and perception were deliberate now, as if she was nobody's fool. No wonder Colette's been so spiteful, she thought. Supermodel, eh?

She stood at the front window, looking out over Admiral Drive. A solitary vehicle ploughed to and fro across the children's playground, turning up mud. The builders had put down asphalt at one stage, but then the surface had seemed to heave and split, and cracks developed, which the neighbours stood wondering at, leaning on the temporary fence; within a week or two weeds were pushing through the hardcore, and the men had moved in again to break up what remained with pneumatic drills, dig out the rubble and reduce it back to bare earth.

Sometimes the neighbours accosted the workmen, shouting at them over the noise of their machines, but none of them got the same story twice. The local press was strangely silent, and their silence was variously attributed to stupidity and bribes. From time to time the knotweed rumour resurfaced. 'You can't keep down knotweed,' Evan said. 'Especially not if it's mutated.' No actual white worms had been spotted, or none that anyone had admitted to. The residents felt trapped and baffled. They didn't want public attention, yet they wanted to sue somebody; they thought it was their entitlement.

Al caught sight of Mart, down at the children's playground.

He was wearing his brickie's hat, and he appeared so suddenly in the middle distance that she wondered if he'd come up through one of the secret tunnels the neighbours were speculating about.

'How are you doing?' he yelled.

'OK.' Her feet were moving sideways and every which ways, but by tacking to the left then abruptly changing course she managed to manoeuvre herself down the hill towards him. 'Are you working here, then, Mart?'

'I've been put on digging,' he said. 'We're remediating, that's the nature of it and the job description. Did you ever have a job description?'

'No, not me,' she said. 'I make it up as I go along. So what's remediating?'

'You see this soil?' He pointed to one heap. 'This is what we're taking off. And you see this?' He pointed to another heap of soil, very similar. 'This is what we're putting down instead.'

'So who are you working for?'

Mart looked wild. 'Subcontracting,' he said. 'Cash in hand.'

'Where are you living?'

'Dossing at Pinto's. His floor got put down again.'

'So you got rid of the rats?'

'In the end. Some pikey come round with a dog.'

'Pikey?'

'You know. Gypsy fella.'

'What was his name?'

'He didn't say any name. Pinto met him down the pub.'

Al thought, if a man is always no more than three feet from a rat – or is it two? – how does that feel from the rats' point of view? Do they spend the whole of their lives in trembling? Do they tell each other nightmare stories about a gypsy with a terrier on a rope?

'How's the old shed?' Mart said. He spoke as if it were some foolish indulgence of his youth.

'Much as you left it.'

'I was thinking I might get the odd night there. If your friend had no big objection.'

'She does have a big objection. So do the neighbours. They think you're an asylum seeker.'

'Oh, go on, missus,' Mart said. 'It's just for when Pinto says, Mart, take a walk. Then we could have a chat again. And if you've got the money we could get a takeaway.'

'Are you remembering your pills, Mart?'

'On and off. They're after meals. I don't always get a meal. It was better when I was living in your shed and you was bringing a tray and reminding me.'

'But you know that couldn't go on.'

'Because of your friend.'

I will continue to do a good action, she thought. 'Wait there, Mart,' she said. She went back into the house, took a twenty out of her purse. When she got back, Mart was sitting on the ground.

'They're going to be waterjetting the sewers soon,' Mart said. 'It's due to complaints and concerns.'

'You'd better look busy,' she said. 'Or you'll get the sack.'

'The lads have gone on their lunch,' Mart said. 'But I don't have a lunch.'

'Now you can get one,' she said, handing over the banknote.

Mart stared at it. She thought he was going to say, that's not a lunch. She said, 'It represents a lunch. You get what you want.'

'But I'm barred.'

'Your mates will go for you.'

'I'd rather you made me a lunch.'

'Yes, but that's not going to happen.'

She turned and plodded away. I want to do a good action. But. It won't help him to hang around here. On the doorstep of the Collingwood she glanced back at him. He was sitting on the ground again, in the freshly dug soil, like a gravedigger's assistant. You could spend your life trying to fit Mart together, she thought. There's no cause and effect to him. He feels as if he might be the clue to something or other, made up as he is out of bits and pieces of the past and the fag end of other people's phrases. He's like a picture where you don't know which way up it goes. He's like a walking jigsaw, but you've lost the box lid to him.

She was closing the front door, when he called out to her. She stepped outside again. He loped towards her, his twenty screwed up in his fist. 'Forgot to ask you. If in case of a terrorist outrage, could I come in your shed?'

'Mart,' she said warningly, and began to close the door.

'No, but,' he said. 'It was at the neighbourhood watch last week.'

She stared at him. 'You went to the meeting?'

'I sneaked in the back.'

'But why?'

'Keep my eye on Delingbole.'

'I see.'

'And the message was, in case of terrorist outrage or nuclear explosion, go indoors.'

'That seems sensible.'

'So if there's one of those, can I come back and live in the shed? You're supposed to stock up with a first-aid kit to include scissors, a wind-up radio, but I dunno what one is, and tins of tuna fish and beans, which I have, plus a tin-opener to open them with.'

'And then what do you do?' She thought, I wish I'd gone to this meeting.

'Then you sit tight, listen to the radio and eat your beans.'

'Till such time as?'

'What?'

'I mean, when is it safe to come out?'

Mart shrugged. 'I suppose when Delingbole comes round and tells you. But he might not ever tell me because he hates me. So I'd just starve to death.'

Alison sighed. From under his brickie's hat, Mart rolled a fallow eye at her. 'OK,' she said. 'How about this? In case of terrorist outrage or nuclear explosion, never mind the shed, you can come and live in our house.'

'But she won't let me.'

'I'll tell her you're my guest.'

'That won't make no difference.'

He shows sense, Al thought.

'A bloke was here,' he said, 'looking for you. Yesterday. In a van.'

'Oh, that would be the courier,' she said. They were expecting some more party packs from Truro.

'You was out.'

'Funny he didn't leave a card. Unless Colette picked it up and didn't say.'

'He didn't leave a card, he didn't leave a trace,' Mart said. He clapped his belly. 'How about tea?'

'Mart, get back over there and start digging. These are testing times. We've all got to put a bit of effort in.'

'You wouldn't give me a hand, would you?'

'What, with the digging? Look, Mart, I don't do outdoors, horses for courses, I'm in here earning a twenty so I can give it you. What would your mates say if they came back and found me doing your job for you? They'd laugh at you.'

'They laugh at me anyway.'

'But that's because you don't get on with the job. You should have self-respect! That's what's important to all of us.'

'Is it?'

'Yes. That's what people used to call it, now they call it self-esteem, but same difference. People are always trying to take it away from you. Don't let them. You have to have backbone. Pride. So! You see! Get digging!' She stumped away, then stopped and turned. 'This man, Mart, this courier, what did it say on the side of his van?' As an afterthought, she added, 'Can you read?'

'I can,' Mart said, 'but not a plain van with no writing. It didn't say his name or anything. There was mud up the side of it, though.'

'So did he speak to you? I mean, did he have a box that he was wanting to leave, did he have a clipboard or one of those computers that you sign on, you know?'

'He had boxes. He opened the back doors and I looked in. He had boxes stacked up. But he didn't leave any.'

A terrible uprush of fear swept over her. She thought her new heart pills prohibited such a feeling. But seemingly not.

'What type of bloke was he?' she said.

'He was one of them type of blokes what always hits you. The kind that, you're in a pub, and he says, oi, mate, what you looking at? and you say nothing mate, and then he says—'

'Yes, I get the picture,' Al said.

'—and then the next thing you know is you're in the hospital,' said Mart. 'Having yourself stitched together. Your ears all sliced and blood down your jersey, if you have a jersey. And your teef spitting out of your head.'

In her own room, Alison took an extra heart pill. For as long as she could endure, she sat on the edge of the bed, hoping that it would take effect. But her pulse wouldn't slow; it's remarkable, she thought, how you can be both bored and frightened at the same time. That's a reasonable way, she thought to describe my life with the fiends: I lived with them, they lived with me, my childhood was spent in the half-light, waiting for my talent to develop and my means of making a living, knowing always, knowing always I owed my existence to them; for didn't a voice say, where d'you fink your mum gets the money to go down the shop and get instant mash, if it ain't from your uncle Morris; where d'you fink your mum gets funding for her little bevvy, if it ain't from your uncle Keef?

She took off her clothes: peeling them wetly from her body, dropping them on the floor. Colette was right of course; she should be on a diet, any diet, all the diets at once. If TV, as people said, put extra weight on you, then she would look like – she couldn't think what she would look like, something ridiculous, faintly menacing perhaps, something from a sci-fi channel. She felt her aura wobbling around her, as if she were wearing a giant's cape made of jelly. She pinched herself. The thyroid pills had not made any instant impact on her flesh. She imagined how it would be if she woke up one morning, and she had shed layers of herself, like someone taking off a winter coat – then two coats, then three . . . She took handfuls of flesh from here and there, repositioned and resettled them. She viewed herself from all angles, but she couldn't produce a better effect. I try my best with the diets, she said to herself; but I have to house so many people. My flesh is so capacious; I am a settlement, a place of safety, a bombproof shelter. 'Boom,' she said softly. She swayed on her feet, rocked back on her heels. In the long mirror she watched herself, rocking. When she was accustomed to her reflection, inured to it, she turned her back; craning her chin over her shoulder, she could see the raised, silver lines of her scars. In hot weather like this they seemed to puff and whiten, whereas in winter they seemed to shrink, redden and pull. But perhaps that was her imagination. In her imagination, someone said, 'The tricky little bitch. We'll show her what a knife can do.'

Cold sweat sprang out across her back. Colette was right, Colette is right, she has to take me in hand, she has to hate me, it is important someone hates me. I liked it when Mart came and we got the takeaway, but I should have left it all for him. Though in all conscience I didn't do it for the sake of the spare ribs. I did it because I wanted to do a good action. Colette never does a good action because she is being thin, it is what she does instead. See how she has starved herself, just to teach me, just to shame me, and see how impervious I am to example. In the last week or two, Colette's wheat-coloured clothes had hung on her like bleached sacks. So cheer up, Al thought, we can go shopping. We can go shopping, me for a bigger size and Colette for a smaller. That will put her in a good mood.

The phone rang, making her jump. She sat down, naked, to take the call. 'Alison Hart, how may I help you today?'

'Oh, Miss Hart . . . is that you in person?'

'Yes.'

'So you are real? I thought you might be a call centre. Do you offer dowsing?'

'It depends what for. I do missing jewellery, old insurance policies, concealed wills. I don't do lost computer files or any type of electronic recovery. I charge a flat-rate call-out fee, which depends on your area, and then after that I work on a no-find no-fee basis. I do indoor work only.'

'Really?'

'I'm not suited to distances, or rough terrain.'

'But it's the outside that's worrying us.'

'Then you need my colleague Raven, who specialises in earth energies, neolithic burials, mounds, caverns, burrows and henges.'

'But you're in my area,' the woman said. 'That's why I rang. I'm going by your telephone code in your ad.'

'What is it you're actually looking for?'

'Actually, uranium,' the woman said.

Al said, 'Oh dear. I do think it's Raven you want . . .' I expect he'll be branching out, she thought, if these poisonings continue: knotweed, the bad drains. He'll be branching out into sludge and toxic seepages, and detecting the walls of underground installations. If there were walls beneath my feet, she thought, if there were occult silos and excavations, cavities blasted in the earth, would I know? If there were secret chambers and bricked-in culs-de-sac, would I sense them?

'Are you still there?' she asked the client. She imparted Raven's details; his email, and so on. It was hard to get the woman off the phone; she seemed to want some sort of free extra, like, I'll throw you in a tarot reading, pick one card of three. It's a while since I unwrapped the cards, Al thought. She said to the woman, I really ought to go, because I have, you know, another client coming in a – well, fifteen minutes, and oh dear – what is that smell? Oh dear, I think I've left something on the stove . . . she held the phone away from her ear, and still the woman talked, and she thought, Colette, where are you, get this woman off the line . . . she threw the receiver down on the bed and ran out of the room.

She stood on the landing, naked. I never did any science at school, she thought, any chemistry or physics, so I can't advise these people about the likelihood of aliens or rabies or uranium or knotweed or anything at all really. Imagine, she said to herself, Morris let loose in a laboratory . . . all his friends trapped in a test tube, amalgamating and reacting against each other and causing little puffs and whiffs. Then she said to herself, don't imagine, because it is imagining that gives them the door to get in. If you were thinner they would have less space to live. Yes, Colette was right and right again.

She knelt down, and leaned forward, and tucked her head down by her knees. 'Boom!' she said softly. 'Boom!' She crunched herself down as small as she could go, and said to herself a phrase she did not know she knew: *Sauve qui peut.*

She rocked her body, back and to, back and to. Presently she felt stronger: as if a shell, as if the back of a tortoise, might have grown over her spine. Tortoises live for many years, she thought, they outlive human beings. No one really loves them for they have no lovable qualities but they are admired just for lasting out. They don't speak, they just don't utter at all. They are OK as long as no one turns them upside down and shows their underside, which is their soft bits. She said to herself, when I was a child I had a tortoise for a pet. The name of my tortoise is Alison, I named it after me because it is like me, and with our slow feet we walk in the garden. With my tortoise at weekends I have many enjoyable times. The food of my tortoise is bollocks grass and blood.

She thought, the fiends are on their way, the question is how fast and who is first. If I cannot enjoy a nice childhood thought about a tortoise I might have had but didn't, then I can expect Morris will shortly be limping in my direction though I believed he had gone on to higher things. Unless I am the higher things. After all, I tried to do a good action. I try to be a higher thing myself, but why does something inside me always say, but? Thinking *but*, she squashed herself down hard. She tried to put her chin on to the carpet, so she could look up, as if she were emerging from her shell. To her surprise – she had not tried this sort of thing before – she found it anatomically impossible. What came naturally was to tuck her head into her shielding spine, her plaited fingers protecting her fontanelle.

In this position Colette found her, as she scampered lightly up the stairs, coming back from a meeting with their tax adviser. 'Colette,' she said to the carpet, 'you were right all along.'

These were the words that saved her; protected her from the worst of what Colette could have said, when she extended a cool hand to help her up and finally, admitting the task beyond her, brought a chair upon which Alison could place her forearms, and from there lever herself into a position that seemed like an undignified sexual invitation: and from there, upright. One hand was spread across her heaving diaphragm, another crept down to cover her private parts – 'which I've seen, already, once this week,' Colette snapped, 'and once too much, thank you, so if you don't mind getting dressed – or at least covering yourself up decently, if the idea of getting dressed is too challenging – you might come down when you're ready and I'll tell you what Mr Colefax has to say about short-term savings rates.'

For an hour, Alison lay on her bed to recover. A client called for a tarot reading, and she saw her cards so clearly in her mind that really, she might as well have jumped up and done it and earned the money, but she heard Colette making tactful excuses, taking the client into her confidence and saying that she knew she would understand, the unpredictable demands placed on Alison's talent meant that she couldn't always give of her best, so when she said she needed rest, that must be respected . . . she heard Colette book the woman in for a callback, and impress on her the fact that she must be standing to attention when it came, ready for Alison, even if her house were on fire.

When she felt able, she sat upright; she ran a tepid bath, and dipped herself in and out of it, and felt no cleaner. She didn't want hot water, which would make her scars flare. She lifted her heavy breasts and soaped beneath them, handling each one as if it were a weight of dead meat that happened to adhere to her chest.

She dried herself, put on the lightest dress she owned. She crept downstairs and, by way of the kitchen, into the garden. The weeds between the paving had withered, and the lawn was rock hard. She looked down; snaky cracks crossed the ground. 'Ali!' came the cry. It was Evan, out poisoning his own weeds, his spray slung like a bandolier across his bare chest.

'Evan!' She moved stiffly, patiently towards the fence. She was wearing her fluffy winter slippers, because her swollen feet wouldn't go into any other shoes; she hoped Evan wouldn't notice, and it was true he didn't notice much.

'I don't know,' he said, 'why did we ever pay the extra five k for a garden due south?'

'Why did we?' she said heartily, buying time.

'Personally I did it because I was told it would boost the resale value,' Evan said. 'And you?'

'Oh, the same,' she said.

'But we couldn't have known what climate change had in store, eh? Not the most of us. But you must have known?' Evan giggled. 'What's tomorrow, eh? Ninety-eight and rising?'

She stood in the doorway of Colette's room, where she did not usually intrude: she stood and watched Colette, who was gazing into her computer screen, and she talked to her, in a good-humoured, light sort of way. She said, the neighbours seem to think I have supernatural knowledge of what the weather's going to be, and some of them are ringing me up to search for uranium and dangerous chemicals, I've had to say I don't do that, I've handed them on to Raven, but today's been quite good and quite busy, I've got lots of repeat telephone business, I know I always say to you I prefer face to face, but you always said, it limits you, it really limits you geographically and basically you can do it fine over the phone if you learn to listen hard, well, you're right, Colette. I have learned to listen hard and in a different way, you were right about that as you have been right about everything. And thank you for protecting me today from my client, I will phone her back, I will, you did the right thing, you always do the right thing, if I took notice of you, Colette, I would be thin and rich.

Colette saved her screen, and then, without looking at Al she said, 'Yes, all that is true, but why were you naked and curled into a ball at the top of the stairs?'

Al padded downstairs in her furry slippers. Another red, blazing evening had come; when she went into the kitchen, it was filled with a hellish light. She opened the fridge. To her knowledge, she had not eaten that day. Can I please have an egg? she asked herself. In Colette's voice, she said, yes, just one. There was a sound behind her, a little tapping noise. Painfully – every bit of her was stiff and aching – she moved herself round, to look behind her; round again, to take in the whole room. 'Colette?' she said.

Tap-tap. Tap-tap. It was coming from the window. No one was there. She crossed the room. She looked out into the garden. It was empty. Or seemed so.

She unlocked the back door and stepped out. She heard the train rumbling through Brookwood, the distant background roar of Heathrow, Gatwick. A few drops of rain fell, hot swollen drops. Lifting her head, she called out, 'Bob Fox?' The rain plopped on to her face and ran backwards into her hair. She listened. There was no reply.

'Bob Fox, is that you?' She gazed out into the milky darkness; there was a fugitive movement, towards the back fence, but that could be Mart, seeking shelter from some civic catastrophe. I could have imagined it, she thought. I don't want to be premature. But.

ELEVEN

You can understand it, she thought. Fiends would be attracted to any site where there's diggings, workings, companies of men going about men's business, where there's smoking, betting and swearing; where there are vans running around, and trenches dug where you could conceal things. She lay on the sofa; the tarot cards slid from her hands and fanned out on the carpet. She levered herself upright, dabbing at her face, to see how the cards had fallen. The two of pentacles is the card of the self-employed, indicating uncertainty of income, restlessness, fluctuation, an unquiet mind, and an imbalance between the output of energy and the inflow of money. It is one of those cards so doubled and ambivalent in its meanings that if you draw it reversed it hardly matters much; it then suggests mounting debt, and the swing between paralysed despair and stupid overconfidence. It's not a card you want to draw when you're making next year's business plan.

Colette had got her online these days, emailing predictions around the globe and doing readings for people in different time zones. 'I'd like to make you a global brand,' Colette said. 'Like . . .' Her sentence had tailed off. She could only think of fat things, like McDonald's and Coca-Cola. In Al's belief, the four of swords governed the Internet. Its colour was electric blue and its influence bore on people in a crowd, on the meetings of groups, on ideas which had mass appeal. Not all the psychics agreed; some backed the claims of the four, five and six of cups, which govern secret areas of knowledge, recycled concepts and work pursued in windowless rooms such as cellars or basements. As read by Mrs Etchells, the four of swords indicated a short stay in hospital.

The weather broke; it thundered, then rained hard. The water ran down the patio doors in scallops and festoons. Afterwards, the gardens steamed under a whitening sky. Then the sun struggled through and the cycle began again, the build-up of unbearable heat. But if you looked into the crystal ball you could see shifting cloud banks, as if it were making its own weather.

'I don't understand it,' Colette said, peering in. 'I cleaned it yesterday.'

She read for Colette and said, oh look, the two of cups. Colette said, wait, I know that one, that means a partner, that means a man for me. Her optimism was endearing, Al supposed. The spread was short on the major arcana, as if Fate wasn't really bothered about Colette.

Colette yelled, 'Silvana on the phone. Are you up for team psychics?'

Al picked up the phone by her own computer. 'Oh, Silvana,' she said. 'What's team psychics then?'

Silvana said, 'It's a way to keep the excitement going, we thought. Up on the stage, twenty minutes, in and out, no time to get into anything deep and sticky; you're on, you're off, you leave them asking for more. Six times twenty minutes with shortest possible changeover is two hours, add in twenty minutes' interval, and you're away by ten thirty, which means everybody can get home the same night, nice hot chocolate and a cheese toastie, tucked up in your own bed by midnight, which means you're fresh the next day and up with the lark and manning the phones. Which looks to me like a good deal all round.'

'Sounds all right,' Al said, cautiously.

'We'd have come to you first off, except wossname, Colette, she's always so offhand and snotty.'

Yes, I'm afraid she is, Al thought, which is why I was last pick—

'—which is why you were last pick for the hen parties,' Silvana said. 'But anyway, no hard feelings, Mandy said I should try you. She said one thing about Al, she's nobody's fool but she is the forgiving type, she says, there's no malice or harm in her anywhere. So our problem is, we've advertised Six Sensational Psychics, but Glenora's dropped out.'

'Why?'

'She had a premonition.'

'Oh, she's always having those. She should get over herself. Where is it?'

'The Fig & Pheasant. You know. The steakhouse.'

Oh dear. Not one of Colette's favourite venues.

'So it's who?'

'Me, Cara, Gemma, Mrs Etchells, Mandy and then you.'

'You're a bit light on men. Can't you phone Merlyn?'

'We did. But his book came out, and he's gone to Beverly Hills.'

It put Colette in a temper, the whole thing: the news about Merlyn, the insult of being called up last, and the fact that they would be performing at short notice in a so-called banqueting suite, cleared for the occasion, where beyond the wall a mega sports-screen in the bar would be roaring with football chants, and in the 'family area' a bunch of low-rent diners would be grimly hacking their way through honey-basted chicken kebabs.

She made her feelings known.

Alison drew the Papessa, with her veiled lunar face. She represents the inward world of women who love women, the pull of moods and gut feelings. She represents the mother, especially the widowed mother, the bereft feme sole, the one who is uncovered and abject and alone. She represents those things which are hidden and slowly make their way to the surface: she governs the virtue of patience, which leads to the revelation of secrets, the gradual drawing back of the velvet cloth, the pulling of the curtain. She governs temperature fluctuation and the body's deep hormonal tides, besides the tide of fortune which leads to birth, stillbirth, the accidents and freaks of nature.

Next morning, when Colette came downstairs, her temper had not improved. 'What's this? A fucking midnight feast?'

There were crumbs all over the worktop, and her precious little omelette pan lay across two rings of the hob, skidded there as if by some disdainful hand which had used and abused it. Its sides were encrusted with brown grease and a heavy smell of frying hung in the air.

Alison didn't bother to make excuses. She didn't say, I believe it was the fiends that were frying. Why protest, only to be disbelieved? Why humiliate yourself? But, she thought, I am humiliated anyway.

She rang up Silvana. 'Silvy, love, you know at the Fig & Pheasant, will there be a space to set up beforehand, you know, my easel and my picture?'

Silvana sighed. 'If you feel you've got to, Al. But frankly, darling, a few of us have remarked that it's time you retired that photo. I don't know where you got it done?'

Oh, you *wish*, Al thought, you wish you did, you'd be

round there like a shot, getting yourself flattered. 'It will have to do me for this week,' she said, good-humouredly. 'OK, see you tomorrow night.'

Next day when they came to pack the car, they couldn't find her silk: her silk, her apricot silk for draping the portrait. But it's always, always, she said, in just the same place, unless it's in the wash, and to prove to herself it wasn't she turned out her laundry basket, and then turned out Colette's. Her heart wasn't in it, she knew it had vanished, or been filched. For a week she had noticed the loss of small objects from her bathroom and dressing table.

Colette came in. 'I looked in the washing machine,' she said.

'And? It's not there, is it?'

Colette said, 'No. But you might like to look for yourself.'

In the kitchen, Colette had been running the extractor fan, and spraying room freshener. But the odour of burst fat still hung in the air. Al bent down and looked into the washing machine. Her hand shrank from it, but she picked out the object inside. She held it up, frowning, It was a man's sock, grey, woolly, the heel gone into holes.

So this is what it's led to, she thought, Morris going on a course. It's led to him sucking away my silk and my nail scissors and my migraine pills, and taking eggs out of the fridge and frying them. It's led to him intruding his sock into Colette's sight: and soon, perhaps, his foot. She looked over her shoulder, as if he might have materialised entirely; as if he might be sitting on the hob and taunting her.

Colette said, 'You've had that vagrant in.'

'Mart?' How wrong can you be?

'I've seen him hanging around,' Colette said, 'but I draw the line at his actual admission to the premises, I mean his using the cooking facilities and our utilities. I suppose that would account for the lavatory seat left up, which I have found on several occasions over the last few days. You have to decide who's living here, Alison, because it's him or me. As for the frying, and the bread that was obviously brought in somehow, that will have to rest with your own conscience. There isn't a diet on this earth that allows the wholesale consumption of animal fats and burning another person's pan. As for the sock – I suppose I should be glad I didn't find it before it was washed.'

The Fig & Pheasant, under a more dignified name, had once been a coaching inn, and its frontage was still spattered with the exudates of a narrow, busy A-road. In the sixties it had stood near-derelict and draughty, with a few down-at-heel regulars huddled into a corner of its cavernous rooms. In the seventies it was bought out by a steakhouse chain and Tudorised, fitted with plywood oak-stained panels and those deep-buttoned settles covered in stainproof plush of which the Tudors were so fond. It offered the novelty of baked potatoes wrapped in foil with butter or sour cream, and a choice of cod or haddock in breadcrumbs, accompanied by salad or greyish and lukewarm peas. With each decade, as its ownership had changed, experiments in theming had succeeded each other, until its original menu had acquired retro-chic, and prawn cocktails had reappeared. Plus there was bruschetta. There was ricotta. There was a Junior Menu of pasta shapes and fish bites, and tiny sausages like the finger that the witch tested for plumpness. There were dusty ruched curtains and vaguely William Morris wallpaper, washable but not proof against kids wiping their hands down it, just as they did at home. In the sports bar, where smoking was banned, the ceilings were falsely yellowed, to simulate years of tobacco poisoning; it had been done thirty years ago, and no one saw reason to interfere with it.

To get to the function room you had to push through the bar, past the winking fruit machines. Colette got a round in, counting on her fingers: Gemma, Cara, Silvana, Natasha, four large vodka tonics, include me in and make that five, sweet sherry for Mrs Etchells and a fizzy water for Alison. The internal walls were thin, porous; at the noisy re-enactment of early-evening goals the rooms seemed to rock, and cooking smells crept into the nostrils of the sensitives as they gathered in an airless hutch behind the stage. The mood was militant. Mandy read out the order. 'I'll only do twenty minutes because of my arthritis,' Mrs Etchells said, and Mandy said, 'Look, love, you were only doing twenty minutes anyway, that's the whole idea, it's like a tag team, or passing the baton.'

'Oh, I couldn't do anything like that,' Mrs Etchells said.

Mandy sighed. 'Forget I spoke. You just do your usual. You can have a chair on stage if you want. Colette, do you think you could find her a chair?'

'That's not my job.'

'Perhaps not, but couldn't you show a bit of team spirit?'

'I've already agreed to do the microphone. That's enough.'

'I'll get Mrs E a chair,' Al said.

Mrs Etchells said, 'She never calls me granny, you know.'

'We can go into that another time,' Al said.

'I could tell you a story,' Mrs Etchells said. 'I could tell you a thing or two about Alison that would knock your socks off. Oh, you think you've seen it all, you young 'uns. You've seen nothing, let me tell you.'

When the card Papessa is reversed, it hints that problems go deeper than you think. It warns you of the hidden hand of a female enemy, but it doesn't oblige by telling you who she is.

'Let's kick it off, shall we?' said Cara. From beyond the wall came a long roar of 'Go-o-o-al'.

* * *

It's raw, this kind of work, and near the knuckle: unsupported by music, lighting, video screen, it's just you and them, you and them and the dead, the dead who may oblige or may not, who may confuse and mislead and laugh at you, who may give you bursts of foul language very close up in your ear, who may give you false names and lay false trails just to see you embarrassed. There's no leeway for a prolonged course of error and no time to retrieve a misstep, so you must move on, move on. The punters all think they are talented now, gifted. They've been told so often that everyone has dormant psychic powers that they're only waiting for the opportunity for theirs to wake up, preferably in public. So you have to suppress them. The less they get to say, the better. Besides, the psychics need to avoid any charge of complicity, of soliciting information. Times have changed and the punters are aggressive. Once they shrank from the psychics, but now the psychics shrink from them.

'Don't worry,' Gemma said. 'I won't stand for any nonsense.' Her face grim, she stepped out to begin.

'Go, girl!' Cara said. 'Go, go, go!'

It was a low platform; Gemma was only a step above her audience. Her eyes scoured them as if they were a bunch of criminals. 'When I come to you, shout up. Do not say your name, I don't want to know your name. I want no information from you but yes or no. I need a minute, I need a minute of hush please, I need to attune, I need to tune into the vibrations of spirit world.' Time was she would have told them to hold hands, but these days you don't want them to strike up alliances. 'I have it, I have it,' Gemma said. Her face was strained, and she tapped the side of her head, which was a mannerism of hers. 'You, have I ever seen you before, madam?'

'No,' mouthed the woman. Colette stuck the mike under her nose.

'Can you give us that again, loud and clear?'

'NO!' the woman roared. Gemma was satisfied. 'I'm going to give you a name. Answer yes or no. I'm going to give you the name Margaret.'

'No.'

'Think again. I'm going to give you the name Margaret.'

'I did know a girl called—'

'Answer yes or no!'

'No.'

'I'm going to give you the name Geoff. Can you take that?'

'No.'

'Geoff is standing here by my side. Can you take that?'

'No,' the woman whimpered.

Gemma looked as if she were going to fly from the stage and slap her. 'I am going to give you a place. I am going to give you Altrincham, Cheshire, that is to say Greater Manchester. Can you take Altrincham?'

'I can take Wilmslow.'

'I am not interested in Wilmslow. You, can you take Altrincham?' She jumped from the stage, gestured to Colette to hand her the microphone. She paced the aisle throwing out names, Jim, Geoff, Margaret. She spun a series of questions that dizzied the punters, she tied them in twisting knots with her 'yes or no, yes or no'; before they could think or draw breath, her fingers were clicking at them, 'No need to think it over, darling, just tell me, yes or no.' Yes breeds further yes and no breeds yes too. They haven't come out for the evening to say no. People aren't going to go on and on refusing her offers, or with a contemptuous hitch of her shoulders she will move on to the next prospect. 'Yes? No. No? Yes.'

A loud humming began inside Al's head; it was the brush of skin as a thousand dead people twiddled their thumbs. God, it's boring, this, they were saying. Her mind wandered.

Where's my silk? she wondered. Whatever has Morris done with it? Her photograph on its easel looked bare without it. In the picture her smile looked thinner, almost strained, and her glowing eyes seemed to stare.

Gemma swished past her, coming off to a spatter of applause. 'On you go, take your time,' Silvana said to Mrs Etchells. Mrs Etchells toddled forward. As she passed Alison, she muttered again, 'Never called me granny.'

'Get out there, you batty old witch,' Gemma breathed. 'You next, Cara.'

'What a joy to see your faces,' Mrs Etchells began. 'My name is Irene Etchells, I have been gifted with second sight from an early age, and let me tell you there has been a great deal of joy in my life. There is no place for gloom when we reach out to spirit world. So before we can see who's with us tonight, I would like you all to join hands, and join me in a little prayer . . .'

'She's up and running,' Silvana said, satisfied.

A moment or two, and she was eliciting symptoms from a woman in the second row left: palpitations, light-headedness, a feeling of fullness in her abdomen.

Gemma stood in the wings, prompting, 'Yes or no, answer yes or no.'

'Let her do it in her own sweet way,' Alison sighed.

'Oh, I can't do with that yes-no malarkey,' Mrs Etchells said; apparently to no one. The woman with the fullness paused, and looked offended. 'There's a gentleman coming through from spirit who's trying to help me. He begins with a K, can you take a K?'

They began negotiations. Kenneth? No, not Kenneth. Kevin? Not Kevin. 'Think, dear,' Mrs Etchells urged. 'Try and think back.'

In the house before Al had left that evening, there had been further signs of a creeping male presence. There had been a whiff of tobacco and meat. As she was getting changed she had stepped on something with her bare foot, something rolling, round and hard. She had picked it up from the carpet; it was the gnawed stump of a pencil, the kind of pencil someone used to wear behind his ear. Aitkenside? Or Keef?

'It's Keith,' Mrs Etchells said. 'K for Keith. Do you know a Keith, dear?'

I used to know one, Al thought, I used to know Keef Capstick, and now I've created him, brought him to mind, his pals can't be far behind. She stood up, her breathing tight, wanting to get out. The room had a close smell, damp and medicinal, like mould under a box lid.

On stage Mrs Etchells was smiling. 'Keith is suggesting an answer to your problem, dear. About your swollen tummy. He says, well, madam, are you in the pudding club?'

There was a yelp of laughter from the audience: of indignation, from the woman in the second row left. 'At my age? You must be joking.'

'Chance would be a fine thing, eh?' said Mrs Etchells. 'Sorry, dear, but I'm only passing on what the spirits tell me. That's all I can do, and what I'm bound to do. Keith says, miracles can 'appen. Those are his exact words. Which I have to agree with, dear. Miracles can happen, unless of course you've had a little op?'

'Dear God,' Gemma whispered, 'I've never known her like this.'

'Had more than one sherry,' Mandy said.

'I'd have smelled it on her breath,' Silvana snapped.

'Have you placed Keith, yet?' Mrs Etchells asked. 'He's laughing, you know, he's quite a joker. He says, you wouldn't catch him wiv his trousers down in your vicinity, but some geezers don't bother. They say, you don't look at the mantelpiece when you're poking the fire.'

There was a puzzled silence in the hall; laughter from

some; from others a hostile mutter. 'They're turning,' Silvana said, a warning in her voice. 'Can we get her off?'

'Leave her be,' Mandy said. 'She's been working with spirit more years than you've had hot dinners.'

'Oops,' said Mrs Etchells. 'Somebody's got their wires crossed. Now I look at you, dear, I see you're not of an age for any how's-your-father. Let's clear the vibrations, shall we? Then we'll have another go at it. You have to be able to laugh at yourself, don't you? In spirit world there's lots of laughter. After the sunshine comes the rain. A chain of love links us to the world beyond. Let's just tune in and have a little chat.'

Alison peeped out. She saw that Colette stood at the back of the room, ramrod-straight, the mike in her hand. 'There's a gentleman in the back row,' Mrs Etchells said. 'I'm coming to you, sir.'

Colette looked up, her eyes searching the platform for guidance. Her difficulty was clear. The back row was empty. From the wings Silvana cooed, 'Mrs E, dear, he must be in spirit, that gentleman, the audience can't see him. Pass on, dear.'

Mrs Etchells said, 'That gentleman at the back, on the end there, have I seen you before? Yes, I thought I had. You've got a false eye now. I knew something was different. Used to wear a patch, didn't you? I remember now.'

Alison shivered. 'We must get her off,' she said. 'Really, Mandy, it's dangerous.'

A little louder, Silvana called, 'Mrs Etchells? How about some messages for the people in front?'

The audience were turning round, craning their necks and swivelling in their seats to see the empty back row: to giggle and jeer.

'Aren't they ungrateful!' Cara said. 'You'd think they'd be glad of a manifestation! There's obviously somebody there. Can you see him, Al?'

'No,' Al said shortly.

Mrs Etchells beamed down at the hecklers. 'Sometimes I wonder what I've done to be surrounded with so much love. God gave us a beautiful world to live in. When you've had as many ops as me you learn to live for the moment. As long as the youngsters are willing to listen and learn, there's hope for this world. But now they're only willing to put dog shit through your letter box, so I don't see much hope. God has put a little light inside of us and one day we will rejoin the greater light.'

'She's gone on automatic,' Cara said.

'Which one of us is going to get her?' Mandy said.

'Mrs Etchells,' Silvana called, 'come on now, time's up. Come on for your cup of tea.'

Mrs Etchells flapped a dismissive hand towards the wings. 'Ignore that raddled little madam. Silvana? That's not her name. They none of them have their right names. She's light-fingered, that one. She comes into my house to collect me, and the next thing is, the milk money's gone, the milk money that I left behind the clock. Why does she give me a lift anyway? It's only because she thinks I'll leave her something when I go over. And will I? Will I buggery. Now let us link hands and pray. Our prayers can put a chain of love around—' She looked up, dumbfounded; she had forgotten where she was. The audience shouted up with various silly suggestions: Margate, Cardiff, Istanbul.

'I've never seen such unkindness,' Mandy breathed. 'Listen to them! When I get out there, I'll make them sorry they were born.'

Silvana said, 'She has a nerve! That's the last lift she'll get from me.'

Al said quietly, 'I'll get her.'

She stepped out on to the platform. The lucky opals gleamed dully, as if grit were embedded in their surface. Mrs

Etchells turned her head towards her and said, 'There's a little flower inside us that we water with our tears. So think of that, when sorrows come. God is within all of us, except Keith Capstick. I recognise him now, he had me there for a minute, but he can't fool me. He only once did a good action and that was to drag a dog off a little girl. I suppose God was within him, when he did that.'

Alison approached, softly-softly, but the stage creaked beneath her.

'Oh, it's you,' Mrs Etchells said. 'You remember when you used to get belted for playing with knitting needles?' She turned back to the audience. 'Why did her mum have knitting needles? Ask yourself, because she never knitted. She had 'em for sticking up a girl when she's in trouble, you don't have to do that these days, they vacuum it out. She stuck a needle up herself but the baby never come out till it was good and ready, and that was Alison here. You'd see all manner of sharp objects in her house. You'd go in and the floor would be all rolling over with little dead babies, you wouldn't know where to put your feet. They all brought their girlfriends round, Capstick, MacArthur, that crew, when they found themselves with a bun in the oven.'

So, Al thought, my brothers and sisters, my half-brothers and -sisters: every day, when I grew up, I was treading on them.

'There was hardly anybody up that way knew the joy of motherhood,' Mrs Etchells said. Al took her arm. Mrs Etchells resisted. Sedately, she and Mrs Etchells tussled, and the audience laughed, and gradually Al inched the old woman towards the edge of the platform and behind the scenes. Colette stood there, a pale, burning figure, like a taper in fog.

'You could have done something,' Al complained.

Mrs Etchells shook off Al's hands. 'No need to molest me,'

she said. 'You've pulled my nice new cardigan all out of shape, you've nearly had the button off. No wonder they're laughing! A laugh's all right, I like a laugh, but I don't like people pointing fun at me. I'm not going back out there because I don't like what I've seen. I don't like who I seen, would be a better way to put it.'

Al put her mouth close to Mrs Etchells' ear. 'MacArthur. Isn't it?'

'Yes, and the other bloody shyster. Bob Fox. All along the back row.'

'Was Morris with them?'

Mandy said, 'Cara, you're next, go on.'

'Not me,' Cara said.

Mrs Etchells sat down and fanned herself. 'I've seen something you wouldn't want to see in a month of Sundays. I saw Capstick at the back there. And the rest. All that old gang. I recognised them large as life. But they've got modifications. It was horrible. It turned me up.'

Mandy stepped out on stage. Her chin jutted and her voice was crisp. 'There will be a short delay. One of our sensitives has been taken ill.'

'How short?' a man shouted. Mandy gave him a baleful glance. 'As short as we can contrive. Have some compassion.'

She turned her back on them. Her heels clicked, back to the hutch. 'Al, it's for you to decide, but I don't like the feel of Mrs Etchells' blood pressure, and I think Colette should call an ambulance.'

'Why me?' Colette said.

'Colette could drive her,' Cara said. 'Where's the nearest A & E?'

'Wexham Park,' Colette said. She couldn't resist supplying the information, but then added, 'I'm not taking her anywhere on my own. Look at her. She's gone weird.'

Said Mrs Etchells, 'I could tell you a thing or two about

Emmeline Cheetham, no wonder the police were always round her place. She was a big drinker and she knew some terrible people. Judge not, that ye may not be judged. But there is a word for women like her and that word is prostitute. Soldiers, we all know soldiers – Tommies, no harm in 'em. Have a drink, have a laugh, we've all done it.'

'Really?' Silvana said. 'Even you?'

'But no two ways about it. She was on the game. Gypsies and jockeys and sailors, it was all the same to her. She used to go down to Portsmouth. She went off after a circus once, prostituting herself to dwarfs and the like, God forgive her, foreigners. Well, you don't know what you'll catch, do you?'

'Quick!' Mandy said. 'Loosen her collar. She can't get her breath.'

'She can choke for all I care,' Silvana said.

Mandy struggled with the buttons of Mrs Etchells' blouse. 'Colette, call 999. Al, get out there, darling, and keep it going for as long as needed. Cara, go through into the bar and find the manager.'

Al stepped out on to the stage. She took in the audience, her gaze sweeping them from left to right, front row to back, to the back row which was empty; except for a faint stirring and churning of the evening light. She was silent for a long moment, letting their scattered wits regroup, their attention come to rest. Then she said, slowly, softly, almost drawling, 'Now where were we?' They laughed. She looked back at them, grave; and slowly let her smile spread, and her eyes kindle. 'We'll drop the yes and no,' she said, 'since tonight has not turned out the way we expected.' She thought, but of course I have expected it, I have done nothing but expect it. 'I suppose it teaches us,' she said, 'to expect the unexpected. It doesn't matter how many years experience you have, spirit can never be anticipated. When we work with spirit we are in the presence of something powerful, something we don't completely understand, and we need to remember it. Now I have a message for the lady in row three, the lady with the eyebrow piercing. Let's get the show back on the road.'

Behind her, she heard the slamming of doors. Manly cheers burst through, from the sports bar. She heard snatches of voices, a moan from Mrs Etchells, the low rumbling voices of ambulance men: she heard Cara wailing, 'She's left her chakras open. She'll die!'

They drove home. Colette said, 'They took her out on a stretcher. She was a bad colour.'

Al glanced down at her hands, at the leaden sheen of her rings. 'Should I have gone with her? But somebody had to hold the evening together.' She thought, I didn't want that shower in the back row following me, not to a public hospital.

'She was breathing all wrong. Sort of gasping. Like "urg – ee, urg – ee . . ."'

'I get the picture.'

'Silvana said, she can snuff it for all I care, she can rot in hell—'

'Yes.'

'She said, "I've bloody had enough of it, running around after her like a nanny, have you got your door keys, Mrs Etchells, have you got your teeth in, have you got your spare pad for the toilet" – did you know Mrs Etchells had an irritable bladder?'

'It might come to all of us.'

'Not to me,' Colette said. 'If I can't get as far as the lavatory, I'll top myself. Honestly. There's only so far you can sink in self-esteem.'

'If you say so.'

They drove in silence, to the next traffic light. Then Al

lurched forward in her seat; her seat belt dragged her back. 'Colette,' she said, 'let me explain to you how it works. If you have lovely thoughts you get attuned to a high level of spirits, right? That's what Mrs Etchells always said.'

'I wouldn't call that a high level of spirit, the one who said that old biddy was up the duff.'

'Yes, but then a spirit—' she gulped, she was frightened to name him, 'but then a spirit, you know who he was, had broken in on her, like a burglar – she couldn't help it, she was just transmitting his message. But you see, Colette, some people are nicer than you and me. Some people are much nicer than Mrs Etchells. They do manage to have lovely thoughts. They have thoughts that are packed inside their head like the chocolates in an Easter egg. They can pick out any one, and it's just as sweet as the next.'

The lights changed; they shot forward. 'What?' Colette said.

'But other people's heads, on the inside, the content is all mixed up and it's gone putrid. They've gone rotten inside from thinking about things, things that the other sort of people never have to think about. And if you have low, rotten thoughts, not only do you get surrounded by low entities, but they start to be attracted, you see, like flies around a dustbin, and they start laying eggs in you and breeding. And ever since I was a little kid I've been trying to have nice thoughts. But how could I? My head was stuffed with memories. I can't help what's in there. And with Morris and his mates, it's damage that attracts them. They love that, some types of spirits – you can't keep them away when there's a car accident, or when some poor horse breaks its leg. And so when you have certain thoughts – thoughts you can't help – these sort of spirits come rushing round. And you can't dislodge them. Not unless you could get the inside of your head hoovered out. So if you ask why I have an evil spirit guide instead of an angel or something—'

'I don't,' Colette said. 'I've lost interest. I'm past caring. I just want to get in and open a bottle of wine.'

'—if you ask why I have an evil guide, it's to do with the fact that I'm a bad person, because the people who were around me in my childhood were bad. They took out my will and put in their own. I wanted to do a good action by looking after Mart, but you wouldn't let me—'

'So everything's my fault, is that what you're saying?'

'—and they wouldn't let me because they want the shed to themselves. They want me, and it's because of me that they can exist. It's because of me that they can go on the way they do, Aitkenside and Keef Capstick as well as Morris, and Bob Fox and Pikey Pete. What can you do? You're only human, you think they'll play by earthside rules. But the strong thing about airside is that it has no rules. Not any we can understand. So they have the advantage there. And the bottom line is, Colette, there are more of them than us.'

Colette pulled into the drive. It was half past nine, not quite dark.

'I can't believe we're home so early,' Al said.

'We cut it short, didn't we?'

'You could hardly expect Cara to go on. She was too upset.'

'Cara gets on my tits. She's a wimp.'

Al said, 'You ask why I have an evil spirit guide, instead of an angel. You might as well ask, why do I have you for my assistant, instead of somebody nice?'

'Manager,' Colette said.

As they stepped out of the car, Pikey Paul, Mrs Etchells' spirit guide, was weeping on the paving by the dwarf conifers that divided them from Evan next door. 'Pikey Paul!' Al said. 'It's years since I seen you!'

'Hello, Alison dear,' sniffed the spirit guide. 'Here I am, alone in this wicked world. Play your tape when you get in. She's left you a few kindly sentiments, if you want to hear them.'

'I'm sure I shall!' Alison cried. She sounded, in her own ears, like someone else; someone from an earlier time. 'Why, Paul,' she cried, 'the sequins is all fell off your jacket!'

Colette removed Al's portrait from the boot of the car. 'They're right,' she said. 'You need to get this picture redone. No point in fighting reality, is there?'

'I don't know,' Al said to her, temporising. Said Paul, 'You might fetch out a needle and a scarlet thread, darling girl, then I can stitch up my glad rags and be on my way to my next post of duties.' 'Oh, Pikey Paul,' she said, 'do you never rest?' and 'Never,' he said, 'I'm on my way to link up with a psychic in Wolverhampton, would you know anyone who could give me a lift up the M6?'

'Your nephew is around here somewhere,' she said, and he said, 'Never speak of Pete, he's lost to me, I want no truck with his criminal ways.'

She stood by the car, her hand resting on its roof, her face entranced.

Colette said, 'What's the matter with you?'

'I was listening,' she said. 'Mrs Etchells has passed.'

Torches crept over Admiral Drive. It was the neighbourhood watch, beginning their evening search, among the cow-parsley meadows that led to the canal, for any poor wastrels or refugees who had grubbed in for the night.

Colette played the messages on the answering machine; several clients wanting to set up readings, and Mandy's cool level voice: 'on a trolley in the corridor . . . didn't linger . . . mercy really . . . given your name as next of kin.' She took down the messages; once she had shot her first draught of sauvignon blanc down her throat, she wandered into the sitting room to see what Al was doing. The tape recorder was in action, emitting chirps and coughs. 'Want a drink?' Colette said.

'Brandy.'

'In this heat?'

Al nodded. 'Mrs E,' she said, 'what's it like there?'

'It's interactive?' Colette asked.

'Of course it is.' She repeated, 'Mrs E, what's it like in spirit?'

'Aldershot.'

'It's like Aldershot?'

'It's like home, that's what it's like. I've just looked out of the window and it's all happening, there's the living and there's the dead, there's your mum reeling down the road with a squaddie on her arm, and they're heading for hers to do the unmentionable.'

'But they've demolished those houses, Mrs Etchells. You must have been past, you only live down the road. I went past last year, Colette drove me. Where my mum used to live, it's a big car showroom now.'

'Well, pardon me,' said Mrs Etchells, 'but it's not demolished on this side. On this side it looks the same as ever.'

Alison felt hope drain away. 'And the bath still in the garden, is it?'

'And the downstairs bay's got a bit of cardboard in the corner where Bob Fox tapped on it too hard.'

'So it's all still going on? Just the way it used to?'

'No change that I can see.'

'Mrs Etchells, can you have a look around the back?'

'I suppose I could.' There was a pause. Mrs Etchells' breathing was laboured. Al glanced at Colette. She had flung herself on to the sofa; she wasn't hearing anything. 'Rough ground,' Mrs Etchells reported. 'There's a van parked.'

'And the outbuildings?'

'Still there. Falling down, they'll do somebody a damage.'

'And the caravan?'

'Yes, the caravan.'

'And the dog runs.'

'Yes, the dog runs. Though I don't see any dogs.'

Got rid of the dogs, Al thought: why?

'It all looks much the same as I remember,' Mrs Etchells said, 'not that I was in the business of frequenting the back of Emmeline Cheetham's house, it wasn't a safe place for an old woman on her own.'

'Mrs Etchells – listen now – you see the van? The van parked? Could you have a peep inside?'

'Hold on,' Mrs Etchells said. More heavy breathing. Colette picked up the remote and began to flick through the TV channels.

'The windows are filthy,' Mrs Etchells reported.

'What can you see?'

'I can see an old blanket. There's something wrapped up in it.' She chuckled. 'Blow me if there isn't a hand peeping out.'

The dead are like that; cold-blooded. Nothing squeamish left in them, no sensitivities.

'Is it my hand?' Al said.

'Well, is it, I wonder?' Mrs Etchells said. 'Is it a little chubby baby hand, I wonder now?'

Colette complained, 'It's like this every summer. Nothing but repeats.'

'Don't torment me, Mrs E.'

'No, it looks like a grown-up woman's hand to me.'

Al said, 'Could it be Gloria?'

'It could at that. Now here's a special message for you, Alison dear. Keith Capstick has got his balls armour-plated now, you'll not be able to get at 'em this time. He says you can hack away all bloody day, with your scissors, carving knife or whatever you bloody got, but you'll not get anywhere. Excuse my language, but I feel bound to give you his very words.'

Alison clicked off the tape. 'I need a breath,' she said to Colette. 'A breath of air.'

'I expect there'll have to be a funeral,' Colette remarked.

'I expect so, I don't suppose the council will agree to take her away.'

'Oh, I don't know. If we doubled her up and put her in a black bag.'

'Don't. It's not funny.'

'You started it.'

Colette made a face behind her back. Alison thought, I have seen, or I have dreamt of, a woman's body parts wrapped in newspaper, I have seen men's hands smeared with something glutinous and brown as they unloaded parcels from the back of the van, wobbling packages of dog meat. I have heard a voice behind me say, fuck, Emmie, got to wash me hands. I have looked up, and where I thought I would see my own face in the mirror, I saw the face of Morris Warren.

She went out into the garden. It was now quite dark. Evan approached the fence, with a flashlight. 'Alison? We had the police out earlier.'

Her heart lurched. She heard a low chuckle from behind her; it seemed to be at knee height. She didn't turn, but the hair on her arms stiffened.

'Michelle thought she saw somebody snooping about your shed. You had that tramp, didn't you, broke in? She thought it might be him again. Take no chances, so she called them out. Constable Delingbole came in person.'

'Yes? And?'

'He checked it over. Couldn't see anything. But you can't

be too careful, when you've got kids. That type want locking away.'

'Definitely.'

'I'd throw away the key.'

'Oh, so would I.'

She stood waiting, her hands joined at her waist, the picture of patient formality, as if she were Her Majesty waiting for him to bow out of her presence.

'I'll be getting in, then,' Evan said. But he shot her a backward glance as he crossed his balding lawn.

Alison turned and stooped over a large terracotta pot. Bending her back, she heaved it aside, managing only to roll it a few inches. The gravel beneath appeared undisturbed; that is to say, no one had dug it up. She straightened up, rubbing the small of her back. 'Morris,' she said, 'don't play silly beggars.' She heard a scuffling; then the chuckle again, faintly muffled by the soil, coming from the very depth of the pot.

TWELVE

Next morning, when she was eating her low-salt corn flakes with skimmed milk, Morris put his head around the door. 'Have you see Keith Capstick?' he asked. 'Have you seen MacArthur? He has a false eye and his earlobe chewed off, and he wears a knitted weskit? Have you seen Mr Donald Aitkenside?'

'I think I'd know them, if I saw them.' The skin of her entire body crept at the sight of him, as if there were a million ants walking under her clothes; but she wasn't going to let him know she was scared. 'Have you forgotten who you're talking to?' she said. 'Anyway, why the formality? What's this about *Mister* Aitkenside?'

Morris puffed up his chest, and tried to straighten his buckled legs. 'Aitkenside's got made up to management. Aren't you informate with our new terms of employment? We've all got our training under our belt and we've all been issued wiv notebooks and pencils. Mr Aitkenside's got certificates, too. So we're supposed to be foregathering.'

'Foregathering where?'

'Here is as good as any.'

'What brings you back, Morris?'

'What brings me back? I have got a mission. I have got a big job on. I have got taken on a project. You've got to retrain these days. You've got to update yourself. You don't want to go getting made redundant. There's no such thing any more as a job for life.'

Colette came in with the post in her hand. 'Usual catalogues and junk mail,' she said. 'Mayan calendar workshop, no thanks . . . shamanic requisites by return . . . What about mixed seeds from Nature's Cauldron? Henbane, wolfsbane, skullcap, hemlock?'

'Some might blow over to next door.'

'That's what I was thinking. By the way, do you know you're on the phone from eleven till three?' Al groaned. Morris, squatting before the empty marble hearth, glanced up at her and began to roll up his sleeves. 'And we've had a call from those people near Gloucester, saying are you going on the Plutonic symbolism weekend? Only they need to know how many to cater for.' She laughed nastily. 'And of course, they count you as double.'

'I'm not sure I want to go away by myself.'

'Count me out, anyway. They say it's in an idyllic location. That means no shops.' She flicked through the letters. 'Do you do exorcisms for eating disorders?'

'Pass it on to Cara.'

'Will you go over to Twyford? There's a woman got a loose spirit in her loft. It's rattling around and she can't get to sleep.'

'I don't feel up to it.'

'You're entitled to postpone things if you've had a bereavement. I'll call her and explain about Mrs Etchells.'

A light blinked at Al from a corner of the room. She turned her eyes and it was gone. Morris was scuttling fast across the carpet, swinging on his knuckles like an ape. As he moved, the light moved with him, a crimson ripple, sinuous, like an exposed vein; it was Morris's snake tattoo, lit and pulsing, slithering along his forearm as if it had a life of its own. 'Tee-hee,' Morris chuckled.

She remembered what Mrs Etchells had said: 'They've got modifications. It turned me up.'

Colette said, 'Are you having that yogurt, or not?'

'I've lost my appetite.' Al put her spoon down.

She phoned her mum. The phone rang for a long time, and then after it was picked up there was a scuffling, scraping sound. 'Just pulling up a chair,' Emmie said. 'Now then, who is it and what can I do for you?'

'It's me. I thought you'd like to know my grandma's dead.'

'Who?'

'My grandma. Mrs Etchells.'

Emmie laughed. 'That old witch. You thought she was your grandma?'

'Yes. She told me so.'

'She told everybody that! All the kids. She wanted to get 'em in her house, captive bloody audience, innit, while she goes on about how she's had bouquets and whatnot, little op, chain of love, then when the time's right she's offering 'em around the district to all-comers. I should know, she bloody offered me. Same with you, only the lads got in early.'

'Now just stop there. You're saying my grandmother was a—' She broke off. She couldn't find the right word. 'You're saying my grandmother was as bad as you?'

'Grandmother my arse.'

'But Derek – Derek *was* my dad, wasn't he?'

'He could of been,' her mother said vaguely. 'I think I done it with Derek. Ask Aitkenside, he knows who I done it with. But Derek wasn't her son, anyway. He was just some kid she took in to run errands for her.'

Al closed her eyes tight. 'Errands? But all these years, Mum. You let me think . . .'

'I didn't tell you what to think. Up to you what you thought. I told you to mind your own business. How do I know if I done it with Derek? I done it with loads of blokes. Well, you had to.'

'Why did you have to?' Alison said balefully.

'You wouldn't ask that question if you were in my shoes,' Emmie said. 'You wouldn't have the cheek.'

'I'm going to come over there,' Al said. 'I want to put a few straight questions to you. About your past. And mine.'

Her mother shouted, 'You hear that, Gloria? She's coming over. Better bake a cake, eh? Better get the fancy doilies out.'

'Oh, you're not on that again, are you?' Al's voice was weary. 'I thought we'd got Gloria out of our lives twenty years ago.'

'So did I, pardon me, till she turned up on me doorstep the other night. I never had such a thunderclap. I says, Gloria! and she says, hello, and I says, you've not changed a bit, and she says, I can't say the same for you, she says, give us a fag, I says, how'd you track me down in Bracknell? She says—'

'Oh, Mum,' Alison yelled. 'She's DEAD.' I said it, she thought, I uttered the word no sensitive ever uses: well, hardly ever. I didn't say passed, I didn't say gone over, I said dead, and I said it because I believe that when it comes to dead, Gloria is deader than most of us, deader than most of the people who claim to be dead: in my nightmares since I was a child she is cut apart, parcelled out, chewed up.

There was a silence. 'Mum? You still there?'

'I know,' said Emmie, in a small voice. 'I know she's dead. I just forget, is all.'

'I want you to remember. I want you to stop talking to her. Because it's driving me round the twist and it always did. It's not as if you made a living out of it. So there's no use fooling yourself. You may as well get it straight and keep it straight.'

'I have.' Emmie sounded cowed. 'I have, Alison. I will.'

'So do you want to come to Mrs Etchells' service?'

'Why?' Emmie was mystified. 'Is she getting married?'

'We're burying her, Mum. I told you. Cremating. Whatever. We don't know what her wishes would have been. I was hoping you could shed some light, but obviously not. Then as soon as that's over, we're going to sit down and have a heart-to-heart. I don't think you're fit to live on your own. Colette says you should be living in a warden-assisted bungalow. She says we ought to make you a care plan.'

'You hear that, Gloria?' said Emmie. 'We'll have to polish the silver, if Lady Muck is coming to tea.'

For a few days the fiends were faintly present, flickering at the corner of her eye; throughout her whole body, they left their mark. It's as if, she thought, they're walking in one by one, and wiping their feet on me. Her temperature dropped, her tongue furred up with a yellow-green coating. Her eyes looked small and bleary. Her limbs tingled and she lost sensation in her feet; they still seemed intent on walking off, leaving the whole mess behind, but though the intention was there, she no longer had the ability.

Morris said, got to get the boys together. We will be wanting a knees-up, seeing as Etchells is fetched away, and we are fully entitled in my opinion, there's one we can tick off, well done, lads, there weren't no messing about with Etchells.

'You arranged it?' she said. She had hoped their appearance in the back row of the dem might be coincidental; or rather, the kind of coincidence with unpleasant events that they liked to arrange for themselves.

'Course we did,' Morris boasted. 'What is our mission? It is to track down useless and ugly people and recycle them, and with Etchells we have made a start. I says to Mr Aitkenside, do you mind if I kick off the project wiv a bit of personal business, and he says, Morris, old son, if I could give you the nod I would, but you know it is more than my skin's worth, for you know old Nick, his temper when he is roused, and if you don't go right through the proper procedure and your paperwork all straight he will take a pencil and ram it through your earhole and swivel it about so your brain goes twiddle-de-dee, he says, I seen it done, and Nick has a special pencil that he keeps behind his ear and it makes it more painful. I says to him, Mr Aitkenside, sir, upon my mother's life I would not ask you to take any such risk of having your brain twiddled, forget I asked, but he says, Morris, old son, we go back, he says, we go back, you and me, I tell you what I'll do for you, when I happen to catch old Nick in a mellow mood, let us say we have had a good session in the back bar at the Bells of Hell, let us say Nick has won the darts, let us say we have had a barbecue on the back lawn and the great man is feeling at ease with himself, I'd say to him, Your 'ighness, how would it be if my friend and yours Morris Warren were to do a bit of personal business, a bit of tidying up he has left over? For Nick was in the army, you know, and he likes things tidy.'

'What army?' Al said.

'I don't know.' Morris sounded impatient. 'The army, the navy, the forces, innit, bomber command, special boat squadron, there's only one army, and that's ours. Will you stop interrupting?'

'Sorry.'

'So it all worked out just like Mr Aitkenside said it would, and I got leave, and off I go, rounding up a few of the lads *as* I go, and we pop up there and give the old biddy the fright of her life—'

'What had she ever done to you?'

'Etchells? She put me out in the street. She kicked me off spirit guide, she wanted Pikey Paul with his shiny outfits, Poncey Paul as I call him, if he wasn't the uncle of Pete who is a mate of mine, I could cast aspersions there, I really could. I had to live in a builder's skip, under an old broken fire-place, till I could happen to move in with you.'

'It's a long time to hold a grudge.'

'It's not a long time, when you're dead and you've bugger all else to do. You can't treat a guide like that – maltreat him, and it comes back on you. So anyway . . . we got ourselves down the Fig & Pheasant, we tampered with the optics and nipped the little girls' bottoms that was serving behind the bar, we strolled into the function room cool as you like and then we lined up on the back row. Etchells – blimey, you should have seen her face.'

'I did.'

'But you didn't see our modifications.'

'So what are those? Apart from your tattoo?'

'Lifelike, innit?' Morris said. 'I got it done when we was on a spot of R & R in the Far East. We got leave halfway through our course. Still, you ain't seen nothing till you seen young Dean. We oldsters, we've got enough to sicken folk as it is, by God have we a collection of scars, there's Mac with his eye socket and his chewed-off ear and Capstick with his private problem that he don't like mentioned. Pikey Pete booked in to have his teeth filed, but Dean said, you could get that earthside nowadays, mate, you could get your teeth filed and your tongue slit. Oh, but Dean did rib him! So Capstick says, I'll show willing, I'll lay my money out, so he's had his hair stood on end and his tongue rasped, but the youngsters don't think nothing of that. They've all got these new tongue extensions. You can have it hung further back so it's retractable, or you can have your palate heightened so your tongue rolls up neatly till required. Now Dean has opted for the last one, it costs you but it's more neat and tidy, doesn't slide out when you're walking, and Mr Aitkenside is teaching him to take a pride in his appearance. He's going for the full scroll-out, so he'll have to wear a guard till he gets used to it, but he claims it's worth it, I dunno. He's gone in for his knees swivelled as well, so he's walking backwards when he's walking forwards, you have to see it to appreciate it, but I can tell you it's comical. Mr Aitkenside has got six legs, so he has got six boots, that's because he has got made up to management, that's all the better for kicking them with.'

Colette came in. 'Al? Cara's on the phone – do you think Mrs Etchells would have liked a woodland burial?'

'I don't think so. She hated nature.'

'Right,' Colette said. She went out again.

Al said, 'Kicking who?'

'Not just kicking, kicking out. We are chasing out all spooks what are asylum seekers, derelicts, vagrants and refugees, and clearing out all spectres unlawfully residing in attics, lofts, cupboards, cracks in the pavement and holes in the ground. All spooks with no identification will be removed. It ain't good enough to say you've nowhere to go. It ain't good enough to say that your documents fell through the hole in your breeches. It's no good saying that you've forgot your name. It's no good pretending to go by the name of some other spook. It's no good saying you ain't got no documents because they ain't invented printing yet, you got your thumbprint, ain't you, and it's no good saying they cut off your thumb, don't come that, they all say that. Nobody is to take up room they ain't entitled to. Show me your entitlement or I'll show you the boot. In Aitkenside's case, six boots. It's no good trying to bamboozle us because we have got targets, because Nick has set us targets, because we have got a clear-up rate.'

Al said, 'Is Nick management?'

'You're joking me!' Morris said. 'Is Nick management? He is the manager of us all. He is in charge of the whole blooming world. Don't you know nothing, girl?'

She said, 'Nick's the Devil, isn't he? I remember seeing him, in the kitchen at Aldershot.'

'You should have taken more notice. You should have been respectful.'

'I didn't recognise him.'

'What?' Morris said. 'Not recognise a man wiv a leather jacket, asking for a light?'

'Yes, but you see, I didn't believe in him.'

'That's where you was under a mistake.'

'I was only a girl. I didn't know. They kept throwing me out of the RE class, and whose fault was that? I hadn't read any books. We never got a newspaper, except the ones the blokes brought in, their racing paper. I didn't know the history of the world.'

'You should have worked harder,' Morris said. 'You should have listened up in your history lessons, you should have listened up in your Hitler lessons, you should have learned to say your prayers and you should have learned some manners.' He mimicked her: '"Is Nick the Devil?" Course he's the Devil. We have only been under pupillage with the best. Who have you got to put up against him? Only mincy Mandy and the rest, they're not worth MacArthur's fart. Only you and string bean and that sad bastard what used to live in the shed.'

As the week passed, her parade of business as usual became less convincing, even to Colette, whom she sometimes caught gazing at her dubiously. 'Is something troubling you?' she said, and Colette replied, 'I don't know that I trust that doctor you saw. How about a BUPA health check?'

Al shrugged. 'They'll only talk about my weight again. If I'm going to be insulted, I'm not paying for it. I can get insults on the NHS.' She thought, what the doctors fail to realise is that you need some beef, you need some heft, you need some solid substance to put up against fiends. She had been alarmed, climbing out of the bath, to see her left foot dematerialise. She blinked, and it was back again; but she knew it was not her imagination, for she heard muffled laughter from the folds of her bath towel.

That was the day they were getting ready for Mrs Etchells' funeral. They had opted for a cremation and the minimum of fuss. A few elderly practitioners, Mrs Etchells' generation, had clubbed together for a wreath, and Merlyn sent a telegram of sympathy from Beverly Hills. Al said, 'You can come back to mine afterwards, Colette's got some sushi in.' She thought, I ought to be able to count on my friends to help me, but they'd be out of their depth here. Cara, Gemma, even Mandy – they've had nothing like this in their lives, they've never been *offered.* They've sold spirit services; they haven't been sold, like me. She felt sad, separate, set apart; she wanted to spare them.

'Do you think in spirit she'll be at her best age?' Gemma said. 'I find it hard to picture what Mrs Etchells' best age might have been.'

'Sometime between the wars,' Mandy said. 'She was one of the old school, she went back to when they had ectoplasm.'

'What's that?' Cara said.

'Hard to say.' Mandy frowned. 'It was supposed to be an ethereal substance that took on the form of the deceased. But some people say it was cheesecloth they packed in their fannies.'

Cara wrinkled her nose.

'I wonder if she left a will?' Colette said.

'No doubt behind the clock, with the milk money,' Gemma said.

'I hope you're not looking at me,' Silvana said. She had threatened to boycott the ceremony, and only turned up out of fear that the other sensitives might talk about her behind her back. 'I don't want anything from her. If she did leave me anything, I wouldn't take it. Not after those wicked things she said about me.'

'Forget it,' Mandy said. 'She wasn't in her right mind. She said herself, she saw something in the back row she couldn't stomach.'

'I wonder what it was,' Gemma said. 'You wouldn't have a theory, Al, would you?'

'Anyway,' Mandy said, 'somebody ought to see about her affairs. You've still got a key, Silvy?' Silvana nodded. 'We'll all come over. Then if there's no will in the obvious places, we can dowse for it.'

'I'd rather not, myself,' Al said. 'I try to steer clear of Aldershot. Too many sad memories.'

'There would be,' Mandy said. 'God knows, Al, I don't think any of us had what you'd call a regular upbringing, I mean, when you're a sensitive it's not like a normal childhood, is it? But those kind of old people tend to keep cash lying about. And we'd want a responsible witness. A relative ought to be present.'

'I'm not,' Al said. 'A relative. As it turns out.'

'Don't listen to her,' Colette said. If there were any bundles of fivers to be picked up, she didn't see why Alison should lose out. 'It's just what her mum's been putting into her head.'

'Didn't your mum want to come today?' Gemma asked.

But Alison said, 'No. She's got a house guest.'

Guilty – knowing they'd been fed up with Mrs Etchells, knowing they were glad to have her off their patch – they let the conversation drift; back to discounts, to advertising rates, to websites and to suppliers. Gemma had found a place on the North Circular that undercut the Cornwall people on scrying kits. 'Nice cauldrons,' Gemma said. 'Very solid. They're fibreglass, of course, but as long as they look the business. You don't want to be lugging cast iron around in the boot of your car. They go from mini to three gallon. Which is going to set you back a hundred quid, but if that's what you need, you've got to invest, haven't you?'

'I don't do much with Wicca any more,' Cara said. 'I got bored of it. I'm more interested in personal development, and ridding myself and others of limiting beliefs.'

'And are you still rubbing people's feet?'

'Yes, if they'll sign a disclaimer.'

'It can't be very nice, remembering the womb,' Gemma said.

There was a feeling among them, in fact, that nothing about the day was very nice. Mandy's nose kept twitching, as if she could smell spirits. Once the sushi and meringues were consumed, they showed no wish to linger. As they parted on the doorstep, Mandy took Al's arm and said, 'If you want a bolt-hole, you know. You can soon be down in Hove. Just pick up the car keys and come as you are.'

She was grateful for Mandy's tact. She obviously had her suspicions that Morris was back, but she didn't want to say anything in case he was listening in.

Sometimes Morris's voice was in her head; sometimes she found it on the tape. Sometimes he seemed to know everything about their past life together; he would talk, reprising the Aldershot days, running them back on a kind of loop, as if, like Mrs Etchells at the dem, he'd gone on automatic.

She tried every means she knew to tune him out; she played loud music, and distracted herself by long phone calls, going through her contacts book for the numbers of psychics she had known years ago, and calling them up to say, 'Hi, guess who?'

'Al!' they would say. 'Have you heard about Merlyn? He's gone to Beverly Hills.' Then, 'Shame about Irene Etchells. Sudden, wasn't it? I never quite got it straight, was she your gran, or not? Did you ever trace your dad? No? What a shame. Yes, Irene dropped in, I was just cleaning my crystal, and whoops, there she was, swimming about inside. She warned me I might have to have a little op.'

But, as she chatted, the past was chatting inside her: how's my darling girl? Mrs McGibbet, poxy little boxer, Keef, are you my dad? If you're going to chuck up go outside and do it. Fuck, Emmie, I've got to wash me hands. Dogmeat, Gloria, Gloria, dogmeat: there's an evil thing you wouldn't want to see. Round and round it went: there's an evil thing you wouldn't want to see at all. Morris was giving her earache, about the old days: the fight game, the scrap-metal game, the entertainment game. All the same, she felt there was something he wasn't saying, something that he was holding back, perhaps some memory he was teasing her with. At other times, he seemed to be hazy about who he was addressing; he seemed to be talking to the air.

He said, 'Have you seen MacArthur? He's the cove that owes me money. If you see him you'll know him, he's missing one eye. Have you seen young Dean? He's got his head shaved and Rule Britannia stamped on it. Have you seen Pikey Pete? I've been down the waste ground and Pete ain't there. Been up the waste tip, civic amenity they call it now, I expect to see him rummaging but he's not. Totting you call it, totting's in his blood, together wiv scrap metal, his uncle were the biggest scrap-metal merchant in the Borders in the old days.'

'The Borders,' she said, 'that's a bit out of the way for you, how did you get up there then?' and Morris said, 'Circus used to go up that way, didn't it? Then in later years when I got kicked out of the circus I got a ride off Aitkenside. Aitkenside and his truck was always very handy, if you wanted picking up, if you want dropping off, post yourself by the side of a major trunk road and Aitkenside will be there. Very handy, a truck like that, when you've got boxes, when you've got a consignment, a van is very nice for a small consignment but nowadays we are trucking spookies by the score, gel. We bring 'em in by the hundreds, they are migrating from the east for a better life. But we charge, mind, and at the same time as we're bringing 'em in we are kicking 'em out, it's all part of the same racket, now you might not understand that but if you'd been on a course with Nick he'd make you understand: Comprenez? he'd say and hang you up by your feet until you answered yes. Now Aitkenside is management we have incentives for good work. We have vouchers to spend on modifications and we have family leisure breaks. We pack off on the weekends to the country, and we make crop circles. We fly over the fields and we make high-pitched whistling sounds, causing alarm to farmers and ramblers. We go on theme parks, that's what they call a fair these days, and we hang off the rides and lie by night unscrewing the screws to cause fatalities. We go out to golf clubs to dig up the greens and they think we're moles. Only you don't want to go on a driving range, a spirit can get tangled up easy in them big nets. That's how we found young Dean, we had to rescue him. Somebody shouted "old Nick's coming" and Dean being new, he panicked and run off, he run head first into one of them nets, well, where his head would be. It was Aitkenside what extricated him, using his teef.' Morris cackled. 'Old Nick, if he sees you where he didn't ought, he will spit your bollocks on his toasting fork. He will melt you on a brazier and sip the marrow out your bones.'

'Why did you get kicked out of the circus?' she asked. 'I never heard that before.'

Morris didn't answer. 'Got kicked out of the circus,' he said. 'Got kicked out of the army. Got kicked out of Etchells' place and had to live in a skip. Story of my life. I don't know, I don't feel right in myself till I meet up with Pete. Maybe there's an horse fair. Do you reckon there's an horse fair? Maybe there's a cockfight somewhere, Pete enjoys that.'

When she saw MacArthur again, materialising in the kitchen after this gap of many years, he had a false eye, just as Mrs Etchells had suggested. Its surface was lustrous but hard, and light bounced from it as it did from the surface of her lucky opals on the days when they refused to show their depths. Morris said, 'Say what you like about MacArthur but he was an artist wiv a knife. I seen him carve a woman like a turkey.'

The tape unspooled in the empty room, and Morris, speaking from the distant past, could be heard puffing and grunting into the microphone, as if he were carrying a heavy and awkward burden. 'Up a bit, left a bit, mind the step, Donnie – right, I've got her. You grab your corner of the blanket there . . . steady as she goes. Fuckit, I'm going in the kitchen, I've got to wash me hands. They are all over sticky stuff.'

Colette came in from the garden, indignant. 'I've just been in the shed,' she said. 'Mart's been back. Come and look, if you don't believe me.'

Alison went down the garden. It was another of those hot, clammy days. A breeze stirred the saplings, bound to their posts like saints secured for burning, but the breeze itself was fevered, semi-tropical. Al wiped her hand across her forehead.

On the floor of the shed were a scatter of Mart's belongings: a tin-opener, some plastic cutlery nicked from the supermarket café, and a number of rusty, unidentifiable keys. Colette scooped them up. 'I'll pass these on to PC Delingbole. Perhaps he can reunite them with their owners.'

'Oh, don't be so spiteful!' Alison said. 'What did Mart ever do to you? He's been kicked out of any place he could call home. There's no evil in him. He isn't the sort to cut a woman up and leave her in a dirty van.'

Colette stared at her. 'I don't think you ought to go to Aldershot,' she said. 'I think you ought to have a lie-down.' She ducked out of the Balmoral, and stood on the lawn. 'I have to tell you, Alison, that I am very disturbed at your behaviour lately. I think we may have to reconsider the terms of our arrangement. I'm finding it increasingly untenable.'

'And where will you go,' Alison jeered. 'Are you going to live in a shed as well?'

'That's my business. Keep your voice down. We don't want Michelle out here.'

'I wouldn't mind. She could be a witness. You were down and out when I met you, Colette.'

'Hardly that. I had a very good career. I was regarded as a high-flyer, let me tell you.'

Alison turned and walked into the house. 'Yes, but psychically, you were down and out.'

On the way to Mrs Etchells' house, they did not speak. They drove through Pirbright, by the village green, by the pond fringed with rushes and yellow iris; through the black-shaded woodlands of the A324, where bars of light flashed through the treetops to rap the knuckles of Colette's tiny fists clenched on the wheel: by the ferny verges and towering hedges, by deep-roofed homesteads of mellow timbers and old stock-brick, the sprinklers rotating on their velvet lawns, the coo of wood pigeons in their chimney stacks, the sweet smells of lavender and beeswax wafting from linen press, commode and *étagère*. If I walked out on her now, Colette thought, then with what I have got saved I could just about put a deposit on a Beatty, though to be frank I'd like somewhere with a bit more nightlife than Admiral Drive. If I can't live here where the rich people live I'd like to live on a tube line, and then I could go out to a club with my friends and we could get wrecked on a Friday like we used to, and go home with men we hardly knew, and sneak off in the mornings when only the milk floats are out and the birds are singing. But I suppose I'm old now, she thought, if I had any friends they'd all have kids by now, they'd be too old for clubbing, they'd be too grown-up, in fact it would be their kids that would be going out, and they'd be sitting at home with their gardening manuals. And I have grown up without anyone noticing. I went home with Gavin once, or rather I pressed the lift button to his hotel floor, and when I tapped at his door he looked through his spyhole and he liked what he saw, but would anybody like me now? As the first straggle of the settlement of Ash appeared – some rotting sixties infill, and the sway-walled cottages by the old church – she felt penetrated by a cold hopelessness, which the prospect before her did nothing to soothe.

Much of the district had been razed; there were vast intersections, grassy roundabouts as large as public parks, signs leading to industrial estates. 'Next right,' Al said. Only yards from the main road, the townscape dwindled to a more domestic scale. 'That's new.' She indicated the Kebab Centre, the Tanning Salon. 'Slow down. Right again.'

Between the 1910 villas some new-built terraces were

squeezed, bright blue plastic sheeting where their window glass would be. On a wire fence hung a pictorial sign that showed a wider, higher, loftier and airier version of the building it fronted: LAUREL MEWS, it said, MOVE IN TODAY FOR NINETY-NINE POUNDS. 'How do they do that?' Al said, and Colette said, 'They offer to pay your stamp duty, your surveyor's fees, all that, but they just stick it on the asking price and then they tie you into a mortgage deal they've picked out, you think you're getting something for nothing but they've got a hand in your pocket at every turn.'

'They want their pound of flesh,' Al said. 'Pity. Because I thought I could buy one for Mart. You'd think he'd be safe, in a mews. He could keep that sheeting over the windows, so nobody could see in.'

Colette hooted. 'Mart? Are you serious? Nobody would give Mart a mortgage. They wouldn't let him near the place.'

They were almost there: she recognised the dwarf wall, its plaster peeling, the stunted hedge made mostly of bare twigs. Mandy had pulled her smart little soft-top off the road, almost blocking the front door. Gemma had given Cara a lift, and she and Silvana were parked in the road, bumper to bumper.

'You want to watch that,' Silvana said, indicating Mandy's car. 'In a neighbourhood like this.'

'I know,' Mandy said. 'That's why I pulled as close as I could.'

'So where do you live, that's so special?' Colette asked Silvana. 'Somewhere with security dogs?'

Mandy said, trying to ease relations, 'You look nice, Colette. Have you had your hair done? That's a nice amulet, Cara.'

'It's real silver, I'm selling them,' Cara said promptly. 'Shall I send you one? Postage and packing free.'

'What does it do?'

'Sod all,' said Silvana. 'Silver my arse. I had one off her.

It makes a dirty mark round your neck, like a pencil mark, looks as if somebody's put a dotted line round for snipping your head off.'

Colette said, 'I'm surprised anyone notices it. Against your natural deep tan.'

Silvana put the key in the door. Alison's heart squeezed small inside her chest.

'You nerved yourself, love,' said Mandy in a low voice. 'Well done.'

She squeezed Al's hand. Al winced as the lucky opals bit into her flesh. 'Sorry,' Mandy whispered.

'Oh, Mand, I wish I could tell you the half of it.' I wish I had an amulet, she thought, I wish I had a charm against the stirring air.

They stepped in. The room felt damp. 'Christ,' Silvana said, 'where's her furniture gone?'

Alison looked around. 'No milk money. No clock.'

In the front parlour, nothing was left but a square of patterned carpet that didn't quite meet the sides of the room, and an armchair hopelessly unsprung. Silvana wrenched open the cupboard by the fireplace; it was empty, but a powerful smell of mould rushed out of it. In the kitchen – where they had expected to find the crumbs of Mrs Etchells' last teatime – there was nothing to find but a teapot, unemptied, on the sink. Alison lifted the lid; a single tea bag was sunk in brown watery depths.

'I think it's obvious what's happened here,' Gemma said. 'I believe if we inspect the windows at the back we'll find signs of forced entry.' Her voice faded as she walked down the passage to the scullery.

'She used to be married to a policeman,' Cara explained.

'Did she?'

'But you know how it is. She got involved in his work. She tried to help out. You do, don't you? But she got strangled once too often. She lived through the Yorkshire Ripper, she had all sorts of hoaxers coming through, she used to report them to his seniors but it didn't stop her having to walk about all day with an axe in her head. She gave him an ultimatum, get out of the CID, or we're history.'

'I suppose he wouldn't quit,' Colette said.

'So he was history.' Al sounded awed.

'She left him, moved down south, never looked back.'

'She must be older than she says, if she was married when it was the Yorkshire Ripper.'

'We're all older than we say.' Gemma was back. 'And some of us, my dears, are older than we know. The windows are intact. They must have got in upstairs. The back door is locked.'

'Funny, to come in upstairs, if you're going to make off with the furniture,' Colette said.

Alison said, 'Colette is nothing if not logical.' She called out, 'Pikey Pete? You bin in here?' She dropped her voice. 'He's part of a gang that used to run about round here, Mrs Etchells knew them all. He's what you call a totter, collects old furniture, pots and pans, anything of that sort.'

'And he's in spirit, is he?' Gemma said. She laughed. 'That explains it, then. Still, I've never seen such a wholesale teleportation of anybody's goods, have you?'

'It's a shame,' Al said. 'It's just plain greedy, that's what it is. There are people earthside could have used the things she had. Such as nutmeg graters. Toby jugs. Decorative pincushions with all the pins still in. She had a coffee table with a glass top and a repeat motif of the Beatles underneath, printed on wallpaper – it must have been an heirloom. She had original Pyrex oven dishes with pictures of carrots and onions on the side. She had a Spanish lady with a flouncy skirt that you sat on top of your spare loo roll. I used to run to her house when I wanted to go to the toilet because there was always some bloke wanking in ours. Though God knows why they were wanking because my mum and her friend Gloria was always ready to give them hand relief.'

Mandy put an arm around her. 'Shh, lovey. Not easy for you. But we all had it rough.'

Alison scrubbed the tears out of her eyes. Pikey Paul was crying in the bare corner of the room. 'It was me what gave her that Spanish lady,' he said. 'I won it on a shooting stall in Southport on the pleasure beach. I'd a lift all the way from Ormskirk and down the East Lancs Road, and then I had the malfortune to be picked up by a chap in a truck called Aitkenside, which was the origin of the sad connection between my fambly and yours.'

'I'm sorry, Pikey Paul,' Alison said. 'I do sincerely apologise.'

'I carried it all the way down the country wrapped in a cloth, and Aitkenside he would say, what's that you've got between your legs, employing the utmost ambiguity, till finally he made a dive for it. So I held it out of the way, the dolly, above my head while Aitkenside had his way, for I wasn't about to get Dolly spoiled, and I had a good inkling as to his nature, for those men's men they are all the same.'

'Oh, I do agree,' said Alison.

'For it is all they can think of, those men's men, rifling about in a boy's tight little matador pants till they can find his wherewithal. But still and all it was worth it. You should have seen Irene smile, when I gave her the presentation. Oh, Paul, she said, is that dolly all for me? I never told her of the perils I'd been assaulted with. Well, you don't, do you? She was a lady. I don't say you're not, but Mrs Etchells wouldn't have understood a thing like that. Whereas now it's more the modern style. They're all at it. They don't like to miss any pleasure. They're having extensions so they can fuck themselves, and whores will be out of business.'

'Pikey Paul!' said Alison. 'Keep it low! Don't talk so obscene. You never used to have such a filthy tongue in your head!'

'They're queueing up for multiple tongues,' Paul said. 'I seen 'em. What I say is mild, believe me. You want to hear 'em in the years to come. No sentence will be clean.'

'I can believe it,' Alison said. She began to cry. 'All the same, Paul, I wish I'd had a spirit guide like you. Morris never brought me a present. Not so much as a bunch of flowers.'

'You should have kicked him out,' Paul said. 'You should have kicked him out like Mrs Etchells kicked him out. Soon as she saw my Spanish dolly, she hoisted him up in her arms – she was sinewy in those days, and you know how squat he is – she carried him down the road and she dumped him in a skip. Then she come back and cooked us some pancakes. I was uncommonly fond of pancakes with syrup, but now I lay off 'em, as I've to watch my waistline, which don't we all. Now I was looking for a place to call my own, and I had a billet where I could come and go, ask me no questions and I'll tell you no lies, she was easygoing, was Mrs Etchells. We was suited – that's how you could express it. Little op, chain of love, joys of motherhood, she never varied it and why should she? Meanwhile, I got on with my own life. She had a stack of testimonials, handwritten, some of them in real fountain pen by titled people, stacked up in that sideboard there.'

'What sideboard?' Al said.

'That sideboard that one of my fambly has removed, namely Pikey Pete.'

'He should be ashamed,' Alison said. The sensitives, acting on instinct, or by training, had formed a semicircle around Al, aware that she was experiencing a manifestation. Only Colette walked away, bored, and stood with drooping head, her fingers flaking yellowed paint from the front window sill. Silvana rubbed and rubbed at a spot below her jawline: trying, perhaps, to ease her teak-coloured line of tan into the tint of her flesh. The women stood, patient, till Pikey Paul vanished in a dull red flash, his suit of lights depleted, bagged at the knee and sagged at the seat, his aura – trailing on the air – resembling no more than a greasy smear of old-fashioned men's hair cream.

'That was Pikey Paul,' Al said. 'Mrs E's guide. Unfortunately he didn't say anything about the will.'

'OK,' said Cara. 'Dowsing it is. If it's here at all, it can only be under the lino, or slid behind the wallpaper.'

She opened her beaded satchel, and took out her pendulum. 'Oh, you use a bobber,' Mandy said, interested. 'Brass, is it? I swear by a Y-rod, myself.'

Silvana took out of a carrier bag what looked like a length of lavatory chain, with a metal nut on the end. She glanced at Colette, as if daring her to say something. 'It was my dad's,' she said. 'He was a plumber.'

'You could be done for carrying that around,' Gemma said. 'Offensive weapon.'

'Tools of her trade,' Mandy said. 'Did you get your sight from your dad, then? That's unusual.'

'Alison doesn't know who her dad was,' Colette said. 'She thought she had it worked out, but her mum knocked her theory on the head.'

'But she's not the only one,' Mandy said. 'I believe that in your case too, Colette, what's on the birth certificate isn't quite the same as what's in the genes.'

Al's been gossiping, Colette thought: and yet she said it was all in confidence! How could she? She stored it up, for a future row.

'I don't even have a birth certificate,' Al said. 'Not that I know of. To be honest, I'm not really sure how old I am. I mean, my mum gave me a date, but it might not be true.

I can never remember my age when things were done to me or when things happened. It's because they always said to me, "If anybody asks, you're sixteen, right?" Which is confusing when you're about nine.'

'Poor love,' Mandy breathed.

'You must be recorded somewhere,' Colette said. 'I'll look into it. If you had no birth certificate, how did you get a passport?'

'That's a point,' Al said. 'How did I? Maybe we can dowse for my documentation, when we're done here. OK, look, ladies, you do down here, don't forget to take that armchair apart. I'll go and check upstairs.'

'Do you want somebody with you?' Gemma asked.

Mandy said in a low voice, 'Let her have some privacy. Doesn't matter whether she was her gran or not, she looked up to Irene Etchells.'

Pete had stripped out the stair carpet, so the creak of each tread carried to the women back in the parlour and, as their pendulums twitched, each tiny impulse registered an answering twitch in Alison, just above her diaphragm. The rooms were bare; but when she opened the wardrobe, a row of garments still hung there, close-covered against moths. She parted their calico shrouds; her hand brushed silk and crêpe. They were Mrs Etchells' performance gowns, from her days of triumph on distant platforms. Here was a peacock green faded to grey, here a rose pink faded to ash. She examined them: crystal beads rolled beneath finger and thumb, and a scatter of pewter-coloured sequins drifted to the floor of the wardrobe. She leaned in, breathing the smell of cedar, and began to scoop them into her cupped hand, thinking of Pikey Paul. But as she straightened up, she thought, no, I'll buy him new. I'm patient for sewing, as long as its spirit sewing, and he'll appreciate something more shiny than these. I wonder why Pete left her frocks? Probably thought they were worth nothing. Men! He had plundered the saggy polyester skirts and the cardigans that Mrs Etchells usually wore; and these, Al supposed, he would be selling on to some poor Iraqi grandma who'd lost everything but what she stood up in, or somebody who'd been bombed out in the Blitz; for in spirit world, wars run concurrently.

She let the sequins drift, between her fingers, to the bare boards, then picked two empty wire hangers from the wardrobe. She wrenched them out of shape, formed each into a rod with a hook for a handle, and held them in front of her. She followed their guidance into the back room. They bucked and turned in her hand, and while she waited for them to settle she looked out of the uncurtained window on to the site of urban clearance beyond. Probably going to build a mews, she thought. For now, she had a clear view of the back plots of the neighbouring street, with its lean-tos and lock-up garages, its yellowed nylon curtains billowing from open windows, its floribundas breaking through the earth and swelling into flagrant blood-dark bloom: a view of basking men throwing sickies, comatose in canvas chairs, their white bellies peeping from their shirts, their beer cans winking and weakly dribbling in the sun. From an upper storey hung a flag, ENGLAND red on white: as if it could be somewhere else, she thought. Her eye carried to the street beyond, where on the corner stood municipal receptacles for the sorting and storage of waste, disposal bins for glass, others for grass, others for fabrics, for paper, for shoes: and at their feet clustered black sacks, their mouths tied with yellow tape.

The rods in her hands convulsed, and their hooks cut into her palms. She followed them to the corner of the room, and at their direction, laying them down, she tore into a foot of rotting linoleum. Her nails clawed at a seam, she inched two fingers under it and pulled. I should have a knife, she thought, why didn't I bring a knife? She stood up, took a deep breath, bent again, tugged, tugged. There was a crack, a splintering; floorboards showed; she saw a small piece of paper, folded. She bent painfully to scoop it up. She unfolded it, and as she did so the fibres of the paper gave way, and it fell apart along the folds. My birth certificate, she thought: but no, it was barely six lines. First a blurred rubber stamp: PAID TO. Then *Emmeline Cheetham* was written beneath, in a florid, black hand: *The Sum of Seven Shillings and Sixpence*. Underneath came another stamp, at an angle to the above, RECEIVED WITH THANKS: and then in her mother's youthful hand, her signature, *Emmeline Cheetham*: below that, IN WITNESS THEREOF: *Irene Etchells (Mrs)*. Beneath the signature, the paper had a brown indentation, as if it had been ironed briefly on a high setting. As the nail of her little finger touched the scorch mark, the paper flaked away, leaving a ragged gap where the mark had been.

She kicked the divining rods away from her feet, and went downstairs; clattering, tread by tread. They were gathered in the kitchen, turned to the foot of the stairs and awaiting her arrival. 'Anything?' Mandy said.

'Zilch. Nix.'

'What's that? That paper?'

'Nothing,' Al said. She crumpled the paper and dropped it. 'God knows. What's seven shillings and sixpence? I've forgotten the old money.'

'What old money?' Cara said.

Mandy frowned. 'Thirty-three pence?'

'What can you get for that?'

'Colette?'

'A bag of crisps. A stamp. An egg.'

When they went out, pulling the front door behind them, Mandy stood aghast at the sight of her car. 'The sneaky bastards! How did they do that? I kept looking out, checking.'

'They must have crawled,' Silvana said. 'Unless they ran up on very little legs.'

'Which, sadly, is possible,' Alison said.

Mandy said, 'I cancelled a half-day of readings to get here for this, thinking I was doing a favour. You try to do a good action, but I don't know. Dammit, where does it get you?'

'Oh well,' Cara said, 'you know what Mrs Etchells used to say, as you sow shall you reap, or something like that. If you have done harm you'll get it back threefold. If you've never done any harm in your life, you've nothing to worry about.'

'I never knew her well,' Mandy said, 'but I doubt that, with her long experience, Irene thought it was that simple.'

'But there must be a way out of it,' Al said. She was angry. 'There must be a route out of this shit.' She took Mandy's arm, clung to it. 'Mandy, you should know, you're a woman of the world, you've knocked about a bit. Even if you have done harm, if you've done really bad harm, does it count if you've done it to evil people? It can't, surely. It would count as self-defence. It would count as a good action.'

Colette said, 'Well now, Mandy, I hope you're insured.'

'I hope I am too,' Mandy said. She freed herself from Al. Tenderly, she passed her fingers over her paintwork. The triple lines were scored deep into the scarlet, as if scraped with a claw.

Tea, tea, tea! said Colette. How refreshing to come into the cleanliness and good order of the Collingwood. But Colette stopped short, her hand on the kettle, annoyed with herself. A woman of my age shouldn't be wanting tea, she thought. I should be wanting – I don't know, cocaine?

Alison was rummaging in the fridge. 'You're not eating again, are you?' Colette said. 'It's coming to the point where I'm getting ashamed to be seen with you.'

There was a tap on the window. Alison jumped violently; her head shot back over her shoulder. It was Michelle. She looked hot and cross. 'Yes?' Colette said, opening the window.

'I saw that stranger again,' Michelle said. 'Creeping around. I know you've been feeding him.'

'Not lately,' Alison said.

'We don't want strangers. We don't want paedophiles and homeless people around here.'

'Mart's not a paedophile,' Al said. 'He's scared to death of you and your kids. As anybody would be.'

'You tell him that the next time he's seen the police will be called. And if you don't know any better than aiding and abetting him, we're going to get up a petition against you. I told Evan, I'm not too happy anyway, I never have been, two single women living together, what does that say to you? Not as if you're two girls starting out in life.'

Colette lifted the steaming kettle. 'Back off, Michelle, or I'm going to pour this over your head. And you'll shrivel up like a slug.'

'I'll report you for threatening behaviour,' Michelle said. 'I'll call PC Delingbole.' But she backed away. 'I'm going round right now to see the chairman of the neighbourhood watch.'

'Oh yes?' Colette said. 'Bring it on!'

But when Michelle had ducked out of sight, she slapped the kettle down and swore. She unlocked the back door, and said, 'I've had enough of this. If he's in there again I'm going to call the police myself.'

Alison stood by the kitchen sink, swabbing up the hot water that Colette had spilled from the kettle. Out in the garden there was seething activity, at ankle height. She couldn't see Morris, but she could see movement behind a shrub. The other spirits were crawling about, prone on the lawn, as if they were on some sort of military exercise. They were hissing to each other, and Aitkenside was gesticulating, as if urging the others forward. As Colette crossed the grass they rolled over and kicked their legs; then they rolled back and followed her, slithering along, pretending to nip her calves and slash at them with spirit sticks.

She saw Colette push at the door of the Balmoral, and step back. Step forward, and push again. Her face turned back towards the house. 'Al? It's stuck.'

Al hurried down the garden. The spirits edged away and lay in the verges. Dean was whistling. 'Cut that out,' Morris said, speaking from within his bush. 'Watch and observe. Watch how she goes now. Now she says to string bean, well, what's sticking it? Is it swollen up wiv damp? String bean says, what damp, it ain't rained for weeks. Watch 'em now. Now she pushes. Watch how she breaks out in a sweat.'

'There's something heavy behind the door,' Al said.

Dean giggled. 'If she was any good at predictionating, she'd know, wouldn't she? What we've done?'

Al crouched down and looked in at the window. It was dusty and smeared, almost opaque. Behind the door was an area of darkness, a shadow: which thickened, took on form, took on features. 'It's Mart,' she said. 'Stopping the door.'

'Tell him to get away,' Colette said. She banged on the door with her fist, and kicked it. 'Open up!'

'He can't hear you.'

'Why not?'

'He's hanged himself.'

'What, in our shed!'

There was a spatter of applause from the margins of the lawn. 'I'll call 999,' Colette said.

'Don't bother. It's not an emergency. He's passed.'

'You don't know. He might still be breathing. They could revive him.'

Al put her fingertips against the door, feeling for a thread of life through the grain of the wood. 'He's gone,' she said. 'Goddammit, Colette, I should know. Besides, look behind you.'

Colette turned. I still forget, Al thought, that – psychically speaking – Colette can't see her hand in front of her face. Mart was perched on the top of the neighbours' fence, swinging his feet in their big trainers. The fiends now roused themselves, and began to giggle. By Al's feet, a head popped up out of the soil. 'Coo-ee!'

'I see you turned up, Pikey Pete,' Al said. 'Fresh from that little job of yours at Aldershot.'

'Would I have missed this?' the fiend replied. 'Rely on me for a nice noose, don't they? I had a great-uncle that was a hangman, though that's going back.'

Dean lay on top of the shed on his belly, his tongue flapping like a roller blind down over the door. Morris was urinating into the water feature, and Donald Aitkenside was squatting on the grass, eating a sausage roll from a paper bag.

'Ring the local station and ask for PC Delingbole,' Al said. 'Yes, and an ambulance. We don't want anybody to say we didn't do it right. But tell them there's no need for sirens. We don't want to attract a crowd.'

But it was school-out time, and there was no avoiding the attention of the mums bowling home in their people carriers and SUVs. A small crowd soon collected before the Collingwood, buzzing with shocked rumour. Colette double-locked the front door and put the bolts on. She drew the curtains at the front of the house. A colleague of Delingbole's stood at the side gate, to deter any sightseers from making their way into the garden. From her post on the landing, Colette saw Evan approaching with a ladder and his camcorder; so she drew the upstairs curtains too, after jerking two fingers at him as his face appeared over the sill.

'We'll have the media here before we know it,' Constable Delingbole said. 'Dear oh dear. Not very nice for you two girls. Forensics will be in. We'll have to seal off your garden. We'll have to conduct a search of the premises. You got anybody you could go to, for the night? Neighbours?'

'No,' Al said. 'They think we're lesbians. If we must move out, we'll make our own arrangements. But we'd rather not. You see, I run my business from home.'

Already the road was filling with vehicles. A radio car from the local station was parked on the verge, and Delingbole's boy was attempting to move back the mothers and tots. The kebab van was setting up by the children's playground, and some of the tots, grizzling, were trying to lead their mothers towards it. 'This is your fault,' Michelle shouted up at the house. She turned to her neighbours. 'If they hadn't encouraged him, he'd have gone and hanged himself somewhere else.'

'Now,' said a woman from a Frobisher, 'we'll be in the local paper as that place where the tramp topped himself, and that won't be very nice for our resale values.'

Inside, in the half-dark, Delingbole said, 'Do I take it you knew him, poor bugger? Somebody will have to identify him.'

'You can do it,' Al said. 'You knew him, didn't you? You made his life a misery. You stamped on his watch.'

When the forensic team came, they stood thigh-deep in the low, salivating spirits that cluster at the scene of a sudden or violent death. They stood thigh-deep in them and never noticed a thing. They puzzled over the multiple footprints they found by the shed, prints from feet that were jointed to no ordinary leg. They cut Mart down, and the length of apricot polyester from which they found him suspended was labelled and placed carefully in a sealed bag.

'He must have taken a long time to die,' Alison said, later that night. 'He had nothing, you see, Mart, nothing at all. He wouldn't have a rope. He wouldn't have a high place to hang himself from.'

They sat with the lamps unlit, so as not to attract the attention of the neighbours; they moved cautiously, sliding around the edges of the room.

'You'd have thought he could have jumped on the railway track,' Colette said. 'Or thrown himself off the roof of Toys 'Я' Us, that's what they mostly do round Woking, I've seen it in the local paper. But oh no, he would have to go and do it here, where he would cause maximum trouble and inconvenience. We were the only people who were ever kind to him, and look how he repays us. You bought him those trainers, didn't you?'

'And a new watch,' Al said. 'I tried to do a good action. Look how it ended up.'

'It's the thought that counts,' Colette said. But her tone was sarcastic, and – as far as Alison could discern her expression, in the gloom – she looked both angry and bitter.

In spirit, Mart had looked quite chipper, Al thought, when she saw him perched on the fence. When she sneaked into the kitchen, in search of supper, she wondered if she should leave him out a plate of sandwiches. But I suppose I'd sleepwalk in the night, she thought, and eat them myself. She believed she caught a glimpse of him, behind the door of the utility room; livid bruising was still fresh on his neck.

Later, as she was coming out of the bathroom, Morris stopped her. 'I suppose you think we was out of order?' he said.

'You're an evil bastard, Morris,' she said. 'You were evil when you were earthside, and now you're worse.'

'Oh, come on!' Morris said. 'Don't take on! You're worse than your bloody mother. We wanted a laugh, that's all. Not as if the cove was doing much good this side, was he? Anyway, I've had a word with Mr Aitkenside, and we're going to take him on to clean our boots. Which is currently young Dean's job, but with Mr Aitkenside getting fitted with the sets of false feet, Dean could do with some assistance. He has to start at the bottom, you know, that's the rule. I reckon he'll shape up. He's no more gormless than Dean was when we picked him out of the golf net. If he shapes up, in about fifty years he might get to go on spirit guide.'

'Don't expect me to thank you,' said Al.

'That's just like you, innit?' Morris said. His features convulsed with spite, he bounced up and down on the landing. 'No bloody gratitude. You talk about when I was earthside, you give me the character of an evil bastard, but where would you be if it weren't for me? If it hadn't been for me the boys would have cut you up a bloody sight worse. You'd be disfigured. Aitkenside said, she has to learn respect for what a knife can do, and they all said, all the boys, quite right, she has to learn, and your mum said, fine, you carve her, but don't go carving her face, the punters won't like it. She said, it's all very well your squabbles, but when you gentlemen have all got bored of her, I've still got to sell her on, ain't I? And I supported her, didn't I? I backed her up. I said to Aitkenside, quite right, show her what's what by all means, but don't make her into a bloody liability.'

'But Morris, why did they do it?' Al cried. 'What did I ever do to you? I was a child, for pity's sake, who would want to take a knife and slice up a child's legs and leave her scarred?' I must have screamed, she thought, I must have screamed but I don't remember. I must have screamed but no one heard me.

'There was nobody to hear,' Morris said. 'That's why you

have to have an outbuilding, innit? You have to have an outbuilding or a shed, or a caravan if you can't manage that, or at least a trailer. You never know when you need to show some little shaver what's what, or hang some bugger what's getting on your nerves.'

'You haven't answered me,' Al said. She stood in his path, fingering the lucky opals as if they were weapons. He tried to swerve past her, but her aura, welling out and smothering him, forced him back. Gibbering with frustration, he condensed himself, and slid under the carpet, and she stamped on him saying, Morris, if you want to keep your job, I want some answers. If you don't give me answers I'm going to give up this game. I'll go back and work in a cake shop. I'll work in the chemist like I used to. I'll scrub floors if I have to. I'm going to give it up and then where will you be?

'Ho,' said Morris, 'you don't frighten me, gel, if you go and work in the chemist I shall make myself into a pill. If you get a job in a cake shop I shall roll myself into a Swiss roll and spill out jam at inopportune moments. If you try scrubbing floors I will rise up splosh! out of your bucket in a burst of black water causing you to get the sack. Then you will be wheedling me around like you used to, oh Uncle Morris I've no spending money, oh Uncle Morris I've no money for me school dinners, I've no money for me school trip. And all the time going behind my back with the same sob story to MacArthur, and whining for sweeties to Keith. Too generous by half, that's Morris Warren. The day I was taken over, there wasn't five bob in my pocket. I was taken over and I don't know how, taken over wiv money owing to me.' Morris began to whimper. 'MacArthur owes me. Bill Wagstaffe owes me. I've got in my black book who owes me. Bloody spirits is devious, innit? Always some reason they can't pay. "My pocket vaporised. Holy Bloody Ghost got my wallet." So there I was turning up airside, they says, turn out your pockets, and when they saw that was all the money I had to my name they bloody laughed. They said, you don't work you don't drink, me old mate. That's the rule here. Then I got put on spirit guide. First I got Irene Etchells, and then you. God help me. I say God help me but the bugger never does. That's why I bother wiv Nick, wiv Nick you get a career opportunity. You get sent on courses.'

'If you get promoted,' Al said, 'nobody will be happier than I will. The only bit of peace and quiet I had was when you were on your course.'

'Peace and quiet?' Morris yelped. 'How could you have peace and quiet? Wiv a past like yours? Not ten years old, and a man's testicles on your conscience.'

'What testicles?' Alison yelled.

Across the landing, Colette's door opened. She stood in her bedtime T-shirt, very white and severe. 'That's it,' she said. 'I don't intend to spend another night under this roof. How can I live with a woman who has rows with people I can't see, and who stands outside my bedroom door shouting "What testicles?" It's more than flesh and blood can stand.'

Alison rubbed her forehead. She felt dazed. 'You're right,' she said. 'But don't be hasty.'

'It's simply not acceptable conduct. Not even by your standards.'

Alison moved her foot, so Morris could slide from under it. 'At least wait until the morning.'

'I don't believe it's safe to wait until morning. I shall pack a small bag and I shall send someone for the rest of my things in due course.'

'Who?' Al said, in simple wonderment. 'Who will you send?' She said, 'You can't just rush off into the night. That's silly. You owe it to me to talk it over.'

'I owe you nothing. I built your business up from scratch.

It was a blundering amateur mess when I came on board.'

'That's what I mean. Come on, Colette! We've been through such a lot.'

'Well, from now on you're on your own. You've got plenty of company, I would have thought. Your special sort of company.'

'I've got my memories,' Al said. 'Yes. That's fine.'

She turned away. I won't entreat you any more, she thought. She heard low voices from downstairs. It sounded as if Aitkenside and the rest had come in and were making themselves a snack. Colette closed her door. Al heard her talking. For a moment she stood still, in astonishment. Who has she got in there with her? Then she realised that Colette was using her mobile phone, and was making arrangements to depart.

'Wha?' Gavin said. 'Who's this?' He spluttered, coughed, blew his nose twice; he sounded like a bear that has been hibernating at the bottom of a pit.

'It's not that late,' she snapped. 'Wake up, Gavin. Are you awake? Are you listening to me? This is an emergency. I want you to get me out of here.'

'Oh,' said Gavin, 'it's you, Colette. How've you been?'

'I've been better. I wouldn't ask, except I need to get out right now, and I need somewhere to stay, just for tonight. I'm packing a bag right now.'

There was a silence. 'So let me get this straight. You want me to come over there?'

'Yes. At once.'

'You want me to drive over there and get you?'

'We used to be married. Is it too much to ask?

'Yes, no, it's not that . . .' He broke off. To consult Zoë, perhaps? Now he was back on the line. 'The problem's my car, you see, it's – well, it's in the garage.'

'What a time to pick!' she snapped. 'You should have a little Japanese one like us, never lets us down.'

'So why don't you, you know, get in it . . . ?'

'Because it's hers! Because she's the owner and I don't want a dispute. Because I don't want her near me, or anything that belonged to her.'

'You mean Fat Girl? Are you running away from her?'

'Look, I'll call a cab. Only be ready to let me in when I get there. It may take a while.'

'Oh, I've got wheels,' Gavin said. 'I can come. No problem. As long as you don't mind it. I mean, it's not my usual standard.'

'Gavin, come now, in whatever you happen to be driving.'

She clicked the phone off. She put her hand on her solar plexus, and tried to breathe deeply, calmly. She sat on the side of the bed. Vignettes from her life with Al ran through her mind. Alison at the Harte & Garter, the day they got together: arranging the sugar straws and pouring the milk. Alison in a hotel in Hemel Hempstead: trying on earrings at the dressing table, between each pair dabbing at her earlobes with cotton-wool balls soaked in vodka from the minibar. Alison wrapped in a duvet, on the night the princess died, her teeth chattering on the sofa of the flat in Wexham. As she hauled down a bag from the top of the wardrobe and pushed into it a washbag and some underwear, she began to rehearse her explanation to Gavin, to the world. A vagrant hanged himself in the shed. The air grew thick and my head ached. She stamped outside my room and shouted 'What testicles?!' She snapped her bag shut, and lugged it downstairs. At once she thought, I can't turn up like this, what about Zoë, she'll probably be wearing designer lingerie, maybe a one-off a friend has made for her, something chiffon, something silk, I wouldn't like her to see these sweatpants, she'll laugh in my face. She ran upstairs, took off her clothes, and stood before her open wardrobe, wondering what she could find to impress a model. She glanced at her watch: how long would it take Gavin to get over from Whitton? The roads will be empty, she thought. She dressed; she was not pleased by the result; maybe if I do my make-up, she thought. She went into the bathroom; painstakingly she drew two eyes and a mouth. She went downstairs again. She found she was shivering, and thought she would like a hot drink. Her hand reached for the kitchen light switch, and drew back. We're not supposed to be here; the neighbours think we left. She crossed the room, and began to inch up the kitchen blind.

It was three thirty, and already the short midsummer darkness was becoming a smoggy haze. Aluminium barriers had been erected around the Balmoral, and on them a line of magpies was bouncing, as if they were sharing a joke. Behind her, she heard a footstep on the vinyl floor. She almost screamed. Al crossed the kitchen, bulky in her voluminous cotton nightgown. She moved slowly, as if drugged, hypnotised. She slid open the cutlery drawer, and stood looking down into it, fingering the knives and forks.

This is the last of it, Colette thought. A phase of my life ends here; the hidden clink-clink of the metal from inside the drawer, the conversational sound of the birds, Alison's absorbed face. Colette crossed the room and passed her without speaking. She had to push past, she felt: as if Al's white gown had swelled out to fill the room, and the substance of Al's flesh had swollen with it. In the distance she heard the sound of a car. My chariot, she thought. Gavin may not be much of a man, but he's there for me in a crisis. At least he's alive. And there's only one of him.

From the kitchen, Al heard the front door close behind Colette. The letter box opened, keys dropped to the carpet, the letter box flipped shut. That was a bit dramatic, Al thought, there was no need for her to do that. She limped to a kitchen chair, and sat down. With some difficulty, she raised one calf and crossed her ankle over the opposite knee. She felt the drag and pull on the muscle beneath her thigh, and she had to hang on to her shin bone to stop her foot sliding off and back to the floor. She bent her back, hunched forward. It was uncomfortable; her abdomen was compressed, her breath was squeezed. It's a pity Cara's not here, she thought, to do it for me, or at least to instruct me in the proper technique; she must have got her diploma by now. I'll just have to rub away and hope for the best; I'll have to go back by myself, back to Aldershot, back to the dog runs and the scrubby ground, back to the swampish waters of the womb, and maybe back before that: back to where there is no Alison, only a space where Alison will be.

She felt for the underside of her toes, and delicately, tentatively, began to massage the sole of her foot.

THIRTEEN

At some point on your road you have to turn and start walking back towards yourself. Or the past will pursue you and bite the nape of your neck, leave you bleeding in the ditch. Better to turn and face it with such weapons as you possess.

Her feet feel more swollen than usual. Perhaps she's kneaded them too hard. Or perhaps she's just reluctant to walk down this road, back through her teenage years, fire-side chats with Emmie, happy schooldays, kindergarten fun. She hears Colette drop her keys through the door. Back, back. She hears the engine of a small car, struggling uphill on Admiral Drive: it's Gavin.

Back, back, back to yesterday. The police are searching the house. Colette says, what are you looking for, Constable Delingbole, surely you don't think we've got another corpse? Delingbole says, rather self-conscious, would you not call me that any more? I'm Sergeant Delingbole now.

Lovely house, the policewoman says, looking around. Alison says, can I make you a cup of tea? and the police-woman says, oh no, you've had a fright, I'll do the tea.

Al says, there's lemon and ginger, camomile, Earl Grey or

proper tea, there's a lemon in the fridge and semi-skimmed, there's sugar on the top shelf there if you want it. Sergeant Delingbole plunges a long stick down the waste disposal, fetches it up again and sniffs it. Just routine, he says to Al. By the way, that's quite a set of knives you've got there. I love those Japanese ones, don't you? So chic.

The policewoman says, what do these houses come in at, then?

Back, back. Her fingers are pressed to the door of the shed, feeling for Mart's pulse. She is coming down the garden towards the Balmoral. Colette is gesturing that the door is stuck. She is standing at the sink swabbing the spilled water. The kettle is boiling. Michelle's face appears. Back, back. They are closing the door on Mrs Etchells' house. As you sow so shall you reap. She is holding a piece of paper with a scorch mark. Her head is in the wardrobe and she is breathing in camphor, violets, a faint body smell persisting down the years. They always said to me, if anyone asks you're sixteen, right? I can never remember my age when things were done to me or when things happened. I'm not sure how old I am.

With each step backwards she is pushing at something light, tensile, clinging. It is a curtain of skin. With each step the body speaks its mind. Her ears pick up the trickle and swish of blood and lymph. Her eyes turn back and stare into the black jelly of her own thoughts. Inside her throat a door opens and closes; no one steps in. She does not look into the triangle of shadow behind the door. She knows a dead person might be there.

She hears a tap-tap: a knuckle on glass. 'Are you there, Mr Fox?' she says. She always says 'Mister': when she remembers. The men say, here, you bloody tell her, Emmie, tell her politeness costs nothing.

There is a noise which might be crockery smashing, and a chair being knocked over. A door in her mind opens, and at first, once again, no one enters. She waits, holding her breath. It might be Keef, or it might be Morris Warren, or it might be their mate MacArthur, who always winks at her when he sees her.

But it's her mum who staggers in, rights herself with some difficulty. 'Whoops!' she says. 'Must be my new pills. Blue, they is. That's unusual, ain't it, blue? I says to him at the chemist, are you sure these are right? He says, lovely shade, he says, not blue, you'd not call that blue. It's more heliotrope.'

She says, 'Mum, did Donnie Aitkenside leave you any wages when he went off this morning? Because you know that magic shilling that we have to put in the gas meter? He took it with him.'

Her mum says, 'Donnie? Gone?'

'Yes,' she says, 'he was creeping downstairs with his shoes in his hand, and he took our shilling for the gas. I thought maybe it was his change.'

'What in the Lord's name is the girl talking about now, Gloria?'

'If we don't have that shilling we need real money for the meter. It's cold out and I haven't had my breakfast.'

Her mother repeats, 'Donnie? Gone?'

'And if he's not paid you, we've no money for my dinner money.'

'And who gave you permission to call him Donnie, you stuck-up little madam? If a child such as you talked back in my day there'd be bloody blue murder.'

She says, there is anyway, innit? It's bloody blue murder every day here. Her mum says, there you go again, if he takes his belt off to you I'll not be surprised, I'll not be the one holding him back, I'll tell you: and there, thumping her fist on the wooden draining board, her mum is saying what they'll do, what they'll do and what they won't, how they're going to thrash her till she's the texture of a jellyfish and she has to crawl to school on her belly: till she begins to wail and cry and say, but what can I eat for my breakfast? and her mum says, corn flakes if there's no gas, and she says, but there's no milk, and her mum says, so am I black and white, am I stood in the fucking meadow, and if not, what leads you to believe I am a fucking cow?

And that concludes it. It has to. Emmie falls over, knocked out by the force of her own sentence. She goes to school on an empty stomach. The lesson is scripture and she is thrown out to stand in the corridor. She is just standing there, doing no wrong. The headmaster sees her. 'You again!' he bellows. She draws down the secret flaps, the membranes that cover her ears, and watches him gesticulating at her, his forehead creasing with fury. At playtime Tahera buys her a bag of crisps. She hopes they will give her a school dinner on credit but she doesn't have a token so she is turned away. She says, the dogs have eaten my token, but they laugh. She gets half of a quarter of a marmite sandwich from Lee. On her way home she keeps her eyes down, searching the pavement for a magic shilling: or any money really, or a pin to pick up. She just thinks she sees a pin when wham! she walks straight into MacArthur. Hello, Mr MacArthur, she says. All the day you'll have good luck. He stares at her, suspicious. He says to her, your mam says you need a lesson. He puts out his hand, grabs her right nipple and twists it. She cries out. There's one, he says, do you want me to do the other side? He winks at her.

Daylight has come to Admiral Drive. Dare she pull back a curtain? She is stiff and cold, except for her feet, which are burning. She limps into the kitchen. For a moment she stands paralysed before the gas rings, thinking, how will I light them, when Aitkenside has taken our shilling? Then she depresses the ignition switch and the blue flame leaps up. She pours milk into a pan and sets it on the flame.

The telephone rings. It will be Colette, she thinks, wanting to come back. The cooker's digital clock glows green, lighting the kitchen tiles with their frieze of fishes, lighting their slippery scales. Don't be silly, she says to herself, she'll barely be arrived in Whitton yet. She had thought a much longer time had elapsed: years. She stands with her cold hands stretched over the pan, and lets the machine take the call. Her message plays: there is a click. She thinks, it is the neighbours, trying to trick me into picking up; they want to know if I'm here.

Tentatively, she pulls up the kitchen blind. The clouds are charcoal and thick and grey, like the smoke from burning buildings. The full moon burrows into them, and is immersed, swallowed. There is a tension headache at the back of her neck and, at the auditory rim, a faint high-pitched singing, like nocturnal wildlife in an equatorial forest, or God's fingernail scraped against glass. The sound is continuous, but not steady; it pulses. There is a feeling that something – a string, a wire – is being stretched to its limit. She lowers the blind again, inch by inch, and with each inch the years fall away, she is in the kitchen at Aldershot, she is twelve, thirteen, but if anyone asks, she is sixteen of course.

'Mum,' she says, 'did you run away with a circus?'

'Oh, circus, that was a laugh!' Her mum is merry from three strong lagers. 'Your uncle Morris was in that circus, he did sawing the lady in half. He wanted me to be sawed but I said, Morris, on your bike.'

'What about Gloria?'

'Oh yes, they sawed Gloria. Anybody could saw her. She was that sort of girl.'

'I don't know what that sort would be. The sort of girl who lets herself be sawn in half.'

'Yes, you do,' her mum says: as if she is prompting her to remember. 'They was always practising on you. Morris, he liked to keep his hand in. Used to say, you never know when the old tricks will come in useful, you might have to turn your hand to it again. Many's the time I seen your top half in the scullery and your bottom half in the front room. I seen your left half out the back in the shed and your right half God knows where. I says to Morris, I hope you know what you're doing, I want her stuck together before you leave here tonight.'

Mum takes a pull on her can. She sits back. 'You got any ciggies?' she says, and Al says, 'Yes, I got some here somewhere, I nicked 'em for you.' Her mum says, 'That's nice: it's thoughtful. I mean, some kids, they only go nicking sweeties, just thinking about themselves. You're a good kid, Ali, we have our ups and downs, but that's in the nature of mother and daughter. We're alike, you see. That's why we don't always see eye to eye. When I say alike, I mean, not to look at obviously, plus we're not in the same class when it comes to brains, you see, I was always quick when I was at school, and as for weight I was about half the weight of a whippet, whereas you, I mean, you're not the sharpest knife out of the drawer, you can't help that, love, and as for your size it's no secret some men like that type, MacArthur, for instance. When I took his deposit on you, he says, Emmie, it's a good thing you're not selling her by the pound.'

She asks, 'Did MacArthur say that?'

Her mum sighs; her eyelids flutter. 'Al,' she says, 'get me one of my new blue pills. The helicopter ones. Would you?'

What year is this? Al runs a hand over her body. Has she breasts now, or just the promise of them? There is no point, when it comes to your own flesh, trying to knead it into precision; flesh doesn't yield that kind of answer. She pours the hot milk on to a spoonful of instant coffee. Then she is too weak to do any more, and she sits down.

'They used to disappear you,' Emmie says. 'For a laugh. Sometimes you'd be gone half an hour. I'd say, here, Morris, where's Alison? That's my only daughter you've disappeared. If she don't come back I'll sue you.'

'And did I?' she says. 'Come back?'

'Oh yes. Else I really would. I'd have seen him in court. And Morris knew it. There was all sorts of money tied up in you. Trouble is with me I couldn't keep me books straight.'

'You didn't have books. You had a vase.'

'I couldn't keep me vase straight. Bob Fox was always dipping in it. And then the boys fell to quarrelling about who was to go first at you. MacArthur put down his deposit, but oops! You see, I had borrowed money off Morris Warren. Morris said money owed counts for more than money down. And he wouldn't leave it alone, I'm owed this, I'm owed that.'

Al says, 'He's still the same.'

'But then Keith Capstick got in anyway, before either of them could do the business, on account of your turning to him after the dog-bite. The ones that weren't there when the dog broke in, the ones that didn't witness it, they couldn't understand the way you was wiv Keith, making up to him and kissing him and all. So there was bound to be disputes. So then they was mired in a three-way fight. And MacArthur come first versus Keith, and Keith got a pasting.'

'But Morris, he just maintained the same, Keith Capstick owes me money, Mac owes me – he said Bill Wagstaffe owed him, I could never see how that was, but I suppose it was a bet on the horses and boys will be boys. Morris said, I will go to my grave buried with my little black book saying who owes me what, I will never rest till I get my money back, dead or alive.'

'I wish I'd known,' Alison says. 'If I'd known all he wanted was a refund, I could have written him a cheque myself.'

'And Aitkenside,' her mum says, 'was overseeing it all. Thank the Lord for Donnie Aitkenside. He was advising me, like. But then how was I supposed to make a living, after you was offering all-in for a shilling? I even lent you my nightdress, and that's all the thanks I get.'

'You said I was a good kid.'

'When?'

'A while back.'

'I changed my mind,' says Em, sulking.

Her coffee is cold, and she raises her head to the tap, tap, tap. Mr Fox, are you there? Are your friends with you? Click by click, she lifts the kitchen blind. Dawn: there is a dazing light, a bar of thunderous black across the sky: hailstones are falling. These summers since the millennium have been all the same: days of clammy unnatural heat, sapping to the will. She puts her fingers against her forehead and finds her skin damp; but she couldn't say whether she's hot or cold. She needs a hot drink, to banish that deep internal quaking; I could try again, she thinks, with the kettle and a tea bag. Will the police come back? She hears the neighbours chanting – OUT OUT OUT – a swell of distant voices, like a choir.

'Jesus,' Colette said. 'Where did you get this clapped-out dodgem car?'

'My garage lent it. It's only temporary. A courtesy car.' Gavin looked at her out of the tail of his eye. 'You look done in,' he said.

'Done in,' she said. 'Tired out.'

'Washed up,' Gavin offered.

'Look, I realise this isn't convenient for you. I promise I won't be in your way. I just need a few hours to catch up on my sleep, then I can think straight. I'll soon put my life to rights. I'm by no means penniless, I just need to work out how to extricate myself from my ties with Alison. I may need to see a solicitor.'

'Oh. She in trouble?'

'Yes.'

'Small businesses going under all over the show,' Gavin said. 'Easy to run up a tax bill. They claim there's not a recession, but I dunno.'

'What about you, did you get fixed up?'

'Bit of contract work. Take it as it comes. Here and there. As and when.'

'Hand to mouth,' she said.

For a while they drove in silence. The suburbs were beginning to wake up. 'What about Zoë?' Colette said. 'What will she think about me turning up like this?'

'She'll understand. She knows we used to be related.'

'Related? If that's what you call it.'

'Married is a relation, isn't it? I mean, you're related to your wife?'

'She's got no cause for jealousy. I shall make that perfectly clear. So don't worry. It's just for the emergency. It's strictly temporary. I'll make sure she knows that. I'll soon be out of her way.'

'Anyway,' her mum says, 'Gloria got sawed once too often. And then they had to get rid of her, didn't they? It wasn't even on the premises, that was the big nuisance of it. They had to fetch her back as consignments. But then the dogs came in handy, didn't they? But Pete said, you got to watch them dogs now, Keith. You got to watch dogs, once they have got a taste for human flesh. Which was proved, of course. With the dog flying out at you. And then the way he cleaned his dish, when you served him up a slice of Keith.'

She leaves the house now, young Alison, she leaves the house at Aldershot, kicking open the back door that is swollen with damp. MacArthur sees her go. He winks at her. It has rained that day and the ground is soft underfoot as she makes her way towards the lock-up garages.

Emmie says, 'Where there is waste ground, there is outbuildings. It stands to reason. That's where the boys used to keep their knocked-off ciggies and their bottles of spirits, they was always bringing in spirits by the case. Oops, I think I've spoken out of turn now, it's a good thing MacArthur's not around, he'd have walloped me one, do me a favour and don't mention to the boys it was me what told you—'

'I'm not the police,' Al says.

'Police? That's a laugh. They was all in on it, only you don't want to mention it to MacArthur, I'll only get my eye blacked and my teef knocked out, not that I have any teef, but I wouldn't like a smack in the gums. Police used to come round, saying I'm after the whereabouts of MacArthur, I'm attempting to locate a gypsy fella name of Pete, they was having a laugh, they weren't locating, all they was wanting was a rolled-up fiver in their top pocket and a glass of whisky and lemonade, and if I couldn't oblige them, on account of I'd spent me last fiver and you'd drunk the lemonade, they'd say, well now, Mrs Cheetham, well now, I'll just get my leg over before I depart your premises.'

She walks past the van, young Alison, the van where Gloria rests in pieces: past the dog run, where Harry, Blighto and Serene lie dreaming: past the empty chicken runs, where the chickens are all dead because Pikey Pete has wrung their necks. Past the caravan with its blacked-out windows: back to the hut where she lies and howls. She peeps in, she sees herself, lying bleeding on to newspaper they've put down: it will be hygienic, Aitkenside says, because we can burn them once she's clotted.

Aitkenside says, you'd better stay off school, till it scabs over. We don't want questions asked into our private business. If they say anything to you, say you was trying to jump barbed wire, right? Say you did it scrambling over broken glass.

She lies, moaning and thrashing. They have turned her over on her back now. She screams out: if anybody asks I'm sixteen, right? No, officer, sir, my mummy is not at home. No, officer, sir, I have never seen this man before. No, officer, sir, I don't know that man either. No, sir, for certain I never saw a head in a bath, but if I do I will be faithfully sure to come to the station and tell you.

She hears the men saying, we said she'd get a lesson, she's had one now.

The telephone again. She won't answer. She has lowered the kitchen blind, in case despite the new locks the police have installed the neighbours are so furious as to swarm over the side gate. Colette was right, she thinks, those gates are no good really, but I don't think she was serious when she mentioned getting barbed wire.

She goes upstairs. The door of Colette's room stands open. The room is tidy, as you would expect; and Colette, before leaving, has stripped the bed. She lifts the lid of the laundry basket. Colette has left her soiled sheets behind; she stirs them, but finds nothing else, not a single item of hers. She opens the wardrobe doors. Colette's clothes hang like a rack of phantoms.

They are in Windsor, at the Harte & Garter. It is summer, they are younger, it is seven years ago, an era has passed. They are drinking coffee. She plays with the paper straws with the sugar in. She tells Colette, a man called M will enter your life.

At Whitton, Colette's hand reached out in the darkness of the communal hall; accurately, she found the light-switch at the foot of the stairs. As if I'd never been away, she thought. In seven years they say every cell of your body is renewed; she looked around her and remarked, the same is not true of gloss paintwork.

She walked upstairs ahead of Gavin, to her ex-front door. He reached around her to put the key in the lock; his body touched hers, his forearm brushed her upper arm. 'Sorry,' she said. She inched aside, shrinking herself, folding her arms across her chest. 'No, my fault,' he said.

She held her breath as she stepped in. Would Zoë, like Alison, be one of those people who fills up the rooms with her scent, a person who is present even when she's absent, who sprays the sheets with rose or lavender water and who burns expensive oils in every room? She stood, inhaling. But the air was lifeless, a little stale. If it hadn't been such a wet morning, she would have hurried to open all the windows.

She put her bag down and turned to Gavin, questioning.

'Didn't I say? She's away.'

'Oh. On a shoot?'

'Shoot?' Gavin said. 'What do you mean?'

'I thought she was a model?'

'Oh yes. That. I thought you meant like on safari.'

'So is she?'

'Could be,' Gavin said, nodding judiciously.

She noticed that he had placed his car magazines on a low table in a very tidy pile. Other than that, there was very little change from the room she remembered. I'd have thought he'd have redecorated, in all these years, she said to herself. I'd have thought she'd have wanted to put her stamp on it. I'd have thought she'd throw all my stuff out – everything I chose – and do a makeover. Tears pricked her eyes. It would have made her feel lonely, rejected, if she'd come back and found it all changed; but the fact that it was all the same made her feel somehow . . . futile. 'I suppose you'll want the bathroom, Gav,' she said. 'You'll have to get off to work.'

'Oh no. I can work from home today. Make sure you're all right. We can go out for a bite of lunch if you feel up to it later. We could go for a walk in the park.'

Her face was astonished. 'A what, Gavin? Did you say a walk in the park?'

'I've forgotten what you like,' he said, shuffling his feet.

In the corner of Colette's room, where the air is turbulent and thickening, there arises a little pink felt lady whom Al has not seen since she was a child.

'Ah, who called me back?' says Mrs McGibbet.

And she says, 'I did, Alison. I need your help.'

Mrs McGibbet shifts on the floor, as if uncomfortable.

'Are you still looking for your boy Brendan? If you help me, I'll swear I'll find him for you.'

A tear creeps out of Mrs McGibbet's eye, and makes its way slowly down her parchment cheek. And immediately a little toy car materialises by her left foot. Alison doesn't trust herself to pick it up, to handle it. She doesn't like apports. Start on that business, and you'll find some joker trying to force a grand piano through from the other side, pulling and tugging at the curve of space-time, wiping his boots on your carpet and crying, 'Whew! Blimey! Left hand down a bit, steady how she goes!' As a child, of course, she had played with Brendan's toys. But in those days she didn't know how one thing led to another.

'I don't know how many doors I've knocked on,' says Mrs McGibbet. 'I've tramped the streets. I've visited the door of every psychic and sensitive from here to Aberdeen, and attended their churches though my priest told me I must not. And never a sighting of Brendan since the circus fellas put him in a box. He says, "Mam, it is the dream of every boy to join the circus, for hasn't my sister Gloria a costume with spangles? And such a thing was never seen in these parts." And that was true. And I didn't care to spell out to him the true nature of her employment. So he was taken on as box boy.'

'They put him in a box?'

'And fastened round the chain. And box boy will burst out, they said. A roll on the drums. The audience agog. The breath bated. The box rocking. And then nothing. It ceases to rock. The man MacArthur comes with his boot, oi, box boy!'

'Was MacArthur in the circus?'

'There wasn't a thing that MacArthur wasn't in it. He was in the army. He was in the jail. He was in the horse game, and the fight game, and the box game. And he comes with his boot and kicks the side of the box. But poor Brendan, he makes not a murmur; and the box, not an inch does it shift. And a deadly silence falls. So then they look at each other, at a loss. Says Aitkenside, Morris, have you ever had this happen before? Says Keith Capstick, we'd better open it up, me old china. Morris Warren protests at the likely damage to his special box, but they come with a lever and a bar. They pull out the nails with pliers and they prise off the lid. But when they open it up, my poor son Brendan is gone.'

'That's a terrible story, Mrs McGibbet. Didn't they get the police?'

'The police? Them? They'd be laughed out of the place. The police are the king of boxes. It is well known in every nation that people who trouble them disappear.'

'That's true,' Alison said. 'You've only to watch the news.'

'I would help you out,' the little lady said, 'with your memorising and all, but I'm sure the topic of MacArthur's eye is not a topic for decent people. I'm sure I wasn't looking, though I do recall the man MacArthur lying drunk as a lord on your mammy's couch, for though I might have shifted his head to see if Brendan was under the cushion, if he then fell back into his stupor I barely recall. And if the man they call Capstick was incapable too, lying with his head under the table, I'm sure I was too busy to notice. I can't recall at all you stooping over them vermin and patting their pockets, hoping for a shilling to roll out, for I wouldn't know where the minimart was or what sort of sweeties you were fond of spending on. Now one or the other might have roared "bleeding thief", but then it could have been "bleeding Keith", for I can't claim I was paying attention – and you wouldn't mention to them, would you, that it was me, McGibbet, that told you nothing at all about it, for I'm in mortal fear of those fiends? I'm sure I wasn't seeing a little girl with a pair of scissors in her hand, snipping about a man's private parts. I'm sure I was too busy about my own business to notice whether that was a fork you were carrying, or that was a knife, and whether you had a spoon in your pocket, or whether your mouth was bristling with pins. I'm sure I wouldn't have known if you were carrying a knitting needle, for there were several on the premises, but I'm sure I was too busy seeking my boy Brendan to know whether you had opened the drawer and took one out. And I wouldn't say I saw you go down the garden to feed the dogs, neither. If I hadn't been peeping under the furniture as was my habit, I might have seen a smile on your face and a bowl in your hand, and a trickle of blood running down each arm. But your age I couldn't swear to, it was no more than eight years, nine or ten. And I never saw the fella called Capstick run out and collapse on the ground at the side of the house, shouting, ambulance, ambulance! Nor did I see Morris God curse him Warren and the other bloody bleeder come up at the trot, his name I don't suppose would be Aitkenside. I didn't notice them haul up Capstick by his oxters and dump him in the bath that was kept out on the road in front of your mother's premises. There was a deal of shouting then, but it was that sort of neighbourhood, so I couldn't say he was crying out to the whole street, where's my bollocks, find the fuckers for they can stitch them back on, beg your pardon but that's the exact truth of what he might have said at the time, if I had been able to hear above the racket. And Morris Warren said something back to him, I dare say, but I wouldn't like to quote you his words, which were too late I regret my son, for your bollocks are all eaten by the dogs, they cannot sew them back when they are swallered, not to my way of thinking, and to my way of thinking they are swallered good and proper and the dogs have cleaned their bowls. And he, Morris Warren, it's possible he could not forbear to laugh, for he had told Capstick he should not interfere with your good self without paying money for it, and now you get paid out, he said, and now you get what's coming to you, the little girl herself pays you out for being a dirty bugger.'

I paid him, Alison thought. At least one of the fiends is paid out. Or did I pay out two? 'Mrs McGibbet,' she urged, 'go on.'

'I'm sure,' said Mrs McGibbet, 'I never heard the moment Morris Warren ceased to laugh. I never looked in the dog's bowl curious to see what they were eating, for if you came near them they'd bite your leg off. And therefore I couldn't have noticed MacArthur's eye plop off a spoon and fall into a dish – surely I must have dreamt it, for such a thing could never be. And if your little self, no more than eight, nine, ten years old, were to have cried out, "Now wink at me, can you, you bloody bastard?" I wouldn't have known it because

I was searching down the back of a cupboard for Brendan. And if Mr Donald Aitkenside ran down the road in a panic, I wouldn't have seen him. Still less the fella they call Pikey Pete jump in his van and drive screaming in all directions at once.'

Al walks down the road. She is, eight, nine, ten. Once again she hasn't got her swimming kit or her gym shoes or anything else she should have for school. Lee and Tahera are just behind her, then comes Catherine Tattersall; she looks back for Catherine, who is lagging, and there on the pavement she sees MacArthur's eye, rolling along. 'Look,' she says, and they say, what? She points. 'Look at that,' she says, 'at that.' Catherine steps right on MacArthur's eye, and squashes it into the ground. 'Yeachh!' Al says, and turns aside. 'What's up wiv you, Al?' Catherine says. When Al looks back, the jelly has bounced back again, to a perfect orb, and MacArthur's eye continues to roll along.

It followed her to school one day, it was against the rule:
It made the children laugh and play, to see an eye at school.

It is evening. She is coming home from school. At the street corner, the half-crippled little bloke called Morris Warren leans against the wall. Eff off, she says under her breath. As she approaches, she expects him to reach out and make a grab at her breasts, as this is his usual habit. She prepares to swerve; that is her usual habit, too.

But today he doesn't grab. He just looks at her; and as he looks, he almost falls over. It seems as if his crooked legs won't support him; he grabs the wall for support, and when he speaks, his tone is amazed. He says, 'Take off his bollocks, yes! But take out a cove's eye? I've never heard of it before.'

She bangs into the house, casting a glance down into the stained bathtub, thinking, I better get something and scour that out, it looks bad. Emmie comes at her as soon as she gets in the door: 'I saw MacArthur's eye on a spoon, I saw MacArthur's eye on a fork.'

'Which?'

'I saw you standing there with a knitting needle in your hand, young lady. He didn't deserve that. He was only doing what men do. You was all over Capstick when he pulled the dog off you, but then you was all over MacArthur when he bought you sweeties. So what was he to think? He used to say, Emmie, what have you bred there, she'll do anything for a bag of chocolate raisins.'

Al sits in her kitchen, her kitchen at Admiral Drive. Older now, suddenly wiser, she asks the empty air, 'Mum, who's my dad?'

Emmie says, 'Leave off, will you!'

She says, 'I cannot rest till I know. And when I know, then possibly I still cannot rest.'

'Then you have to ask yourself what's the use,' Emmie says. 'I dunno, girl. I would help you, if I could. It could be any one of 'em, or it could be six other fellas. You don't see who it is, because they always put a blanket over your head.'

Back, back, go back. She is at Aldershot. Darkness is falling, darkness is falling fast. The men are moving a bundle of something. They are passing it between them. It is limp, doll-sized, swaddled. She pulls the blanket aside with her own hand, and in its folds, dead-white, waxy, eyes closed tightly, she sees her own face.

And now back she goes, back and back, till she is smaller and smaller, before she can walk, before she can talk: to the first wail, the first gasp: to the knitting needle pricking her skull and letting in the light.

At Whitton, Colette opened the wardrobe. 'Where are Zoë's things? Surely she doesn't take everything with her when she travels?'

A pity. She had been looking forward to trying her clothes on, when Gavin went to work. She wished he would clear off, really, and let her go through all the drawers and cupboards; instead of hanging about in a sheepish way at the back of her and sighing like that.

Back and back. There is an interval of darkness, dwindling, suspension of the senses. Al neither hears nor sees. The world has no scent or savour. She is a cell, a dot. She diminishes, to vanishing point. She is back beyond a dot. She is back where the dots come from. And still she goes back.

It is close of day, and Al is plodding home. The light is low and greyish. She must make it before dark. Clay is encrusted on her feet, and beneath them the track is worn into deep ruts. Her garments, which appear to be made of sacking – which may, indeed, be sacks – are stiffening with the day's sweat, and chafing the knotty scars on her body. Her breath is coming hard. There is a stitch in her side. She stops and drinks from the ditch, scooping up the water with her fingers. She squats there, until the moon rises.

In the kitchen Colette was opening cupboards, staring critically at the scanty stocks. Zoë, she thought, is one of those people who lives on air, and has no intention of putting herself out to cook for Gavin; which is a mistake, because left to himself he reverts to fried chicken, and before you know where you are he's bursting out of his shirts.

She opened the fridge, she pushed the contents about. What she found was unappealing: a half-used carton of full-fat long-life milk, some Scotch eggs, a lump of orange cheese which had gone hard, and three small blackened bananas. 'Didn't anyone ever tell Zoë,' she said, 'not to keep bananas in the fridge?'

'Feel free,' Gavin said.

'What?'

'Look in all the cupboards, why don't you? Look in the dishwasher. Don't mind me. Look in the washing machine.'

'Well, if it's empty,' she said, 'I'll just pop in one or two things of mine that I brought with me. I didn't like to leave my laundry behind.'

He followed her into the sitting room as she went to pick up her bag. 'You're not going back then?'

'No chance. Gavin, excuse me, don't stand in my way.'

'Sorry.' He sidestepped. 'So won't you miss her? Your friend?'

'I'll miss my income. But don't worry. I'll get it sorted. I'll ring up some agencies later.'

'It's quiet,' Gavin warned.

'Anything at your place?'

'My place? Dunno.'

She stared at him, her pale eyes bulging slightly. 'Gavin – correct me if I'm wrong.' She squatted and opened her bag. 'Would I be near the truth if I said you're still out of a job?'

He nodded.

She plucked out her dirty washing. 'And would I be near the truth if I said you made Zoë up?'

He turned away.

'And that rust bucket out there, it really is your own car?'

Damn, she thought, isn't that just typical, he's more

embarrassed about the car than everything else put together. Gavin stood rubbing his head. She passed him, went into the kitchen with her bundle.

'It's temporary,' he said. 'I traded down. But now you're back—'

'Back?' she said coldly. She bent down and retrieved a grey sock from the washing machine. It was a woolly sock, the kind you darn; the heel had gone into holes. 'How long were you intending to leave it before you told me Zoë didn't exist?'

'I thought you'd work it out for yourself. Which you did, didn't you? I had to say something! You went on about this Dean guy and the rest. Dean this and Donnie that. I had to say something.'

'To make me jealous?'

'Yes. I suppose.'

'I only mentioned Dean once, as far as I remember.'

'He going to come after you, is he?'

'No,' she said. 'He's dead.'

'Christ! Really? You're not winding me up?'

She shook her head.

'Accident, was it?'

'I believe so.'

'You'd lost touch? I'm glad he's dead. Suppose I shouldn't say it. But I am.'

She sniffed. 'He was nothing to me.'

'I mean, I hope he didn't suffer. Kind of thing.'

'Gavin, is this sock yours?'

'What?' he said. 'That? No. Never seen it before. So what about this psychic stuff, have you given it up?'

'Oh yes. That's all finished now.' She held up the sock to examine it. 'It's not like you usually wear. Horrible grey thing. Looks like roadkill.' She frowned at it; she thought she'd seen the other half of the pair, but couldn't think where.

'Colette . . . listen . . . I shouldn't have told you lies.'

'That's all right.' She thought, I told you some. Then, in case she seemed to be excusing him too readily, she said, 'It's what I expect.'

'Doesn't seem like seven years. Since we split.'

'Must be. Must be about that. It was the summer that Diana died.' She walked around the kitchen, her finger dabbing at sticky surfaces. 'Looks like six years and three hundred and sixty-four days since you gave these tiles a wipe down.'

'I'm glad now we didn't sell up.'

'Are you? Why?'

'It makes it like before.'

'Time doesn't go backwards.'

'No, but I can't remember why we split.'

She frowned. Neither could she, really. Gavin looked down at his feet. 'Colette, we've been a couple of plonkers, haven't we?'

She picked up the woolly sock, and threw it in the kitchen bin. 'I don't think women can be,' she said. 'Plonkers. Not really.'

Gavin said humbly, 'I think you could do anything, Colette.'

She looked at him; his head hanging like some dog that's been out in the rain. She looked at him and her heart was touched: where her heart would be.

Admiral Drive: Al hears the neighbours, muttering outside. They are carrying placards, she expects. Sergeant Delingbole is speaking to them through a megaphone. You can't scare Al. When you've been strangled as often as she has, when you've been drowned, when you've died so many times and found yourself still earthside, what are the neighbours going to do to you that's so bloody novel?

There are several ways forward, she thinks, several ways

I can go from here. She accepts that Colette won't be back. Repentance is not out of the question; she imagines Colette saying, I was hasty, can we start again, and herself saying, I don't think so, Colette: that was then and now it's now.

Time for a shake-up. I'll never settle here after so much name-calling and disruption. Even if, when all this dies down, the neighbours start to cosy up to me and bake me cakes. They may forget but I won't. Besides, by now they know what I do for a living. That it's not weather forecasting; and anyway, the Met Office has moved to Exeter.

I could ring an estate agent, she thinks, and ask for a valuation. (Colette's voice in her ear says, you ought to ring three.) 'Miss Hart, what about your shed, which is of local historic interest? And what about the black cloud of evil that hovers over your premises. Will you be leaving that?'

Memories are short, she thinks, in house sales. She will be forgotten, just like the worms and voles who used to live here, and the foetus dug in under the hedge.

She calls Mandy.

'Natasha, Psychic to the Stars?'

'Mandy, Colette's walked out.'

'Oh it's you, Alison. Oh dear. I foresaw as much, frankly. When we were at Mrs Etchells', looking for the will. I said to Silvana, trouble there, mark my words.'

'And I'm on my own.'

'Don't cry, lovey. I'll come and get you.'

'Please. For a night or two. You see, the press are here. Cameras.'

Mandy was puzzled. 'Is that good? For business, I mean?'

'No, I've got vigilantes. Demonstrators.'

Mandy clicked her tongue. 'Witch-burning, isn't it? Some people are so narrow-minded. Are the police there?'

'Yes.'

'But they're not trying to arrest you, or anything? Sorry,

silly question. Of course not. Look, I'll bring Gemma for a bit of muscle.'

'No. Just come yourself.'

'Take a nice hot bath, Al. Unplug the phone. Spray some lavender around. I'll be there before you know it. I'll have you out of there. A bit of sea air will do you good. We'll go shopping for you, give you a makeover, I always thought Colette gave you bad advice. Shall I book you a hair appointment? I'll line up Cara to give you a massage.'

Three hours later, she is ready to leave the house. The police have not had much success in dispersing the crowd; they don't, they explain, want to get heavy-handed. Sergeant Delingbole says, what you could do, probably it would be for the best, would be to come out with a blanket over your head. Al says, do you have an official blanket you use for that, or can I choose my own? They say, feel free: the policewoman helpfully runs upstairs and looks out at her direction her mohair throw, the raspberry-coloured throw that Colette bought her once, in better times than these.

She places it over her head; the world looks pink and fuzzy. Like a fish, or something newborn, she opens her mouth to breathe; her breath, moist, sucks in the mohair. The policewoman takes her elbow, and Delingbole opens the door; she is hurried to a police vehicle with darkened windows, which whisks her smartly away from Admiral Drive. Later, on the regional TV news, she will glimpse herself from the knee down. I always wanted to be on TV, she will say, and now I have; Mandy will say, well, bits of you, anyway.

As they swing on to the A322, she pulls aside the woollen folds and looks around her. Her lips itch from their contact with the throw; she presses them together, hoping not to smudge her lipstick. Sergeant Delingbole is sitting with her, for reassurance, he says. 'I've always been fascinated,' he says. 'The paranormal. UFOs. All that. I mean, there must be something in it, mustn't there?'

'I think you tried to come through,' she says, 'at one of my dems. Couple of years back. Just after the Queen Mother passed.'

'God bless her,' says Delingbole automatically, and Alison answers, 'God bless her.'

The day has brightened. At Worplesdon, trees drip on to the fairways of the golf club. The policewoman says, 'The cloud's lifting. Might see some action at Wimbledon this afternoon.'

Al smiles. 'I'm sure I couldn't say.'

Before they reach Guildford, they pull into an out-of-town shopping centre. The exchange takes place in front of PC World. Mandy clip-clips towards the white van: high-heeled pastel courts in pistachio green, tight pale jeans, fake Chanel jacket in baby pink. She is smiling, her big jaw jutting. She looks quite lined, Al thinks; it is the first time in years she has seen Mandy in full daylight. It must be Hove that's aged her: the sea breezes, the squinting into the sun. 'Got the consignment?' says Mandy, breezy herself: and Delingbole opens the back door and gives her his arm to help her out of the van. She tumbles to the ground, her sore feet impacting hard.

The soft-top stands by, lacquered once again to a perfect, hard scarlet. 'There's a new nail bar at the end of our road,' Mandy says. 'I thought after we've had some lunch we could pop in and treat ourselves.'

For a moment Al sees her fist, dripping with gore; she sees herself, bloody to the elbows. She sees, back at Admiral Drive, the tape unspooling in the empty house; her past unspooling, back beyond this life, beyond the lives to come. 'That will be nice,' she says.

MORRIS: And another thing you can't get, you can't get a saveloy.

CAPSTICK: You can't get tripe like you used to get.

DEAN: When I get my tongue-guard off, I'm going for a curry.

MORRIS: You can't get a decent cuppa tea.

DEAN: And then I'm going to get a swastika studded into it. I can hang it over walls and be a mobile graffiti.

MART: Tee-hee. When Delingbole comes you can wag it at him and then bugger off.

AITKENSIDE: Etchells could make a good cuppa.

CAPSTICK: She could. I'll give her that.

MORRIS: By the way, Mr Aitkenside.

AITKENSIDE: Yes? Speak up.

MORRIS: I only mention it.

AITKENSIDE: Spit it out, lad.

MORRIS: It's a question of fundage.

AITKENSIDE: Warren, you have already tapped me for a sub. When I look in my wages book I find it ain't the first time either. You are spending in advance of your entire income, as far as I can see. It can't go on, me old mate.

MORRIS: I don't want a sub. I only want what's due.

MACARTHUR: He's right, Mr Aitkenside. It ain't fair that Pete should keep all the money he got from Etchells' personal effects, seeing as we all helped to frighten her to death, and especially me rising up with my false eye rolling.

AITKENSIDE: Pete! What you got to say about this?

Pause.

Where is he?

CAPSTICK: Bugger me. Taken to the road. His wodge of cash wiv him.

MORRIS: Ain't that his sort all over?

BOB FOX: What can you expect, Mr Aitkenside, taking on pikeys?

AITKENSIDE: Don't you tell me how to do my job, lad! I've got a diploma in Human Resources from Nick himself. We are working towards equal opportunities for all. Don't tell me how to recruit, or you'll be knocking on windows for all eternity.

CAPSTICK: We'll have to contact the missus, then. If we want our cut. She'll nail down Pikey for us. He likes her. He can't keep away.

AITKENSIDE: Pardon me, but I don't know if you'll see your missus again.

DEAN: You've pissed her off good and proper.

CAPSTICK: What, not see her? Who we going to medium-ise, then?

BOB FOX: Morris? Morris, speak up. It's you in charge of this fiasco.

MORRIS: You can't get decent vinegar, neither. You go in for vinegar, there's bloody shelves and shelves of the stuff. There's only one sort of proper vinegar, and that's brown.

CAPSTICK: Morris? We're talking to you.

AITKENSIDE: It was you, Warren, according to my ledger, what requested to have that crustie hanged, that lived in her shed.

MORRIS: He was on my manor! Only just got a proper outbuilding, where I can put me feet up evenings, and some geezer with an hat moves in.

AITKENSIDE: But what did you fail to see, my son? You failed to see he was her good deed.

WAGSTAFFE: A good deed in a naughty world.

AITKENSIDE: That you, Wagstaffe? Bugger off, we're talking.

MORRIS: Besides, you was all agreeable. Oooh, Morris, you

said, let's have an hanging, haven't had a good hanging in years, it'll be a right laugh when the little bugger kicks his feet!

AITKENSIDE: You failed to see that little bugger was her good deed. And what's the result? She's looking to commit a few others. They get the habit . . . see? They get the habit. It's sad. But they get the taste for it.

MORRIS: So she don't want to know us no more?

AITKENSIDE: I very much doubt it, old son.

MORRIS: But we go back, me and the missus.

Pause.

I'll miss her. Be on my own. Won't be the same.

CAPSTICK: Oh, leave off, do! Bring on the bloody violins! You wouldn't think so well of her if she'd had away your balls.

MACARTHUR: You wouldn't think so well of her if you'd seen your eye on her spoon.

DEAN: You can get another place, Uncle Morris.

MORRIS (*sniff*): Won't be the same, Dean lad.

AITKENSIDE: Not the bloody waterworks! Pull yourself together, Warren, or I'll demote you.

Morris is sobbing.

AITKENSIDE: Look . . . Morris, old son, don't take on . . . oh, blast it, ain't nobody round here got a bleeding handkerchief?

WAGSTAFFE: Any handkerchief in particular?

AITKENSIDE: Wagstaffe? Put a sock in it. Listen, lads, I've an idea. Maybe she'll come back if her dad asks for her.

Pause.

MACARTHUR: Who is her dad, then?

CAPSTICK: I always thought it was you, MacArthur. I thought that's why she took your eye out.

MACARTHUR: I thought it were you, Keef. I thought that's why she took your bollocks off.

AITKENSIDE: Don't look at me! She's not my daughter, I was in the forces.

MORRIS: She can't be mine because I was still in the circus.

PIKEY PETE: She can't be mine—

MORRIS: Oh there you are, Pete! We thought you'd scarpered. Give a dog a bad name and hang him! We thought you had made off with the emoluments.

PIKEY PETE: —I say, she can't be mine, because I was in jail for painting horses.

CAPSTICK: Painting horses?

PIKEY PETE: You paint one racehorse to look like another, innit?

MORRIS: Don't the paint run off, Pikey, when there's a downpour?

PIKEY PETE: It's an old Romany skill. Anyway, she ain't mine.

CAPSTICK: She ain't mine, because I was in the nick too.

MACARTHUR: And me. Serving five.

AITKENSIDE: So who's left? Bob Fox?

BOB FOX: I never did nothing but tap on the window.

Pause.

MACARTHUR: Got to be that Derek bloke. Innit.

AITKENSIDE: Couldn't have been. Bloody errand boy? He never had no money. Emmeline Cheetham, she didn't do it for free.

MACARTHUR: True. You made sure of that.

CAPSTICK: Not like these girls you get these days, eh, Dean?

MORRIS: So who's left?

Pause.

MACARTHUR: Oh, blimey.

MORRIS: Are you thinking what I'm thinking? Only the great man himself!

CAPSTICK: Well, knock me down with a feather.
MORRIS: I never had such a thunderclap.
PIKEY PETE: You don't want to mess with the fambly of Nick. Because Nick he is a fambly man.
Pause.
CAPSTICK: What would he do?
AITKENSIDE: Dear oh dear.
MORRIS: The worst thing that can befall a spirit is to be eaten by old Nick. You can be eaten and digested by him and then you've had your chips.
BOB FOX: You can't get chips like you used to. Not fried in proper lard.
AITKENSIDE: Shut it, Bob, there's a good lad?
CAPSTICK: What, you get et? You get et by Nick? And you don't get another go around?
MORRIS: If he pukes you up you can reform and have another go, but otherwise you're et and that's all.
MACARTHUR: And that's all?
MORRIS: El finito, Benito.
PIKEY PETE: Here, shall we do the share-out of these notes? It's the proceeds from Etchells' furniture. Lads? Where you going? Lads? Wait for me . . .

October: Al is travelling, in the autumn's first foul weather. There are mudslips and landslides, there are storm drains burst, a glugging and gurgling in sumps, conduits and wells. There are fissures in the river beds, there are marshes, swamps and bogs, there are cracked pipes and breached sea walls, and outswells of gas on the bubbling flood plain. There is coastal erosion, crumbling defences, spillage and seepages: where the saline and swift-rushing tide meets the viscid slime of swollen sewers, there the oceans are rising, half a metre, half a metre, half a metre onwards. On the orbital road the hazard lights of collided cars flash from the hard shoulder.

Cameras flash on the bridges, there is the swish of the wipers against drenching rain, the mad blinking eyes of the breakdown trucks. 'On we go!' Alison calls. 'Sevenoaks, here we come.'

They are singing, Alison and the two little women: a few music-hall favourites, but hymns, mostly, for it's what the little women like. She didn't know any of the words, but they have taught her.

'Show pity, Lord! For we are frail and faint:
We fade away, O list to our complaint.
We fade away, like flowers in the sun;
We just begin, and then our work is done.'

Maureen Harrison says, 'Have we been to Sevenoaks?' and Alison says, 'Not with me, you haven't.' Maureen says, anxious, 'Will we get our tea there?' Alison says, 'Oh yes, I hear in Sevenoaks you get a very good tea.'

'Just as well,' says Maureen's friend from the back, 'because I could have brought my own Eccles cakes.'

'Cakes,' says Maureen, 'we've had some lovely cakes. Do you remember that one you bought me once, with a walnut on top? You can't get cakes like that these days. Here, lovey, I'll make you one. On your birthday. I always made you a cake on your birthday.'

'That would be nice,' says Maureen's friend. 'And *she* can have some too.'

'Oh yes, we'll give *her* some. She's a lovely girl.'

Alison sighs. She likes to be appreciated; and before these last weeks, she never felt she was. They can't do enough for her, the two old ladies, so happy they are to be together again, and when they are talking in the evening, from under a rug and behind the sofa they praise her, saying that they never had a daughter, but if they had, they would have wanted a bonny big girl just like Al. Whenever they set off in the car, they are so excited she has to make them wear incontinence pads. She cries, 'Are your seat belts on, girls? Are your buttons all sewn on tight?' And they shout, 'Yes, Miss!' They say, 'Look at us, riding in a motor vehicle, a private car!' They will never get tired of the orbital road, no matter how many times they go round it. Even if some image from her former life washes up – the fiends escaping Admiral Drive, vestigial heads trapped under the fences, multiple limbs thrashing, feet entangled in their tongues – even if some moment of dismay fades her smile, chills her, tightens her grip on the wheel or brings a shiny tear to her eye – even if she misses a junction, and has to cross the carriageway – the little women never complain. They say, 'Look at her hair, and look at her lovely rings, look at her frock and look at how she pedals the car – you'd think it would tire her out, but you can't tire her out. Oh, I tell you, Maureen Harrison, we've landed on our feet here.' And Maureen adds, 'Where our feet would be.'

Her mobile phone rings. It's Gemma. 'How's tricks? Staines? The 27th? I doubt it, but I'll check my diary when we pull in. *We*? Did I say we? No, not Colette. God forbid. I meant me and my new guides. Colette's gone back to her husband. Near Twickenham. He used to be a, you know, what do they call it, one of those men who sets traps. Sort of gamekeeper.'

'Near Twickenham?' Gemma says, surprised, and Al says, 'No, in a former life.'

He was a man, she thought, who kept dogs, but not for pets. A terrier man. Digs out the earths, lays down poisons for hapless small creatures trying to earn a living. 'I didn't care for him,' she says, 'when I ran into him in Farnham.' You shouldn't leave bait about for it attracts entities, the slow grub and creep of legless things, feral crawlers looking for wounds to suck or open minds to creep inside. You shouldn't leave traps, for you don't know what will spring them: severed legs, unclaimed and nameless feet, ghouls and spectres looking to stitch themselves together, haunting the roads looking for a hand, an ear, for severed fingers and dislocated thumbs.

She has been, herself, of course, a snapper-up of unconsidered trifles. She doesn't remember, really, if she saw MacArthur's eye in a dish; though she's been trying to remember, just to keep the record straight. It might not have been in a dish; it might have been on a plate, a saucer, a dog bowl. She remembers she had her spoon in her hand, her fork. 'Business?' she says. 'Business is booming, thanks for asking, Gemma. Give or take the odd quiet midweek, I'm booked out till next Feb.'

There are terrorists in the ditches, knives clenched between their teeth. There are fundis hoarding fertiliser, there are fanatics brewing bombs on brownfield sites, and holy martyrs digging storage pits where fiends have melted into the soil. There are citadels underground, there are potholes and sunken shafts, there are secret chambers in the hearts of men, sometimes of women too. There are unlicensed workings and laboratories underground, mutants breeding in the tunnels; there are cannibal moo-cows and toxic bunnikins, and behind the drawn curtains of hospital wards there are bugs that eat the flesh.

But today we are going to Sevenoaks, by way of Junction 5: to see whom fortune favours today. Will it be the brave, or is it the turn of the bloody? Will they be queuing to have their palmprints taken, the legion of the unbowed? Softly the cards are shuffled, whispering to the crimson cloth. A knight in armour is galloping from the battle: or to it. A dog climbs the wheel of fortune, while a monkey descends. A naked girl pours water into a pool, and seven stars shine in the evening sky.

'When is it teatime, Miss?' the little woman enquires; and then, 'Pedal faster, Miss, see if you can beat that one!'

Alison checks her rear-view mirror. She pulls out to overtake a truck, she puts her foot down. She moves into the fast lane, half hidden by the spray. Unmolested, unobserved, they flee before the storm. If the universe is a great mind, it may sometimes have its absences. Maureen Harrison pipes up from the back: 'This cake we're having: could we have it iced?'

P.S.

Ideas, interviews & features …

About the author

About the book

Read on

Expanding Our Sympathies

Louise Tucker talks to Hilary Mantel

You have lived abroad and in various parts of England. Where is home, and why?
I have lived in the south-east since 1985, but still somehow feel this is a temporary arrangement. But the north-west, where I grew up, has changed a good deal. So I don't know where I belong, or even if it's in England at all; but I don't mind that. I think it's good to have an outsider's eye. And the past lives in people, as much as places. I like to know where I come from, but it doesn't dictate where I may go.

What did you want to be when you grew up?
A man.

What, or who, made you a writer?
Circumstance and chance; poor health, unfitting me for more active trades; the desire to read books that didn't seem to exist, and wouldn't exist, unless I wrote them.

How did you start your first novel, and how long did it take?
The first novel I wrote was not the first I published. I began *A Place of Greater Safety*, which is a novel about the French Revolution, in 1974, which was the year after I left university. I had completed two drafts by the end of 1979. It then gathered dust on a shelf until 1991, when I tidied it up for publication (and retyped the enormous MS) in the course of a summer when I survived on very little sleep, permanently distorting

my work habits. My first published novel, *Every Day is Mother's Day*, came out in 1985. It took me around two years, on and off; I changed country part way through, moving from Africa back to England and then on to Saudi Arabia.

Nothing's ever been straightforward, but why should it be? The writing of the story becomes part of the story.

The supernatural, in all its manifestations, has featured in many of your books. Does it fascinate you personally as well as professionally, and if so why?
When I was a child I believed our house was haunted, and so – worryingly – did the grown-ups. I was often very frightened, and the imprint of that fear stays with me; but I try to use it constructively now. The good thing about being a writer is that you take your bad experiences and make them pay.

> ‘The good thing about being a writer is that you take your bad experiences and make them pay.’

Where and how did you start your research on psychics? Did you try all that Alison offers, from palmic and tarot readings to sensitive stage-shows, and were you ever surprised by the results?
I saw my first 'psychic show' in Windsor, at the Harte & Garter – just as Colette does, in the novel. I attended out of curiosity. I was more taken by the medium than by her messages. I wondered what her private life was like.

I tried, within limits, to understand ▶

Expanding Our Sympathies *(continued)*

◀ what it would be like to be Alison. I got myself a teach-yourself-tarot book, and worked conscientiously. I learned to be a 'reiki healer' in the course of a weekend, and have a pretty certificate to show for it. I experienced a 'past life regression'. And no, the results didn't surprise me. I don't take up an attitude to Alison's trade. I am not a believer or unbeliever.

Towards the end of the book, when TV psychics have become popular, the narrator says 'the punters all think they're talented now, gifted'. Do you, like the punters, think that we all have such gifts in some way?
I dislike people who make claims for themselves, unless they are founded on evidence. My experience, such as it is, suggests that people who are keen on discovering their psychic powers are too interested in themselves to succeed. It's a bit like writing, really. Some people are excessively interested in 'being a writer', and they think more about their persona than about their work and its content. This is usually a recipe for disappointment.

" I got myself a teach-yourself-tarot book, and worked conscientiously. I learned to be a "reiki healer" in the course of a weekend, and have a pretty certificate to show for it. I experienced a "past life regression". "

What made you decide to include contemporary deaths and tragedies in the book, such as Princess Diana's death and September 11th?
It's a novel set firmly in its time and place, and it would have been false to create characters who never watch the news and don't respond to contemporary events. Besides, Diana's passing brought about an emotional convulsion in our national life; it gave rise to

a huge, primitive, heartfelt cry of mourning. No one concerned with collective sensibilities could ignore its importance. If you want to write about 'the state of the nation', you have to study dreams and nightmares, as well as returns from the opinion polls. You can't omit the emotional and the irrational.

'You had to guard the words that came out of your mouth and even the words as they formed up in your mind,' thinks Alison when Colette talks about Morris, and thus, in spirit terms, invites him and his negativity back. Is this suggesting that positive thinking can keep spirits or negativity at bay?
I don't think this passage is so much about positive or negative thinking as about Alison's superstitious feeling that to give birth to a scenario in your mind is to admit the possibility that it will play out in reality – whatever, for Alison, 'reality' means. Again, I think there's a link with the process of writing. When a writer creates a character, she first pulls the character out of herself; it comes out of her experience of life, and from the back rooms of her imagination. Then she lets the character grow, she enhances it, points it in a useful direction, puts it to work. Next, the traits of the character who has been created feed back into the writer, and change her. All your characters are you, and (as your writing progresses) you are all your characters. I think this is what happens with Alison and the Fiends. Their vilest act can only be as vile as the worst act she can imagine. ►

LIFE AT A GLANCE

Author photograph © John Haynes

BORN

Derbyshire, 1952

EDUCATED

Village school, convent grammar, LSE and Sheffield University

FAMILY

Married, no children

CAREER

Patchy – social worker, shop assistant, barmaid, teacher, film critic, novelist

TOP TEN FAVOURITE NOVELS

Kidnapped
R.L. Stevenson

Huckleberry Finn
Mark Twain

Another Country
James Baldwin

Things Fall Apart
Chinua Achebe

The Good Soldier
Ford Madox Ford

Blood Red, Sister Rose
Thomas Keneally

I, Claudius
Robert Graves

Effi Briest
Theodor Fontane

The *Sword of Honour* trilogy
Evelyn Waugh

Angel
Elizabeth Taylor

◄ *Beyond Black* is extremely dark and yet equally very light. How do you manage to balance your tone so that it never descends into farce?
I don't balance it, consciously. I trust that the humour and horror will distribute themselves naturally, as they are distributed in life.

How did writing this book change you, if at all?
I think every book changes you, as a writer – if it doesn't, you have to ask yourself if you are just marking time. The story of Alison took much longer than I thought it would, and was more difficult to tell than I thought it would be. I knew already that the tendency was for material to deepen over time; you begin on a comedy, then you start to hear the faint plaintive note within it. The horrors of Alison's childhood revealed themselves to me a piece at a time, as her memory reveals them to her, and as I reveal them to the reader. I didn't want to force or distort the process. So I was aware I was taking risks with fictional form, with reader satisfaction. I knew I could make a tight, smart, shipshape little book – I've done that before. Here I wanted to know if I could make something that seemed to follow the natural curve of memory, the curve of the slow awakening of thought; and if I could do this through a main character who is intelligent but not educated, natural and not sophisticated, generous and not mean, giving and not taking. It had to feel like Al's book, not Hil's book. It's for the reader to decide if this peculiar risk was worth taking.

What do you think the purpose of fiction is, if any? Is it simply entertainment or does it have a moral dimension too?
I think good fiction expands our sympathies, asks us to consider people and places and circumstances very remote from our own, and asks us to consider how we would act and what we would feel if we were in their shoes. Much wickedness stems from our failure to imagine other people as fully human, and as our equals. So, yes – I think fiction does have a moral dimension. But of course, if it is not also entertaining, no one will read it and it will have no effect at all.

What has been the most satisfying part of your career? And the most frustrating?
This may sound childish, but I will never forget the day on which I learned my first novel was accepted. I was in Saudi Arabia at that time; an airmail letter brought the news. It was early afternoon. I opened the letter and when I tried to speak, my mouth moved but no words came out. Until then, I thought that it was only in stories that people were 'speechless with shock', or 'dumb with delight'.

Each novel breeds its frustrations. But frustration is usually the prelude to a breakthrough. When I'm in the process of frustration, I always manage to forget that.

Who are your influences?
I don't write novels about pirates or Highland rebels, but I think Robert Louis Stevenson formed my notion, as a child, of what a story ought to be like. ►

A WRITING LIFE

When do you write?
Whenever an idea strikes.

Where do you write?
Wherever I am. Usually on public transport.

Why do you write?
Good question.
Habit/need to earn money/curiosity about what I will say next/hope of doing something good.

Pen or computer?
Pen first, as I write all ideas first in notebooks. But the screen seems as natural as paper.

Silence or music?
Sometimes I put on music, but I screen it out; I only hear it if my writing is not flowing.

How do you start?
With spirit and dash, but with an error; I usually rewrite the beginning.

And finish?
Softly: I have to go back after a few days, and work it up.

Do you have any writing rituals?
None.

A WRITING LIFE cont.

Who is your favourite living writer?
Oliver Sacks.

If you weren't a writer, what would you do?
I'd be a spy.

Expanding Our Sympathies *(continued)*

◀ What do you do when you are not writing?
When would that be? Writing is not a trade that gives you holidays. In *Who's Who* I put my 'recreation' as 'sleep', but that's not wholly true, as I do a lot of work during dreams.

What are you writing next?
I have a medium-term project, a short non-fiction book called *The Woman Who Died of Robespierre*, but what I'm working on most urgently is a novel called *The Complete Stranger*, set in Africa during the late 1970s. It is a love story, and I've never done one of those. ■

Revering the Gone-before

by Hilary Mantel

Imagine an evening in early summer, and a hundred people packed into the back room of a Tudorized chain eatery, which might ten years ago have been a country pub, but isn't now … as everywhere in England, the country shrinks, the town expands. The thriving and busy town of Slough – not such a benighted place as it sounds, but not an artist's delight either – now creeps its tentacles into rural Buckinghamshire. We have come together, we hundred or so, to listen to a medium calling up the dead. He has enough confidence to stand up on a stage, in a public demonstration, to prove to us that there is a life beyond this one: that our ancestors are watching over us; that the dead know what we do, Monday to Friday and through the weekend; that they care what we do; that they can talk to us, and hear us speak.

All this – as a belief system – I find threatening, unlikely, and slightly repulsive. But I cannot deny that the medium works hard. He is a man of forty or so, overweight and pasty, his shirt trying to crawl out of the waistband of his trousers. He turns from side to side, ponderous, unlikeable, his cupped hands soliciting compassion; he spreads his arms, showing dark patches of sweat, trying to unite us in a universal hug. We stare back at him, glassy-eyed, faintly bored.

He makes contact with someone whom he says has died (and won't we all?) with breathing difficulties. He gasps, he holds his chest, you can see the cold perspiration ▶

Revering the Gone-before *(continued)*

◀ bead on his face; he is forced to re-enact the dead man's final moments. He's a con-artist, maybe. But what a strenuous way to make a living! He seems, he is, physically distressed; he is not in charge of himself, something else is in charge. This is not acting, I think; or if it is, the Royal Shakespeare Company might consider hiring him to give them lessons.

If it's not acting, what is it? None of the 'messages' he has given to members of the audience have been a success. There is no doubt that *he* believes in what he is doing; he is working, he is suffering, he is getting nothing back. Why have they come out tonight, these paying customers? Presumably they want to believe. They are ready to be convinced, surely? They are open-minded, would that be the word? As the medium recovers from his latest, strenuous bout with death, he changes tack, focuses on a young girl towards the back of the room. 'Yes, you, dear,' he says, and he won't be diverted. He has things to tell her; but she's vacant, surly, seventeen. She can hardly be coaxed to speak up.

> ❛ Some people take to the internet and research their family tree. Some go to "psychic fayres". Most of us – let us leave aside those who have aristocratic pedigrees – wonder where we came from. ❜

'I have your grannie here,' he tells her. 'She has a message for you. I have your granddad. But I can't quite get their names.' He begins flailing around, in a way familiar to me, because I've been to a few of these psychic shows. 'Is it Anne? Do they call her Annie? Is it Alice? I'm getting two syllables, begins with A, could it be Amy?'

At this point the punter's supposed to chip in. She's supposed to do her bit, supply the name. We all wait, necks craning, ears straining: will-she-won't-she?

'Speak up, darling!' the man begs.

Then, shrugging, she begins to speak. She doesn't know, she says, the name of her grandmother. Or her grandfather. She seems surprised that he would think she should. What are they, to her?

I brood about it later, rehearse it in my mind. As the interaction continued – as the medium tried to prompt her, as she stonewalled him – it became clear that, no, she was not adopted; she was not kidnapped, displaced, not an immigrant, a refugee; she was just a little lass from Slough whose memory didn't stretch back much beyond last year. Why should it? What interest did old dead people hold for her?

I had already been writing *Beyond Black* – or at least, taking notes for it – for a year or so, going to different 'demonstrations' to see professional psychics at work. I was always as much interested in the audience as the performer. Some members of the audience had very personal questions they needed to ask: they had experienced a sudden, untimely or unexplained death. Others were less traumatized: they wanted, I thought, a sense of connection.

Don't we all? Some people take to the internet and research their family tree. Some go to 'psychic fayres'. Most of us – let us leave aside those who have aristocratic pedigrees – wonder where we came from. A woman in Derbyshire, at a talk I gave once, said to me: 'I'm like you, love; I come from a long line of nobodies.' It's important to me to know that I come from a line of Derbyshire nobodies, who married Irish nobodies. I revere the ▶

' The thing that frightens me most is confiscation of history. If you don't own the past, and can't speak up for it, your past can be stolen and falsified, it can be changed behind you. I am interested in the way people remember, and just as interested in the way they won't remember. '

Revering the Gone-before *(continued)*

◀ gone-before, even if I can't talk to them. But the little lass in Slough showed me what I most fear; a lack of roots that doesn't even define itself as a lack. She lived in a town where few people really come from. A town where people just ended up. She had no interest in what happened before she was born. I think it didn't seem real to her. Only the present was real.

It was this fright I received – on a summer evening outside Slough – that drove the book. The thing that frightens me most is confiscation of history. If you don't own the past, and can't speak up for it, your past can be stolen and falsified, it can be changed behind you. I am interested in the way people remember, and just as interested – since that night – in the way they won't remember. I already had the character of Alison; I knew her present, and wondered about her past. I wondered if she remembered her childhood; if she had permission to remember. What 'psychics' tell you about their early years is usually bland and sunny. When I glimpsed, in my imagination, Alison's past, I got another fright.

That's really nasty, I thought. It has power. I'll write it. Fear's such powerful fuel. ■

' When I glimpsed, in my imagination, Alison's past, I got another fright. That's really nasty, I thought. It has power. I'll write it. Fear's such powerful fuel. '

Have You Read?

Other books by Hilary Mantel

Giving Up the Ghost

A wry, shocking and unique autobiography of childhood, ghosts, illness and family. From childhood daydreams to the reality of family secrets, her father's mysterious disappearance and an adulthood blighted by medical neglect, Mantel uncovers the losses that wrenched her from the patterns of the past and drove her to forge her own path. Winner of Mind Book of the Year 2004.

The Giant, O'Brien

Charles O'Brien flees Ireland for England and, he hopes, a future as a sideshow exhibit. But his enormous size attracts the attention of John Hunter, celebrated surgeon and anatomist who buys dead men from the gallows and babies' corpses by the inch. Hunter is determined to dissect this giant, but Charles needs to keep body and soul together in order to reach heaven. This book is based on the true story of an eighteenth-century Irish giant, Charles O'Brien, who was, despite his best efforts, eventually dissected by the surgeon John Hunter. His bones still hang in the Museum of the Royal College of Surgeons in Lincoln's Inn Fields.

A Place of Greater Safety

'Household names come out of households,' said a perceptive reviewer of this novel of the French Revolution. Great historical figures have their private – even their hidden – lives. Robespierre, Danton and the journalist Camille Desmoulins are the three main figures in this novel; in five years of ►

Have You Read? *(continued)*

◀ revolution they lived as hard as most people do in a natural lifespan. Their lovers, wives, sisters lived with them; in some cases they died with them.

Every Day is Mother's Day
Evelyn and Muriel Axon are a reclusive mother and daughter, barricaded into their filthy (and haunted?) house. They never go out; yet somehow, it seems, Muriel is pregnant. Who can possibly be the father? Isabel, their young social worker, is distracted by her own family problems and by her hopeless affair with Colin, a married teacher. How will she get into the Axon house? Will she be in time to defuse the crisis that must occur when Muriel's baby is born?

Vacant Possession
Muriel Axon is about to re-enter the lives of Colin Sidney and Isabel Field. It is ten years since her last tangle with them, but for Muriel this is not time enough. There are still scores to be settled, truths to be faced and a certain amount of vengeance to be wreaked.

Fludd
Fetherhoughton is an isolated village, poor and superstitious, located in the north of England in the 1950s; it is earthy, stolid, yet it seems adrift in its own dream. Father Angwin, gentle and anxious, is a parish priest who has lost his faith. His only (chaste) bond of sympathy is with Sister Philomena, a passionate young Irish nun. But she is a prisoner in the convent, and he is a prisoner of habit. One stormy night a stranger appears

at the door of the priest's house, wrapped in a black cloak and carrying a black bag. Who is Fludd? Is he a curate? Is he an angel? Is he perhaps a devil? Or is he something stranger than any of these? 'I have come to transform you,' he says. 'Transformation is my business.'

Winner of the Winifred Holtby Prize, the Cheltenham Festival Prize and the Southern Arts Literature Award.

A Change of Climate
Anna and Ralph Eldred live happily in the Norfolk countryside. To the outward eye they are a contented, middle-aged couple who have raised four happy children and devoted themselves to helping others. But in the course of one summer their peace is almost destroyed, as echoes of their early career in Africa come to haunt them, and it becomes evident that, in their present life, something or someone is missing.

Eight Months on Ghazzah Street
Frances Shore is a cartographer by trade, but when her husband's work takes her to Saudi Arabia she finds herself unable to map the Kingdom's areas of internal darkness. The streets are not a woman's territory – confined in her flat, she finds her sense of self begin to dissolve. She hears whispers, sounds of distress from the 'empty' flat above her head. As her days empty of certainty and purpose, her life becomes a blank – waiting to be filled by violence and disaster. ▶

Have You Read? *(continued)*

◀ ***An Experiment in Love***

It was the year after Chappaquiddick, and all spring Carmel had watery dreams about the disaster. Now she, Karina and Julianne were escaping the dreary north for a London University hall of residence. Awaiting them was a winter of new preoccupations – sex, politics, food and fertility – and a grotesque tragedy of their own.

Winner of the Hawthornden Prize

Learning to Talk

A semi-autobiographical collection of stories drawn from life in the 1950s in an insular northern village. For the child narrator, the only way to survive is to get up, get on, get out. ■

If You Liked This, Why Not Try More From *The Perennial Collection*

The American Boy
Andrew Taylor
WINNER OF THE CWA HISTORICAL DAGGER FOR FICTION

London 1819: Thomas Shield is tutor to a young American boy and the boy's sensitive best friend, Charles Frant. When a brutal crime is committed, Shield finds himself drawn into a deadly tangle of sex, money, murder and lies – a tangle which grips him even tighter as he struggles to escape it. And what of the strange American boy at the centre of events – what is the secret of the boy named Edgar Allan Poe?

Eve Green
Susan Fletcher
WINNER OF THE WHITBREAD FIRST NOVEL AWARD

Following the death of her mother, eight-year-old Evie is sent to a new life in rural Wales. With a sense of being lied to she sets out to discover her family's dark secret – unaware that when a local girl vanishes there is yet more darkness to come. Years later she remembers that first Welsh summer: her lies, her anger, her reckless search for Rosie's abductor and the lessons she learnt – about trust, identity, guilt and how to survive when love is gone.